WELCOME TO
JIMMY'S PLACE

A SUSPENSE NOVEL

MICHAEL MAYO

coffeetownpress

Kenmore, WA

A Coffeetown Press book published by Epicenter Press

Epicenter Press
6524 NE 181st St. Suite 2
Kenmore, WA 98028.
www.Epicenterpress.com
www.Coffeetownpress.com
www.Camelpress.com

For more information go to: www.epicenterpress.com
www.mike-mayo.com

Welcome To Jimmy's Place
Copyright © 2022 by Michael Mayo

ISBN: 9781684920266 (trade paper)
ISBN: 9781684920273 (ebook)

Printed in the United States of America

For Marcia

The speakeasy was quietly decorated and happily illuminated, and both the pretense of secrecy and the presence of women enforced quiet behavior and good manners. When Repeal came we had the sense to apply the lesson and a good bar today is indistinguishable from a good speakeasy of 1930.

Bernard DeVoto, *The Hour: A History of the Cocktail* (1948)

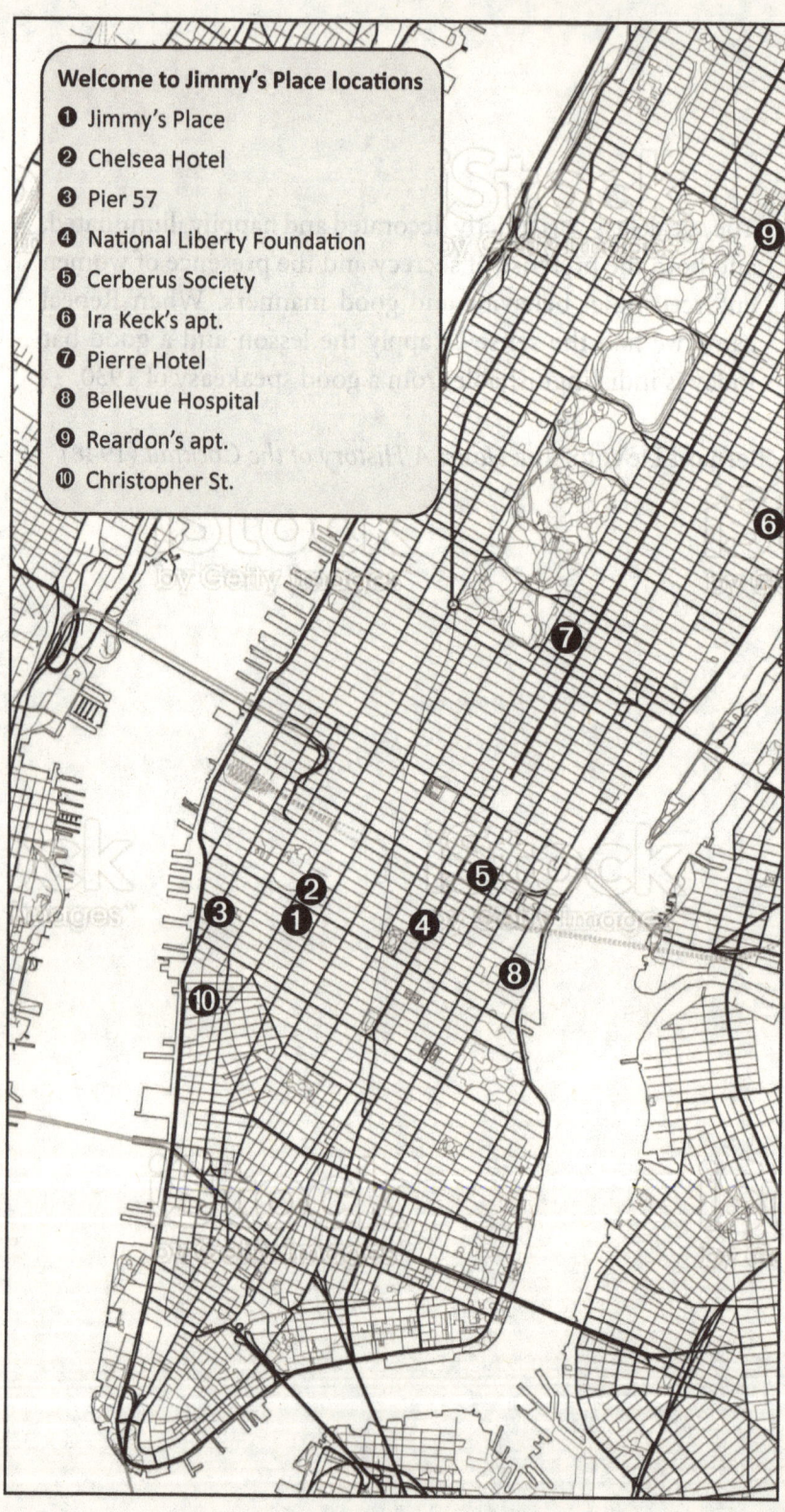

Welcome to Jimmy's Place locations

❶ Jimmy's Place
❷ Chelsea Hotel
❸ Pier 57
❹ National Liberty Foundation
❺ Cerberus Society
❻ Ira Keck's apt.
❼ Pierre Hotel
❽ Bellevue Hospital
❾ Reardon's apt.
❿ Christopher St.

Chapter One

JUNE 5, 1934

The first guys they sent to kill me weren't so good. That's what happens when you hire cheap, but you could see why they thought it. Two big goons, armed, against one short good-looking gimp with a stick—ought to get the job done, right?

It happened about half past one in the morning. Business had been on the slow side so we closed Jimmy's Place early. I was walking back to the Chelsea. The sidewalk on that part of West Twenty-Second Street is narrow. On one side you've got steps going up to the stoops of the brownstones and iron fencing in front of the doors to the lower floors. Trees close to the curb on the other side.

The two men were trying to read a little map that they were holding up under a lamppost near the corner. The map might have been one of those that they give you on the double decker tourist buses, but these two didn't look like tourists. Heavy-set guys, maybe thirty or forty, hard to say at night. Regular clothes, suits and hats. They'd been drinking, not drunk, not sober. I knew the look, but something wasn't right, something about the way they were standing. Then one of them nudged the other when he saw me and they both stared at me.

The first one pulled the map away from the other. He switched on a big friendly grin as he stepped quick toward me. His right hand was under the map. If I'd been farther away, I might have turned and run. But it was too late and maybe the bad mood I was in had something to do with it. Hell, in a situation like that you want to be the guy that lands the first shot, anyway.

I gripped the stick with both hands, brought the tip up and lunged at him as hard as I could. He wasn't expecting it and hesitated. I aimed at the

1

middle of his tie and tried to drive the tip of the stick straight through his body. If he really was from out of town, welcome to New York.

He staggered back and fell into the guy behind him. The knife he'd been hiding clattered to the sidewalk. I kept pushing forward, lowered my shoulder and stabbed him again. He reached for the stick. I reversed it and rammed the crook end into his neck. He went backward and landed on his side choking and grabbing at his throat. No threat there. I went for the second guy.

He was reaching inside his coat as he backpedaled. I switched my grip, got in close and cracked his arm and his head twice. Jab to the soft spots, strike to the hard. The second one caught him near his eyes and drew blood on his forehead.

By then I could hear the first goon stumbling to his feet and running away. Realizing he was alone, the second goon sprinted the other direction.

I stood there under the lamppost looking one way, then the other until I was sure they were gone and my own excitement calmed down. Without thinking, I picked up their hats. I noticed then that the second guy had bled on the front of my shirt and my coat sleeve. The bastard.

Over the next day or so when I told people in Jimmy's Place about it, they'd shake their heads and say that with the end of Prohibition and Repeal, everything was changing. You wouldn't be surprised by something like that a few blocks away, west of Ninth Avenue, but here? What're you going to do?

If I'd thought more about it, I might have figured that those two had been waiting for me where I walked just about every night. But I didn't think about it. I had other things on my mind. And like I said, those were the first guys. They got better.

• • •

For me it started with those two goons under a streetlamp. But the men behind it would say it began two years before that, with the Lindbergh kidnapping. Yeah, that's the same time I met Connie. These things are never as simple as you want them to be.

It was Sunday, March 6, 1932, five days after the kid was snatched. By then, the news had sunk in and it was all anybody talked about. You've got to remember that those were the blackest days of the Depression with millions of men out of work and nobody doing anything to help them.

Then the son of the most famous man in the world was stolen from his bedroom, and everybody learned about it right away from the radio and in newspapers. Yeah, a lot of rich people were being held for ransom in those days, but when it happened to the most famous people on earth, it rattled everybody, rich and poor, legit and crooked. It wasn't just regular people like Connie and me who felt like the world had gone completely crazy. On the East Side of Manhattan, a few wealthy men were just as scared as the rest of us. And they could do something about it, or so they thought.

For the moment, don't worry about how I know all this. I'll explain by and by.

That was the Sunday the blizzard hit the East Coast. It shut the city down by midafternoon. These guys were in the most exclusive men's club in the city, the Cerberus Society. Don't bother trying to look it up, you won't find anything. It's not like the Knickerbocker Club or the Metropolitan. These men were in one of those walnut-paneled rooms with a big toasty fireplace, and leather wingchairs. There was a sideboard with bottles of hundred-year-old brandies and a humidor filled with Havanas wrapped in silk bands with an CS monogram. I've got no use for the cigars, but I've had the brandy. It's not bad. There's still about an inch left in the bottle I stole.

Chapter Two

In the spring of 1934 when this crazy business started, I was distracted and cranky.

First, that bastard Roosevelt had ended Prohibition. I know, it's funny that I hated the guy so much and then when all this was over, I saved him. Go figure. You see, without Prohibition, for the first time in my young life, I was trying to make a living without breaking whatever laws they'd decided to enforce at the time. Until then, I'd applied myself to stealing cars, handling bribes for cops and politicians, fixing a World Series and selling alcohol. As long as Jimmy Quinn's Place was a speak, I paid off the right men and didn't worry about regulations and the like. Once they made booze legal, I had to grease more palms and I also had to get permits and pass inspections and do a hundred other damn things I'd never had to think about if I wanted to keep the place open.

Second, Connie was in Paris. That's why I was cranky. It happened like this. About three years before, Connie Nix had been working as a maid for my old friend Walter Spencer at the Pennyweight mansion in New Jersey. That didn't pan out so she came to be a waitress at the speak. Within a year she knew as much about running the place as I did. She worked hard. She suggested changes that made money right away. I'd never have figured out that painting the women's bathroom and putting in better lights, mirrors and fixtures would make such a big difference. And when she helped with the nightly count and the books, her skim was reasonable. The place was doing well enough that I didn't mind. Hell, I expected it. For a time after the Crash, I lost money just about every week and had to tap my savings to stay open. I did what I had to do and never missed a payroll.

But then last year, Connie and I got ourselves involved in a strange situation out on Long Island that I still can't explain. It had to do with

Willie Seabrook, the famous writer, adventurer and drunk. The story's complicated and I've already told it. The point is that when it was over, Connie had taken possession of this fancy gold egg.

I remember the Sunday afternoon we took a good look at the thing for the first time. We went in early and took it out of the safe in my office. I could tell she was really excited to see it. Things had been damned dicey the day before when she lifted it. She found it on the floor where I'd knocked it, wrapped it up in a handkerchief and stuffed it into a pocket. A little later, smart girl that she was, she stuffed it into the deep pocket of my topcoat. I didn't know it was there. After we got back to the city, she stashed it in the safe.

We put it on my desk and unwrapped it under the good reading light. Sitting on its side, the egg was about four inches long and two or three inches tall, bigger than most chicken eggs. It looked like it was made out of gold and it was heavy enough to be gold. There was a clear, shiny, deep green enamel design like leaves with tiny diamonds all over. The round end was hinged and when you opened it, there was a tiny green and gold car inside with wheels that rolled.

She said, "What do you think it's worth?"

I couldn't say. Connie chewed her lip and looked worried. I was worried, too, and I could tell what she was thinking.

You see, when the egg turned up missing, the previous owner claimed she didn't care. She said she'd always found the thing ostentatious and it didn't mean anything to her. I believed her. Well, I believed her when she said it, but was she saying the same thing after she'd thought it over? The woman was wealthy enough that losing something like that wasn't going to cause her to skip a lunch, but you never know. Connie and I hashed it out. She wanted to turn it into cash as fast as she could to pay for a trip to Paris. I told her to go slow.

"To do this right, you're going to have to let three or four of those pirates down on Canal Street examine it. If it really is valuable, word is going to get about that it's on the market. That might get the cops interested, and I know it will get a lot of other guys interested—guys who'll do whatever they have to do to get it."

"You're saying I should just leave it in the safe. For how long?"

That's exactly what I wanted her to do. Let it sit for a year, then nose around to see what's what. But I knew she wouldn't buy it.

"You've got to be careful. Let me make some calls tomorrow, see if I can set something up. I've had dealings with some guys."

"Do you trust them?"

"Of course not."

• • •

Connie didn't know about my savings, my inheritance. She knew about Mother Moon, but not what she left me.

Mother Moon raised me. She told me she was my aunt. My parents emigrated from Ireland where they'd been told that my mother's older sister, Mother Quinn, owned a tenement in Hell's Kitchen. She'd have a place for them. That was true but by the time they got here, Mother Quinn had taken a trip out west and married a Chinaman. Then she was Mother Moon. She came back with a baby girl she named Fantan Perfect Jasmine. She never explained what happened to Mr. Moon and I never asked. I was born in her place. My real mother died a couple of years later and not long after that my father wandered off. I can't honestly say I remember them.

Mother Moon took me over. You see, everybody who lived in her building either paid rent or worked for her—adults and kids. There were usually dozen or so small fry who took orders from her. Some sold newspapers but more of us were sent out to steal from shop owners who hadn't kept up with their payments or had done something to get on the bad side of Alderman Jimmy Hines and the local cops. They told her who needed persuading and she cut us loose.

I wasn't a good shoplifter. I was too small to carry much but I was fast, really fast, and I knew my way around that part of the city pretty good. When I was eight or nine, Mother Moon arranged for me to work as a runner for Arnold Rothstein, the gambler and fixer who had his hand in a lot of business. To do that I stayed around whenever he thought he might need to send a message or answer one or have something picked up. When he got into poker or pool games that could last for ten or twelve hours, I'd sit in corners waiting. And watching and listening. I didn't understand much of what I saw and heard but I got some of it. I'd be there when he got the telephone call or when some guy came to tell him something. Then he'd send me off to see so and so at this hotel or that restaurant, and give him something or get something from him and bring it back.

I don't know how much A.R. or the Brain, as he was called, paid Mother Moon but it must have been pretty good. I hadn't been working for him long before she moved me into a better room upstairs. It wasn't as nice as Fanny's—what else would we call a girl named Fantan Perfect Jasmine?—but I wasn't sharing it with five other kids and I thought that was pretty great.

When I asked Mother Moon what Rothstein was paying, she said that she was taking care of it for me and she'd see to it that I had enough in my pocket. Then she'd give me a nickel or a dime. She kept track of the other work I came to do later and always expected at least half of what I took in. Of course, I made sure that my skim was reasonable.

What I'm getting at is that over the years I worked for him, Rothstein gave Mother Moon a lot of money. She held it until the most terrible weekend of my life in 1928 when both of them died. Rothstein got plugged in the Park Central Hotel. I was there. The shots scared me and I ran and fell in the street and ruined my right knee. A few days later, the pain of her cancer dulled by the opium I'd brought her, Mother Moon died on her daybed. In her will she left the building to Fanny and ten thousand dollars to me. That was a hell of a lot less than A.R. had shelled out for my services over the years. After they'd taken her body away and I could get into her room alone, I found another six thousand dollars she'd hidden in her strongbox and twenty-four uncut diamonds and emeralds, each wrapped in a little piece of white paper. They were inside the pillow on the daybed that fit the small of her back.

Mother Moon didn't trust banks. I didn't either but I had to trust a safety deposit box at the Harriman National on Fifth Avenue. It had been good enough for Rothstein.

I took five of the stones to jewelers in the Diamond District on Canal Street and found out they were quality stuff, not the best but very good. Over the years, I'd sold six of them on Canal Street when I needed cash. I spread them around the merchants, not wanting to be known as a guy who had a lot of quality goods stashed away somewhere. But I probably had a reputation, anyway. Those guys talked to each other. They knew who Jimmy Quinn was and when I went into their little shops, they knew I was there for business.

On the Monday after Connie lifted the egg, I found my address book in the desk and looked up the numbers of three guys—Leo Leonard & Sons,

Vincent Daddiego, and Basil Bogolomov. Connie listened in when I called them. I told them that I had an unusual piece of gold and I wanted to know if they might be interested in making an offer. Each of them said he'd be ready whenever I got there. Connie smiled when she heard that. Then I called down to the bar and asked Arch Malloy to come up to my office. Connie raised her eyebrows. I said, "You'll see."

Arch came to work at the speak a few months after Connie. He was a garrulous old gent who surprised me every time he opened his mouth. He was one of guys who'd read just about everything and was happy to tell you about it. Now, some guys like that, you know they're shitting you but I never caught Arch spinning a story that turned out to be a total lie, or, as he might put it, "airy persiflage." That means light bantering talk. I looked it up.

Arch sat in the chair next to Connie and looked at the thing wrapped in a handkerchief on my desk. A curious smile ticked up behind his soup strainer mustache. He didn't say anything.

I said, "How'd you like to come in early tomorrow and earn some overtime?"

"Of course."

Connie unwrapped the egg.

The soup strainer ticked again. "Oh, my."

"We're taking this dingus down to Canal Street to get some estimates on what it might be worth. I don't expect any trouble but it can't hurt to have another guy with a gun."

He leaned forward and reached for the egg. "May I?"

Connie nodded.

He picked it up carefully, turning it in his hands to look at every part of the surface. He put in back on the desk, opened the catch and let the little car roll out. He held that up to the light and used a fingernail to lift the hinged sides of the hood. There was a tiny engine inside. The doors opened to show a chauffeur in the front seat and a man and woman in the back. All of it gold. The clothes were painted in different colors.

Arch said, "I've heard of eggs like this that were made for the Russian royal family before the revolution but I've never seen one."

He rolled the car back inside the egg and closed it. "If it's one of those it could be worth almost anything. But even if it's not, if it's real gold... I see why you want another gun."

Chapter Three

Tuesday, December 5, 1933, was a memorable day.

At ten o'clock that morning, Connie, Arch and I caught a cab to Canal Street.

I didn't get down that way very much. When I started dealing with the jewelers, the little storefronts that lined the street were always busy. After the Crash it quieted down, like the rest of the country. But we weren't interested in the street-level stores. The guys I dealt with didn't have signs. You had to know they were upstairs, and you didn't waltz in.

It was a cold day, threatening rain. I remember Connie had on a long coat and she carried a little Walther .22 in the pocket. I had the egg wrapped in the handkerchief in one pocket of my topcoat and a Detective Special in the other. Arch usually used a Luger he'd stolen. I don't know where he carried it. To anybody who cared to look, we were three ordinary people, not threatening anybody, not skulking and snaking around like we've got something hot to unload. No, we were well dressed locals, probably down there to buy something for the little lady.

We went to Bogolomov first, figuring if the egg was Russian, he'd be most likely to know. To get to his place, you went to a single unmarked metal door set back from the street between two storefronts. There were four buttons and a speaker grille by the door. I pressed the second one. A moment later a scratchy voice said, "Yes."

"Quinn."

"A moment."

Sometime later, we heard steps and a thin pissed-off blonde opened the door. I'd never seen her before. It was always Bogolomov or his wife. Then I remembered somebody saying that she died. The blonde turned without speaking and stalked down a short dark hall to the stairs. We went up two flights to the shop. She banged on the door and Bogolomov let us in.

He was a skinny older guy with a fringe of white hair around a shiny bald head. He wore his glasses on a chain around his neck. The pissed-off blonde looked to be in her twenties, a doxy with wavy hair held by a jeweled clip, rouged cheeks, lipstick and nail polish. She said something to him in Russian, and gave us the once-over. He answered her, sounding like he was asking a question. She lit a cigarette and ignored him. It didn't take Dr. Freud to figure what was going on.

There were three glass cabinets in that room with rings, bracelets and necklaces. Bogolomov took us through another thick metal door to a second room where he kept the good stuff and then on into his work room filled with tools and equipment I didn't know.

He sat at a table beneath a bright light. "So, you said gold. No stones this time? What have you brought me?"

I unwrapped the egg and put it on the table. The old jeweler put on his glasses and leaned down for a close look. I couldn't tell if he was impressed but he was intrigued. He opened it up, then took a magnifying glass to the car. He used a small flashlight to look closely at the inner wall of the egg, and he looked at each of the little diamonds through a loupe. He measured the egg and the car with calipers, and weighed them on a scale.

He spent about half an hour on it. Finally, he took off his glasses and said, "There are faint marks on the flat base of the egg and the bottom of the automobile that say 24-carat. I can test for this. The egg and the automobile weigh 380 grams. It is decorated with a deep translucent green floral design studded with seventeen small diamonds. Four appear to be missing. I'd have to remove the stones to get accurate weight and clarity. Also, you can just make out a double-headed eagle on the base. That is the Fabergé hallmark, but I am almost certain that this is not one of the Imperial eggs. I have not seen one myself but they are described as being much more elaborate than this egg."

Connie said, "How much is it worth?"

I wanted to elbow her. She was going too fast.

"Gold is $35 an ounce but even if it is not Fabergé, it is well crafted and certainly worth much more. If you could let me speak with a colleague, I might be able to make a more accurate offer."

I said, "Leonard wants to see it."

Bogolomov blew a raspberry. "Leonard will serve you coffee and tell you how beautiful your girlfriend is. He will beat the bush for an hour before he says that he will give you a thousand dollars."

Yeah, that was how Leonard operated. "What about Daddiego?"

Bogolomov shrugged and dismissed Daddiego with a wave. "If you wish to waste your time."

Connie surprised us by standing up quick. She wrapped the egg in the handkerchief and gave it to me. "We need to know more than this," she said, and then, as sweet as she could sound, "Thank you so much for your valuable time, Mr. Bogolomov. We'll be in touch."

"Quinn," he said, "Be reasonable. We have much to discuss."

"No, you don't talk to Jimmy. You talk to me. The egg is mine."

"A thousand pardons. I assumed that since I have always dealt with Mr. Quinn and he contacted me that he was in possession of the object."

"Of course, but you'll have to excuse us. We have other appointments. Here." She handed him one of the new cards I'd had printed. "If you'd like to make an offer, call Jimmy's Place and ask for Miss Nix."

• • •

Turned out Bogolomov had it right with Leo Leonard. His place was in the same block, also on the second floor, and the woman who worked with him had been there ever since I'd been selling him stones. He gave us coffee and picked up straight away that he needed to be talking to Connie. He examined the egg just like Bogolomov had and said that it was clearly a cheap imitation of an Imperial egg, and he hoped she hadn't paid too much for it. Connie didn't answer. It took him an hour to say that he was sorry but the best he could offer was a grand. Connie gave him a card.

Across the street, Vincent Daddiego's building had a doorman who let us in and called up to his shop. We took a self-service elevator to the third floor. Daddiego and his partner were dealing with two other guys I knew a little. They worked for Joe Adonis and were looking at a couple of big diamond rings for themselves. We nodded to each other. Daddiego left them to his partner and took us to his back room and went through the same process as Bogolomov and Leonard with the egg. Then he asked Connie if he could test the gold. He rubbed the edge of the base on a flat piece of stone, and put a drop of acid on the faint gold streak it left. It was 24 carat.

At the end, he said, "It's an interesting piece. I'm not sure what to make of it. The hallmark might be a forgery but I doubt it. I've seen it before. It could well have been made by an apprentice in the Fabergé shop as a test or assignment. Maybe they meant to remove the diamonds and melt it down. On its own, the car might attract attention but the market for this kind of bauble is down, like everything else."

He stared at it and frowned. "I'll give you $1,500 for it. I doubt you'll find anyone here who'll offer more."

Connie handed him a card and said she'd consider it.

• • •

Back on Canal, I hailed a cab. Before I got in, I looked up at the window of Bogolomov's shop across the street. The pissed-off blonde doxy was staring at us. When we got back to the speak, Connie had a message to call Bogolomov. He said he'd give eleven "on the matter we discussed," because you never know who could be listening in. She told him she had an offer of fifteen. He said he'd call back.

After that, all of us settled down to work. We thought it might be busy for a Tuesday, because the papers were saying that Utah was finally about to vote to repeal the Eighteenth Amendment. That would mean Prohibition would be officially ended in New York, and Jimmy's Place would be legal. Well, almost half-legal.

You see, I'd had two inspections by the State Alcoholic Beverage Control Board. After the first one, I made the changes that the guy demanded and I passed the second one. I had the paperwork to prove it but they hadn't issued the official certification. And, if you wanted to be technical about it, I wasn't supposed to be selling my stock either. That was the liquor, wine and beer that I bought off the boat from Meyer Lansky, Charlie Luciano and Owney Madden. Once selling a drink was legal, the stuff was supposed to come from a bonded warehouse after the taxes had been paid.

I heard that a few guys were going to give their inventory away, but those were the guys who'd been selling bad booze all along—panther piss that had been cut with stuff you don't want to think about, much less drink. I didn't deal in that. I sold the real thing and charged at least twice as much for it as any place in that part of town.

Because that Tuesday was going to be such a historic night, I thought that the regulars might find reason to stop by. They did. All the tables were filled and they were two deep at the bar. Most of them knew about the changes that were coming but we still handed out more than a hundred of the new cards.

Those cards replaced the ones I got when I bought the place from Carl Spinoza in 1928. The originals said "Quinn's Place" because everybody thought of it as Spinoza's, and they were membership cards. If Fat Joe Beddoes didn't recognize your face through the little spy door in the front door, you had to show him a card to get in. Now, as I experienced it, Prohibition really wasn't enforced, at least not by the city cops as long as they got their due. There were Feds who'd try to shut you down. But they had to get in. Izzy and Moe were the ones everybody knew. They dressed up as women one night but Fat Joe recognized them and told them to fuck off. Hell, Fat Joe told everybody to fuck off. That happened before I bought the place and I heard him tell the story a thousand times.

My point is that now with the place going legit, we decided to change the name.

One night back in October after we closed, Marie Therese, Frenchy, Connie, Arch and I sat down together. We asked Fat Joe to join us but you know what he said. Anyway, we talked about the changes that were coming and what we had to do. First thing was to get a sign. Until then, we didn't need one. It was a neighborhood bar. Everybody knew where it was. Connie suggested a green canvas awning over the steps down from the sidewalk. Wouldn't cost much and we could put the name on three sides. Maybe a couple of little spotlights so you could read it at night. And a matching awning over the front door of the Cruzon Grill upstairs so anybody who didn't know would figure that they were connected. But what should the name be? The old cards said it was Quinn's Place but nobody called it that. In the neighborhood, it was just Jimmy's. Thus, Quinn's Place became Jimmy's Place.

Marie Therese said we should replace the overhead and wall lights with something more indirect and flattering. Connie said we should replace the old bar stools with new ones that were a few inches shorter and padded so women would be comfortable on them. While we were at it, we should take down the painting of the coy naked young lady that had been behind the bar since before Carl Spinoza owned it. Frenchy and Arch said they liked her. Connie and Marie Therese said women didn't like it and if we took it down, and put up more mirrors and lighting there, the place would look more inviting. Arch took the picture home.

We also refinished the floor and the mahogany bar, and put in new booths and tables. When you added in what I'd paid the plumbers and electricians, becoming a legitimate businessman was turning out to be the most expensive thing I'd ever done.

• • •

They'd put up the awning while we were down on Canal Street that Tuesday. All the regulars said it looked great and I have to say I was surprised to see a lot of new faces. Patrolmen Norris and Mahan showed up early. They were my beat cops. Mahan had replaced Cheeks when he retired. I got on well enough with both of them. We'd talked it over and agreed that the place being legal really didn't change anything. I slipped them a few bills every week. They got their drinks on the house and I expected them to keep a close eye on things. When we had problems with the odd obnoxious drunk, they'd lend a hand and keep it on the QT. If they learned about something that might interest me, they made sure I heard about it first from them.

They were the ones who told me a week before that whenever booze became legal, Commissioner Bolan was going to announce that he was putting more than a hundred men around Times Square to keep it quiet. But nobody was going to roust a place doing business as usual.

By ten, we had a full house. I was working behind the bar with Frenchy. Arch, Connie and Marie Therese were taking orders and serving drinks. I don't remember who was in the coat room. Fat Joe was still at his spot by the door but now he was letting everybody in. I told him that soon enough, he'd have to do some real work, not just sit there on his butt and curse the customers while he kept the riff-raff out. I saw Detective Ellis making his way through the crowd to me. Gordon's on ice for him. Ellis was just crooked enough to know who you could work with in any department of the city government. I'd been paying him what he called a "retainer" to ease the way with the right guys to do my inspections and permits. He was my most dependable and unprofitable regular.

Ellis grabbed his gin and said something to a guy sitting at a table. The guy got up. Ellis stood on his chair and tapped on his glass with a spoon until everybody quieted down. He knocked back a slug of gin and said, "Hear ye, hear ye, hear ye," his cop voice loud. "Chief Inspector John O'Brien has personally instructed me to tell you that he received a teletype this evening at 9:20 informing him that the great state of Utah has just voted to repeal the 18th Amendment. That drink in your hand is now legal!"

The crowd burst into applause. Then Ellis helpfully added, "And the next round is on the house!"

Chapter Four

Late that night, actually early Wednesday morning after we'd closed, Connie said she wanted to come to my room at the Chelsea. She did that some nights, not every night and it surprised me then because we were both exhausted. She wanted to talk and she'd brought a bottle of Hennessy Five Star from the bar. We both knew Five Star was Willie Seabrook's favorite brandy. Seeing it reminded me of the crazy business we went through with him. She poured two glasses, hers short. I suggested we drink them in bed. She made me sit in my reading chair. I knew what she was going to say.

"I want to sell it. I want you to come to Paris with me."

"I want to go to Paris with you but I can't. Not now. Too much is changing every day. You saw that tonight. Too many decisions. Haven't even got the distributors straightened out. A year from now I can go but not now. You know all this."

I didn't admit to her or myself that I wanted her help with those decisions. I also knew how much she wanted to go. "I'm not sure about putting the egg on the market either."

"Don't try to talk me out of this."

"I'm not. Wait to find out if Bogolomov comes up with another offer. You should do that anyway."

"All right, but Marie Therese and I have discussed this. She says she knows a girl in Montreal who's planning to go to Paris this summer. I could travel with her and we could get a place together. Marie Therese and I worked it out. For six hundred dollars I could afford to stay for three months."

A few years ago, a young woman wouldn't have thought about doing something like that on her own but times change, and with Connie, well, she was never going to be told what to do. Hell, she rode from California to New Jersey on a train by herself. When she saw a chance at something better, like working for me, she took it. And when she had a chance to go to Paris, she was going to take it.

But her leaving then was the last thing I wanted. I sipped the good brandy and tried to figure how to say what I'd been thinking ever since I saw the damned egg.

"You're going to go to Paris then. That's settled. This summer."

She finished her brandy, sat on my lap and started to unbutton my shirt. I helped.

"And you'll let me take care of the egg," I said.

She stopped unbuttoning. "How?"

"I got an idea."

• • •

The truth is the egg worried me. I was afraid that if Connie sold it, whoever bought it would do something stupid and I'd wake up one morning to see a headline that read:

Imperial Russian Egg
Thought Lost by Wealthy Widow
Found in Pawn Shop

From there, the cops would have no trouble tracing it back to me. The other people involved in the dicey business that put the egg in Connie's pocket were either dead, missing, rich or famous. That left Connie and me.

And there was the pissed-off blonde doxy. She was just too interested in us. I had to figure Bogolomov told her everything about the egg. I didn't know her and I had no reason to trust her. Joe Adonis might know something too. He was one of the top men in Charlie Luciano's mob and even though he didn't need to do it for money, he always liked jewelry. Kept his hand in stealing and fencing the stuff. If his guys mentioned anything and he asked me about it, I wouldn't be able to say no. I had to figure that word was out on Canal Street that Jimmy Quinn had a nice-sized gold dingus, and that spooked me.

Thinking like that took me back to my time working for Rothstein. I usually didn't know what I was carrying for him, but there was a good chance it was valuable, and I knew I was responsible for it. There were guys who tried to take it away from me. More than once. None of them got anything, and I'm not bragging when I say that. I was good at what I did and, hell, I'm proud of it. But my point is that I learned to pay careful attention to everything on the street. It's hard to describe now, but I was able to widen my focus on people and things around me without swiveling my head around or gawking at tall buildings like some appleknocker. I tried to ignore normal street noise and listen for anything I hadn't heard before, and I was usually a little bit scared. Like I said, it's hard to describe now. It's just something I knew when I was ten years old.

Having the damn egg brought that fear and wariness right back. I didn't like it but, hell, it had served me before.

• • •

I got up early on Wednesday and set to work on my plan for the egg. Connie was back up in her room on the fifth floor. I broke out a new medium gray three-piece from F.R. Tripler, one of your better haberdashers, with a fresh starched white shirt and a deep translucent green silk tie. Had a couple over easy at the hash house next door and was at the Bowery Savings Bank when they opened their doors. That's where I kept my goods in a safety deposit box that I rented when I heard a rumor that the Harriman Bank was going to go bust. I always dressed better when I went to the bank. A.R. said that you want to look sharper than any society toff or businessman who assumes he's better than you. Another piece of advice that's served me. A well-cut suit impresses women, too, and, yes, I was thinking that might help later that day with Connie.

Bogolomov called that afternoon and offered seventeen. We were in the office with the egg on the desk between us. Connie jumped out of her chair and did a little dance. I called Daddiego. He went up to seventeen fifty. I called Leonard. He said that he'd made his best offer the day before. Connie wanted to try to get Bogolomov and Daddiego bidding against each other face to face but I talked her out of it. I was still worried about what could happen if we let go of it.

"I tried to explain that you need to let this thing cool off."

She made a face.

"How about this? You sell the egg to me." I took an envelope stuffed with cash out of my breast pocket and put it on the desk.

"That's two grand. You go to Paris and you're not broke when you get back. A year from now I sell my egg and make a profit."

I watched her working her way through her options and her questions. She picked up the money, took a couple of tens out of the envelope and held them up to the light. Felt the paper. "You've got two thousand dollars?" She sounded suspicious.

"Yes."

"What about Bogolomov and Leonard?"

"I tell them a third party heard about the egg and made a substantially higher offer. He showed up here. With cash. We don't know how he found out about it. Word must have got out after our visit on Tuesday. He wanted to take possession immediately."

The best lies are almost the truth.

"What if Bogolomov and Daddiego are both lying? What if the egg is worth a lot more, and a year from now you're able to sell it for three or four thousand?"

She was serious. She was talking about money.

"Then you'll be wrong to sell it."

I let her work with that. "Or maybe you can persuade me to make a better offer."

I was serious. I was talking about sex.

We left the egg in the safe and went downstairs to work. That night in my room in bed, she said she'd take the two thousand. We were naked, sipping the Five Star, covers kicked away. The way the light hit her reminded me of another time with another woman named Connie. That had been before I met this Connie, and it was the last time that Connie and I were in bed together. The memory made me shiver.

• • •

The next day I called Bogolomov and Daddiego and spun my story about them being outbid by a third party. Daddiego sounded relieved, like he didn't have to think about it anymore.

Bogolomov was not happy.

Statement by Michael Patrick Reardon; Saturday, July 14, 1934; 11:34am.

Stenography and typescript by Provisional Operative T.S.

Also present: Detective Theodora Opperman and Miss Louise Deavers, a Negro girl who acts as Mr. Reardon's caretaker.

[Note: Subject is ill and partially blind. He speaks slowly. He is easily tired and sips morphine at irregular intervals. T.O.]

The Cerberus Society was founded in 1895. It is housed in an unassuming five story building at 249 East 35th St. From the street it appears to be a single narrow private address, but the Society also occupies the buildings on either side. Facilities for the removal of incriminating evidence are located in the basement.

A staircase on the first floor leads to the library and dining room on the Mezzanine. Stanford White designed the building's thick paneling and insulation so that even the loudest sounds cannot be heard on the street. On the floors above the Mezzanine are the card room, billiard room, opium parlor, and bedrooms for members' use with their prostitutes, catamites and victims. I have been told that the Latin inscription above the library fireplace translates "Within these walls all is permitted." Members take that to mean they are beyond all civil and religious laws. No one can punish them for anything that is done there. For 43 years I witnessed the members' attempts to live up to that sentiment and, I am ashamed to say, I helped make sure knowledge of those actions did not go beyond those walls. For that and many other sins, I hope this confession or testament will bring some understanding. I cannot ask for forgiveness and expect none.

Unlike most private clubs, membership in the Society is strictly by invitation. No man may apply though many have made inquiries. Members bring potentially like-minded men to dine, drink or attend social functions. Other members take their measure of the man. If a guest is then put forth for membership, two of the three Governors must approve. The man is then offered a place in the Society. Annual dues and special expenses are easily twice those of the city's more established clubs. Even at that, the Governors underwrite the Society's operating expenses. I know. I kept the books. The Governors control every aspect of the Cerberus Society. The original Charter states that each of the three founders is a Governor. He may pass his office to his oldest son or another member agreed to by the other two Governors if he chooses to retire. If a member wishes to offer a suggestion about a change to the Society or an idea for a new activity, he presents it to the Governors in writing. They seldom approve. If a member offends the sensibilities of other members and the Governors, he will be reprimanded once. A second reprimand results in removal from the membership roll and expulsion. This has never happened.

During my tenure membership was limited to fifty. In recent years it has declined.

Members come from the wealthiest of the wealthy men in the city. They are also the most ruthless and competitive. Because of that, many of them have been denied membership elsewhere. Beyond the pleasures of the fleshpots that the Society offers, the members are brought together by their resentment of other men of the same or lesser status who have rebuffed them. They share a sense of their individual righteousness and superiority. One of the founding Governors said, "Inside each successful man there lies a beast. It must sometimes be allowed to roam, lest it destroy him from within."

Staff is limited to the Major Domo, two Stewards, Sergeant at Arms, his assistant, and two Chefs. For larger events, temporary help is engaged. Luncheon and dinner are served. Prohibition did not exist for the Cerberus Society. Our stock of the finest spirits, wines and beers is far superior to any other club's and was regularly replenished during the dark years.

The dining room and library of the Cerberus Society are paneled in black walnut. In the library, members are cosseted in leather wingback chairs. In the evening, the room is usually illuminated only by small pools of light from the reading lamps and, in winter, from the fireplace. Members often gather there to discuss the news of the day—the devastation of the Depression, the rising threat of Communism, and the possibility of an American transition to the fascist ideas that appear to have saved Italy and are taking root in Germany.

Before the Crash, the talk was primarily of business. As the Depression continues, members' talk more often turns to these political matters. Unlike the discussions that take place in union halls, cafes or speakeasies, members of the Cerberus Society are fully prepared to use their wealth to make changes that would benefit them. On more than one occasion, I have heard them say that if it takes drastic measures to save the nation, so be it. Though they disagree on many issues they are one in their belief that words without actions are useless.

[The subject fell asleep at 12:06pm. T.O.]

Chapter Five

I can't really describe that time between the night in December when I bought the egg from Connie and June when she sailed for Havre. There was so much going on that most days I was running from one thing to another before the first one was finished and while I was doing that, there were two other things I should have been doing. Or I was waiting for a painter or a fire inspector or some other guy I had to grease. Then at night I worked behind the bar.

On slow afternoons, Marie Therese and Connie planned her trip. The girl Marie Therese knew in Montreal was Celeste Cassidy. Celeste was going to a special school in Paris. Her father owned three grocery stores. Her mother was an old friend of Marie Therese from France. The older women started writing letters and telegrams to each other. Connie and Celeste did the same thing, and Connie was talking about her like an old friend before she even met her. Marie Therese wrote to half a dozen friends in Paris. Air mail, no less. One of them arranged for someone to meet their ship at the dock in France. Two other friends said they knew of apartments. It took Marie Therese and Madame Cassidy two weeks to decide on the one that was "most appropriate." Connie set up an account with American Express and used it to send her first month's rent. Marie Therese managed to get a deal on tickets with the French Line. It wasn't a great deal, but they had a Tourist class cabin on the *S.S. Champlain* leaving on June 3 and returning on September 20.

Connie read fashion magazines to find out what clothes they would be wearing in Paris. She and Marie Therese scoured Russeks and Gimbels and B. Altman for weeks, but they wound up not getting much. Instead Connie bought a couple of outfits for the ship and a set of good luggage. She said she'd get what she needed in Paris.

Once they had those details set, Connie locked herself in my office for two hours on an afternoon in April and wrote to her mother back in California to tell her what she was doing. Connie had written to her a few times before and never got an answer. I know because she told me. After she finished that letter, there were a lot of crumpled pieces of stationery in the trashcan. She gave me the letter to put in the box. I could tell it was only one page.

You see, her mother didn't agree with Connie going east to work for the Pennyweights and that wasn't the first time they had it out with each other. But when Connie decided to leave home, she was sixteen and her mother didn't try to stop her. Yeah, she lied about her age. She lied about a lot of things, like the rest of us.

As for Jimmy's Place, business dropped off after that first night of being almost legal but, according to the receipts we were gaining customers. You see, once my competition was able to stock the same good brands I'd been selling, I had to lower the prices I'd been charging. But I still had one other thing that had always set Jimmy's Place apart. Variety.

More than half of my customers were locals who knew what they liked and ordered the same drink every time they came in. But since we'd been the only source of good liquor and wine in that part of town for more than five years, we also attracted your more serious and prosperous booze hounds who'd put up with my top-drawer prices for something they couldn't find anyplace else. I knew that if I wanted to keep catering to them, I had to look for new things. Arch Malloy was aces at that.

The old guy had been just about everywhere in the world and at every stop he acquainted himself with the local product. Scotch and Irish whiskey, of course. With rum and gin, he could hold forth for hours. Brandies nobody had ever heard of, akvavit, schnapps—Arch had an opinion. He could even discuss the finer points of vodka and tequila, and nobody drank those. The problem was finding a distributor who could get the stuff for us.

Using the inventory we had on hand, we were able to put up an impressive display of bottles and labels behind the bar once we had the new lighting and mirrors in place. But that brought up another problem.

After years of letting honest speaks do as they pleased, the new Alcoholic Beverage Control board decided to take it seriously if they caught you selling product that you hadn't paid taxes on. They called it contraband, so I had to keep my old stock out of sight if the wrong guys were inspecting the place. One more thing I had to worry about.

All of it—locating the product, buying it in the right quantities, letting people know we had it—took time and work. And money. I'd never handed out so much cash so fast in my young life. The box at the Bowery Savings Bank was getting sparse. Looked like a fifty-fifty proposition that Repeal could put me out of business.

At first though, everybody was so glad Prohibition was over that most nights had a good, happy feeling. It wasn't as roisterous as it had been the night before Roosevelt was inaugurated back in March. Everybody was over the moon for him, then. By the next spring it seemed like the same people thought he was doing everything wrong. Despite of the alphabet soup of agencies and such that he dreamed up, a lot of men were still out of work. Nobody was complaining more than the bankers who supported him before the election. The same guys who stood behind him on the platform in Washington said he was going too far with his financial reforms. But everybody else, regular people, wanted to celebrate Repeal. The fact that I was having to work behind the bar during the week told me business was better. First, there were more women in the crowds, and we were seeing more of them coming in with friends, women friends, not as couples.

I'd noticed it without understanding it until one night in late April right before Connie left. It was midweek, around eight o'clock. Four girls came in and took a table. The way they were laughing, it figured this wasn't their first stop. Connie waited on them. They ordered a quart bottle of champagne and made it clear to anyone who could hear them that they were celebrating the engagement of a tall girl with brown hair. The first bottle went down fast and they ordered a second right away. Sometime later, the tall girl got up and came to the bar. She found room at the end, motioned me over and asked for a Manhattan. She wore a well-cut expensive outfit and a diamond on her left hand.

As I mixed, I said, "Enough of the bubbles?"

She made a face. "I never really cared for it, to tell you the truth. Gives me gas."

I laughed. She took a sip of the drink and liked it. "You know, it's funny.

I live a couple of blocks away and I've been seeing this place for years but this is the first time I've been inside. My fiancé told me it was owned by a gangster. But I noticed the green awning out front and this," she looked around, "this is really nice."

"Glad you like it. Hope you come back."

"Are you…?"

I gave her a card from my vest pocket. "Jimmy Quinn."

"Oh no, I'm so embarrassed," she said, not at all embarrassed, with a big laugh that made Connie cut her eyes at us.

"This joint is safe enough. Nobody's been shot here since last week."

She put the card in her handbag and slid a dollar across the bar for a seventy-five-cent drink. I pushed it back. "This one's on the house. Congratulations. Hope to see you again."

She smiled and said, "I might just do that," before she went back to her table.

Connie gave me a look. That night she came to my room.

• • •

We were in bed, and I was in no mood to talk, when she said, trying to sound playful, "Are you going to be making time with that long drink of water while I'm gone?"

I pulled her close and started kissing my way down from her neck. She grabbed my hair and said, "Are you?" like she expected me to tell the truth.

"I was being polite to a new customer. She said she lives in the neighborhood and hasn't been in the place because she heard it was owned by a gangster."

Connie laughed. "You know, I can believe that. I remember the first time I saw it, that night we drove into the city because you 'had business to take care of.' Mrs. Pennyweight brought me along to look after little Ethan because she was afraid to leave him with Flora. We spent hours driving around in the rain while you left to see people without explaining what you were doing. Mrs. Pennyweight was ready to strangle you. Then you left me and Oliver at two in the morning in the Bowery."

"I really know how to show a girl a good time."

She was talking about the night right after I met her, when she was working as a maid for Mrs. Pennyweight. I had agreed to watch Spence and Flora's son but I had to straighten things out with a cop who laid a beating on me and shut my place down for a night. That's the only time I was ever closed down and it really doesn't count because the cop was crazy and we were only closed for a few hours.

"And you said yes as soon as I offered you a job."

"Yeah, I couldn't believe it myself. What a dope."

Chapter Six

As it happened, the timing of Connie's trip stunk. You see, she'd paid for her tickets in March. They were set, couldn't be changed. Then I learned that the day she was going to leave, Saturday, June 3, was likely to be the busiest and most profitable ever for Jimmy's Place. It happened like this. Celeste Cassidy and her mother were going to take the train from Montreal to Penn Station two days early, Thursday. Connie and Celeste would get to know each other and see the city on Friday. Saturday morning, they'd board the *S.S. Champlain* at Pier 57 and head for France. Sweet guy that I am, I said that Connie and Marie Therese could take the weekend off. We didn't count on the entire U.S. Navy being in town at the same time, but that's what President Roosevelt wanted.

Back in the Great War, he'd been Secretary of the Navy or something and once he got in the White House, he started building ships. To show them off to the world, he invited eighty warships to steam into New York Harbor for him to review. A hundred thousand people were expected to be on hand to watch. That night, the ships would berth in the city and on Saturday, thirty-five thousand thirsty sailors would be cut loose. The papers said the last time that many sailors hit the town at one time was in 1918.

Marie Therese said they'd change their plans. Still being Mr. Sweet Guy, I said no, you find a couple of girls to fill in, and you and Connie take the weekend off. That's what we did.

• • •

Celeste Cassidy and her mother got to Penn Station on schedule. Connie and Marie Therese met them. I'd hired a car and driver for them while they were going to be in town because I couldn't stray far from the bar. They drove to the Chelsea where Madame Cassidy had booked a room and then the four of them set out to see the town. I worked with Frenchy and Arch to pack as much extra product as we could in the cellar. Arch said it had been his experience that sailors went for cheap rum and beer, so we loaded up with them and extra ice. It took the better part of the day.

Later that afternoon I was in my office when Bogolomov called. By then it had been four, five months since I spun my story for him.

He said, "I would like to get in touch with the buyer of the egg. I will give you twenty dollars if you can arrange for me to speak with him, preferably in person but via telephone will do if I can be assured that indeed he has possession of the egg."

The call surprised me. Bogolomov had sounded hot under the collar the last time we talked, but not like it was anything serious. "Why are you so interested now?"

I heard a rustle like he was putting his hand over the mouthpiece and talking to the pissed-off blonde doxy.

"I have obtained more information about the possible source of the egg. But to be certain, I need to examine it again. I cannot say more, but this is a serious offer, Mr. Quinn. We have been doing business for many years. I promise you it would be to your benefit to allow me to speak to the new owner. If there is a new owner."

O.K., Bogolomov saw through my story about the other buyer. Ignore that. What do I do? I was still worried that if the cops ever got their hands on the egg, it would come back to me, and if it was as valuable as Bogolomov was hinting, then the cops would take it seriously. But, if it was worth that much, hell, maybe it was worth the risk. I could use the money. I said, "I can get in touch with him. Let me see what I can do."

"Very well. Do not be surprised if you hear from Daddiego. Other parties may become involved also."

What the hell?

• • •

After I hung up, I went to the Chelsea, showered and changed into my lightest tropical worsted, fresh shirt, and flowered tie topped by a Panama. I strolled back and checked in at the bar. Not too busy then but it was shaping up to be a good night. The two girls Marie Therese had hired were there. They looked like they were old enough to know what they were doing. Frenchy said they were fine. He told me that patrolmen Norris and Mahan had been by while I was gone. He'd given them a fiver to keep an extra eye on that place over the weekend. One thing I didn't have to take care of. When I told Fat Joe that he'd have to move bottles and kegs later, he said that wasn't his fucking job. I said it was his fucking job now if he wanted to have a fucking job and I didn't want to hear anything more about it. Fat chance.

By then, it was after seven. Connie and Marie Therese and the Cassidys had reservations at the Cruzon Grill. I went down to the cellar and found a decent bottle of French wine. Up in my office, I straightened my tie and took the back stairs to the kitchen. Vittorio had put them at the best six-top. I stopped at the door where I could see them through the glass.

Like Marie Therese, Madame Cassidy was a small, bright woman. She and her daughter were both attractive with dark hair and pale complexions. They had the same nose. Madame Cassidy split her attention between Marie Therese and her daughter. Celeste and Connie were huddled together, yakking away. Connie looked terrific. I gave Vittorio the wine and told him to bring four glasses.

Marie Therese jumped up when she saw me and made introductions. Madame Cassidy pulled a chair over and told me to sit next to her.

"Thank you so much for the car. It can be exhausting to see the city. Henri, the driver, even took Celeste's big trunk to ship. This is the most wonderful thing you have done for us." Connie beamed.

I asked Madame Cassidy if her room was all right. She said it was. She hadn't been to the city for a long time and she was surprised by how much had changed. First trip for Celeste but she didn't have that bowled-over look you see on some people. Connie said Celeste had been accepted at a famous art school in Paris. They'd been to the tower on the Chanin Building and they saw Times Square but they couldn't get down to the Battery because of the crowds trying to find a way to see the ships.

When their food arrived, I said I had to get back to work. Connie grabbed my sleeve before I could leave. She leaned close so nobody could hear her and asked how busy it was downstairs.

"We're doing fine. Have a good time."

She pulled me closer and smiled. "You are such a son of a bitch."

"Don't sound so surprised."

• • •

If it wasn't our busiest Friday night, it was close. No sailors but more out-of-towners than usual. They kept me and Frenchy moving behind the bar. A little after ten, Marie Therese and Connie came in. Connie took drink orders. Marie Therese replaced me. I loaded dirty glasses into the dumbwaiter and went downstairs to help Arch. We brought up more ice, mixers and gin.

Connie and I got back to the Chelsea an hour after last call. She came to my room.

I stripped off my clothes and got in bed while she made a real production of turning on the bedside light, pouring two Five Stars for us, and getting ready. She took her clothes off piece by slow piece. I sipped brandy and appreciated the show. Shoes first. Jacket folded over the back of my easy chair. Blouse untucked. Skirt unbuttoned and unzipped next, folded twice and placed next to the jacket. Blouse unbuttoned as she walked around the room and talked about this and that. Blouse shrugged off, draped over the chair. Brandy put on the table as she sat and unsnapped her stockings and rolled them off. Then the slip came off and even more slowly, the brassiere and underwear.

She drained the brandy, strolled over smiling to the bed and slid in beside me. "Roll over," she said, "I'm going to rub your back."

That didn't happen often and it was always the beginning of an interesting night. She sat on my back and worked on my shoulders and neck. "This is what Mr. Big Spender gets for springing for a Packard and driver. Pretty snazzy, all right. Celeste thinks my boyfriend is very handsome and rich."

"She's half right."

She worked on my shoulders for a little longer, then stretched out my arms. To rub them, she had to lean over my back until she forgot about what she was doing and laid down on me. She knew I liked that part. Sometime later, she sat up and told me to turn over.

As she got comfortable and rubbed my chest, she said, "That tall girl you were talking to the other night, she'll be back."

"Maybe."

"She will. I know it. By herself. What are you going to do then?"

"I don't know," I said, "but I know what I'm going to do now."

I grabbed her hips hard and pulled her up the way she liked. Her mouth twisted into a wicked smile that matched mine. She shoved my shoulders down and we pulled and pushed against each other until she twisted and I rolled over on top of her.

. . .

She was gone when I woke up Saturday. I showered, shaved and put on an older suit that was comfortable to work in. Vittorio's guys sent a plate of salami and eggs to my office. I ate as I went over last night's receipts. They were good. More was coming in than going out for a change. If the rest of the weekend was the same… I didn't let myself think about that. I got the cash, checks and IOUs sorted, and was back at the Chelsea when the car arrived.

Connie and I took the jump seats facing Madame Cassidy, Marie Therese and Celeste on the ten-minute drive to Pier 57. Marie Therese and Madame Cassidy were teary. Celeste was still taking in the sights. Connie reminded me about the dozen things that she'd been reminding me about for a week.

There was a wide paved area off Eleventh Avenue in front of the pier. It was thick with cars and taxis and a couple of buses unloading people. Two cops directed traffic. The driver knew the routine and jockeyed the big Packard to a lane on the right. The closest cop waved him on. We stopped in front of a big open structure that covered the pier. The *Champlain* towered over it. A couple of stevedores approached the car. Our driver waved them off and whistled. A guy in a French Line uniform pushed a cart over and opened the Packard's trunk. He looked at the girls' tickets, checked the tags on their luggage and wheeled the bags away. Celeste, Madame Cassidy and Marie-Therese went on into the boarding area. The older women wanted to go aboard and see the ship. I begged off. Connie stayed back when they left. I saw that she was crying, and it made her mad. She wrapped her arms around my neck and said, "Oh hell, I swore to myself that I wouldn't do this."

I took off my hat and kissed her for a long time.

Before she let go, she whispered, "Be good while I'm gone if you know what's good for you."

She was ready to leave and I almost didn't say anything.

"Listen, there's something I've got to tell you. Yesterday afternoon, Bogolomov called. He says he wants to make another offer on the egg. Maybe. First he wants to talk to the new owner."

It surprised her as much as it surprised me. "What does that mean?"

I shrugged. "He says he got more information about it and he wants to look at it again. He sounded pissed. I don't understand that either."

"What are you going to do?"

"I'll think of something. Maybe I'll tell him the new owner took the egg to Europe but has promised to be back in the country in six months."

She frowned and thought before she said anything. "I'm not going to go. It's not too late. I can get my bag."

"No," I sounded more sure of myself than I meant to. "You're going to go. You've got to go. You've been wanting to do this ever since you got to know Willie, ever since you read his book, I guess. With you and Willie, there's just something, I don't know how to say it but you've got to do this. You won't be happy here until you do and maybe it won't make you happy and you'll need to keep going places... oh hell, I don't know what I'm saying."

We probably talked it out some more then but I don't remember what we said. Connie got on the ship and sailed off to France.

That Saturday night Jimmy's Place was packed with sailors. Arch was right about the rum and cheap beer. We only had two fights. I saw that the first one was building. Before it started, I ducked under the leaf in the bar and got between the two guys. I told them to take it outside and we were almost at the door when they went for each other. Fat Joe and I tossed them out onto the sidewalk and whistled down Norris and Mahan. The second got to the yelling stage. The two guys' shipmates told them to can it and they all left. The guys at that end of the bar were disappointed. They wanted to see a fight.

When Marie Therese and I counted the evening's take, we'd made more money than we had since I bought the place. Maybe being a legitimate enterprise was going to work.

Three nights later, the goons with the map and the knife under the lamppost tried to kill me.

Continuation of statement by Michael Patrick Reardon; Saturday, July 14, 1934; 2:55pm.

(Personnel same as morning session.)

Stenography and typescript: T.S.

The library of the Cerberus Society is a graceful quiet room where older members gather to read, talk and enjoy our stock of the finest brandies, sherries, cordials and cigars. It is separated from the dining room by thick paneled walls and sliding doors that are much heavier than normal.

The dining room tends to be boisterous in the evening, especially when the younger members congregate. For a period of several years, a group of them participated regularly in "Heights of Degradation" dinners in which they attempted to outdo each other in disgusting acts. Those ended only after the Governors threatened mass expulsions. Those excesses were replaced by motion picture screenings when films that would never be shown at the Biograph or Odeon were made available to the members.

It is common for the younger members to use the dining room to advance a seduction. A man might bring a coquette or perhaps his fiancée for dinner at the Society knowing that later, on his silent command, the Steward will slip a philter into her drink. This potion was concocted by a member whose family fortune comes from the chemical industry. He has generously made it available to any member who requests it. On evenings when a young gentleman is planning to make use of this amenity, word spreads and the dining room is packed. Those members understand what is happening when he takes his young lady upstairs to "break her in." The lucky man knows that he is in for a good round of back-slapping when he comes downstairs.

That congratulatory spirit is seldom in evidence when members bring their catamites. Many of those young men and boys do not need any narcotic inducement to be led upstairs. It can be more difficult to deal with the uncooperative ones.

Upon occasion, members of a violent bent allow their predilections to go too far, resulting in severe injuries, injuries that often require surgical treatment. Three times, to my knowledge, young men and women have been killed in the bedrooms or have been so horribly damaged that they expired soon after they were taken away. They were common street mongrels. Doubtless they may have been missed by someone, but the staff made sure that no trace of their presence at the Society was left in the building, and the bodies were disposed of. I understand they are beneath Long Island Sound.

Drug overindulgence by the members is a more common problem for the staff. Several members have been taken by a private ambulance service to Doctor's Hospital where they are discreetly admitted and treated. Payment for all services is handled through a third party to ensure that the Society remains anonymous. Only one member has died from his use of drugs on the premises. The Sergeant-at-arms and I were able to keep the body on ice over the weekend, and then to quietly move it to his office where he was discovered at his desk Monday morning. There was never even a hint of a police inquiry. The Governors make it quite clear to the members that they will be billed for all medical expenses and debris removal.

Those expenses can be substantial. Of course, the Society makes regular payments to the local precinct to see that any inquiries into its activities are scotched quickly and thoroughly. Rumors of the Society's existence have reached the press. I cannot say exactly how these reporters and gossip mongers were dissuaded. I know that no newspaper or magazine has ever mentioned the Society in print. Beyond vague blind items in Winchell's broadcasts that could mean anything, its existence has never even been hinted about on radio or in newscasts.

Chapter Seven

Business continued to be good after the fleet left town. Much as I liked the money we took in from the sailors, we couldn't do that kind of work every night or even every weekend without bringing in more people. As it was, I wound up hiring two girls right away to take Connie's place.

Katherine O'Neal, one of Marie Therese's friends who worked that weekend, said she'd come in on Thursday, Friday and Saturday. Her husband didn't want her to do that but they needed money. Anne Green took the other four nights. She was another stray that Marie Therese collected, a war widow. At first, I didn't think she'd work out.

When Marie Therese brought her in to see me for the first time, she wasn't wearing any makeup and her dark hair was pulled back tight. Heavy clothes, glasses with big round lenses. She said she was from Chicago. She worked in two speaks there.

"Both of them were bigger than this, not as nice though. I moved here with my boyfriend. He's a musician."

It was the middle of the morning, before we were open. I explained the hours to her and the deal we had with a cab company for a ride home if she worked late. I said she would be replacing a girl who was taking some time off. She'd be back in September but that wasn't anything to worry about. If she liked it here and we liked her, we'd work something out.

Anne Green blinked once, pushed up her glasses. "That's fine, and, by the way, don't worry about these cheaters. I just use them to see, and I can dress better, too. I know how to get tips."

She'd do.

Marie Therese said, "Can you start tonight?"

• • •

The second time they tried to kill me, it started with a telephone call in my office. It was about half past four on a Friday afternoon, June 15, more than a week after the first guys. And remember, I still thought that was nothing but a botched mugging. Still, it shows you just how ignorant I was about being a legitimate businessman that I didn't figure out right away that something wasn't on the up and up with the call. The guy on the other end said he was with the "Special Licensing Division" of the Alcoholic Beverage Control Board. Sounded like a young guy with an accent I'd never heard.

"I've got your E-35 form in front of me. There's one piece of information we need that's missing. Maximum cubic feet of storage, and you didn't initial subsection c on page two. Almost everyone overlooks that. The form is much too confusing and it's easy to miss."

I had no idea what an E-35 form was. I'd filled out dozens of forms over the past months, some of them twice. This guy sounded sympathetic so I said I could give him the dimensions of the cellar and if he could fill it in for me, I'd make sure he knew how thankful I was. He said, "Believe me, if it was that easy I wouldn't be bothering you on a Friday afternoon. But we can straighten this out easily enough if you can get to our office before five."

"I can't get to City Hall by then."

"Oh, our office isn't in City Hall. They just moved us to Union Square. Where are you?" I heard shuffling papers. "I see from the form you're on West Twenty-Second. You'll never get a cab this time of day, but if you catch a BMT train at the Twenty-Third Street Station you can be here in ten, fifteen minutes. We're the next stop."

"That's cutting it tight."

"I'll tell you what, my wife is expecting me but I'll stay a few minutes late. I've got hundreds of these E-35s on my desk and I want to get them to my boss on Monday. The office is at the corner of Seventeenth Street and Broadway, on the second floor, a block and a half from the station." I scrawled down the address.

"It's up to you. I can return the form by mail or I can submit it as is and they'll send another inspector."

"I'll be there." I grabbed my hat and stopped on the way out to cadge a couple of subway tokens from the register. Yeah, we let regulars pay with tokens.

That time on Friday afternoon, the sidewalks were clogged and the closer I got to the subway steps, the slower my time. On the stairs going down to the narrow side platform, I saw a downtown train stopped with its doors open. As I got to the platform, a large woman in a blue raincoat and a big black hat pulled down over her ears stepped in front of me and slowed down. She limped and as I tried to pass her, she lurched into me. She was so damn big she nearly knocked me over. She stumbled along, staggering like a drunk through the crowd and I couldn't get past her. People were pushing against her as they tried to get out of the station and that slowed me down more. I hadn't got halfway to the train when the doors closed. By then I was steamed at her, at the goddamn unfairness of having to deal with the liquor board on a Friday afternoon, at everything.

Looked like most of the people on the platform made that train. I got right up to the edge of the track wondering how long I'd have to wait for the next one and if I'd make it in time. I checked the scrap of paper I'd written the address on. Got a little closer to the edge before more people crowded around me. I was not going to miss the next train. Kept one eye on the uptown end of the tunnel, waiting on that first light.

Then there it was. The guy next to me saw the light, too, and he moved a step to his left. Looked like he might be a guy who rode this train every day, so I stayed close to him. As the light got brighter and we heard the rattle, the crowd thickened around me, people pushing at my shoulders and trying to get a hip in front of me. I didn't let that happen and so I was right at the edge of the platform as the train came out of the tunnel and the big rush of air hit me in the face.

That's when somebody shoved me in the back. Not a bump, a hard push right between my shoulder blades. If I hadn't had both hands on my stick and the stick planted, I would've gone over. As it was, with the extra support of the cane and rubber soled shoes, my feet didn't slip and my shoulder hit the guy next to me.

He yelled, "Hey, watch it, fella," as the train rumbled in front of us.

I looked back but everybody was trying hard not to notice that anything was going on between me and the guy. He glared at me. I glared at him. We got on the train and moved away from each other. I fumed all the way down to Union Square. You're my size, you get bumped a lot, but you never like it.

• • •

Back on the street at Union Square, I checked my watch. Just after five. I hurried across the Square to Seventeenth Street. The building on the corner was a medium-sized office building. Lot of guys leaving. I went in through a revolving door and found the directory on the lobby wall. That's when I started to think something hinky was going on. According to the directory, there were offices for a dental supply company, a mailing service, and a secretarial school on the second floor.

The guy on the telephone had said the office just moved there. Maybe they hadn't changed the directory. I hoofed it up to the second floor. Most of the offices were closed and locked. No ABC Licensing Division. The only office still open was the dental supply place. The secretary who was putting everything away said she didn't know anything about an ABC licensing division in the building. All the other businesses on the second floor had been there since she started working there, and she was ready to leave. I checked the offices on the third and fourth floors. All locked, no licensing division.

Yeah, something was hinky, and right then I got the crazy idea that Bogolomov was behind it. Was there anybody else who'd pull a prank like this? Plenty of guys had reason not to like me, but I couldn't come up with anybody I'd honked off recently. Except Bogolomov.

I wasn't about to go down into that damn subway again, so I walked back to Jimmy's Place. On the sidewalks that old wariness from my time with Rothstein came back stronger than ever. And as I thought about, I saw just how wrong everything about the telephone call was. First, those guys didn't call. They had my number but they did everything by mail. Either you got your permit for this or that, or they returned the form with a big red DENIED stamped across it.

Somebody was pulling my leg. I figured when I got back to the bar I'd find some guy I knew with a smirk on his mug. But no, nothing. The only thing was a telegram on my desk.

DOCKED IN HAVRE. TRAIN TO PARIS. APT. TINY. PARIS FINE.
LOVE CONNIE

It was close to six by then. The place was filling up. I ditched the coat, buttoned up my vest, put on an apron, and took a shift behind the bar. Arch Malloy came up from the cellar and said he needed to talk to me when I had a minute. The place filled up nicely. Frenchy and I stayed busy and so did Marie Therese and Katherine O'Neal. The tall girl with brown hair came in with a couple of her friends. They had wine. She had a Manhattan. We smiled and nodded to each other. Marie Therese gave me a slant-eyed look when she got their drinks. A couple of hours later when business quieted, I went downstairs to find out what Arch wanted.

He said we might have a problem. "You remember that feller Croydon? Said he could get all the kraut wines we need?"

"Yeah, he's supposed to bring a load by tomorrow morning."

Arch shook his head. "No, got a message from him while you were gone. He said there's something wrong with the prices he gave us and he wants us to come to his warehouse."

Hell, I thought, this day is just one damn thing after another. "Did you talk to him?"

"No, Katherine took the call." Arch dug into his pocket and handed me the note she'd written. "Croydon says $ change. Talk to JQ Sat 10 am? Pick up wine at 442 E. 90. will need truck."

Croydon had come in earlier in the week. Young guy. Said he was new to the distribution business and he was trying to make contacts. Seemed eager enough and the catalog he showed me and Arch looked to be product we could sell. When I told Vittorio about it, he said the same. Prices were about a dollar a bottle less than we were paying for the French stuff. We agreed that he'd bring four cases by on Saturday morning for Arch and Vittorio to sample. If it was as good as he claimed, we'd talk quantities.

"Katherine said he was apologetic. He didn't give her a telephone number. Do you have it?"

I shook my head. "Let's do this, Frenchy brought his truck today. If he doesn't need it tomorrow, I'll drive him and Marie Therese home to Brooklyn tonight and bring the truck back here. We can check the wine in the morning and I'll pick them up tomorrow afternoon."

"I'll meet you here at 9:30. Want to finish sorting the old stock we've got behind the false wall? With two of us, it shouldn't take more than an hour."

"Why not?"

By the time I got back upstairs, the tall girl with brown hair and her friends were gone.

Chapter Eight

Saturday morning, I strapped on my knee brace and put on old work clothes. Had a quick breakfast of bread, cheese and coffee in the kitchen of the Cruzon Grill, and went down to my office to recheck Friday's final count. It was another good night. I noted down the totals and took out enough to cover the wine, assuming Croydon hadn't jacked up the prices and Arch O.K.ed the goods.

When he got there, we opened the heavy gate between the loading area and the alley where I'd parked Frenchy's truck. I backed the truck out. Arch relocked the gate and we drove uptown. Traffic seemed heavy for a Saturday but I didn't get out much in the morning, so I really couldn't say. We started north on Park, then went over to Third Avenue, and then to First Avenue when we got up into the eighties. Arch went on about the different kinds of wine this guy said he had.

"I can't say they're to my taste but the ladies love them. I recall a summer in the Austrian Alps when many an afternoon began with a tall blue bottle and ended in a feather bed that accommodated the two of us quite comfortably. Oh, she was a lively girl. But I see by your face that I shouldn't be mentioning that now, should I, not with your inamorata so far away."

"Just tell me where the turn is." Arch could go on for hours like that and much as I enjoyed listening to him and learning new words, that day I wasn't in the mood. I did wonder if inamorata began with an "i" or an "e."

Farther uptown, the neighborhood changed from residential to industrial with garages, auto parts shops, ice companies and such on the narrow cross streets. We were close to Ninetieth and Arch told me to turn right when a dusty black four-door sedan whipped past me on the left and screeched into a hard right turn. I had to stand on the brakes or hit him. Arch cursed. The light turned red. As we waited for the cross traffic, we heard horns blaring. Sounded like the bastard was pissing off other guys, too.

When the light changed, I turned right and hadn't gone more than ten yards when the dusty sedan pulled away from the curb and stopped, blocking the street. I stood on the brakes a second time for the bastard. Both front doors opened and two guys got out, reaching under their coats. They did not mean me well. I yanked the shifter into reverse and gave the truck as much gas as I could. It threatened to stall so I feathered the gas and clutch, and it still took long slow seconds to groan back down the street. I couldn't see much in the mirror when I checked it. If I was going to hit somebody on First Avenue, I was going to hit him. The two guys sprinted toward us, aiming pistols. I stomped the gas pedal to the floor, but the old truck was slower than they were.

Then the third guy appeared. He stepped out between two parked cars on my left and stared straight at the other two guys. As I backed past him, he smoothly raised a pistol, and took a shooter's stance with his left hand supporting his right. The driver of the dusty sedan saw him and triggered a couple of fast wild shots. The third man paid no attention and put a bullet through him. Before the driver fell, the man turned his shoulders and shot the other guy twice with two carefully spaced shots. I didn't see what happened after that. I gave up trying to use the little rearview mirror and twisted around to look through the back window as the deafening reports boomed in the narrow street.

Maybe the sound of the shots was enough to make people stop on First Avenue. The intersection was clear. Horns were blaring as I skidded to a stop, cranked the wheel around and headed north as fast as the truck would go. What the hell was happening?

A few blocks later, Arch released his death grip on the wooden dashboard and let out a long breath. "Who's your guardian angel?"

"I didn't know I had one. None of this makes any sense."

We had to go a couple of blocks north before I could turn around. If there were any police sirens, I didn't hear them. Arch and I didn't say much as we drove downtown. I kept thinking about the egg. This had to have something to do with the goddamn egg. We got back to Jimmy's Place and locked the truck in the loading area. As soon as I opened the back door, we heard somebody knocking on the front. I gimped behind the bar as quick as I could and found the old .44 hog leg that was hanging from a nail. I cocked it before I opened the little spy door. It was Croydon, the wine guy.

"Good morning, Mr. Quinn. The juice is in my car. Shall I bring it in here or pull around back?"

I took a deep breath and tried to sound normal. "Take it to the alley. We'll meet you with a hand truck."

Arch raised his eyebrows. I shrugged. "Don't say anything. Let's see what his wine's like."

Arch pointed at the big pistol. "Does that thing work?"

"I don't know. It came with the place when I bought it. Ask Frenchy."

We went to the back door. I opened the gate and checked the alley while Arch brought a hand truck up from the cellar. Nothing in the alley. Croydon was driving a Ford sedan. He pulled in beside Frenchy's truck. We unloaded four wooden cases and took them straight into the bar. Croydon was just as eager as he'd been before.

"For a minute there, I thought I had the time wrong for our meeting. When nobody answered, I thought maybe it was Sunday we'd said."

Arch said, "We had something to tend to downstairs. Now, what have we here?" He popped open a case and took out a bottle. "Yes, I remember this."

Croydon pulled out a corkscrew. I got glasses and called Vittorio on the house telephone. He came down and the three of them sat at a four-top to discuss the product. Croydon offered me a glass. I said no and asked to see his invoices. He dug them out of his salesman's case.

"These are the same prices you gave us when you were here before, right?"

"Of course."

The information at the top of the form said that J. Patrick International Wine Importers was in Paramus, New Jersey. I asked him if they had any offices or warehouses in the city. No, he said, too expensive. Arch's eyebrows popped up again. They were getting a real workout.

Arch and Vittorio said the wines were everything Croydon had promised, so we took what he'd brought and placed an order. Vittorio said he'd make up some cards to promote the new stuff. He could have the cards on every table if Croydon could deliver more that afternoon. He headed back to New Jersey a happy salesman. Arch and I went up to my office. I told him to help himself to a brandy. He did and settled on the divan. "I believe it was about two weeks ago that you were accosted by ruffians after we closed."

I hadn't thought about that. "Yesterday, I got sent on another snipe hunt. Guy called saying he was with the ABC board. Said I could hurry to his office and complete a form that wasn't right. Suggested I take a train from the Twenty-Third Street Station. Some son of a bitch tried to shove me in front of the train, and the address he gave me was phony."

"Just like today."

"Figure it has something to do with the egg. Couldn't be anything else." Arch knew that I'd bought it from Connie. He didn't know about Bogolomov calling back and wanting to make a new offer until I told him.

Arch shook his head. "You say it has to be the egg, but if Bogolomov or anyone wants it, it does them no good to kill you. Not meaning to pry, but you have told me something of your background and I have heard stories, exaggerations I'm sure, but colorful enough to suggest that someone in your past might still feel that he has a score to settle. Perhaps someone who has been incarcerated and recently released."

I wanted to disagree but couldn't. "Let's talk about this later, after we close. Don't say anything to any of the others yet. Not 'til we know what's going on."

"Of course."

"And you understand I wouldn't have asked you to come with me this morning if I had any idea that somebody was going to be shooting."

It looked like he smiled behind the soup strainer. "It's not the first time."

By then, it was almost time to open, so I drove to Brooklyn and picked up Frenchy and Marie Therese. On the way back, I told them that somebody was messing with me. The whole business about the wine prices had been a bad joke or maybe something more serious, I wasn't sure. Whatever was happening, they should let me know if they noticed anything else out of the ordinary. Marie Therese said she'd talk to Katherine O'Neal and find out more about the telephone call. They let me out in front of the Chelsea. I managed to make it inside without anybody taking a shot at me.

• • •

That evening I chose one of my older suits. Since I was spending so much time behind the bar in apron, vest and shirtsleeves, my better suits were wasted. Not that I looked bad, mind you, but I knew that I'd be lugging dirty glasses and spilling beer and booze, so what was the point? And now somebody was trying to kill me.

I'd been in that position before when I was up to something illegal and I knew there was a good chance somebody would try to stop me. That's why the work paid so well. But not knowing why this was happening, that bothered the hell out of me. So I paid more attention when I was out on the sidewalk, just like I did when I worked for Rothstein. Going to Jimmy's Place I took the long way and used a section of the alley I avoided because somebody piled garbage there.

Marie Therese stopped me as soon as I came in and said I should talk to Katherine O'Neal. Send her up to the office, I said.

Mrs. O'Neal was about forty, plump and nice-looking. She knew how to tease customers and did fine on tips. That night, she looked worried.

"I don't know what Marie Therese told you but it looks like somebody was playing a joke on me with the telephone call about changing the wine delivery, a mean joke or maybe something worse. Tell me about the telephone call. Was it a man or a woman?"

Seeing that she wasn't being called on the carpet she sat down and said, "It was a man." She hadn't been there when Croydon came in so she wouldn't have recognized his voice.

"Did he say who he was?"

"No, I don't think so. I'd have put it down if he had. He said the prices he gave you had changed and he wouldn't be able to bring the wine here. You had to go to his warehouse."

"Was he angry or was he sorry he screwed up?"

"It was more that he was insistent and it was really important that I get this message to you, and you had to be at that address on Ninetieth Street."

"Young? Old?"

"Young, and the way he talked, it sounded like he wasn't from here."

Sounded like the guy who claimed to be with the ABC board.

Mrs. O'Neal said, "What kind of joke are you talking about, anyway?"

"A couple of guys shot at me and Arch," I said, hoping she didn't decide to quit on the spot.

She shrugged. "Marie Therese said it might get interesting."

We went downstairs. The place was filling up. I found Fat Joe at his place by the door and told him we'd had some trouble that morning. "Check anybody looks like he might be carrying a gun."

He snorted. "All the fucking broads you got coming in here, you want I should look in their handbags?"

"This isn't a joke," I said. "Somebody took a shot at me. You let in anybody with a gun and I find out, it's your goddamn job. Remember that."

He grumbled and cursed again, but he always did that.

I went behind the bar, put on my apron and tried to smile like I meant it. Nobody wants a bartender to look like he's sizing up every customer. No, a bartender has to have an easy smile. He's got to be a guy you're comfortable with, a guy who knows how to make your drink, delivers it with an extra touch of something, and then knows when to leave your alone. He's got to be able to do a dozen things at once and never look like he's rushed. Frenchy pulled it off night after night as well as anybody I've ever seen. I was getting better.

That Saturday night, I acted like I knew what I was doing but I found myself scanning the room, looking for that one guy who was looking at me funny. Couple of times, I caught Arch doing the same.

The new wines sold well and it turned out to be the third straight good Saturday. After we closed, I toted up the count and put the day's take in the safe. Then I took out the .38 and brought it downstairs. After we finished cleaning up, and everybody else had gone, Arch and I sat down at a two-top with a bottle of Irish and two clean glasses. For the first time since I saw those guys with their guns, I relaxed a little. Both of us were tired from a day that had started fifteen hours ago but we hadn't had the time or privacy to talk it through. Arch poured and said, "What do we know?"

"We know somebody's trying to kill me."

"No, what do we know about what happened this morning? Exactly what did we see? Were those the same men that attacked you the first time?"

"No, those guys were heavier."

"What kind of car were these guys driving?"

I started to answer and realized I didn't know.

Arch said, "It was a Buick with a New York license plate. Didn't see the number. What about the men? What did they look like?"

"Medium height, I guess. Hats pulled low. Had guns. That's about all I noticed."

"The man on your side was wearing a black suit and a boater. The one on my side had a short jacket, no tie, and he was wearing a cap. They were white, maybe Italian—not swarthy or colored. They weren't as fast as they should have been getting out of the car because they were looking around for witnesses."

"If they'd been following us since we left here, I would have noticed. That means they were waiting for us, probably on First."

"That's an assumption. We'll get to it presently. What about the third man, your angel?"

"Right-handed. White. Experienced gunman."

"Another assumption."

"No, an observation. He didn't flinch when the Buick driver shot at him. He aimed carefully, spaced his shots, and all three of them hit."

Arch agreed. "What else?"

"Bareheaded. He looked like all the guys you see who have been out of work a long time. Sunburned face. His shirt was green, light green. No coat, I think."

"Living rough, maybe. What about his gun? I didn't see it but it sounded like a .45."

"It was. Damn near deafened me. Here's another assumption. He was waiting for them. I didn't get a good look at him but if he was somebody I knew, I think I would've recognized him. So, figure he wasn't there to help me, he was there to get them. Did we stumble into the middle of a gunfight?"

Arch shook his head. "Not a chance." I didn't buy it either.

"Now, what can we deduce from all this?" he asked. "First, several people are involved. You said that yesterday, the man who said he was from the ABC Board called you around four thirty. Within what, fifteen minutes you were in the subway station where one person or more were waiting for you. A large woman kept you from getting on the train that was already on the platform."

"Yeah." Son of a bitch.

"Did you see her face? No. Then, before you returned here, the same man telephoned again to lure you to the warehouse that doesn't exist on Ninetieth Street."

That made the hair on my arms stand up. Arch went on. "Therefore, we know that at least four people have been working together—the man on the telephone, the woman on the platform, probably a man on the platform who shoved you and who might also be one of the men in the Buick, and the other man in the Buick."

I started to understand the way Arch was thinking.

"We know they are well organized because minutes after the attempt on the subway platform failed, they called again to initiate the next attempt on Ninetieth Street. They're also familiar with your movements and the basic operation of this establishment."

"As for how they're doing it, with the first two goons on the sidewalk, it was easy. Anybody who came into the place a few times would see that I leave every night around the same time and usually walk back the same way. And anybody would know about the problems I've had with the ABC Board. I talk about them with regulars all the time."

Arch said, "When Croydon came in the first time with his catalog, there must have been half a dozen customers around us. Remember, one of them butted in saying he knew all about Alsatian wines."

"Here's another assumption. They're trying to hide what they're doing. The guys at the streetlight, everybody would've thought that was just a mugging that went bad. The subway would've been chalked up as an accident. Happens a few times every year. Today it was a beef between me and my 'Known Associates.'"

Arch nodded. "And we've got to assume that they're going to try again."

I nodded. We drank. I probably should have been more scared than I was then, but I was confused. Like I said, I'd put myself in situations before where guys tried to kill me, but I knew the risk I was taking and why I was doing it. That night I didn't know anything. It confused me. And being confused made me angry. About as angry as I've ever been, and I tried to tamp it down. This was serious. Anger wouldn't help. I had to think. I had to be careful.

Arch said, "What're you going to do?"

I drained my glass. "Damned if I know, but just to be on the safe side, I'll spring for another cab to get us home."

Arch called the cab company while I checked the locks and gathered the Sunday papers. It was around three when we left. The hack let me out in front of the Chelsea and took Arch back to his place downtown. I went up to the third floor and took out my keys. That's when I realized where I was and what I was about to do. It wasn't hard to get to the third floor from the sidewalk, and there was a narrow iron balcony across the front of the building that made it even easier to get in through a window on the lower floors. A couple of years before, some guys busted into my room. They did not mean me well either. The way it ended up, three of them were dead and they ruined a good carpet.

I gimped back to the stairs and climbed to the fifth floor. I knew there'd been a reason I told Connie not to give up her room.

My inamorata's place had been closed for two weeks. It still smelled like her. When I snapped on the reading light, I saw that she'd left it neat. Drawers and closet door closed. Her winter clothes were folded and stacked in the dresser or hanging in the closet. Not much left in the bathroom, but it still smelled like her, and it made me miss her. But it was good that she was gone with all this going on.

It took a long time to go to sleep.

Chapter Nine

It was after noon on Sunday when I went back down to my rooms. The .38 in my mitt, I unlocked the door. The heavy curtains were drawn so I couldn't really see anything until I turned on a light. If somebody had been there, he hadn't disturbed anything that I could see. I showered and packed a valise that I took upstairs to Connie's room. Seemed reasonable to stay there until I knew what the hell was going on.

Over a bagel and a schmear at the corner hash house, I mulled over what Arch and I had talked about, and decided it had to be Jimmy's Place they wanted, whoever they were. Ixnay the golden egg. Not too many people knew that when I bought the joint from Carl Spinoza, I got the whole brownstone. My lawyer at the time was a shyster named Jacobson. He had been Mother Moon's lawyer, and he'd been bailing me out when I was arrested since I was six years old. I sold four of Mother Moon's stones and Jacobson worked out the deal to buy the building through a company he set up for me. He did it without involving any banks, since I was too young to sign legal papers, and he made sure the taxes were paid. I kept the deed in my safe. Over the years, I'd had one offer to buy me out but it wasn't serious. Still, figure the building was what these guys were after, but when I thought about it, the brownstone was like the egg. Killing me wasn't going to make it any easier for somebody to buy. Unless the idea was to get me so rattled that I'd accept any offer when they made it. That was enough to make my head hurt.

I put off reading the papers until the middle of the afternoon. It was a warm day, and the sun was out, so I left my coat and the .38 in Connie's room. I slipped the German .22 into my pocket, and rolled up my shirtsleeves. Gathered my stick and took the *Times* up the stairs. At the top floor, there was one more set of steps to a heavy metal door. Most of the flat roof had been bricked over. A couple of apartments had doors that opened onto it. There were trees in pots, strings of lights, rocking chairs, tables and canvas canopies stretched out to shade a few places. On an afternoon like that, you'd find twenty or thirty people sitting around up there. I settled in a chair near the railing on the south side looking out over the neighborhood.

The story was at the top of page two in the middle. On one side of it was a story about an actor I'd never heard of being killed when his truck got hit by a train in Connecticut. On the other side was a story about a bunch of communists getting subpoenas from Representative Dickstein to appear before his un-American Activities Committee. The Reds were unhappy with him but then the Reds were always unhappy.

The headline on the story I was looking for was this:

Youths Are Shot Dead
From Passing Truck

One dies at Scene
His Companion
Succumbs in Hospital

Two youths were met by a fusil-
lade of gunfire late this morning
in front of 422 East Ninetieth
St. One was killed and the second
was taken to Bellevue Hospital
where he succumbed to his wounds.
The youths were Albert (Skinny)
Egidio of 111 Harrison Avenue,
Brooklyn, who died on the scene,
and Fred (Ickie) Eccles of 230
Elizabeth Street.
Although Patrolman Netzger
of the East Sixty-Seventh St.
Station was within hearing distance
of the shooting and arrived on the
scene three minutes afterward,

the assailants had fled. Egidio's body was in the street. Eccles had managed to get across the street to the sidewalk.

According to witness Silvey Whitney of 323 East Eighty-Fourth Street, the two youths had parked on the street where they were approached by a small truck. The youths exited their car and the occupants of the truck opened fire and immediately sped away.

Two weapons were retrieved at the scene. Both of the youths have records, according to the police. They said Egidio was questioned about a month ago about the murder of Gandolfo Simonetti who was shot in front of 10 Prince Street.

When Eccles was questioned by a detective in Bellevue he refused to say if he suspected any one of the shooting, declaring, "If I had it coming to me I can take it."

He died later in the afternoon.

So, Egidio and Eccles were a couple of kids. Figure whoever was after me was still not hiring top-shelf talent. Figure that wouldn't last.

That evening I thought about getting a cab but decided no. I knew the neighborhood. I'd see anybody coming for me and I had a pistol. Yeah, I was that foolish, but I guessed right. The kitchen brought me a plate of the chicken that had been the lunch special and a glass of one of the new German wines. Not to my taste, the wine not the chicken.

When Anne Green came in, I asked her to come up to my office. Like Katherine O'Neal she looked worried until I told her she was doing fine, there was something else I needed to talk to her about. She didn't wisecrack with the customers the way Katherine O'Neal did but her tips weren't bad. And she showed up on time. With a little makeup and her hair fixed, she looked a lot better than she did when Marie Therese brought her in. Detective Ellis thought so, too. He'd been coming in more often on nights he knew she was working. I explained about the phony telephone call and what had happened on Saturday morning. Then I showed her the article in the paper.

After she finished it, she said, "You know these guys?"

"Never saw 'em, but this isn't the first thing that's happened. Looks like somebody's after me, but we've always had a rule that there's no guns in Jimmy's Place. If Fat Joe thinks some guy is carrying one, he'll pat him down. Guy objects, he doesn't get in. We've never had a problem, but you ought to know."

She blinked behind the big glasses. "The places I worked in Chicago, stuff like that happened all the time."

• • •

The rest of Sunday was quiet. I told Frenchy and Marie Therese to take the evening off. We closed up at one. I shared a cab with Arch and Anne Green. First stop was the Chelsea. As I got out, I looked up to the third floor and thought I saw a thin line of light between the heavy curtains on one of my windows. There was so much light on the street I wasn't sure I really saw it.

Inside, I crossed the lobby to the desk at the back. Tommy was still working nights. He jumped up as soon as he saw me. Tommy was one of those guys who acted like he knew everything about everybody that they didn't want anybody else to know and he'd love to spill it to you. He'd heard a lot of lies about me and so he thought I was quite the big shot. I stopped for my mail and messages, and asked if anybody had been asking after me. He said no. I pushed a buck across the desk and told him to clue me in if he noticed anything.

He tried to hide his surprise. "What's going on? Is there anything I should know, if you take my meaning?"

"Something's always going on, Tommy, you know that. Just keep an eye out for me, o.k."

On the way up the stairs, I thought that if there was somebody waiting for me in my room, he'd been watching the street. He saw me get out of the cab. He figured that I would be opening the door in a few minutes, and I was tempted to do just that. Hell, I had a .38 and I was tired of being jerked around. So, what was the best thing to do?

Throw the door open and charge on through, gun in hand? Could I figure a way to turn off the lights in the hall and slip in without him seeing me? Get out to the balcony and try to go in through a window? No, if he was already there, he was ready for me.

Fine. The bastard could be ready for me until tomorrow afternoon. I went on up to the fifth floor.

Chapter Ten

It was a little after eleven Monday morning when I got up. Early for me. Figured anybody who might be waiting for me in my rooms could stick with it until I'd had my breakfast. The little .22 in my coat pocket was not a comfort. As I was leaving and locking Connie's door, the next door down opened and a woman hurried out fumbling with her keys. When she saw me, she looked startled.

She was about thirty, slim and well-dressed in a matching jacket and skirt. Dark hair, small hat, low-heeled black shoes, black gloves and a large black leather bag tucked under one arm.

I nodded.

She noticed my stick and said, "You must be Connie's fella. Jimmy."

"Yeah, and you are…?"

"Bernice Friedman. I moved in about a week before Connie left on her trip. She said you might find a use for the room."

The way Connie seemed to get along with every stranger she met, this one probably knew the length of my inseam and what kind of underwear I had on.

She looked at her watch. "Nice to meet you, can't talk now," she said and hustled ahead of me down the hall to the elevator. I took the stairs.

Outside, foot traffic on Twenty-Third Street was heavy. I waited beside the front door and watched it for a time. Nobody I could see was paying any attention to me, so I walked a couple of blocks to the diner that had the best breakfast in the neighborhood and ordered salami and eggs. As I ate, I read a story in the Gotham *Comet* about a teenaged girl who ran off with a bogus prince who was also an ex-con. They met at a poetry party in Greenwich Village. He called himself either Prince or Count Childe de Rohan d'Harcourt. The cops said his real name was Fred London and he'd pulled a year and a half in Sing Sing for extortion. There was a big photograph of the girl, Miss Louise Krist of 116 Washington Place. In the picture, she looked young and pretty.

They'd been gone for a couple of weeks, but the cops said they'd been spotted at a bar where the Prince bragged that "he wouldn't give her up for two million dollars." I doubted that.

I didn't hurry back to the Chelsea. It was well after noon when I opened the door to my room.

I turned on the floor lamp. In that dim light, nothing looked to be out of place. I opened the wardrobe, the closet, the bathroom and the shower curtain around the tub. I checked under the bed and behind the heavy curtains. Opened a window, stuck my head out far enough to see all of the balcony. Nobody there. I put the automatic back in my pocket. No footprints in the carpet pile.

Then I looked at the place more closely. Had anybody been there?

The stuff that collected on top of my dresser looked as messy as it always did. No sign that anybody had gone through the drawers. The little lockbox was still on the shelf in the closet. I opened it and saw that my spare pistol, a .32 Smith, was still there. I kept anything important in the safe or the box at the Bowery Savings Bank. Went through the drawers and compartments of the rolltop desk. I kept nothing important there either. I had one hand on the door and was ready to leave when I stopped and went back. I looked at the second window, the one I hadn't opened. It was unlocked.

I tried to think back over the afternoons I'd spend in the room since Connie left. Unless it was raining, I opened the windows while I read the papers and listened to the radio. You work in a bar that's partially below street level, you appreciate open windows and fresh air. Exhaust fumes add to the romance that is New York. Would I have locked it? Probably not, but I worried over it anyway.

• • •

Monday night nobody tried to shoot me when I walked over to Jimmy's Place and nobody followed me. The mail was waiting on my desk. The expected bills and two things I'd been waiting for. The first was another telegram from Connie. I sliced open the envelope.

PARIS WONDERFUL
ADDRESS: 14 RUE GIT LE COEUR, PARIS
WILL WRITE. MISS YOU. LOVE YOU. CONNIE

I don't know what I'd expected. Telegrams were expensive. She told me what I needed to know in case I changed my mind and decided to visit.

The second thing was a big square envelope from the New York State Liquor Authority. Inside was a typed letter that said, pursuant to Chapter 478, the Division of Alcoholic Beverage Control had decided to grant permission to sell on-premises liquor-by-the-glass at 222 West Twenty-Second Street. And there was the document that proved it, an official license complete with the Great Seal of the State of New York, good for one year.

So, now I was completely legal, except, I guess for the guys I was paying off. There was no going back. You see, until I saw the license, I'd had the idea that somehow, they'd change their minds and make booze illegal again. When I was growing up before Prohibition, there were saloons everywhere. You'd see a couple on every corner in my neighborhood and they were all busy. For a kid they were rough, dangerous places but they were a fact of life. Adults bought food at groceries and restaurants and they bought alcohol at saloons and liquor stores. Then one day, selling a drink was illegal and the saloons and liquor stores closed. It was probably good for me to learn that the law worked that way at a young age, but I still didn't understand it. Once I saw that the saloons reopened in different places and nobody paid any attention to the law, it made more sense.

But then I had a license and I had to admit that I was part of it. Somehow, I was disappointed in myself.

• • •

For a Monday, business was a little livelier than normal. I stayed behind the bar and didn't have much time to talk to the men and women there or to keep an eye on the crowd at the tables. Tuesday was slow. Business picked up on Wednesday. By Thursday, I'd almost convinced myself that I'd been wrong about Saturday. Those two young guys hadn't been after me. They had a beef with the guy who shot them and we got in the middle of it. I tried not to think about the phony telephone call. That lasted until Arch came up to my office. I was sorting out bills and arranging to pay for the ice and beer delivery we'd get the next morning.

Arch said, "Did'ya read the *Times*?"

"I saw that the cops found that girl and the ex-con Prince she ran off with someplace downtown. She wasn't happy about it. Said she was over eighteen and they were married."

"Take a look at this," he said and showed me the paper. It was open to page four. The story was on the top left.

**Accountant Dies
In Subway Fall**

**Mitchell Shea
Struck by Train
at 33rd St. Station**

Pecora Aide

Mitchell Shea, 47 years old,
accountant, of 167 State
Street, Brooklyn, was crushed
to death yesterday between an
I.R.T. subway train and the platform
of the Thirty-Third St. station in
Manhattan.
Police were unable to determine
exactly how the tragedy occurred.
It is believed he had approached too
close to the edge of the platform
as the train entered the station.
George Foster of 200 West 109th
Street, Manhattan, said he saw Mr.
Shea hurrying down the stairs
a few moments before.
The station platform was crowded
with afternoon shoppers waiting on
a train to Brooklyn and lower
Manhattan.
The motorman said he saw the man

topple onto the tracks but before he
could stop the train, the first two cars
had passed over him.
The crew of an emergency squad
removed the body.
Mr. Shea had been working as an
aide for Ferdinand Pecora's Senate
Banking investigation.
Service was tied up for 23 minutes.

"Could be nothing," I said.
"Do you believe that?"
I shook my head. "It doesn't say anything about him being pushed."
"If you'd gone under the wheels, you think they'd mention it in the paper?"
"It doesn't make any sense," I said. "This guy was an accountant from the Bronx. Had nothing to do with me. Do you think somebody's going around pushing guys in front of subway trains for no reason?"
"Just the opposite. The evidence suggests that someone is shoving people in front of trains for a reason that we don't know. Perhaps in poor Mr. Shea's case, it had something to do with his work, though I don't see how you and Ferdinand Pecora could have anything to do with each other."
"We're both short good-looking guys from Chelsea. He doesn't dress as well as I do but he tries. He sent a lot of guys to jail. I worked with some of them, but that was a long time ago."
Arch tapped the paper. "But there is that one detail."
"Yeah," I said. "He was 'hurrying.' Probably nothing."
"Probably."
Neither of us was buying it. But I knew somebody who could help.

Chapter Eleven

Theodora Opperman didn't like me. You couldn't blame her. She was an operative for the Continental Detective Agency, and back when I was doing this and that for A.R., she tried to catch me. Fat chance. Other than that, she was good at her job. I called the agency on Friday and left a message for her. I was in my office when she called back a little before midnight. She sounded grouchy.

"Quinn, I didn't think I'd ever hear from you again. What do you want?"

She'd been involved with Willie Seabrook in the business that put the egg in my safe.

"I want to hire you. Something screwy is going on, or maybe it's nothing, I'm not sure. That's what I want you to find out."

"All right. Should I come to your place?"

"No. Somewhere else. Tomorrow." I didn't like the idea of hiring a detective to begin with, even if she wasn't a real cop and I wasn't ready for anybody else to know about it yet. I figured it was going to turn out to be nothing anyway. No reason to let anybody know about how damn foolish I was.

"There's a diner across the street from the agency on Broadway, the Athenian. Eleven o'clock?"

"Done."

• • •

Saturday morning was cool for June, threatening rain. I wore a light topcoat to walk the dozen or so blocks downtown. It had a big pocket for the .38. I took my time, using the stick more than I needed to. I walked so slow that everybody was moving around me on the sidewalk. Stopped to look in storefront windows every block or so. Nobody tailed me.

I was also keeping an eye out for cops because I was away from my neighborhood and I had the pistol. In the normal course of things, carrying a gun was too much trouble. I got by fine with the stick and knucks. The knucks weren't legal either but they'd been made to fit me and I liked them. Now, I didn't worry if I had a pistol and I was around cops I knew. We understood each other. They knew we handled a lot of cash and I had to take care of it. But the Sullivan Act made it a felony for me to carry a gun in public. If I was stopped by a completely honest cop, I'd be in trouble, but I've never met one of those.

The Athenian was one of those places where the coffee is weak and bitter. The counter and tables were filled. Theodora Opperman was in a booth in the back. I hung my coat, stick and hat on a hook with her umbrella. She was pouring dark tea from a small pot. An old waiter in a stained white jacket shuffled over. I ordered coffee and didn't touch it.

The fat detective was wearing a dark brown jacket and a tan shirt with a bow tie. She squeezed a slice of lemon into her tea and gave me a cop's level stare. "I understand you're legal now." She said it like she didn't believe it.

"Got the papers this week. Stop by and have a drink sometime."

"You do have good booze, I'll give you that. What's your problem?"

I have her yesterday's paper. "Accountant Dies in Subway Fall."

She read it quickly and looked up. "So?"

I still hadn't decided how much I should say. The less she knew about my business the better, but if I didn't tell her enough, she wouldn't know what to ask.

"I want to know more about how this happened. Is there any chance he was pushed?"

Her purse was on the seat beside her. She opened it and took out a notebook and pen. I told her something like that had happened to me a week ago. Somebody bumped me and I almost went off the platform right in front of the train.

"And because of that you want to know about Mr. Shea?"

"No." This was the hard part. "I was on the Twenty-Third Street platform because I got a telephone call from a guy said he was with the ABC Board and if I could get to his office by five, he'd fix my license. But it turns out to be a joke or something. The office isn't there. I'm thinking it's just somebody giving me the business and the subway thing was an accident until I read this." It sounded thin when I said it like that. She wrote in her book.

She said, "That's it?"

"No. Because time was tight when this guy called, I was hurrying, like the paper says this guy Shea was."

"People hurry on the subway every day."

"I know." I felt ridiculous even mentioning it but I still didn't want her to know about the shooting uptown, or the first guys. "Look, do you want this job or not?"

She produced a contract and filled in the blank lines.

"I'll talk to any IRT personnel who were in the station and the motorman and this," she looked at the article. "George Foster, and the first officers on the scene. They'll have more details, but it sounds like you really want to know if there was anything unusual about his being on that platform. Shouldn't be too difficult. Sign this and I'll need a ten-dollar retainer." She pushed the contract and pen across the table.

I gave her a ten-spot. She tucked the signed contract and notebook in her bag. Sliding out of the booth, she said, "Have you heard anything from Mr. Seabrook?"

"He's drying out in a place up in Westchester." She shook her head.

"Yeah," I said. "It won't take. Not with Willie."

Outside on the sidewalk, she squinted at me. "You should know that ever since that night at Mrs. Garner's, I've been keeping an eye out for the golden egg that went missing."

"Has it turned up?"

"Not yet but it will."

"What business is it of mine?"

She shrugged. We weren't fooling each other. "Water under the bridge," she said. "I should have something on this within a day or two. How should I contact you? Telephone after hours? I assume you want to keep this away from your business since you're taking it so seriously."

I shook my head. She tapped my pistol with her umbrella said, "Can it. You wouldn't have that in your pocket for no reason, and who knows? Maybe you need it. You've come to the right woman to find out."

• • •

After I left the detective, I walked west to a Sixth Avenue El station. Took a train downtown to the big Western Union Building on Hudson Street. There were branches all over the city where I could send a telegram, but I didn't know if any of them could get one all the way to Paris. Hell, I'd never sent a telegram to anybody out of the country. The main Western Union Building covered a whole city block between Hudson Street and Broadway.

For normal telegrams, they would send a messenger boy to you and he'd see that whatever you gave him was sent, the same boys that delivered telegrams. You saw them everywhere in their uniforms and caps, some on foot, some on bikes. Mother Moon said she once thought about hiring me out to them until she found out how pitiful the pay was. I mean any kid who could find his way around the city and didn't mind going into some rough neighborhoods from time to time could be a telegraph boy. It took a lot more on the ball to do the same thing for Mr. Rothstein.

Inside the big building, I reread Connie's wire and tried to work out what I was going to say. She'd written that Paris was wonderful, she would write and she loved me and missed me. How should I answer?

BUSINESS GOOD. TALL GIRL CAME BACK. DID NOT TALK TO HER. SOMEONE IS TRYING TO KILL ME.
MISS YOU.

No, too melodramatic. Something more down to earth. I spent a long time staring at the message pad. This is the version I sent.

BUSINESS GOOD. GOT THE LICENSE. REGULARS MISS YOU. ME TOO.
COME BACK SOON.
JQ

By that evening rain was coming down hard enough that I took a cab to Jimmy's Place. The weather slowed business that night, but the kraut wines still sold well, both upstairs and down. Nobody else in my part of town had them. I told Arch we'd order more. The rain continued on Sunday, so it was another slow night. First weekend as a completely legit business and we get rained out. Go figure. Monday was Monday. I'd have sent Anne Green home if Ellis hadn't been there.

The detective called my office on Tuesday, a little after one in the morning.

"I've got part of what you want to know," she said, sounding unsatisfied. "None of the IRT men saw anything until it happened, and they haven't learned anything since then to make them believe it was intentional. They say it happens three or four times a year, almost always around Christmas when trains are crowded with women and children who don't ride every day. Or it's suicides or drunks. Not sure I believe that, except for the drunks, but it's their story.

"I haven't been able to locate George Foster of 200 West 109th Street. He works for the Brooklyn Ash Removal Company. He's out of town now. They expect him back later in the week according to Mrs. Foster. She said that's all he talked about all weekend."

"Anything else?"

"There are only a few people left in Shea's office now that their work is almost over. The secretary, Mrs. Huoy, said that Mr. Shea left that afternoon without speaking to anyone. That was unusual only because he often worked late. But not recently. Shea himself was not married. He lived in an apartment near his mother and sister. They are still too upset to talk about him. How much more do you want the Agency to put into this?"

I thought about that until she said, "Quinn, are you still there?"

"Yeah, I want you to work on this until you're certain you know what happened."

Her short laugh was a bark. "You don't want that. I'm never certain about anything, but you'll get my best shot at it."

She hung up.

As I remember it, I'd put the ear piece back on the switch hook and my hand was still close to the telephone when it rang again. I thought it might be the detective calling back for one more thing she'd forgot. I picked up the telephone and took the ear piece off. It was a man's voice, a young man's voice.

"Quinn?" The voice was low, like he didn't want somebody nearby to hear him.

"Yeah."

"Somebody's trying to kill you. I'll tell you who it is for five hundred dollars. This is the only chance you're going to have to get out of this alive. Get the money ready."

Without taking a second to think, I got mad. "Why the hell should I?" I yelled into the mouthpiece. "Just because some jerk calls and says somebody's after me. Any asshole could do that, and you're not telling me anything I don't know. You gotta make me believe you before I'll do squat."

The line went quiet for a few seconds like he put his hand over the mouthpiece. Then, he went on, his voice still low and even. "This is bigger that you know, Quinn. There are important people involved and they mean business. Just get the money ready. I am your only chance. Nobody else. Just me. Think about that." Click.

I hung up the earpiece and put the telephone back on the desk.

I probably smiled. Things didn't make any more sense but at least I wasn't going crazy and I wasn't making something out of nothing. So, what to do about it? How would Arch go about this? He'd take it apart. What did I know and what could I assume from it?

First, the voice was definitely not Bogolomov or Daddiego or anybody else I knew who was involved with the egg business. The voice might have been the first guy who called, the guy who claimed to be from ABC and sent me down to the subway. I tried to recall how he sounded and decided it was him. O.K., why had he tipped his hand by telling me what they're up to? Obvious answer, he's going to try to kill me again. No, *they're* going to try to kill me again.

Arch and I had figured that several guys and a woman had to be involved. But I couldn't worry about that yet. Figure his next move was to call again and tell me to take the five hundred to someplace where he and the others would finish the job. I doubted they were that stupid.

Chapter Twelve

As soon as I finished the Tuesday count, we closed up and I took the cab with Arch and Anne Green. I spent another night in Connie's room but I couldn't really sleep. Kept going back to the telephone guy and trying to come up with an answer for the next time he called. I got up with first light, went downstairs to my room and put on work clothes. I had a rough idea of what I might do and it would require some cleaning.

There wasn't much foot traffic that early. Nobody followed me into the alley. I let myself in through the back gate and door. First, I went to the cellar. Arch had been rearranging our stock since we'd been dealing with new distributors. I checked the storage area hidden behind the false wall where we'd been keeping the last of our illegal stock. Carl Spinoza built that wall in the early days of Prohibition when he worried about being raided. The area behind it was mostly empty by then, so there was plenty of room for the stuff in the junk room. Cleaning stuff, broken chairs, and this and that tended to wind up there. Took me less than an hour to clear it out. By then it was time for Vittorio's early guys to be showing up. I climbed the back stairs to the kitchen and joined them for eggs, cheese, bread and coffee. You might have been able to get a better breakfast at one of the swanky hotels, but you couldn't find a better cup of coffee in the city.

After we finished, I left a note for Vittorio asking him to give me any old tablecloths he wanted to get rid of. Then I walked back to Connie's room and slept hard until it was time for work.

• • •

That night I went with one of my better suits, a light grey number with a vest that had an inside pocket large enough for the .22. As long as I was wearing my apron behind the bar, you didn't notice it. Finished off with a light blue striped shirt with a white collar and a patterned tie. For a Wednesday, it was a decent crowd. Detective Ellis was in for the second time that week, getting chummy with Anne Green. We were doing better business with a license than we'd done as a speak. A quick look at the customers told me the reason. Half of them were women. Connie and Marie Therese had been right. Remodeling the joint, making it cleaner with more flattering lighting and the awnings out front made women think about us differently. It didn't look like a place run by a gangster. Remembering that, I checked the room for the tall girl with brown hair. She wasn't there.

I mixed drinks, drew beer, opened bottles of kraut wine, and tried not to look like I was eyeballing my customers to sort out the killers. Having run the place for a few years, I thought I was pretty good at sizing up the people who came in. O.K., I probably overestimated myself in that department but I'd learned enough to anticipate the big problems.

Frenchy took over for me at ten. I went up to my office and found a stack of white tablecloths and the day's mail on my desk. No telegram from Connie. I was separating the bills when the telephone rang. Thinking it might be the telephone guy, I rehearsed the little speech I'd been planning before I picked it up. It wasn't the telephone guy. It was Frenchy.

"Boss, there's a customer here'd like to talk to you."

Maybe it was the telephone guy in person. I said I'd be right down and cracked the Venetian blinds over the little window that looks down into the bar. It wasn't the telephone guy. It was the tall girl with brown hair.

I took a moment to straighten my tie and put on my suitcoat. As I was going down the stairs, I thought Connie was right. She said the tall girl would be back. Then I thought that maybe the tall girl came back to kill me.

• • •

She was at the bar drinking another Manhattan. With one hip on the stool, she was about my height. Standing up, she'd be a few inches taller. I signaled to Frenchy and he brought over a glass of seltzer.

I leaned on the bar and said, "Good evening. Good to see you again, Miss...?"

She was wearing a nicely cut lightweight short jacket over a matching dress, and a soft hat.

"Collings. Esther Collings."

Standing closer to her, without the bar between us, I saw that she was a little older than I first thought and prettier than I remembered. "You were in again last week or the week before, weren't you? With some more of your friends."

"That's right, and according to one of them, you didn't tell me the truth." She smiled. "You said you weren't a gangster."

"I think I said nobody had been shot in here recently. And I'm not a gangster."

"Were you ever a gangster?"

"What're you, a lawyer? If you are, I refuse to answer on advice of counsel."

"No, I'm not a lawyer. I'm a buyer for Bonwit Teller."

"That explains the suit."

One eyebrow popped up. "Now I'm supposed to say, 'Oh, this old thing,' but it's not. It's from a new line. Still, I'm surprised you noticed." She held up her empty glass. Frenchy mixed another.

"In my line of work, clothes are important. I pay attention to them."

"Yes, you do," she fingered the edge of my lapel. "This is from Rogers Peet, two years ago. Did your girlfriend pick it out for you?"

"No, I manage to dress myself."

She blushed and drank. "I'm sorry, what a foolish thing to say. It's been a confusing week. I don't know what I'm talking about. Sometimes things are turning out exactly the way you think they should, and then one day, they just stop doing that. And there you are." She blinked back tears and drank. I saw that there was no diamond on her left hand. So, the fiancé was out of the picture. Or she was up to something else.

She shook her head, mad at herself, and opened her purse.

"It's funny. I've really been meaning to come back and introduce myself properly. I meant what I said. I didn't know there was a place as nice as this in the neighborhood. If I'd known about it before, he and I would've come here. Well, I'll never know about that. And now I'm leaving, heading to Paris on the morning tide, as they say."

She put down two dollars and stood. Yeah, she was an inch or so taller. "The way this summer was planned, we'd have set the date, sometime in the fall, and I'd be easing out of the store, but now the wedding's off because he's simply not ready and it wouldn't be fair to me, etcetera etcetera, and everything's falling apart in Paris so somebody has to go over there and straighten it out, and going to Paris is what every girl is supposed to want to do, but it's the last thing this girl wants to do right now but there's nobody else, and her boss says that since this girl finds herself at loose ends, she gets to uproot her life one more time and put out the fire. So, she'll just shut up and smile and do her duty. Right?"

It had all come out in a rush so I didn't say anything. She was still fighting back tears.

She repeated, "Right?"

I said "Right."

"So, this is good-bye." Then she grabbed my head and kissed me. By then, everybody was watching us and nobody was saying anything. After what seemed like ten minutes, she pulled away. Before she let me go, she whispered, "Thank you."

She collected herself, nodded to Frenchy and walked slowly out. The women stared at her with astonishment. The guys close by gave me a round of quiet applause. Marie Therese glared at me.

Chapter Thirteen

The telephone guy called the second time Thursday morning. I was in my office doing the early count before we closed when the telephone rang. It was one-thirty, about the same time he called before. Figure he'd been in the place often enough to know where I was then. I let it ring a few times. Rehearsed my speech to myself.

I picked up the telephone and took the earpiece off the hook. Didn't say anything.

"Quinn?" It was the telephone guy. I let him stew. Said nothing.

"Is this Jimmy—"

"Listen to me," I interrupted and talked fast so he couldn't break in. I tried to keep my voice level, not to sound angry or threatening. I didn't want to scare him, I wanted to pull him in, but I couldn't let him set the rules. "I've got the money. This is what we're going to do. You're going to call me at this number same time tomorrow night and I'll tell you how it will work. From now on, we do this my way if you want a dime from me. I'm going to need names and addresses, proof that you really know what you say you know. First thing, you're going to show me why it's happening. Call tomorrow night. One-thirty. Not before, and I'll tell you what you're going to do to get this money."

I hung up. The telephone rang again a few seconds later. I finished the early count.

• • •

I took the cab with Arch and Anne Green, and went up to my room on the third floor. Opened the windows and curtains to cool the room off. Turned on a couple of lights. If anybody was watching from the street, he knew where I was. Took off my coat and loosened my tie. Poured a tot of

Five Star, thought about Connie and thought again it was good she wasn't there. Found music on the radio. Settled in my chair and went through my half-baked crackpot plan for the twentieth time.

As I saw it, the big problem was that I still didn't really know what was going on or why it was happening. Until I did, I could only react to what "they" did, whoever the hell "they" were. Even if what I was planning worked, would it do me any good? Until I knew more, I was on my own. I was hoping that detective Opperman would find something that explained it, but until then, I wasn't going to involve anybody else or ask them to help. I'd known Frenchy and Marie Therese for a long time, Arch for a couple of years but I couldn't bring them into this yet. Hell, Arch had already been shot at once. He'd probably agree to pitch in, but it wasn't right to ask him.

I remembered a time, years ago, when Spence and I first started stealing cars and delivering bootleg booze. Right at the beginning, I bragged to Meyer Lansky that Spence and I could grab any car he wanted. It was sort of a stupid joke but he took me up on it and said if we got a Packard Twin Six, he'd give us twelve hundred dollars for it—big money in those days when we got fifty bucks for a half-ton truck. Spence and I cooked up a scheme to hijack one from a guy who was bringing in his Twin-Six to get a dented fender fixed at the dealership. One afternoon, we pretended that I was a kid with a broken arm and Spence was my father needing to get me to the hospital. After the guy let us into his car, we threw him out, but he jumped up onto the running board and wouldn't let go of the car until I shoved a pistol into his face.

In that moment when I should have pulled the trigger, I hesitated. I hesitated and he jumped off the car. I think we both realized at the same time what we were doing and thought better of it. I didn't want to kill a guy just to steal his car, and he didn't want to die for it.

Remembering that, I thought about another time, a hot summer night a few years later when Spence and I were out on Long Island. We drove a car from Lansky's garage to pick up a load of Scotch whiskey near a little burg called Patchogue from a speedboat. We used back roads since some of the cops out there weren't on the payroll. On the way out, we noticed that there was a place where the track dipped and rose steeply. The dirt was muddy at the bottom. We said we'd have to watch for it on the way back. With the car loaded down, it would be tricky to negotiate. Good spot to steal a load, too, and in those days, a load of booze straight off the boat was worth thousands of dollars, more than most guys would see in a year. And we were right.

As soon as we left the dock, I started worrying about what I'd do if somebody tried to stop us there, and we talked about different things that could happen. When we reached that spot, the headlights reflected off a big puddle of water at the bottom that wasn't there before, and it hadn't rained. As soon as he saw it, Spence hit the gas and I brought my pistol up. I already had it aimed out the window when a guy on my right came running up toward the car with a shotgun. That time, I didn't hesitate. I shot him twice in the chest. Spence yelled, "Here," and pushed himself back from the wheel. I twisted around in front of him and shot the second guy who was coming from that side. Spence held the car steady down one side, splashed through the water and churned up the other. Once we were away from the place, he held his speed steady. An hour and a half later, we were in Lansky's garage.

I guess the reason I thought about those times that night in my room is that I knew there are some things you shoot guys for and some things you don't, and you try not to hurt anybody who isn't involved. It would have been wrong of me to shoot the guy for the Twin Six. There was nothing wrong with shooting the two guys who came after me and Spence. Not knowing how things were going to go with the telephone guy, I might have to make the same decision.

It was nearly dawn when I locked up my room and went up to the fifth floor to sleep.

• • •

The weather Friday was strange beyond description. It began with thick warm fog that was so dense it delayed ships that were scheduled to leave that morning. By afternoon it was over one hundred degrees in Central Park. No wonder our business was slow that night. It was still so hot people were sleeping outside. We went through a lot of ice and sold more beer than usual.

At one-thirty on the dot, the telephone rang. I let it go for a few rings before I took the earpiece off the hook.

"This is Quinn."

The telephone guy was angry but still kept his voice down. It was low and threatening. "Don't start thinking you're in charge here. These people mean to kill you and they've got other people behind them who are willing to pay whatever it takes. This is serious. I'm offering you a chance to buy your way out. It's the only one you're going to get. The next time you won't be so lucky." I couldn't place the accent. It was like some of the Southern boys I'd heard, but not exactly.

I didn't say anything.

"Quinn, are you there?"

"I'm here. This is what you're going to do. Come here after we close on Sunday. Two o'clock. Alone. On foot. Unarmed. Come to my place from Eighth Avenue. I'll have a man outside watching you. You won't see him. My man sees anybody else, the deal is off. Bring the proof."

I hung up the earpiece.

After the first call, I assumed this guy was setting up another attempt to get me. Now, I wasn't sure. Maybe he was after money. I chewed on that for a time and decided that for the moment, it didn't matter. If the telephone guy was trying to trap me, I was going to get him first. If he had something to sell, we'd come to an arrangement.

• • •

I went in before anybody else early Saturday and finished my preparations in the cellar. By then, the city was turning into a ghost town. That always happens on those stifling weekends. It hadn't cooled overnight, so nobody slept good. The streets and trains were filled with people heading for the beaches, anyplace cooler. Business would be bad until the heat broke.

That morning I called a guy out on Long Island I'd worked with during Prohibition. He had a boat and he didn't ask questions if somebody needed to dispose of something late at night. My dealings with him had strictly been picking up and delivering product he brought in from ships. I hadn't had anything to do with him for a couple of years and so I wasn't sure what he was doing now. We talked. Like me, he'd found ways to make a living that were more legal than not after Repeal, but the pay wasn't as good. He said he was still interested in the occasional odd job, so if things went the wrong way with the telephone guy, I could take care of a body.

In the evening, I worked behind the bar and paid extra attention to the few guys who came in and might be casing the place. There weren't many of them and none of them stayed long. That night everybody tended to drink quickly and leave. Turned out to be the worst Saturday of the summer.

Before we closed, I had Katherine O'Neal make up a couple of cardboard signs, one for the door and one for the bar, with the new hours. They changed the state laws on us that weekend and said we couldn't open until one o'clock on Sundays and had to be closed by three on Saturday, not that we paid much attention to that. I closed early when business was bad. When business was good, we kept the place open until we got tired.

• • •

Sunday afternoon, I dug out one of my older tropical weight suits from the back of the wardrobe, something I wouldn't miss. I went in around five and asked Vittorio's guys to fix a couple of sandwiches out of whatever they had and wrap them up for later. Business was even worse than Saturday. We closed around midnight. Frenchy and Marie Therese had their truck. Arch and Anne Green took the cab. Before they left I told them that since business was so slow, we wouldn't open until six on Monday. I stayed behind and waited for the telephone guy. It took a couple of hours, and I spent the time thinking about all the ways things could go wrong. The first was that he wouldn't be alone. That wouldn't be a problem if I could get him inside by himself. The doors were solid. The locks were heavy. Hell, guys had tried to bomb the place and it hadn't worked. Looking back now on all the things I didn't think about, I understand how ignorant and lucky I was.

I finished getting ready in the cellar and then waited upstairs. I turned off the lights outside and in the bar. About one thirty, I went out and stood in the shadow of the green awning. Twenty-Second Street was hot and mostly quiet. A lot of people had their windows open. From time to time I heard a voice or a snore or a toilet flushing. The air was hot and still. No rustling leaves. Distant traffic. In the half hour I stood there, I saw three people on the street. All of them climbed the steps to their front door and went in. Just after two o'clock, I saw a figure on the sidewalk coming from Eighth Avenue, a man wearing a straw boater. Appeared to be medium sized, but I couldn't tell at that distance. When he was halfway toward me, I went inside, locked the door and turned on the awning lights. Opened the spy door in the big door. I had knucks on my right hand. Took out the little pistol from my vest pocket.

The telephone guy stepped close to the light. Nervous, looking back up and down the street as he edged toward my door. He took a step forward, then backed off. A moment later he moved into the light and I got a good look at him. He wasn't just scared, he was terrified. When he stopped looking over his shoulder, I saw that he was in his twenties. Clean shaven, pomaded hair, thin. If he'd been a customer, I didn't remember him. He raised his hand to knock.

Before he touched the door, I said, "Take off your hat." It startled him and he stepped back. I said again. "Take off your hat."

He took off the boater and held it with shaking hands. Feathery mustache, pale blue eyes. Well chewed fingernails.

"Now the coat. Take off your coat."

"What? What is this?" He was ready to turn and run.

I tried to sound soothing. "Take off your coat. I want to be sure you don't have a gun." He stammered something. I repeated, "Take off your coat." He dropped it on the step behind him.

"Turn out your pockets" He did. They were empty.

"Now the shirt. Take off your shirt and turn around. Slowly."

"Wait a minute. What is this anyway?" He sounded like he was almost laughing. Nerves.

"You want any money, take off your shirt and turn around. Do it now."

He fumbled with buttons and tore the shirt off without thinking about the tie. Sleeveless undershirt. Pale bony shoulders. Shivering despite the heat.

I said, "All right," and opened the big door. He hurried through and I locked it behind him. I held up a hand, motioning for him to come closer, like I had something to whisper to him. He leaned forward and bent at the waist, reaching down for something. My uppercut started in my knees and hips. The knucks caught him on the edge of the jaw. I hit him so hard the side of his head banged against the door. He crumpled.

Chapter Fourteen

In the movies, when a guy has been knocked out and they want to wake him up, they throw a bucket of water in his face. I didn't have a bucket, but I had a beer pitcher. That did the trick for the telephone guy, Mr. Asa Kirk, if that was his name.

Around two thirty Monday morning, he woke up in the middle of a small brightly lit white room. He was hanging by his wrists from a heavy hemp rope that ran through a hook screwed into a joist over his head and was tied off to another hook in the wall behind him. Looked like the rope or his shoulders had stretched some since I strung him up. His toes were touching the floor. No surprise there. It took all my strength to pull him up off the ground.

I got the idea for putting tablecloths on the walls from Willie Seabrook. He'd done the same thing with sheets in that room a few years before for a different reason. It spooked me then and it still did. Spooked Mr. Kirk, too, judging by his wide-open eyes and the panicked muffled sounds he was making and the way he jerked around on the rope. He couldn't talk because there was a wide strip of adhesive tape over his mouth. His ankles were taped together, and so were his wrists. I'd done that so the hemp rope wouldn't chaff his wrists. Am I a considerate guy or what?

I'd taken off his pants, too. Thought about stripping his underwear but I wanted him to cooperate. Humiliating him wouldn't make that any easier. I waited for a second to make sure he saw me after the water splashed in his face. I didn't say anything. Let him think about what was happening to him. I left and locked the door. That was all I wanted for the moment.

• • •

After I knocked him out, I taped his wrists and mouth. Then I checked the street to make sure nobody else was interested. Collected his coat, shirt and boater from outside, and locked up. When I yanked off his shoes and trousers, I saw that he had a Colt automatic in a holster on his right ankle and a dagger in a sheath on his left. So, that's what he'd been reaching for when I tagged him. I relieved him of those and taped his ankles together. After all that, I dragged him down the stairs to the cellar and elevated him. Once I was sure he'd stay put, I took a look at what he'd brought with him.

His clothes were inexpensive but not cheap, not new, not particularly dirty. I didn't know the labels. Nothing hidden in his shoes. I found a zippered leather key purse and a money clip with three dollars in his jacket pocket. A long leather wallet was in the breast pocket. I laid the stuff out on a counter and was about to look through it when I heard him kicking and making strangled noises. As I unlocked the door, he tried to twist around to look at me but there wasn't enough play in the rope. I eased the door shut and locked it again. I wanted him not to know what was going on and to look at those white walls for a while, a long while maybe.

I left the clothes and shoes in the cellar, collected my stick, and brought the rest of his things up to my office where I could go through them under the desk light.

There were six keys in the purse—all it would hold—and two subway tokens in a small buttoned change compartment. I set it aside. The wallet was more promising. Like the key purse, it had seen use, well-worn but not stiff. He kept it in the breast pocket of his coat and it was curved to the shape of his chest.

The first things that fell out when I opened it were three flyers, the kind that get handed out on the street, each folded twice lengthwise like a letter. The first wanted you to join the Americans for Freedom. The second announced a rally for the Workers Ex-Service League, and the third was Selected Quotes from Hitler's Proclamation to the German Nation. I set them aside with the keys. Tucked into one large pocket was an invoice for a hundred and twenty reams of paper from Second Avenue Wholesale Stationeries. There was a grocery list with it, neatly written on a page torn from a narrow notebook. Coffee, sugar, powdered milk, franks, oatmeal.

There was a pink receipt from Funderburk's Shoe and Luggage Repair at 46 Irving Place for putting new rubber heels on a pair of men's black shoes. Six realty company business cards and a Navy i.d. card made out to

Asa Kirk were in the small pockets on one side. The second large pocket had the two newspaper clippings about the guys getting shot on Ninetieth Street, and the accountant on the subway. There was a third clipping from a New Jersey newspaper about a state assemblyman who died from drinking bad booze. One of my new Jimmy's Place cards was in that pocket, too.

Spread out on my desk, it was a lot to look into. I thought about it for a few more minutes before I went back downstairs. The first thing I did was check the shoes. New rubber heels. So, that much at least was right. Good. I found the roll of tape and unlocked the junk room. At the sound of the door opening, Kirk tried to twist around to see me and started swinging on his rope. I stayed near the wall out of his reach as I moved around to face him. He was no happier.

His face was red and he was sweating so hard his undershirt was soaked and his pomaded hair was matted to his forehead. The small white room stunk of him. He was still making muffled angry sounds. The veins in his temples were popping. He jerked on the rope like he wanted to kick me. Couldn't blame him, I guess. I didn't like this either, but not as much as he didn't like it. I leaned on my stick like this was something I did every day and waited for him to settle down before I spoke.

"I told you to come unarmed. You didn't."

He shook his head and tried to say something.

"I told you to bring proof. You didn't."

He shook his head, and then nodded like he was trying to say he did.

"The newspaper clippings? Those didn't tell me anything I don't already know. You've got to do better than that."

He made more noises like he could do better. I reached up and ripped off the tape. He yelled, cursed and tried to kick me again. "Goddammit, Quinn, you better cut me loose. I'm the only chance you've got to get out of this alive." Spit was flying.

I kept my voice low and level. "Show me your proof."

"You think I brought it here? Knowing you were going to pull something? It's close. I can get it once I've seen the money."

"The cash is upstairs in my safe. What's your proof?"

"The clippings prove that I'm on the level. I know what's going on. You're not getting anything else until I've got the money."

I ripped off another strip of tape. "All right, I'll let you think about that while I decide what to do with you."

He jerked away. "No, wait, don't do that. I'll tell you who's in on it."

I stepped back. "Go on."

He hesitated like he was trying to figure how to lie. Then, "Spig Dolan. He's in charge of part of it because he knows you."

Spig Dolan? I hadn't heard that name in years and I never really knew the guy.

"And Sturdivant, Herk Sturdivant. They're working together, like the other teams."

That second name meant nothing to me. "Why are they trying to kill me?"

"They've been hired to do it. It's part of the big plan, a small part. The plan is bigger than any of us, but it wasn't supposed to be like this. They didn't tell me about it until I had the office set up, and now it's gotten out of hand. The things they're doing now are just nuts. I can't handle this anymore so I'm getting out, you gotta believe me."

"What about Egidio and Eccles, the two guys you sent to kill me on Ninetieth Street? Who shot them?"

"What're you saying?" He acted surprised. "You did."

"Who hired them? What's this 'big plan?'"

"No, you won't believe me if I tell you. I've got to show you. That's the proof. It's close." Sweat was dripping off his face.

What Kirk said made sense. I left him and went to my office. He was talking at me all the way up the stairs but I couldn't understand what he said. I gathered his wallet and weapons, and stashed them in my safe. I took out five hundred in cash and found a straight razor in the box of accumulated stuff I kept there. Folded the bills into his money clip. Back in the cellar, he was still talking. I threw his clothes and shoes on the floor in front of him and yanked the knot loose on the hook. He dropped to the floor. His legs collapsed.

When he tried to stand, I said, "Roll over on your stomach," and sliced through the adhesive tape on his ankles. "Get up." I pulled the rope off his wrists and cut the tape. As he dressed, I backed out of the white room and took the Detective Special out of my pocket.

He edged out and looked around like he expected to see some more guys there. I held up the money. It got his attention. "Look at this. It's your money clip. Go get your proof. You said you wanted five hundred. Here it is. It's yours if this proof is good enough."

Kirk's fingers flexed like he was going to try to snatch the bills out of my hand. He shrugged on his coat and felt for his wallet. "Give me my stuff."

"When you get back." I followed him upstairs.

He talked all the way. "Listen, this will be a lot easier if you come with me. This proof, it's hard to describe, and even if I bring it here you won't really understand it. You gotta come with me."

"Hell, no."

"Then give me my gun back. At least give me that." He was looking really scared by then. "Please."

I opened the front door. "Out."

"You don't understand, this isn't what you think."

"Explain it when you show me the proof."

I locked the door behind him.

Chapter Fifteen

When he hadn't come back by sunrise Monday, I decided that either he'd meant to shoot me with his ankle gun or to use the clippings to lure me out where they could kill me. I tried to sleep on the divan but couldn't. I thought about Connie, about how Asa Kirk looked strung up in the cellar, about Spig Dolan last heard of fifteen years ago during the Black Sox series. Hadn't somebody told me he was in Sing Sing? Paris was eight hours ahead of New York. Connie had already had lunch. What was she doing?

I got up when I smelled coffee from the Cruzon Grill kitchen but went to the cellar, cleared up the tablecloths and rope, and replaced the stuff from the hidden storage area. Then I went up to the kitchen and had eggs and spinach and sausage with Vittorio's guys. It was delicious.

I read the *Times* as I ate. The headlines told me that a million New Yorkers had headed out to Coney Island to get away from the heat. "One man died of heart disease while frolicking in the sunshine and two youths drowned." A couple of John Dillinger's boys in Indiana had pistol-whipped a doctor who refused to give them a fix after he'd patched up a bullet wound. Hitler had executed two hundred Storm Troops that weren't toeing the line. In France, a military court acquitted five guys who'd been shot by a firing squad in the Great War. These five were part of a veteran unit that refused to go over the top of their trench to be slaughtered by German machine gun fire. The commanding officers chose the five at random and the War Council did the dirty work. But this new tribunal said it hadn't been handled right so the executed men were acquitted and each of their widows was given seven cents. And I thought I had it bad. What a wonderful time to be alive.

I took a cup of coffee back to my office and went through the items that Asa Kirk had left for me.

The dagger was about seven inches long with dull edges and a sharp point. The scabbard and straps that held it to his leg were thin leather. The pistol was a Colt .32. The eight-round magazine was full and the gun had been cleaned since it was fired.

The three flyers didn't mean much. They were the kind of thing that some wild-haired guy would shove in your mitt when you happened past a rally or speech by another wild-haired guy on a soapbox. It looked like the Workers Ex-Service League thought Roosevelt was about to assume dictatorial power and he had to be replaced by a true representative of the people. The Americans for Freedom didn't like FDR either because he had no right to form that alphabet soup of agencies and must be removed from office. The headline on the Selected Quotes from Hitler said they were translated into English for the first time, so that Americans could know the truth that the Jews and Roosevelt were lying about.

The Jimmy's Place card was no help. I'd been passing them out to half the people I served and there was a stack of them at the coat room. I didn't know what the business cards from the realty companies meant, if they meant anything. But if I could find out that Kirk did any business with them, I might find a door that one of his keys would open. I set them aside and thought about how I could use them.

I read through the two clippings from the Times about the guys who'd tried to ambush Arch and me, and the accountant who was killed in the subway. They were the same ones I'd seen. The third, shorter clipping was from the Newark *Evening News* dated December 27 last year. The headline read:

Assemblyman and Neighbors Die,
Bad Liquor Blamed.

ESSEX FELLS, NJ, Dec. 27 – After-Christmas
tragedy invaded a modest home in the borough
of Essex Fells yesterday when a state assemblyman and two neighbors died in convulsions
after drinking "moonshine" liquor. The three
men lived next to each other. Seeking Yuletide
"cheer," the victims bought and then imbibed

in the privacy of their own homes. A few hours
later, there occurred the first of the three
deaths that sent police and physicians
hurrying from their firesides to investigate.

The first death, that of Assemblyman
Horace Lanning, occurred early Christmas
morning; the second and third, brothers
John and Albert Bryson, at noon of the
same day.

Chief W.L. Ambrose of the Essex Fells
police, acting on information he said he
received from the two brothers before death,
raced to their house to find that they had
succumbed to the poison "moonshine."
The bottle was found in Lanning's house.
It is not known where he procured the lethal
liquid. He and the Bryson brothers were
longtime friends.

Democratic Party officials hope to
name his replacement before the legislature
convenes.

It meant nothing to me. I'd never even heard of Essex Fells. Didn't
know where it was. I'd have to get a map of New Jersey to find it.

That left the two names Kirk gave me. Hank Sturdivant meant nothing
to me either. I remembered Spig Dolan from the 1919 World Series
business. That had been a busy time.

Thinking about the series brought back the memory of a day not long
after Mother Moon sent me to work for Arnold Rothstein. I was out on
the stoop of her building spinning some kind of story to a bunch of the
kids about the great brawler Monk Eastman who provided persuasion
when A.R. needed it. Or I might have been talking about Abe Attell,
ex-featherweight boxing champion of the world. He was also around
A.R. whenever he was needed. Both of them were fearsome, legendary
figures in our neighborhood. What I was saying doesn't matter. When
Mother Moon heard me, she rushed out, grabbed me by the ear and
yanked me inside.

Away from the kids, she slapped my face damn hard to get my attention and said, "Remember what I told you. You work for Mr. Rothstein, you don't talk about Mr. Rothstein. Not nothing to nobody never!"

I nodded. She got in my face. "Say it."

"I work for Mr. Rothstein, I don't talk about Mr. Rothstein, not nothing to nobody never."

"Say it again."

"I work for Mr. Rothstein, I don't talk about Mr. Rothstein, not nothing to nobody never."

"That's right. Except…?"

"Except to you."

She tousled my hair. "That's my boy. You're the smart one."

Spig Dolan was a nobody I wasn't never to say nothing to. He was one of the dozens of guys who swarmed around Rothstein whenever something big was in the works. You see, word got about quick when that happened. As a matter of course, Rothstein kept a lot of irons in the fire, and there were always guys who wanted him to go in with them on this or that, but when a really big deal was cooking, A.R. attracted the attention of a different crowd. Then the bankers, businessmen, celebrities, and politicians who had big money to throw around would show up, and then there'd be more guys circling around them, young sports like Spig Dolan looking to cut themselves in or pick up whatever might shake loose.

I say that like I understood it at the time. I didn't. I was a nine-year-old kid who did what Mr. Rothstein told him to do. Ninety percent of the job was carrying messages, sometimes small packages. He let Mother Moon know when he needed me, and she'd tell me to be at Reuben's or Lindy's or wherever he was working. Might be a pool hall or a hotel room where a poker game was going on. I'd go there and stay out of the way and be quiet until he needed something. To the other guys, I was part of the furniture. I always brought peanuts or pretzels because his games usually went on for hours. For the most part, I just sat in corners or against walls and waited. That's hard for a kid but it was my job and it paid well.

I learned what to watch for as the game Mr. Rothstein was playing went on. At any time, a guy might come in and whisper something to A.R. He'd consider it and scratch out a note on a scrap of paper. Then he'd call me over and tell me where to take it. As it happened, when he got involved with the Black Sox Series, I was there at the creation.

It started right after the Liberty Bond business where A.R. hired guys to "steal" war bonds from couriers who were carrying them between brokerage houses and banks, and arranged to be roughed up. But I've already told that story. It ended in the summer of 1919. A.R. left word with Mother Moon for me to meet him at Reuben's early one afternoon. Sometimes he conducted his business there at a table, but when he had something more important going on, he took a private room near the kitchen. That afternoon, the head waiter said he wasn't there yet, but I should wait for him. I ordered a sandwich and took it to his room. I was still eating when A.R. came in with a guy named Franklin Heller. I never saw the man before that afternoon and I haven't seen him since.

There was nothing out of the ordinary about him. I remember a guy about A.R.'s age, thirty-five to forty, clean shaven, short hair, summer suit, boater. A.R. was eating figs out of a paper bag. Heller had coffee. I can't give you a word-for-word of their short conversation. They kept their voices down and I wasn't trying to listen in, but I did hear Heller say, "Gandil can get Cicotte. He needs money. Comiskey won't give it to him."

"They're finally wising up. But this will be complicated. We'll need help. Jimmy, I want you to find Nat Evans. He's probably having lunch at The Alps."

I don't remember if I found him there, and I wouldn't remember the meeting with Heller if it hadn't led to so much more. I didn't even know they were talking about baseball. Those names—Gandil, Cicotte, and Comiskey—just sounded strange to me and stuck in my mind. All I knew about baseball was that I heard a lot of the young sports yacking at Reuben's about the players they had in their pocket and the games they had the fix on. For all their talk, you never saw them with much money and were always on the lookout for a big score. After that meeting with Heller, things went back to normal for a time. By September, A.R. wanted me around every day and most nights. I spent more time dealing with Nat Evans, Nick the Greek and Nicky Arnstein than I had before. As the Series got closer, A.R.'s business picked up. More sports wanted to bet more money and a lot of them wanted to talk to A.R.

Spig Dolan was one of those sports. I didn't know his name then. I knew his face from seeing him at Reuben's and other places Mr. Rothstein "frequented" as they say in the papers. One evening in late September I was heading in to work. A few blocks from Mother Moon's, three young guys stopped me on the sidewalk. I didn't see where they came from, but before I could do anything, there was one right in front of me and two others, really big guys, moving in on either side. They crowded close and backed me up against a storefront. They weren't threatening but they sure weren't friendly either. The one in front of me got down on one knee and gave me a wide smile like he was my old pal.

"You're Arnold Rothstein's boy, aren't you? Sure you are, I seen you with him all the time. I'm Spig Dolan. That probably don't mean nothing to you but it will, I guarangoddamntee you you'll know Spig Dolan. I'm in the same line of work as Mr. Rothstein, and I got something here for you to give to him. It's something he really needs to see. You understand what I'm saying?"

He had heavy eyelids that gave him a sleepy look and a lean face with a cigar stuck in the corner of his mouth. Like the other two, he wore a flashy pinstriped suit and a Homburg. I went from being scared to pissed off as he spoke, and had to force myself not to yell or cause a commotion. You just didn't do that when you worked for A.R. I shuffled my feet and pushed with my elbows at the two guys boxing me in to make a little room.

"We know that Mr. Rothstein's got something big in the works and we can help him with that."

The other two nodded and said something agreeing with him. "You see, he really wants to get this from us, and if you help us out, there's something in this for you, something you'll really like."

The three of the smiled then and I knew they meant me no good. I said, "Yeah, what have you got for me?"

"A bright shiny new nickel," he said like it was more money than I could imagine.

"A bright shiny new nickel, my ass," I said. "Five bucks."

The two other guys laughed. One of them said, "Kid does business like a little kike."

Dolan stood. "See, I told ya, fellas, the kid is smart. He knows this is good for Mr. Rothstein."

He reached around for his wallet, giving me room to slip between him and the guy on his right. The guy grabbed at me and got my cap. By then I was two steps away from them and moving fast. No grown man could catch me. I heard them chasing me for a block before they gave up. 'A bright shiny new nickel?' What a cheap chiseler.

I was going to tell Mr. Rothstein about it, but when I got to Reuben's, he was already talking to Nat Evans and Abe Attell. Attell was saying he'd met a couple of guys who could guarantee that the White Sox would throw the Series to the Cincinnati Reds. They just needed backing and they needed it quickly. A hundred thousand and they were in business. I wondered if it was the same guys I'd run into. Attell said it was a sure thing and A.R. was the only man who could come up with the cash in time. They had to pay off the players soon and get their bets down. Mr. Rothstein said he didn't think it would work and after some more talk, Attell left disappointed. A.R. and Mr. Evans smiled like they were sharing a private joke. Evans said he'd see him at dinner and left. Then Mr. Rothstein made a couple of calls and told me to walk with him to the Hotel Astor in Times Square. He had to meet someone for dinner there.

Two men were waiting with drinks in the crowded lobby. One of them, I learned years later, was Val O'Farrell, a crooked cop turned crooked private detective. He introduced the other man as Judge somebody. As soon as the Maître d' saw Mr. Rothstein, he moved the people waiting for tables to one side and ushered the three of them through.

A.R. had to talk to half a dozen people as we crossed the lobby to the dining room. Spig Dolan and his two pals were there at a table. Dolan made his hand into a gun and pretended to shoot me. A.R. had a table near the front. I headed for a chair against the wall where I always waited at the Astor. Before A.R. could sit, Spig Dolan jumped up and started talking to him. A.R. listened for a while, then said out loud that Abe Attell had already told him and he hadn't changed his mind about their proposition. He was standing up and speaking in a clear voice that anybody could hear. That part of the room went quiet. His answer was still no. Even if they were friends with the players, he wanted no part of their deal. He didn't think it would work, and Dolan should never bother him again about anything.

In all the time I was with him, I never heard Mr. Rothstein talk like that when he was in public. Dolan stalked out. His two pals followed. I turned to go to my seat but A.R. called me to his table. He dropped his voice to his normal private level and told me to find Nicky Arnstein at the new place, the Butterfly Room at the Hotel Pennsylvania. Before I left, he whispered that I might want to let Mother Moon know she should place a bet on the Reds to win the Series.

I didn't tell him that I'd done that more than a month ago. The truth is, I didn't know what it meant, but the night I heard him and Mr. Heller talking about Gandil, Cicotte and Comiskey, I reported it to Mother Moon as soon as I got home.

She got a funny look on her face. She'd been on the pipe that afternoon. "You're sure he said Gandil can get Cicotte and Comiskey won't give him the money he needs. This is important. You're sure about the names?"

"Sure I'm sure. The names are funny, I remembered them. Who are they?"

"They're the men who are going to make me rich."

I don't know how much money she managed to put together. Getting in that early before everybody else in New York knew about it, she should have got seven to one odds. Not that it matters. Whatever she won, she turned it into those twenty-four uncut diamonds and emeralds I found in the pillow on her daybed.

That's all the Black Sox series meant to me. While it was going on, Rothstein wanted me to be available, and so I spent most of the first week of October with him. I made a point of looking for Dolan in crowds because his cornering me like that embarrassed and scared me. I wasn't going to let it happen a second time.

But I never saw him again, and A.R. had nothing to do with him that I knew of. So how in hell could any of that have to do with somebody wanting to kill me fifteen years later? I was more confused than I'd been before the son of a bitch Kirk told me about Spig Dolan.

Chapter Sixteen

Later Monday morning, I was still looking through Kirk's stuff and getting nowhere when the telephone rang. I figured it was him. It wasn't.

Theodora Opperman said, "What are you doing at your desk this early? I've got your preliminary report, and I'm going uptown. I can give it to you in person."

"Fine." No reason not to have her in the place this early. I told Vittorio's guys to send a pot of tea and a cup of coffee to the bar.

The fat detective knocked on the door twenty minutes later. I had set up a two-top with a clean tablecloth. She looked around, maybe impressed a little. It had been three years since she'd been in. "The joint cleans up nice."

"Jimmy's Place is legit. I've got all my licenses."

She sniffed. "Maybe the place is legit, but that's not what you want to hear from me. You want to know about Mitchell Shea."

She took out her notebook, poured tea and squeezed lemon before she went on. "He worked for the Pecora Commission. What do you know about it?"

"Ferdinand Pecora is from the neighborhood. Grew up just around the corner. He was with Tammany for a time but he was never one of the guys I dealt with." I wasn't going to spill to a detective about all the bribes I moved through the place. It seemed like a lot of money to me, but it wasn't even a tiny drop in the giant bucket of the Tammany machine, and she probably knew about it.

"He wasn't there long enough. He moved into the D.A.'s office before the war and the word I heard was that he couldn't be bribed." I didn't really believe that but I never heard anybody bragging they'd put in a fix with him, so it might have been true.

Mrs. Opperman said, "Eventually, he became the chief assistant to the D.A. The boys downtown refused to nominate him for the top job because they couldn't control him. He was in private practice until last year when the Senate Banking Committee hired him to run its investigation into what the big banks and stock brokers did before the Crash."

I remembered seeing his name on the front page of the papers for a while but none of that stuff had anything to do with me, so I didn't read it.

"The long and the short of it is that Mr. Pecora embarrassed several extremely wealthy men and made them extremely angry with him. He got them on the stand before his committee after he'd spent several days looking through their records. Other committees had done the same thing, but they didn't know what to look for and didn't ask the right questions. He did the background work and got them to admit that they'd seen the Crash coming. They made plans for it and so the top dogs squirrelled away millions while their investors and everybody else got stiffed.

"He went after all of them but his main target was City Bank. When it was over a few weeks ago, nothing much was done because those men didn't break any laws. They didn't have to. They'd helped write the laws so they know how to get what they want without breaking them."

"Sounds like you admire the guy."

"Good to see a fellow paisan making a name for himself on the right side of the law."

She saw how I was looking at her. "I'm a wop, first generation. Before I was Mrs. Opperman, my name was Russo. Man like Pecora gets attention for holding their feet to the fire, you've got to admire him."

He did know how to dress, I had to give him that. From the pictures I'd seen, his taste wasn't quite up to mine but he bought well, and he was almost as good looking as me. Probably smarter and certainly more honest.

"What does this have to do with Shea?"

"He worked for Pecora. Until Pecora took over the investigation last year, the committee didn't do anything. Pecora is an experienced prosecutor. He brought on a staff of lawyers, accountants and investigators that showed him where to look to find all the things the banks wanted to hide. Shea was part of that group. If he'd lived a little longer, he'd probably be looking for work now. The investigation is over."

She turned a page in her notebook. "The office is on Madison, a few blocks from the Thirty-Third Street station. He used it every day. It was a little early for him to leave, but like I said, the investigation's work is essentially over."

"The article said he was hurrying. Did you find anything about that?"

"No, there were less than a dozen people in the office. Nobody remembers seeing him leave. You want more?"

I shrugged. I didn't know what I wanted.

"Personal life, Shea lived in Brooklyn near his mother and sister who are the same apartment he grew up in. Father's dead. Sister's a cripple. Shea had a girlfriend in the neighborhood, Millicent Bonner. Seems to have been well-liked. No grudges, and in a neighborhood like that, if there are grudges and feuds, you find out about them right off.

"He went to City College. Smart, ambitious. Worked for accounting firms, real estate companies. Promoted regularly. Well paid. Had a good life insurance policy. Mother and sister are the beneficiaries. Neither of them could have been at the station.

"I've spoken with both of them and I promise you, neither of them was involved with his death. I've seen enough insurance frauds to know when something doesn't smell right. That's not the case with the mother and sister, and there's nobody manipulating them. I've talked with the motorman, Mr. Ernest Klen. He really couldn't tell me anything. He said it happened so fast he never had a chance to stop. The man is still a wreck. Hasn't been back to work since it happened. The IRT investigators cleared him with no questions.

"I can find the reporter who covered it if you want but you'll be wasting your money. Nothing I found suggests anything but an accident. I think your imagination is working overtime, Quinn."

I didn't say anything. Until yesterday, I might have believed her. Now, I had to figure how to ask her to continue digging without telling her more than I wanted her to know. I was quiet too long.

"What is it? There's something you're not telling me."

Feeling like a fool, I said, "Just make sure there's nothing more to know about his hurrying."

She knew I was holding out. "It's your nickel."

• • •

I went back to my office and separated Kirk's donations into four stacks. The first was the three flyers and the invoice for the paper from the wholesale Stationeries. The second stack was the personal stuff—the grocery list, the Navy i.d. card, the money clip and the receipt for the rubber heels. The third stack was the realty company cards. That left the leather wallet and key case, the dagger and pistol, and the Jimmy's Place card. I took the keys out of the case and looked at each of them more closely. No duplicates. All were worn with little nicks and scratches on the dull metal. The two Schlage keys were almost alike. One had a spot of red fingernail polish on the side. There was no lettering or numbering on them or in the case to tell me where to find the lock or door they fit.

I straightened the stacks. I rearranged them. I stared at them some more and thought, What the hell am I doing? I'm not a detective. I don't solve crimes. I commit crimes. Here I am trying to go legit and my place has been legal for less than a week and I kidnap a guy. Knock him out and hang him up in the cellar.

The smart move is to put this stuff away and let Theodora Opperman do what you're paying her to do.

But when I spread out the realty cards, I got an idea.

Chapter Seventeen

"Paraguay?" The young fellow behind the counter at Wadsworth & Company Residential and Commercial Real Estate was sympathetic. "You say your partner is in Paraguay."

"That's right. Left yesterday. I got in from Philadelphia this morning. He's setting up our office here. I have the keys he left for me. They were in his apartment where I'm staying until I've got a place. He left notes about the equipment he's already moved into the new office so that I can have it ready when the orders start coming in. He left me everything I need except the damned address, excuse my French, of the office. It sounds nuts, I know, but that's the kind of guy he is. He comes up with these great ideas like tin mining in Paraguay and he brings in the investors and then dashes off without telling me where we're working. Just between you and me and the wall, he was the same when we were kids. I'll bet dollars to donuts that he grabbed up all the paperwork he had and stuffed it into his briefcase, and his copy of the lease is on the ship with him.

"That leaves me with this stack of cards from the places he contacted, and I'm hoping that somebody will remember working with Asa Kirk."

Wadsworth and Company was the fourth office I'd visited. Most of the addresses were on or near Broadway, beginning around Sixtieth Street and going north to Ninety-Second. If I tried to get to all of them on foot, it would take an entire day, and I didn't think the cockamamie story I'd dreamed up would work over the telephone. I'd have to show up in person if it had any chance, so I took cabs. No sign of Kirk or anyone showing much interest in me as I left Jimmy's Place. I started with Brown Wheelock Harris, then Slawson & Hobbs, and Sharp & Nassoit. I had two more to go. My story about Kirk going to Paraguay was thin beer, but the real estate business was still so slow that people in the offices heard me out and didn't laugh in my face. I told them that if there was any charge for checking their records for the past few months, I'd be happy to pay. Nobody took me up on it.

A middle-aged woman who was reading the *Daily News* looked up when she heard the name Kirk. She said, "I think that's the nice double office on East Twenty… East Twenty-Something… East Twenty-Seventh!"

She pushed her rolling chair away from a desk. There were four desks on the other side of the counter. The office was in a building on Broadway, six stories above the cross street. The young fellow and the woman were the only ones there. I could tell by their hopeful smiles when I opened the door that they were glad to see a potential customer. I had the same reception at every realty company.

She checked the labels on the drawers of a set of file cabinets built into a wall. She pulled one open, thumbed through hanging files and lifted a thin one out. She brought it to the counter and I saw that the tag read "East 27th". The folder was filled with leases. It didn't take her long to find it.

"Yes, indeed, here it is. Fourth floor, double private office with reception room." The young fellow looked over her shoulder and I saw the resemblance. He must have been her son.

"You remember him, Freddy." She rubbed her thumb and fingers together. "Mr. Money Is No Object."

Freddy nodded, looking sad. I tried to read the upside-down lease and saw that it had been signed on January 6.

"Your partner found a very nice office, Mr.…"

"Robinson. James Robinson."

"Mr. Robinson. I remember Mr. Kirk had some unusual requirements. He wanted a nice neighborhood but one that wasn't too busy."

Freddy said, "That's not hard to find these days."

"He wasn't concerned about the rent if the place was right. There were some wonderful offices in prime locations like the Knickerbocker Building, but he wasn't interested. 'Too many prying eyes,' he said."

She read the lease. "Yes, you have it for twelve months with an option to renew at the same price for another year. Are you interested in more space? I'm sure we can help you find it."

"What's the address?"

"Let's see. One East Twenty-Seventh. Corner of Madison." She frowned and turned the lease over. "This is odd. He's listed the company as the National Liberty Foundation. Funny name for a mining operation."

"Like I said, Asa is a funny guy. You never know what he's gonna come up with. Thanks for your help. You really saved my bacon on this."

. . .

On the street, I hailed a southbound cab. Late afternoon traffic was heavy. It was a twenty-minute ride downtown. The late night with Kirk in the cellar and no real sleep caught up with me in the back seat of the hot car. I needed a shower and a change of clothes for work. Kirk's office would wait. I got out in front of the Chelsea. As the taxi pulled away, I heard a loud, sharp whistle, the kind some guys make by curling their tongue. Everybody turned toward the sound. There he was on the other side of Twenty-Third Street, my guardian angel from the shoot-out. People hurrying by him on the sidewalk shied away from the piercing whistle. He stood tall, back straight, shoulders squared, expression fierce, not angry but serious. He was staring at me. Dark sunburned face, still no hat, short white hair, sharp cheekbones and nose, faded green coat with big pockets and a high stiff collar buttoned to the neck. Doughboy's uniform. That's when I started thinking of him as the Soldier.

He stood there not moving until he was sure that I was looking at him. Then his hand chopped the air in a short wave, and he disappeared into the sidewalk flow of people heading east.

. . .

Later as I showered, I tried to work through everything I'd learned from and about Asa Kirk. It was too much to deal with and it threatened to give me a headache, so I stopped thinking. I went with a light tan Palm Beach. It was still too hot for a vest but I needed the pocket for the pistol. Again, nobody followed me to Jimmy's Place. I hoped I'd find a message from Kirk and a telegram from Connie, but not that day. The only surprise was that Katherine O'Neal was trading nights with Anne Green who'd take the next Friday, and that was fine with Katherine. Tips weren't as good on Monday but she didn't care. How long had it been since I'd heard from Connie? One week? Two? I tried to tell myself I wasn't worried or angry or scared.

I stayed behind the bar where I could keep an eye on the front door. I didn't really expect Kirk to come back during business hours, but I wanted to know as soon as he showed up. He didn't. Around eleven, I turned it over to Arch and went to my office. The special at the Grill was meatloaf. They sent down a plate. It settled my stomach. After I'd finished it and done an early count, I took Kirk's belongings out of the safe and went through them again to make sure I hadn't overlooked anything. Got everything out of the wallet, held it under the desk lamp, and pulled the pockets wide open. Nothing. I did same with the leather key case and got the same result.

The telephone rang after midnight. I picked up, still hoping it was Kirk. It was Theodora Opperman.

"There's nothing more to tell," she said. "I was able to find George Foster, the man who saw Shea 'hurrying' on the platform. I couldn't meet him but I spoke to him by telephone. He said there was really nothing unusual about the way Shea was moving. People do that every day on the subway. Foster thinks people hurry too much. His exact words are 'there's always another train just like there's always another woman.' Is that enough or would you like to give the agency more of your money?"

"Just send me your bill."

She must have heard something in my voice. "What is it, Quinn? I've known all along that there's something you're not telling me. Spill it."

There were a lot of things I could have told her. A guy who says he's part of a plot to kill me had that same clipping in his pocket when he tried to shake me down. His name's Asa Kirk. He disappeared after I strung him up in my cellar, maybe you can track him down. But, no. Instead, I teased her with a little truth.

"There's a lot I'm not telling you because there's a lot going on. I'll take care of it."

She thought before she answered. "The Agency handles unusual cases every day. Keep that in mind." She sounded serious.

• • •

I decided to close around one thirty. Katherine O'Neal and Arch took the taxi. I had Frenchy and Marie Therese let me out at the Chelsea, and spent the night in Connie's room even though it was hotter than mine.

Chapter Eighteen

It was still hot at six thirty Tuesday morning when I left the Chelsea. I was wearing one of my oldest suits, something nobody would notice, and I didn't hurry as I walked east on Twenty-Third. That early, anybody followed me, I'd see him. Nobody did. I stopped at a good diner I knew near the Flatiron Building for coffee and a bagel and schmear. I ate at a counter by the window where I could keep an eye on the street. Nobody paid any attention to me. The papers said ten people had been "prostrated" by the weather and two more had drowned. The big story on the front page was about Shea's boss Ferdinand Pecora giving up his run to be the chairman of something I'd never heard of called the Securities and Exchange Commission. It was supposed to fix the problems his committee had uncovered. Instead, Joe Kennedy was taking over. Go figure.

By the time I finished, traffic was picking up. I cut through a park and walked up Madison to the corner of Twenty-Seventh. That part of the street is three lanes one-way north with narrow sidewalks and tall buildings on both sides, making it feel dark and tight. When people talk about the "concrete canyons" of the city that's what I think of. I was never comfortable there. No room to maneuver if things went wrong. One East Twenty-Seventh was a squarish office building like the others around it, six stories tall, glass doors in the middle. That early those doors were locked. One of Kirk's keys opened them.

Inside it was cooler than the street, and quiet. A soda fountain and drug store took up the first floor. The directory by the elevator listed the National Liberty Foundation on the fourth floor. At least it was there, unlike the ABC Licensing Division. I took the stairs. The elevator would make too much noise, and if anybody was already at work at the Foundation, he didn't need to know there was somebody else in the building. Being careful not to tap my stick, I checked the second and third floors. There were about a dozen offices on each. All of them were dark and more than half were empty with realty company signs on the doors. On the fourth floor, the Foundation and an insurance company for teachers and professors were the only ones with lettering on the frosted glass doors.

Another of Kirk's keys unlocked the National Liberty Foundation. The doors opened onto a reception room with offices on either side. A secretary's desk was cluttered with a big Pitney-Bowes postage meter, telephone, stacks of paper, envelopes, and narrow pamphlets with buff covers. One part of the desk had been opened for a typing table and a tall Royal typewriter. An ashtray filled with lipstick smeared butts was beside it. The pamphlets had titles like "The National Liberty Foundation. A Statement of Principles by Brandon Pelltierre III," "The Fate of the Bonus Army: Proposed Legislation for President Roosevelt by Brandon Pelltierre III," and "Socialized Government and the Threat of Planned Economy by Basil Willsson, attorney." The rest were just as exciting.

Five cardboard boxes were on the floor behind the desk. It looked like the secretary had been addressing envelopes and stuffing them with pamphlets. The boxes were labeled Civic Organizations, College Libraries, Newspapers, Business Groups, Government Agencies, and Men's Clubs. Without disturbing anything on the desk, I tried the drawers. Nothing but office supplies and restaurant lunch menus. The only other things in the reception room were a coatrack and umbrella stand.

The first office door I tried was locked. One of Kirk's Schlage keys opened it. If the secretary's room was meant for work, this one was for a guy who wanted to enjoy himself. Console radio. Wool carpeting, worn down in front of a six-foot sofa. Cigar butts in the ashtray. Dirty glass with half an inch of what smelled like cheap Scotch. Padded highbacked chair, polished wooden desk with a matching cabinet behind it. No sign of work at that desk. Just a blotter, another ashtray, and telephone. The desk was locked but looked like it would be easy to force. Maybe later.

A large closet with folding louvered doors was empty except for two wooden cases of King's Ransom Scotch.

The second office was the same size as the first. It was unlocked and somebody had been through it. No carpeting, no cabinet, no radio, no booze. The closet held metal shelves that were half filled with more cardboard boxes of pamphlets. Empty easel in one corner. Simple Steelcase desk, drawers pulled open and empty. Even the trashcan was clean. Figure this was Kirk's office. Looked like he wasn't planning to come back.

More evidence that maybe the kid had been telling the truth. He was working with Spig Dolan on some big deal. Part of the big deal involved killing Mitchell Shea and some drunken schmuck in New Jersey and now me. Then something scared Kirk or maybe he just realized late in the game that he didn't have the stomach for killing. So, he decided to get out and put the touch on me to bankroll his getaway. Then, what? Maybe after my friendly persuasion, he decided to cut his losses and hotfoot it out of town. Maybe his partners tumbled to his plans to amscray. Maybe he decided to study for the priesthood.

By then, it was close to eight o'clock when some ambitious early riser might show up to work. I had to figure that anybody who'd been working with Kirk knew who I was and what I looked like, so it was time to leave. But first, I noted down the numbers of the empty offices beside the Foundation, and the names and addresses of the restaurants from the secretary's menus. And since there was such a large stack on her desk, I took one of the pamphlets, the Foundation's Statement of Principles.

I walked back to Jimmy's Place taking the same slow care I had before. The sidewalks were busier but I was sure nobody followed me. On the way, I thought over what I'd seen. I knew the pamphlets and the flyers I'd found in Kirk's wallet were political, and the guy they'd killed out in New Jersey was an assemblyman. An assemblyman was something like an alderman, I figured. And Mitchell Shea had worked for Ferdinand Pecora, and Pecora pissed off bankers for politicians. But that was all I could say about the subject. I paid no attention to politics unless it had something to do with the legality of alcohol. To me, politicians were men I delivered bribes and kickbacks to.

All right then, I thought, you don't know about politics but the guys at the National Liberty Foundation do, and they're trying to kill you, so you damn well better educate yourself.

• • •

In my office, I waited until ten to make the call. He picked up on the first ring.

"Wadsworth Realty. Fred Dean speaking."

"This is Jimmy, uh, James Robinson. I was in yesterday about the office my partner rented."

"Yes, Mr. Kirk who's off in Paraguay."

"That's right. I found the place and was able to get in. As I suspected, Asa underestimated how much space we're going to need."

"Oh?" He liked hearing that. "How can we help you?"

"I see that the offices on either side are empty."

"Yes, we're handling both of them, and another on the third floor. I think we could offer you a very attractive rate."

After fifteen minutes of the usual back and forth and this and that, we arrived at a price for a short-term lease. Since Mr. Kirk and the Foundation had already been approved and since I would be using cash, there was no reason they couldn't have the paperwork filled out for my signature that afternoon. I said I'd be there at one.

• • •

Later, I walked several blocks east, making sure nobody was following before I flagged down a cab and went to Wadsworth Realty. When we'd finished, I had a copy of the new lease and two sets of keys to the offices that shared walls with both of the Liberty Foundation offices. Back at the Chelsea, I cleaned up and changed into a more presentable suit for work. With the heat and it being July third, I had an idea it would be a slow Tuesday. I was right.

Around ten thirty, we got a sudden heavy rain, and the crowd cleared out by eleven. I told Frenchy and Marie Therese and Anne Green to leave early and asked Arch to help me clean up. After the others had gone, I locked the front door and went behind the bar. Arch cleared the tables and we sent the last load of dirty glasses up to the kitchen in the dumbwaiter. I got the bottle of the good Jameson down from the top shelf and put it on the bar with two glasses. Arch's mustache twitched. This didn't happen often.

"Have you got a few minutes to talk?"

"Is it about Connie?"

"No. Sit down. Have a knock and pour one for me. I'm going to finish up and do the count. Take a look at these and tell me what you make of them when I'm finished." I handed him the pamphlet and the three flyers I'd taken from Kirk's wallet.

I took the day's cash and IOUs from the register, checked the locks in back, and straightened the cellar. Upstairs, the kitchen was empty and Vittorio had locked his door. The count was what I'd expected. I put it in the safe and took out Kirk's wallet. I left the pistol and the dagger. Back downstairs, Arch had moved to a four-top. He was concentrating on the Liberty Foundation pamphlet. I poured a knock and waited for him to finish.

He put it down on top of the flyers. "You're going to explain these?"

"Sure. But first, tell me what they are. I mean, you see stuff like the flyers all the time. Some guy on the sidewalk handing them out won't let you pass 'til you take one, then you throw it away. I read these and I understand the words but I don't know anything about the stuff they're talking about except that they're trying to sell me something, and they all hate that son of a bitch Roosevelt."

"You hate him because he made you change the way you do business. They hate him because they want to toss him out and take over themselves. But where to start? Tell me what you understand of politics."

"Politics is about who's in charge, who you've got to pay off to do business."

"That does cut to the nub of it, but it doesn't really help us here. Is there anything in these flyers that you do understand?"

I shook my head.

"The one about the Nazis says the Germans are a peace-loving people who want to set their economy aright, and the Nazi Party has a plan to rebuild from top to bottom. Eyewash. This one from the Americans for Freedom, it sounds like they're edging up to the Nazis, saying that Roosevelt is such a dangerous character that he's got to be removed before the next election."

He put it down and held up the pamphlet. "The National Liberty Foundation doesn't go as far. If you can dig your way through the clotted prolix prose of Mr. Brandon Pelltierre III, and that's damned difficult to do, you find that he is saying that everything possible legally must be done to stop or slow Roosevelt down. Elect new candidates that will fight the good fight against him, put in new judges, challenge everything he proposes in the courts.

"And finally we have the Workers Ex-Service League. They, bless 'em, are Reds, angrier than some but ready for the workers of the world to unite, rise up and seize the reins of industrial production and unseat the illegitimate administration. They'd tell you that they are the enemies of the Nazis, but strip away the slogans and it's the same sheepdip."

Prolix. Sheepdip, I'd have to look those up.

Arch drained his whiskey and poured another. "Now it's your turn. I have to suspect that all of these have something to do with attempts on your life and the unfortunate accountant who met his end on the Thirty-Third Street subway platform."

I put the wallet on the table between us. "A week ago, a guy called here and said that he was working with a group that's trying to kill me. For five hundred bucks, he'd tell me all about it. He called a couple more times, we agreed to meet here Sunday night after we closed. We did. Turns out he's a young guy named Asa Kirk. We discussed the situation. He told me a few things about what was going on but said he'd have to show me evidence that was nearby to explain any more. I relieved him of this wallet and some other odds and ends, and sent him off to produce his proof. Haven't seen him since. The flyers were in the wallet. So was that clipping about the accountant that you showed me, and another clipping from a New Jersey paper about a guy that died after drinking bad booze last Christmas. I found the pamphlet at the office where Kirk works."

Arch said, "Wait a minute. You're getting ahead of yourself. Go back to Kirk coming here Sunday."

I did, but I couldn't explain it without telling him about hiring the Continental detective, finding Kirk's office, and the rest of it.

It took me an hour and two more knocks to get to, "This afternoon I went back to the realty company and rented the office next to the Foundation."

"What are you going to do with it?"

"Maybe nothing. I just want to find out who these guys are. Kirk said they were part of something bigger."

"You said someone from your days with Rothstein was involved."

"Spig Dolan. He wanted a piece of the Black Sox series."

"Did you have anything to do with him after that?"

"No. I saw him around but A.R. never did any business with him that I knew of. Dolan was one of those guys who's always hustling and looking to pick up an easy dollar. Dozens of them were trying to talk to Mr. Rothstein every day."

"The other man, Herk Sturdivant?"

"Never heard of him."

"And the Continental detective, the Opperman woman, you trust her?"

"Met her three years ago when I got to know Willie Seabrook. He hired her. I told you about it."

"And you're sure the man you saw outside the Chelsea was the same one who shot the young gunmen who waylaid us?"

"No question about it. He wanted to be sure I saw him."

"Perhaps then, we can assume or hope that he is on our side."

"Not 'our' side. They're not after you."

"We don't know that, but we do know two other things. First, when they tried to shoot you, they tried to shoot me. Ergo, I am involved. Second, you are my friend. I help my friends when they need it. You need it now."

His mustache twitched and his eyes were smiling. "I've got some ideas about how we can start."

**Continuation of statement by Michael Patrick Reardon;
Sunday, July 15, 1934; 1:34pm.
(Personnel same as Saturday, July 14 sessions.)
Stenograpy and typescript: T.S.**

I have tried to describe the various workings of the Cerberus Society
as I saw them. For 43 years I served the Society, 15 years as a Steward
and 28 years as Major Domo. In that capacity, I kept all of the records
of the Society's activities, rolls, accounting, expenses, purchases,
and income. At the same time, I kept a private journal annotating the
members' more egregious excesses.

On the night of June 6, 1934, the Governors demanded my keys and
told me I was being replaced by Henry Brevet, the boy I trained as Head
Steward. He was as dumbfounded and dispirited by my dismissal as I
was. Henry is not a bad lad but he still needs guidance. The Governors
also said that due to economic circumstances, the pension I had been
promised repeatedly over my tenure was under reconsideration. I now
find myself nearly destitute and in a state of medical desperation so
severe that to pay for my care, I have agreed to tell everything I know to
these young people, everything about the Society and the efforts of the
Governors to remove Franklin Roosevelt from office.

Those efforts actually began before Mr. Roosevelt was a candidate.
It was on a stormy Sunday afternoon in March, 1932, when the city was
still reeling from the news that the Lindbergh baby had been kidnapped.
Until then, the activities of the Cerberus Society had revolved around
the usual carnal debaucheries, as I have described in another part of this
statement, but after the Crash a few of the more serious members, and
both Governors—there were only two Governors for several years after
the passing of one without male heir—used the resources of the Society
to discuss more serious political and economic matters. These men had
watched in horror as Russia fell to communism and Italy to fascism,
though they professed to find much to admire in Il Duce, and the current
rise of Hitler in Germany. All of those forces were at work in America,
so, when the angelic infant son of the most famous man in the world
was kidnapped from his crib fifty miles from where they were sitting,

it seemed to them a sure sign that society as they knew it was about to disintegrate. That afternoon, the four of them, two Governors and two guests, resolved that they would do whatever it took and spend as much as was needed to make sure that the disintegration of the nation did not touch them. If a second Revolution was to come to America, it would be their Revolution.

In the years after the Crash, as the Depression continued and worsened, those more serious older members would sometimes invite experts to speak. These were men who were not to be considered for membership, but would share with the members their particular fields of knowledge. Professors, admirals, generals, explorers, anyone who might inform the members about something that had piqued their interest. The leader of one of the early German-American Nazi organizations, the Free Society of Teutonia, made a speech that impressed several of them. It was in that spirit that the two Governors delved into the possible dangers and opportunities offered by the Bonus Army. It was in late April or May of 1932.

The Governors had learned of men who were skilled at infiltrating these revolutionary groups. They had been working in secret for the Bureau of Investigation and the Attorney General since the 1920s. Their efforts lead directly to the Palmer raids that exposed the radicals and anarchists who blew up the Stock Exchange and sent more bombs to the homes of high government officials. These were the men who would be able to tell them the truth about the Bonus Army.

Chapter Nineteen

The girl was no more than fifteen, seventeen tops. I'd never seen her but I knew she was trouble. She was standing at the front door arguing with Fat Joe. He didn't want to let her in. It was about ten o'clock, Wednesday night. Fourth of July business had been slow, as always, so I sent Frenchy and Marie Therese home. Katherine O'Neal was handling the tables. Arch and I were behind the bar.

Fat Joe looked over and shrugged. What did I want him to do? The girl had a determined look about her. Couldn't tell the color or length of her hair under a cloche hat. She wore a short jacket over a simple print dress. I nodded to Fat Joe and went to the short side of the bar by the door. In the light, I could see that she was almost pretty and she hadn't done anything to doll herself up. She hesitated before she spoke, like she was screwing up her courage.

"Are you Mr. Quinn?"

I said I was. She said, "I'm Jenny Pris Kirk. Where's Asa?" Her accent sounded like his.

She didn't have a handbag. No sign of a gun in either pocket of her jacket. Figure she wasn't there to kill me. "Let's talk in my office."

I untied my apron and told Arch to take over. He said under his breath, "Watch that one, she's a sharp cookie."

• • •

She sat on the divan, her hands twisting a small pink and white handkerchief. In better light, she was prettier, and scratch seventeen. Probably fifteen, sixteen tops. I stayed behind my desk. I could see she was chewing on the inside of her lip. She was worried.

I tried not to sound like I was a cop ordering her around. "Have you got anything that proves you're who you say you are?"

"What do you mean? An identification card?"

"I'm not sure, but you walk in here and you're probably not old enough, and you say you want to know the whereabouts of a party named Asa Kirk. What's he to you?"

"He's my husband." She stuck out her left fist so I could see the thin band.

"Why would I know where he is?"

"Because he works for you."

"He said that?"

Her shoulders slumped, and she put her face in her hands as she realized that whatever he'd told her, he'd been lying. "Something's happened to him, I know it has."

"He was here Sunday night, but he doesn't work for me. Never has. Tell me why you think so."

She said they were from Anacostia, in Washington, D.C. When Asa's father lost his job and couldn't support the family, Asa moved in with an uncle and aunt, Ira and Lois Kirk. Uncle Ira worked for the Department of the Navy. The girl didn't know exactly what he did, but sometimes he needed help and then he was able to hire Asa.

"Two years ago, Asa worked the whole summer for Uncle Ira when the Bonus Army was in town. He helped feed the veterans and their families until the U.S. Army drove them out and burned down the camps they'd set up. It paid so well Asa started talking about our getting married, but after that, work was hard to find so we decided to wait. Uncle Ira was transferred to the Great Lakes Naval Training Center. Aunt Lois didn't go with him so we stayed with her and helped with the kids that she took care of. Then about a year ago, Uncle Ira came back with great news."

She sat up a little straighter. "He told us that what Asa had done with the Bonus Army had been noticed by some important people. They wanted to offer him a job in New York with a company that did specialized government contract work. It was almost like a dream come true for us. Nobody in Anacostia or Washington was hiring, so Asa said yes right away and we got married."

Aunt Lois helped them find an apartment in Brooklyn. They furnished it with things Aunt Lois gave them. Being on their own was exciting at first. That didn't last long. The pay that had sounded so good back in Anacostia didn't go far enough. Even with their aunt's help, it cost so much to move.

"Everything in New York is so expensive, and there are so many Jews and Catholics and foreigners. Sometimes I think Asa and me are the only two people in the building who speak English. We couldn't afford to go to restaurants so I tried to cook, but none of the things I made when we were with Aunt Lois were in the stores there and so it seemed like we were living on frankfurters and oatmeal."

Both items on his grocery list. Maybe the girl was telling the truth.

"The real problem was that Asa's job turned out not to be what he thought it was going to be. To begin with, they gave him a lot of responsibility and a lot of money to work with. He had to set up a bank account and find the right place for a new office operation, and get it approved, and arrange for the equipment they'd need. There would be a secretary coming in, and he had to have everything ready for her. Then he had to buy a car, a brand new DeSoto."

"That's big stuff for a kid," I said. "How old is he?"

"Nineteen."

"And he was in charge of all that?"

"He had a boss but that was the problem. The boss wasn't there."

"You're going to have to explain that to me."

She sighed. "When Uncle Ira told Asa he had the job, he said the boss was Mr. Sturdivant, a man he'd met at the Great Lakes Center. But Mr. Sturdivant managed several projects, and he traveled constantly so Asa probably wouldn't meet him right away. He'd get his instructions by telegraph and sometimes by telephone. That was fine at first, but it's been a year and he still hasn't met Mr. Sturdivant. He does get wires and sometimes Mr. Dolan comes into the office. He says he works for Mr. Sturdivant, too, but Asa has never seen him do anything, and he doesn't trust Mr. Dolan."

Smart kid.

"At first, Asa would tell me all about what he was doing when he came home at night, but for the past few months, he hardly says anything, only that they're asking him to write things and sign things he knows are wrong. He's been creating expense reports for other people. He knows they're false, and it's all making him terribly depressed."

I stopped her and asked what they hired her husband to do.

"He's a whiz at paperwork and bookkeeping. He can type and organize anything. He even wrote Uncle Ira's reports, and he can talk to anybody about anything. People just open up to him."

Maybe that's what he thought was going to happen with me Sunday night.

"We want to go back home, but we haven't been able to save any money. Asa said he'd find some and then we'd be able to leave."

"Where does he work? What's the name of this specialized government contract company?"

"Asa told me the name, the Liberty something, but I don't remember exactly. I guess a wife should know that, but I don't. Anyway, Friday, everything changed."

She smiled a little. "He came home with his briefcase and a Gladstone both stuffed with papers. He said that our worries were over. He was so excited. It was the first time I'd seen him happy in weeks. He said he'd made an arrangement. It would get us five hundred dollars and we'd be able to leave. When I asked him what it was, he said he couldn't tell me, but I should pack a bag and be ready to go on Monday. Asa said we didn't have to worry about the deposit money on the apartment. He'd taken care of that. He was nervous, keyed up all day Saturday. He locked himself in the bedroom with those papers, and he made three trips to the incinerator to get rid of some of them. On Sunday, he was so nervous he didn't even eat. He left around nine and came right back. That's when he told me he was going to see a man named Jimmy Quinn who had a bar on West Twenty-Second Street. There was nothing to worry about but I should know where he was."

"And that's when you started worrying."

She nodded.

"He took the papers with him?"

"In the briefcase. He left the Gladstone with his clothes in our apartment."

That fit with what I found in his empty office. Figure he waited for everyone else to leave Friday afternoon, then crammed every piece of paper that might help him into those two bags as fast as he could. Then he took them home to Brooklyn and sorted through them. Kept what he needed. Burned the rest.

"You don't know anything about what your husband did?"

Looking innocent, she shook her head.

"Like I said, he was here Sunday night. He called me on the telephone a couple of times last week and said that he had something I needed. He offered to sell it to me. We talked a few times and agreed on a price."

"He went out late to use the telephone on the street. I gave him the nickels."

"When he came here Sunday night, he didn't have this thing that he said he was going to bring. We talked some more. He told me enough to make me believe he was telling the truth. He also said this thing he was talking about was close. He'd bring it back. He left and that's the last time I saw him."

"What is it that Asa was talking about?"

"He said some people were trying to kill me. He knew who they were."

I watched her face closely as her eyes opened wide and she sucked in a deep breath. "Why would he say that? I mean, it's ridiculous."

"No, it's not."

"Asa would never be involved with anything like that." She looked like she was shocked by the idea. I couldn't tell if she was acting.

"You just said you don't know what he does. Do you know where he works?"

"No. I mean, I asked, of course, but Asa said I shouldn't ever go to that part of town. It was perfectly safe for him, but it was better for me to stay close to the apartment. He wouldn't just lie to me."

Her lip quivered and her voice got raw. "This is the first time I've been outside of Brooklyn since we moved here. If a nice woman hadn't helped me on the subway I wouldn't have found my way."

That's when the first tears came.

"I don't understand this. Asa wouldn't just leave. He couldn't do that. He knows I don't have any money and Mrs. Klopernick asks about the late rent every time she sees me. Please, Mr. Quinn, there's got to be something you can tell me, something that will help."

She moved to raise her handkerchief to her eyes, but saw that she'd twisted it into a tight wad. I gave her a pocket square. How to play this? I tried to look honest.

"O.K., I'm going to level with you," I lied. "A lot of strange things have been happening to me lately and your husband said he could help me straighten them out. When he left here, he said he was coming back with the proof he'd been talking about. Sounds like it was in that briefcase, but, like I said, he left and he didn't come back. That's all I know."

"Then…" She smiled. "If I could find his briefcase, you'd pay me five hundred dollars for it?"

Honest or not, she was a quick little cookie. "I can't answer that without knowing what's in it, but, sure, if you can help me out with this situation, I'll give you five hundred." As I said it, I wondered if I'd just been really stupid.

"I'm embarrassed to admit this but Asa left with almost all of our money. I don't know what I'm going to do until he gets back…"

Sap that I am, I gave her a fiver and paid for a cab to take her to Brooklyn.

• • •

For the second night, Arch stayed late after we closed. I told him everything the girl said, and we considered it over another small knock of Jameson.

Arch said, "If she is, indeed, his blushing bride and their situation is as she describes it, then it seems unlikely he'd run out on her without the money you promised."

"And if she was shooting straight, then it figures Kirk realized that he'd been set up. His name's on the lease and the registration for a DeSoto. He's signed all the checks. His partners are killing people and if it comes back to that office, he's holding the bag."

Arch said, "Then he sees that the next mark runs a prosperous establishment. He's a known associate of underworld figures and so is unlikely to call in the authorities. A good source of ready cash for him and his bride to make good their speedy departure."

"I've considered that."

"On the other hand, if the little lady is part of the conspiracy that means to do you harm, then she was trying to find out what you know and, perhaps, where he is. For all you know the business about the stuffed briefcase and Gladstone is her invention, along with the rest of her story."

"Or she's smart enough to mix her lies with the truth. Like you said, she's a sharp cookie."

He finished his drink. "Let me have those keys to the offices. I think I'll pay a visit early tomorrow. There's bound to be more to see."

I said the keys were in the safe and we went up to my office. I gave him the keys and spread out the rest of Kirk's things on the desk. I told Arch to look through them. The night before I only showed him the flyers and the clipping, none of the other stuff.

He said, "Did you think to check the heels of his shoes?"

"They were new."

"The Navy i.d. card is not something I'd expect to find here."

"The girl said the uncle works for the Department of the Navy and went to the Great Lakes Training Center."

Arch shrugged. "Anything else?"

"Only these." I got out the dagger and pistol. "He had them strapped to his ankles."

Arch spent a long time looking them over under the desk lamp. "The blade's German, I think, at least I've seen ones like it on the Krauts when they dress up in their marching clothes."

He popped the clip from the pistol and worked the slide. He held it back with one hand and twisted the end of the barrel with the other until the piece came apart. "D'you mind if I borrow this? The damn Luger is impossible to carry without letting any copper you might encounter know that you're armed."

"Take it, it's yours. Looks to be in good condition but I haven't fired it."

He put the gun back together and dry fired it. "This'll do. This'll do just fine."

Chapter Twenty

Arch was right. There was more to see in the Liberty Foundation offices. It seemed likely these guys had been in my place and knew who Arch was, so he went over to the building on East Twenty-Seventh early Thursday morning. He had an apartment down off Ninth Avenue with the other Micks in the Irish section. It was too far to walk so he took the El and got there about half an hour after sunrise. Like I did, he let himself in the front door and took the stairs to the fourth floor.

First, he got into the offices I'd rented two days before, one on each side of the Liberty Foundation. They weren't as elaborate as the Foundation's, just a simple reception room with a desk and a telephone and an office behind it. No carpeting in either. Linoleum tile floor. The office window opened over a narrow alley. That early, the alley was too heavily shadowed for Arch to tell what was on the ground. The other office was on the corner of the building. It had a second window on Madison and cost more, even though it was smaller than the first. That corner office shared a wall with the well-appointed side of the Liberty Foundation. The other office shared a wall with what I thought was Kirk's office.

After he'd looked through "my" offices, Arch unlocked the doors to the Foundation. When he told me about it later, it didn't sound like anything had changed since I'd seen it. The secretary's desk was still stacked with pamphlets. Kirk's desk was still empty. The shelves in his closet were still full of boxes of pamphlets. Since they had so many Arch decided none would be missed, and filled his pockets. Both the secretary's area and the better office had been cleaned. Ashtrays were empty. No dirty glasses.

Before he left, he made a quick drawing of the floorplans of the four offices on the back of a pamphlet. Arch is a hell of a lot smarter about some things than I am.

• • •

Marie Therese, Frenchy and I were getting the place ready to open when Arch showed up around eleven. He joined me behind the bar and told me what he'd been up to.

"Before I do anything else, I want to be sure that there is nothing that connects you personally with that building. You didn't use your real name."

"No, I made the lease part of the agreement that Kirk signed. According to the realty company's notes on that, all of the payments have been made with checks on the Liberty Foundation's account signed by Kirk. They didn't mind taking cash from James Robinson. What have you got in mind?"

"I'll tell you later tonight. I'm going to go back after everyone's left for the day and get a better feel for what's going on. I'll be here to help with closing. Let you know if I've learned anything."

"Fine."

"And one other thing, if what I'm considering comes to fruition, I'll need some money to spread around."

Somehow, I knew that was coming.

• • •

When business slowed after lunch, I took a cab down to the Western Union office on Hudson Street. It had been two weeks since Connie's telegram, her only telegram. Whenever I thought about it, I got angry, then scared, then jealous, then angry again. But when I thought about sending a wire to her, I didn't know what to say.

CONNIE, SOME GUYS ARE TRYING TO KILL ME. I DON'T KNOW WHO THEY ARE OR WHY THEY'RE DOING IT, BUT I KNOW WHERE THEY WORK. ARCH IS COOKING UP SOMETHING.
JQ

No, that wouldn't work. Too long. I wound up sending this.

WEATHER HOT. BUSINESS SLOW. EVERYBODY MISSES

YOU. SEE YOU SOON.

JQ

For the rest of the day, I worried about her, wondered what Arch was up to and got mad all over again at Kirk and his pals. My life had been a hell of a lot simpler when I was an honest criminal.

• • •

When Arch came through the door around midnight, his mustache lifted in a grin and he gave me a thumbs up. Later, after Frenchy and Marie Therese left and Katherine Neal had caught her cab, I opened the Jameson and we sat at a four-top. Arch showed me the floorplan he'd sketched on the back of a pamphlet, and described the layout.

"That's the Foundation's offices in the middle with the double doors, secretary in the center, Kirk's office to the left, Sturdivant's office on the right. The dotted lines indicate those long shallow closets. Your offices are the two on either side. They have a reception area and an inner office. I'll explain why this is important in a minute."

I poured two drinks. He said, "I went back late in the afternoon. All the offices I could see from the street were dark. The building is five stories tall. I checked the second, third and fifth floors. Nobody in any of the offices. Same with the fourth. The Foundation was locked. I waited in the corner office until I heard the cleaning crew get off the elevator. Couple of colored fellows. I introduced myself and asked if there was anything I needed to know about the building since I had just taken an office. They said they swept, emptied trash cans, and cleaned every night. When I asked them if they knew anything about my neighbor, the Liberty Foundation, they clammed up, and said I'd have to talk to their supervisor. They had strict orders not to have anything to do with those rooms. He took care of them himself. That supervisor, Mr. Henderson by name, was working on the fifth floor."

Arch poured another short knock. "Mr. Henderson is also a colored gentleman, about forty, I would say. He actually maintains that building and two others with the help of his son and nephew. He was hired by the building super. I asked about the Liberty Foundation. He was reluctant to talk initially but once I explained that I was not looking for favors and I had a generous employer who, for reasons he would prefer to remain private, would pay for useful information, Mr. Henderson became more involved."

"Do you trust what he says?"

"Yes, we had a long talk. Mr. Henderson is an educated man. He's also industrious and has done well for himself. He said at first, there was nothing unusual about the Foundation. You've seen how sparsely populated that building is. He was glad to have more work. For a few months, everything was fine. He knew that there was a young man in one office, and an older secretary who came in every day. A lot of mail went in and out. The second office was furnished but no one used it. Then the super told him that he was to do the cleaning himself. Apparently, the other tenant, a Mr. Sturdivant, was in the office late one evening and saw that the cleaners were colored. He ordered them out. The next day he told the building super that he would not have any 'yankee nigras' working in his rooms. If all the crews were colored, their boss would have to do his room. The super said he'd take care of that without further enlightening Mr. Sturdivant about Mr. Henderson's complexion."

"Did he tell you anything else about this guy?"

"Not much, but he is a Southerner, and he knows, as Mr. Henderson explained to me, that the word 'nigra' is particularly demeaning. He smokes cigars and favors cheap Scotch. He's not in the office during the day, but does come in at night and he usually has company. Mostly men, sometimes women. Mr. Henderson says that his schedule is irregular. There will be no sign of him for weeks, then he'll be in the office every night.

"Now, you have noticed from my crude drawing here, that your corner office shares a wall with Sturdivant's. On your side, it's an unremarkable wall, no windows, no electrical outlets. On his side, it's the closet where he keeps his cheap Scotch. Wouldn't it be interesting if we could listen in on what he does when he's there at night?"

"What're you talking?"

"You don't know this because there's never been a reason for the subject to come up, but one of my many talents is a modest proficiency at carpentry. And there was an occasion when I was unjustly confined while under his majesty's jurisdiction and had to practice that craft with a degree of discretion."

"I'm still missing something."

"I'd rather show you than tell you. If you could loan me your car, I can start tonight and should be able to finish tomorrow."

I wasn't going to get any more out of him. "The keys are in my office. You know where the garage is."

Chapter Twenty-One

Arch disappeared until Friday night. When he came in around midnight, the booths were full and they were two-deep at the bar. He grabbed an apron and pitched in. I told him to send the dirty glasses up to the dishwasher and help Anne Green with the tables. We didn't have a chance to talk until we closed and everyone else left.

I offered him the Jameson but he shook his head. "Not now. It would be wasted on me, I'm too tired and I've got more to do tomorrow, assuming they don't work on weekends. I'll show you what I've done on Sunday."

Arch had my car outside. He drove me to the Chelsea and went back to his place.

The heat broke on Saturday and that night we were busier than we'd been in a week. By then, I'd given up on seeing Asa Kirk again, but I expected his wife. She didn't show up either. Arch came in around nine. When we had a moment behind the bar, he said he'd finished whatever he'd been up to at the office, and would pick me up at the Chelsea after early Mass. We didn't close until after two. While the rest of them cleaned up, I took the money from the register to my office. I added it to the cash I'd moved to the safe earlier that evening and did the first rough count. It came out to a nice total, one I hadn't seen in a while. That made me remember how Connie had been keeping track of our tally. I found her ledger from the year before and checked the first Saturday in July. Even taking her skim into account, we were up more than twenty per cent. Damn. I couldn't remember what the weather had been like that weekend, but we hadn't had a heat wave like this one. Who knows, I thought, maybe there really is money to be made being legit.

• • •

At nine o'clock Sunday morning, my green Ford coupe was parked in front of the Chelsea. Arch tossed me the keys. "I'd forgotten what a sweet little car this is with the V-8," he said. "You should drive it more."

There was no traffic as we went over to the East side and nobody tailed us. Arch said he'd found a place to park around the corner on Twenty-Eighth. "There's no need to suggest someone might be in the building by parking a car in front of it."

We left it there and walked back without seeing anyone else. I unlocked the front doors and we took the stairs to the fourth floor, making as little noise as we could. We probably didn't need to be so careful. The place had that odd silence of an empty building that made footsteps sound loud. We didn't say anything until we were in the corner office I'd rented. The set up was what Arch had described. Small desk for the receptionist. Door with a pebbled glass panel behind it. We went in and I saw what he'd been doing.

The desk and rolling chair had been pushed to one side. There was a heavy canvas bag of hand tools, a small can of paint, a horsehair hand-broom and dust pan, and three cardboard boxes filled with debris on a drop cloth. The debris was chunks of drywall, plaster, wood and lathe. He said, "I hate to admit it but I don't know for certain that this will work. We'll have to test it. You see, with no one in the other office, I couldn't tell how well sound will carry. You rented this office hoping to learn something of what goes on in the Foundation. We ought to be able to hear them now."

He'd cut a hole in the wall near the floor, a square about sixteen inches on each side, and covered it with a black metal grille.

"It's meant to cover an opening in a ceiling that lets heat rise from a room with a heat source into the room above it. There's a matching grille on the other side. It's in the closet behind the desk. As I see it, there is no chance that Sturdivant or anyone else has paid close attention to the details of that closet when they moved in. If they notice the grille now, they'll think it's always been there. You can see that it doesn't look like new construction. I scuffed it up a bit. Stay here, let's see if it works." Arch left and closed the door behind him.

I pulled the rolling chair closer to the grille. When I turned my ear toward it, I could hear nothing at first, then a faint rattle and a larger rattle as Arch opened a door.

"I'm in Sturdivant's office." His voice was muffled but I could understand it. "The closet doors are open. That's how I found them and left them. Can you hear me?"

"Yes. Close the doors and say something else."

I heard the doors fold shut in their rollers. "And gentlemen in Ireland now abed shall think themselves cursed they were not here and hold their manhoods cheap while any man speaks that fought with us upon St. Crispin's Day."

"O.K., that's easy to hear. Can you talk like a regular person? Sit at the desk. Pretend you're talking on the telephone."

A moment later, the chair creaked. Arch said, "I'm at the desk. I'm picking up the handset. Let's say that I wish to talk about unsavory endeavors that I am attempting to perpetrate against certain parties."

"That's enough. It works." Now, what was I going to do with it?

We moved the desk back where it belonged and carried the tools and trash to the lobby. I brought the car around to the front door and we loaded the stuff into the trunk. On the way back, Arch said, "I've spoken to Mr. Henderson and we've come to an arrangement. I've given him a retainer and we've agreed to a weekly stipend for him and his cleaning crew. If they notice anything of interest in the Foundation's trash or any change in their routine, they'll let me know. Mr. Henderson has the telephone number for Jimmy's Place. It seemed best to have him speak only to me or you."

"For now."

"What's next?" he asked.

"I'm going to talk to a woman about hiring a detective."

• • •

I called the Continental Detective Agency that afternoon and left a message for Theodora Opperman. She surprised me by calling back an hour later. When I told her I had another job, she asked if it had anything to do with the last one.

"It's hard to explain over the telephone," I said. "Can you meet me today?"

"At your place?"

"No. One East Twenty-Seventh, corner of Madison. It's an office building."

"All right." She sounded suspicious. "When?"

"How soon can you be there?"

She said she needed lunch. So did I, and I needed time to figure out how much I had to tell her. We agreed to meet at four. I left a note for Frenchy and Marie Therese that I'd be late that evening, went back to the Chelsea and cleaned up for work. Nobody followed me when I walked back to the diner near the Flatiron Building. I had so-so meatloaf and bad coffee, and was waiting for Theodora Opperman when she got out of a cab at quarter to four. I unlocked the front door and let her in. We climbed the stairs to the fourth floor. She was puffing by the time we got there. All of the offices were still dark. We went into the office Arch had worked on and turned on the lights. Arch had drawn the shades on the windows.

"The office next door belongs to an outfit called the National Liberty Foundation. I want to know what goes on there. Somebody sitting here ought to be able to hear what's being said through that grille. I need him, or her I guess, to write it down."

I waited for her answer. She wasn't buying it. "Give me the rest."

This is where it got tricky. "I've got reason to think the Foundation has something to do with Mitchell Shea. I can't tell you how I know that and I'm not going to make up a lie. Leave it at this, a guy who worked at the Foundation told me somebody there was trying to kill me. He told me that and then he took a powder. If it's true, they know what I look like, so I can't be hanging around here to find out what they're up to."

She still wasn't buying it. "And so you just rented this office which just happened to have this grille where there's no reason for there to be a grille."

"Do you ask this many questions of all your clients?"

"I'm not asking questions, I'm making observations."

"O.K., you've observed."

She thought for a long time. "I'm sure I will have questions but for now, I'll say yes. Whatever else this is, it's a surveillance job. If you want it covered twenty-four hours a day, I'll have to bring in more operatives and that will cost you. If it's just for business hours, I'll handle it myself, maybe one more operative."

"There will probably be some work in the evenings."

She waved that away. "Fine, but there is one thing you've got to tell me. Does this have anything to do with Connie?"

I didn't expect that. Guess she and Connie had got to know each other better than I thought, but then that was Connie for you. "No," I said, "She's out of the country."

The detective laughed. "That explains a lot about how you're acting." She pulled a contract out of her handbag. I gave her keys to the office and the front door. As she filled out the contract, she muttered, "The old man's going to give me hell for this."

Chapter Twenty-Two

On Monday morning, Theodora Opperman was in the office on Twenty-Seventh Street before anyone else. She used a set of lock picks to get inside the Liberty Foundation and gave it a fast look. In her report she said she "gained surreptitious entry." Sounds better than "breaking and entering." The secretary's desk was still piled with pamphlets and envelopes. Mrs. Opperman went through the desk drawers and saw the usual office supplies—letterhead stationery, carbon paper, pencils, typewriter ribbons. In the top drawer, the secretary had left two envelopes paperclipped together with a note that read "Mail Thurs." The first was a mortgage payment. The second was a payment to Consolidated Edison. Mrs. Opperman noted the name and return address. Mrs. James Booth of 504 Benzinger Avenue, Staten Island.

The far office, the one that had been Kirk's, was still stacked with boxes of pamphlets. The other office was the one she was interested in, anyway. She went through it and saw the same things Arch and I had seen.

The drug store on the ground floor opened first. On the fourth floor, somebody unlocked the insurance company around nine, and the secretary arrived at the Liberty Foundation right after that. Mrs. Opperman had the door cracked open enough to see a middle-aged woman going into the office. Mrs. Opperman learned later that she was fifty-three years old, brown hair, brown eyes, five feet five inches tall, weight one hundred and ten pounds. No known arrests or outstanding warrants. She was the only person who came into the office that day. Mrs. Opperman unfolded a blanket she'd brought and stretched out on the floor near the grille. She heard a few muffled sounds she couldn't identify and then typing, fast professional typing. Around eleven, the secretary made a telephone call and the typewriter sounds stopped.

Mrs. Opperman cracked the door open and watched Mrs. Booth walk to the elevator. As the elevator doors closed, the detective hurried down the stairs and reached the lobby as the other woman was leaving the building. Mrs. Opperman followed her a few blocks north on Madison to a Schrafft's where she met another woman. That early, the restaurant wasn't busy and the detective was able to take the small two-top right behind Mrs. Booth. Mrs. Booth ordered the olive and egg sandwich, coffee, and the butterscotch almond sundae. Her friend had creamed codfish on toast and the golden sponge cake. Mrs. Opperman didn't say what she had, but on her bill, she listed a dollar and a quarter for lunch that day.

While they ate, the women talked. Actually, Mrs. Opperman said, Mrs. Booth talked. Her friend listened. Mrs. Booth told her about the church service on Sunday, her husband's indigestion, something called the "three little Sachs" on radio. She barely paused to chew and Mrs. Opperman stopped writing down the things Mrs. Booth found interesting until she got to her work. The secretary said Mr. Pelltierre's newest pamphlet, the one she'd started sending out that morning, was particularly fascinating. It addressed "The Negro Problem."

In her report, the detective wrote that what Mrs. Booth said in the restaurant didn't make sense to her. The woman jumped from "original sin" to "the failure of Marcus Garvey" to "the white man's responsibility," to "internment camps" without explaining any connections, and went straight back to the new shoes she'd seen at Saks but couldn't afford.

After the two women finished and were out on the sidewalk, Mrs. Opperman pretended to be searching for something in her bag as they talked. Mrs. Booth said she'd have to make sure everything had been cleaned up because Mr. Sturdivant was supposed to come in later that week and she could never be sure that those janitors would do their job.

The secretary typed for the rest of the afternoon. After she and everyone else on the floor had left for the day, Mrs. Opperman let herself into the Foundation office again and lifted a copy of "The Negro Problem" before she took the subway back to the Continental Agency's office on Broadway. She made some calls to get Mrs. Booth's particulars, typed her preliminary report, called me and said she had something. She brought it to my place around ten. I was behind the bar. She pointed toward the stairs to my office. I nodded, took off my apron and started after her. Arch stopped me.

"Is that your detective?" he asked.

I said it was and realized that he didn't know her. "She was part of the first business with Willie Seabrook back in thirty-one. You should meet her. Come on."

It was a slow Monday, so Frenchy didn't need help. I told him to send up three good brandies. Arch and I followed the fat detective. She was on the divan, lighting a Fatima. The report and the pamphlet were on my desk.

I introduced the two of them. She gave Arch her usual cold-eyed appraisal. "If there's any paper on you, she knows about it," I said.

Arch said, "Not in this country."

"If you're in on this with Quinn, then you're probably the one responsible for redecorating that office with the grille."

Arch laughed and turned on his brogue. "Don't you have the suspicious nature. In your line of work, I suppose that's to be expected, but really now, you can't be thinking that I'll be so overwhelmed by your charm that I'll confess to some undefined illegality right in front of you like some common criminal. You misjudge me." He sat on the other end of the divan and smiled at her.

The detective looked at me. "Is he always like this?"

"He's just getting warmed up."

I tossed the pamphlet to Arch and took the report. While we were reading, Anne Green brought up the brandies.

When I finished the report, Mrs. Opperman said, "I observed nothing out of the ordinary at that office today, but I am intrigued by this Brandon Pelltierre. His name came up regarding another case I worked more than a year go."

"You know who he is then?"

She nodded. "The case involved a Fifth Avenue furrier who was losing merchandise. His two sons ran the retail side of the business. He was sure that Number Two Son, the younger, was behind it, but he didn't want any police involvement or publicity. He knew the son would suspect any man that he brought into the operation, so I posed as a seamstress doing repairs in the fur storage vault."

She leaned back and sipped her brandy. "It took less than two days to catch him lifting smaller pieces, and it wasn't Number Two Son, it was Number One Son. Every afternoon, he was tucking smaller stoles and such into a raincoat that he carried over his arm. Larger pieces went right out the back door. He was fencing the goods through Little Philly Tomguy. You know him?"

"Yeah, but Little Philly isn't a fence, he's a box man, a safecracker."

"He is and this kid was trying to persuade him that it would be worth his time to crack the vault in his father's store. Second day I worked there, after they closed, Number One Son opens the back door and there's Little Philly. I made him on the spot. They paid no attention to an old woman with a needle and thread while Number One Son gave Little Philly a key to the back door and showed him the fur vault. Now, anybody could see that the vault door was nothing that a good box man couldn't crack in a few minutes. The kid didn't want it to look like an inside job. I reported it to the father that night. The next night I was waiting with two other operatives and we welcomed Little Philly with a nice set of handcuffs. When we threatened to turn him over to the cops, he offered to give us names. He fed us useless palaver until he saw that we weren't interested. Then he came up with this Brandon Pelltierre. Said word was out that this rich fellow was looking for guys who weren't particular about the kind of work they did. Said other guys had told him that Pelltierre was the real McCoy. He promised good money and he wasn't all talk, he came up with the cash. The money was so good guys were falling all over themselves but nobody knew anybody who actually got hired. At the time, nothing came of it. The furrier wasn't going to press charges. Little Philly walked.

"Personally, I thought Little Philly was blowing smoke, but I asked around and found out just how wealthy this Pelltierre is, and how little anybody knows about him. When his name comes up twice in business that ought to have nothing to do with a man of his station, well, that makes him interesting, interesting enough for me to want to know more."

Arch said, "In this case, ma'am, your suspicions are completely justified. Yes, young Jimmy and I have been trying to familiarize ourselves with Mr. Pelltierre's activities. I have read several of his political musings."

Arch held up "The Negro Problem."

"In this one, as he so often does, Mr. Pelltierre begins with a sound idea and runs in the wrong direction with it. His thesis is that bringing Africans to America as slaves is this wonderful country's Original Sin. He seems to think that Negroes are inferior to 'Nordics' as he calls them, but he doesn't spend much time with that. Whatever their status, as he sees it, the 'problem' isn't really them, it's that they're here. He goes over the various 'Back to Africa' movements and tells us why they failed. He thinks those mistakes can be corrected, and with the proper motivation, many American Negroes can be persuaded to return to their 'natural home.' He proposes a variety of payments, reparations, bribes, and inducements to fill ships. After that, if too many of them are still here, he suggests that they be rounded up into internment camps and forced to leave. By the way, he mentions internment camps in other pamphlets as possible solutions for the unemployed and the disgruntled veterans of the Bonus Army."

Mrs. Opperman looked like she didn't believe what Arch was saying.

I said, "It sounds pretty damn screwy to me."

"Oh, it is, but it's part and parcel of Mr. Pelltierre's larger thesis, and that is that American democracy has failed. He believes it was doomed from the beginning because the premise that most people want freedom is wrong. It's true, he says, that a few men who have risen to the top should be free, but most men only think they want to be free. As soon as they're placed in a difficult situation, what they really want is security. Then if they are provided food, shelter, entertainment and creature comforts—by which he means alcohol and sex—they will be content. Then a strong leader will then be able to turn them into an effective labor and military force. Herr Hitler believes much the same."

Chapter Twenty-Three

Early the next morning, Tuesday, Mrs. Opperman was back at the Twenty-Seventh Street office. She wasn't alone. She brought a Provisional Operative who'd been with the Agency less than a year. I don't know her name. All I have are the initials "T.S." on each of the typed pages she turned in as part of the report. She was with the Agency because she was a neighbor of Mrs. Opperman. Lived in the apartment across the hall. No, I don't know where Mrs. Opperman's apartment was. I didn't ask and she didn't tell me. She did say later that T.S. was a teenaged girl who thought it was the greatest thing in the world that she knew a real detective, and a woman no less. The fat woman only told me that because I gave her a double shot of the good brandy. She didn't say this either, but I'd bet a dollar that T.S. waited every day to ambush her neighbor in the hall and get her to tell stories about the adventures she was up to. And I'd bet that Mrs. Opperman pretended to be annoyed at the girl but was flattered at the same time. Of course, T.S. wanted to be a detective herself and asked how to go about it. Mrs. Opperman told her that the first thing she needed to learn was how to type because it was her experience that good detectives spent half their time preparing reports and other paperwork. T.S. took her advice and started secretarial school as soon as she graduated high school. That's where she learned how to take shorthand and that's why she was with Mrs. Opperman on Tuesday morning.

Mrs. Opperman told T.S. that she needed to know what was said in the office next door. She wanted the girl to get in early and to make sure that she wasn't seen entering the office I'd rented. Nobody else should know she was there. There would be a secretary, Mrs. Booth, in the other office. T.S. would probably hear Mrs. Booth typing. Their client was really interested in any conversations that went on. A Mr. Sturdivant was supposed to be in the office. Mrs. Opperman wanted to know anything he and any visitors said. Every word. Take them down on the steno pad and type them up later at the Agency office.

And while T.S. was eavesdropping, Mrs. Opperman went back to the Continental Agency offices down town and got to work on who Brandon Pelltierre III was and what he was about.

Even though Little Philly Tomguy said Pelltierre was looking to hire hard cases, she knew her usual lowlife sources weren't going to be much use to her. Instead, she started by calling guys she knew at newspapers. The crime reporters at the *Herald Tribune* and the *Gotham Comet* didn't know anything about Pelltierre either, but they gave her the numbers of the business writers. The business guy at the *Comet* told her that Pelltierre was a mystery man in the small world of New York's wealthiest.

According to the report she turned in to me, she couldn't get much more than the basic facts at first. The Pelltierre fortune was based on armaments, heavy weapons specifically designed for land, sea and air conflicts. Competitors said that their products weren't the best, but Pelltierre Weapons and Matériel always sent out a large hungry sales force. The men seemed to be at the right places, speaking to the right ears and greasing the right palms before anybody else knew that hostilities were brewing.

The first Brandon Pelltierre moved to New York from Maryland right before the Civil War. He sold to both sides until the South couldn't pay. He built a mansion on Fifth Avenue and another one in Rhode Island and avoided society functions. His son, Brandon II, was an even more relentless salesman than his father. He divided the Weapons and Matériel into different companies, built factories in England and Germany, and doubled the profits of the operation. To keep his wife happy, he became more generous to charitable and civic organizations, but he never appeared in public. The Crash didn't hurt his business. The truth is that after it, he was one of the dozen richest men in the city.

Brandon III was in charge when the Nazis took over Germany. According to the guy at the *Comet* and another writer at the *Wall Street Journal*, nobody could be sure how much the company was selling to the Krauts under the table. Everyone assumed it was considerable. Pelltierre himself didn't have much to do with the business. More than one writer told the detective that the third Pelltierre had enough common sense to realize he could only screw things up if he tried to change anything important and so he let the companies run themselves. His interests lay elsewhere. Brandon III fancied himself a philosopher of politics and wrote his pamphlets while his wife busied herself with good works. If he or anyone in his family had ever supported a political candidate or party, Mrs. Opperman couldn't find it.

When she hinted to the guy at the *Journal* that Pelltierre might be trying to hire guys for strongarm stuff, he told her she had to have him mixed up with somebody else. A man of his position would never be involved in anything like that and Pelltierre's reputation as a dilettante made it more unlikely. But if it turned out that he was into some dirty work, the *Journal* would want to know about it.

She went through the pamphlets Arch had lifted. Like Arch, she found Pelltierre's style so bloated and dull that she couldn't read any of his pieces from beginning to end. Scanning them was enough for her to learn that Pelltierre spent most of his time laying out all the things that politicians were doing wrong, and then saying that the problems could be solved if strong-willed men simply stepped in and took charge.

After a full day on the telephone, Mrs. Opperman figured she wasn't likely to find more, and so she went back to the matter of Mitchell Shea, the accountant who was pushed in front of a subway train. By then, the investigation he'd been working on was over and the committee hearings were done. The office she'd visited a few weeks before had closed. His old boss, Ferdinand Pecora, was in Washington setting up the Securities and Exchange Commission. The Continental Agency's Washington bureau gave her Pecora's telephone number and address. She called his office and was told that he was in meetings for the rest of the day. A secretary said that Pecora's schedule for the next day was tight. She couldn't guarantee that he'd be able to return a call, but if Mrs. Opperman could get to the office in the morning, the boss could probably give her a few minutes.

By then, it was nearly seven o'clock. The detective went back up to the building on East Twenty-Seventh. The Liberty Foundation offices were dark. She unlocked the door to my office and found that T.S. had news. The girl said that for most of the day she heard nothing useful. The secretary Mrs. Booth typed and sometimes talked to other women who, she thought, also worked in the building. She couldn't make out what they said, but it sounded to her like friendly conversation. Then an hour ago, the telephone rang and she distinctly heard Mrs. Booth say "Hello, Mr. Sturdivant." Mrs.

Booth talked and listened for a time and TS thought she heard the woman say "it will be ready" either tonight or tomorrow or tomorrow night. That part just wasn't clear, but T.S. was sure that something important was about to happen and she would be happy to spend the night in the office if she had to.

Mrs. Opperman didn't say so in her report, but she was not about to let youthful enthusiasm go to waste. She told T.S. to stay until nine o'clock. If Sturdivant or anyone else showed up in the Foundation offices, T.S. wasn't to turn on a light or make any noise. There's a possibility, the detective told her, a slim possibility that somebody you might hear in that room is trying to kill our client. You don't take any chances. Just write down every word he says.

• • •

Mrs. Opperman had dinner at Schrafft's ($1.50). Then she went back to her office to pick up the overnight bag she kept there. A taxi took her to Pennsylvania Station where she caught the night train to Washington. At nine o'clock Wednesday morning, she was waiting in Pecora's outer office when he got there.

In her report she wrote that "Ferdinand Pecora initially seemed reluctant to be interviewed, claiming that he had so much work to do, but when told that it concerned the death of his associate Mitchell Shea, he was fully cooperative."

They went into Pecora's inner office. Later, she told me that he was shorter than she expected, not much taller than she was. He was "impeccably" dressed, of course. What impressed her was the intense interest and emotion he had about Mr. Shea. Before she started to question him, he told her about the countless hours of work that his underpaid staff had put in. Like him, a lot of them were immigrants. Nobody expected them to expose the biggest bankers in New York as crooks and liars, but they had. And he was quick to admit that it was his staff's work that gave him the information and ammunition he needed to sweat those guys when he had them on the witness stand before the committee.

She said, "I hope I'm not wasting your time and mine, but the Agency has been hired by a client who has reason to believe that your associate, Mitchell Shea, was murdered, that his death was not an accident. I have not been able to discover anything in his life or his background to make me think that could be possible. Was there anything about his work for your investigation that might have made him a target? I know the investigation really finished a year ago, so I'm grasping at straws with this. What did Mr. Shea do for your commission?"

Pecora told her that Shea was an experienced accountant and so he was able to help guide the staff through the maze of various banks' books. He said "I had only a limited time to go through City Bank's books. Mitchell and other accountants and writers and lawyers helped prepare me for that. But Mitchell also had his own personal story to tell when he came to the commission for the first time. His experience was not the main focus of our inquiry. In fact, it was but a small part of it and it never received the public attention that the larger revelations got. However, it did provide a valuable human element to this massive saga of greed and corruption on a scale that many people simply could not believe."

Mrs. Opperman said that as he told the story, Pecora paced behind his desk and used his hands as he spoke like he was giving a speech to a jury.

Before Michell Shea worked for the commission, he was employed by one of the smaller New York banks. This bank, like many others allowed its top officers and higher-level executives to buy shares of stock and pay for them on an installment plan. Then right before the Crash, when the bank realized it was in trouble, it extended that stock program to lower-level employees. They were pressured to sign on, and to pay for the stock with automatic withdrawals from their paychecks. At the time, men who didn't join the program were being fired. Shea said that the bank sold 30,000 shares at $125 apiece. When the Crash hit, the stock value dropped to less than half of that but the employees had to pay off the original amount. The only way to get out of the payments was to quit—with unemployment at twenty-five percent. For the employees who stuck it out, as soon as they made their last payment and owned stock that was now worth considerably less than they'd paid for it, they were let go. At the same time, the officers and executives were given "morale" loans they'd never be expected to pay off to complete their stock purchases.

That's what happened to Mitchell Shea, but instead of simply walking away, he told the story to Pecora when he applied for a job. During a closed-door hearing, Pecora put Shea's old boss on the stand and forced him to admit what he'd done. Like all the other bankers who appeared before him, this one defended his actions. These were simply prudent business decisions, he claimed. For the bank to survive the Crash, it had to trim its sails. Yes, what happened to Mr. Shea was unfortunate, but there was nothing the least bit improper about the bank's actions and they certainly were not illegal. Pecora was casting an unfair, unflattering light on the bank's legitimate activities.

Eventually, that practice of strong-arming low-level staff to prop up the bank and then firing them came out in the public hearings. But Pecora first learned about it from Mitchell Shea, and it led to the questioning of his old boss. It happened right there in the Washington office. With Shea sitting at his side, Pecora forced the banker to come clean about the legal shakedown.

He said, "I've never seen a man that angry. If he could have killed Mr. Shea right then, I am sure he would have, but that's over now. It is impossible for me to believe that he would hold such a grudge or that he would make an attempt on Mitchell's life."

She asked who this banker was.

Chapter Twenty-Four

Tuesday evening, when the detective was taking the train to Washington, business was slow at Jimmy's Place. I called Anne Green and told her not to come in. Arch was in my office going through Pelltierre's pamphlets. Frenchy was behind the bar and Marie Therese was working the tables and booths. I was at my two-top in the back, reading the papers and doing other important things when Jenny Pris Kirk came in. Since I'd told him to let her in before, Fat Joe didn't stop her. She spotted me, walked straight to my table and sat without waiting to be invited.

"Has Asa been back?" She looked more worried than she had the first time. She wore another thin cotton print dress, light jacket and cloche hat.

I shook my head. "You haven't seen him either?"

"No, it's been more than a week now. I'm sure something must have happened to him. He's never done anything like this before. I mean, he wouldn't just leave without me, would he?"

I didn't say anything. She knew as well as I did that a lot of young guys walked away when they got scared. Or maybe she hadn't learned that. I still wasn't sure what her game was. She acted like a fifteen-year-old girl who'd got married too young and moved to a strange big city full of people who frightened her.

"Mr. Quinn, I hate to do this, but could you see your way to lending me a little more money, just until Asa gets back? Mrs. Klopernick wants her rent and that's twenty dollars for the month."

"You said that he liked the job at the beginning, but then it went bad. How did it go bad? Tell me about that. Something must have happened."

"Oh yes. At first we laughed about it when he told me, because it seemed like a joke. Mr. Dolan came in one day and told Asa that Mr. Sturdivant needed estimated travel expenses for a trip he'd be taking. He said he'd be going to London, Brussels, and Berlin, and there were other cities, too, but I can't remember them. He wanted the prices of first-class travel on steamships and airplanes and trains, hotel accommodations, even a new car that he'd buy in Europe. When Asa asked him when he'd be taking this trip, Mr. Dolan said that wasn't important, he just needed to know how much it all cost. Of course, Asa did it. It took him more than a week. He found the prices, even created an itinerary. I don't remember the exact total he came up with but it was more than fifteen thousand dollars.

"Then when he gave it to Mr. Dolan, he said Mr. Dolan barely looked at it. He was only interested in the fifteen thousand dollars. He didn't say that Asa had done a good job or a bad job, nothing. Asa got really worried then, mostly because he still hadn't met Mr. Sturdivant and it was bothering him. Whenever he asked Mr. Dolan about it, he got the brush off."

"I knew Dolan a long time ago. He was a jerk. But there must have been more than that."

She nodded, looking uncertain. "The next day, Mr. Dolan came back with eight more trips like that one. He said that he needed the same detailed itemized estimates, and he wanted them typed and listed in the same way. Everything had to be done neatly, without any mistakes or typographical errors. It took Asa more than a month, and when he had them ready, Mr. Dolan did the same thing."

"What do you mean?"

"He just went to the last page and looked for the total expenses. Asa said he smiled and said, 'Just the ticket. You did great, kid.'"

"How much money are you talking about?"

"A hundred and six thousand dollars. We laughed at the fifteen thousand, but Asa started worrying that something wasn't right about such a crazy amount of money."

She wasn't batting the breeze. In those days, a guy bringing home five thousand bucks a year was sitting pretty.

"He was already worried before that Friday, three weeks ago."

When he tried to set me up on the subway and then on Ninetieth Street.

"He came home that night and he was scared. He said everything was going wrong and he had to do something, but he didn't know what."

"He was worried because Sturdivant was ordering him to do something illegal?"

She nodded and looked even more scared. "He thought so but he didn't know, not really. He said he wasn't supposed to tell me about his work, but he did."

"What about that last weekend he was with you?"

"He was really excited that we were leaving but something was bothering him, too. He said he couldn't trust anybody and that maybe everybody had lied to him, even Uncle Ira."

Arch came down the back stairs and headed for my table. He stopped when he saw the girl.

"You said if I could find Asa's briefcase, you'd give me five hundred dollars."

"No, I said if it was the proof that your husband said he had, I'd pay five for it. Do you have it?"

She said, "No, but I think I know where it is."

That was the first time I was sure she was lying, and it made me think that maybe everything else she was saying was the truth, that she really didn't know what her husband was up to. That's why I was a sap. I said I'd loan her twenty-five as an advance. Took the money from the register and drew a glass of seltzer on ice for her. I asked Arch to call a cab.

When the cab got there, Arch came over and said, "Mrs. Kirk, I don't think my employer has formally introduced us. I'm Archibald Malloy. Let me walk you to your cab."

He pulled her chair back and took her arm. She blushed and looked flustered at his attention. "I understand this has been a difficult time for you. I remember how I felt the first time I came to this city." He was still yakking away as they went out.

A few minutes later, he ran back to my table and said under his breath, "They know each other!"

"Who?"

"The girl, Mrs. Kirk, and the Soldier, the man who shot those two incompetent gunmen who jumped us. You saw him on the street."

"What're you saying?"

"Just now. You heard that I was giving her a little of the old soft soap to prove just how friendly and trustworthy I am, a shoulder to lean on, so to speak, a mature man who—"

"Arch, get on with it."

"I will but she knows more than she's saying. I told you she's a sharp cookie, no matter how young she is. You show her a little kindness right now, she'll tell you everything."

"The soldier?"

"The impatience of youth. All right, so the taxi is a few feet away. I go up the steps with her, open the door, ask what address I should tell the cabbie. She gives it to me so now we know where she lives, by the way. I inquire about the fare and give it to the man, with a tip. Then I tuck a fiver into her hand and tell her again that I'm always here to help if she needs it, and by now the poor girl is nearly in tears, she's so grateful. Then I send her off and go back down the front steps when I hear the screech of brakes and the cabbie hitting his horn. I climb back up to the street and I see your Soldier standing in front of the taxi. He'd jumped into the street to stop it and he's right there in the headlights. White hair, the doughboy's green blouse. He slaps the hood and goes around to the back seat. I think he's saying something but I can't hear it. She must have heard him because the door swings open, she gets out and they hug each other."

By then Arch was loud enough that people were listening. He lowered his voice. "They were twenty, thirty feet down the street from me. I started toward them but before I'd gone more than a few steps, she and the Soldier got back in the cab and it left."

"Just when you think this can't get any screwier than it is…"

Arch said, "One idea does present itself. Let's talk about it after we close."

"Yeah, and it's about time we clued Marie Therese and Frenchy in on all this."

• • •

We shut down about an hour later. As we finished the cleanup, I took a glass of wine for Marie-Therese—French, not the kraut—a brandy for Frenchy and two whiskies to a four-top. I called them over. Frenchy and Marie-Therese looked at me curiously, maybe a little worried. This wasn't normal. I said, "Remember after those guys uptown took a shot at Arch and me, I told you that something strange seemed to be going on? Well, there is."

I explained about Kirk's calling and telling me that he knew people were trying to kill me and wanted five hundred for the details. He'd come there Sunday night. We talked. He told me a few things. He said he'd come back with his proof and left. After that, nothing. I explained how I'd nosed around after looking through some items he left with me and learned where his office was. I'd rented one next to it and Arch had fixed it up so we could listen in on what was being said.

"And yesterday, I hired a detective to stay in the office and find out what's going on."

Marie-Therese said, "That's why Mrs. Opperman was here. Good."

"I'm telling you all this now because even though I don't really know much more, something is going on, something I don't understand. You know what this place is like as well as I do. Better really. We get our share of unusual characters, but if anything strikes you as too unusual, let me know."

Marie Therese said, "What about that young girl who was here tonight?"

"She's Kirk's wife, and she wants to know where he is. Hasn't seen him since he came here."

Frenchy and Marie Therese looked at each other and shrugged. Frenchy said, "I knew business had been too good. Something's always gonna go wrong."

Marie-Therese cut her eyes at him. "Since we're talking about things that aren't going right, what have you heard from Connie?"

"Nothing. Just that one telegram. Have you?"

"No. Have you written to her?"

"Two wires."

Marie-Therese fretted. "It's not like her."

"With all this, I'm glad she's not here," I said and almost meant it.

• • •

After Frenchy and Marie-Therese left, Arch poured two more whiskies. "The girl told you that she and her husband are from Anacostia, didn't she? And that he helped his uncle feeding the Bonus Army two years ago."

"Yeah."

"Then it's possible that this Soldier was part of that misguided collection of Great War veterans. Their biggest camp was in Anacostia, across the river from Washington, and maybe that's how he knows Mrs. Kirk."

"O.K., what does it mean?"

"I don't know, but here is another item to consider. I have been shoveling my way through the dense and unreadable prose of Brandon

Pelltierre III in his Liberty Foundation pamphlets. The Bonus Army is one of his favorite subjects. He comes back to it time and again with a mixture of admiration at what it tried to do and fear at what it might have accomplished. I can't believe it's a coincidence. Perhaps your detective will be able to tell us something."

He finished his drink. "You know that I talked to Mr. Henderson, the colored gentleman who supervises the janitors, and told him that my generous employer would pay for information about the Foundation. I'll ask him if he knows anything about Pelltierre. That's unlikely, given his views on racial matters, but who knows? Strange bedfellows and all that. And, one more thing. I know three men and women who have been in service to Brahmins of Pelltierre's exalted station. It's likely one of them knows someone who works in the household, or knows someone who knows someone. How much are you prepared to spend for personal information?"

"You decide. Enough to get somebody to spill the goods, but not so much that we get nuts coming out of the woodwork."

Continuation of statement by Michael Patrick Reardon; Sunday, July 15, 1934; 4:10pm.

(Personnel same as Saturday, July 14 sessions.)

Stenography and typescript: TS.

Though I did not realize it at the time, the night of August 14, 1932, marked a significant turning point in the history of the Cerberus Society. That was a Sunday. The presidential campaign was beginning and the Bonus Army had recently been routed from their occupation of Washington. For months, the Governors had been particularly agitated about the movement and what it portended for the upcoming election, particularly Governor Pelltierre. He believed that Herbert Hoover had completely failed to meet the demands of his office, and he held no hope that Roosevelt would do any better. He often referred to Mr. Roosevelt as "an eager Boy Scout, not the leader that the times demand and we must have."

The Governors wanted to know exactly what the Bonus Army actually was. To that end, they had hired a man named Herk Sturdivant who came with a solid record of success from his work as a strikebreaker and as an informant for both the Bureau of Investigation and Naval Intelligence. As veterans in all corners of the nation were beginning to gather and march, Mr. Pelltierre engaged Sturdivant to discover the truth behind the organization's façade when they reached Washington. Throughout the summer, the Governors read all the reports they found in the newspapers and received background information from Mr. Sturdivant every week. Virtually nothing else was discussed in the library. They wanted to know who these men were and what they really wanted. On that August Sunday, after the Bonus Army camp had been destroyed, Sturdivant came to the Society where he turned in his report to the Governors. Members had been told that the building was closed that day.

Sturdivant began with silent film footage of the camps being set up, men marching around the Capitol, and then speeches by a man in a khaki uniform. Following that, he produced tables listing food supplied by different organizations, and estimates of consumption. He placed an easel with a large map of central Washington before the

cold fireplace. Upon the map were the locations where the various
veterans' groups were camped. He had typed copies of a daily journal
he had maintained that detailed the activities of those groups. Near
the end, he handed out copies of his Report Summary. I saved one.
Here are parts of that report from the copy I kept and Sturdivant's
spoken remarks as I remember them:

"In May, 1932, I joined the Maryland Friends and Volunteer Society.
Once the Bonus Army assembled in Washington, I worked with others to
purchase and distribute sandwiches to the large group in the Anacostia
camp. My associate, Jane Doe, presented herself as a 'Boudoir Bolskiviki'
and infiltrated the Workers Ex-Service League or Weasels camp
where she obtained valuable 'pillow talk' on their plans. (Her report
is included.) I conclude from my observations and those of other law
enforcement personnel, that the Bonus Army was composed of roughly
equal percentages miscellaneous white and mulatto, Jew, Negro and
Eastern European. Their living quarters were mixed together at random
with no sense of the natural divisions of races in an orderly society. A
quarter of them were women with a few hundred children. Some of them
were committed to leftist ideas and when their 'peaceful' tactics proved
unsuccessful, they were ready to turn to more violent means.

"They had weapons, explosives and the training to use them. A
report from J. Edgar Hoover states that they had dynamite and a plan
to blow up the White House. A carbon copy of that document and other
intelligence reports are included as addendums to my full report. As you
can see in these photographs, they also had heavier weapons that have
not been reported in the press.

"On the night that Gen. MacArthur ordered that the Bonus Army be
cleared out, I made my way to the center of subversive activity in Camp
Marks. That center was one of the larger huts called a clinic. As you can
see in this picture, the box on the left contains fragmentary grenades.
The device at the foot of the bed, that perforated tube with folding legs,
is a Stokes trench mortar. The objects partially under the bed are the
rounds it fires.

"Gentlemen, from that hut, a mortar round could have struck and
severely damaged the Capitol building. They might not have destroyed it,
but can you imagine what the reaction to that would have been?

"I can see that you find this hard to believe. I was surprised myself when I found the mortar, and I would not have discovered it if the situation in the camp had not been so chaotic due to the speedy advance of Gen. MacArthur's forces across the river."

At that moment, Mr. Sturdivant brought out a long canvas duffle bag that had been on the floor beneath the easel. He unlaced it and took out the mortar in the photograph. He unfolded the two legs to stand it upright as the Governors crowded around it.

He continued. "I brought this with me to show you how serious the threat was and it still is. Yes, the Bonus Army has fallen apart for the moment, but the forces that created it are still here, and it will take another form. You know that. It's why you hired me. We are at a pivotal point. Remember that you have the means to direct the next Bonus Army when it forms. It will not be easy and it will not be inexpensive.

"I know that two of your friends, Mr. Murphy and Mr. Clark, are working with two of their agents to persuade Gen. Smedley Butler to lead the American Legion and force the formation of a new administration. They will fail. I have more realistic ideas that I would like to discuss with you, if you're interested."

Chapter Twenty-Five

It was a warm Wednesday morning so we had the front door open. Frenchy, Marie Therese and I were getting the place ready. Just after eleven, I heard the rattle of a bicycle bouncing down the steps from the sidewalk. I'd been listening for that sound for weeks, and ducked under the bar as the kid came inside. He was wearing a round hat. Western Union messenger.

"Telegram for Marie Therese Reneau."

What the hell? Marie Therese didn't understand it either.

I took the window envelope from the boy, flipped him a penny and handed the wire to Marie Therese.

As he left, the kid muttered, "She gives me a nickel."

Marie Therese ripped open the envelope and read aloud.

"WHY NO WORD? AM ON CHAMPLAIN. ARRIVE WED. JULY 11. WIRE NAME OF HOSPITAL. IF CANNOT CONTACT. LEAVE LOCATION AT FRENCH LINE OFFICE. WILL GO DIRECTLY THERE. CONNIE"

"What's the date on it?"

"Monday," she said, looking confused. I was scared. Coming on top of everything else, this meant something dangerous. First thing, I opened the *Times* to the back pages and found the Shipping and Mails listings. There it was. The *Champlain* had docked an hour ago at Pier 57. No time to try to call the French Line. What would they know anyway?

Marie Therese said, "We drove in. The truck's here."

"Frenchy, open the gate. I'll be right back."

What else did I need to do? Arch wasn't there yet. "Somebody's got to stay here. Call Anne Green or Katherine O'Neal. Get one of them to come in."

"I want to go with you."

"If this is real, if she's here, there won't be room in the truck for four of us. Whatever's going on, something's not right."

She nodded. I went up to my office for my coat and hat. I was grabbing things as fast as I could until I made myself stop. Don't hurry. You never do what you ought to do then. You know this, don't hurry, don't hesitate. Right now, you don't know what you're getting into. If Connie really is on that boat, you've got to find her and then get her someplace safe. What do you need to do that? I pulled up my pantleg and made sure my brace was in the right place, not too loose or tight. I had the kraut automatic in my vest pocket. Got the Detective Special and a stack of cash from the safe. Gimped down the steps and went out the back.

Marie Therese opened the heavy wooden gate and Frenchy pulled the truck into the alley. She grabbed my sleeve. "What's going on, Jimmy?"

"Nothing good."

Looking grim, Frenchy floored it and got as much as he could out of the old pick-up. As he drove, he asked me the same thing Marie Therese had and I still didn't have any answers.

"I got one telegram from her. That's all. I've sent a couple. I don't know what she meant in this one about a hospital."

I worried about a hundred different things and my stomach churned as Frenchy drove. When we got close to Pier 57, I saw that the ship was beside it, and there was a crowd in the loading area, about as thick as it had been the day Connie left. Most of the people were moving out of the big open building. I had no way of knowing how long people had been getting off the boat. If it docked at ten and she got right off, she might already be there in the crowd. I said, "When the guy drove us here before, he used the lane on the right where that cop's standing."

"It's for hired cars and taxis. He's not letting anybody in there."

"Try it anyway." Frenchy edged to the right. The white-gloved traffic cop shook his head, blew his whistle loud and motioned us to the left.

I jumped out and gimped toward him, leaning more heavily on my stick than I needed to. "Excuse me, officer, you see we've got a problem. The car I hired to pick up my girlfriend didn't show up. She's expecting us over there." As I talked, I slipped a bill into his hand. He waved us around. I got up on the running board to see better as Frenchy eased close to the building. How the hell was a short guy supposed to find a short woman in a crowd like this?

Frenchy made space to pull over. I told him I'd be back. The place was an open area about as wide and long as the pier with rough wooden walls and windows up beneath the eaves. There were several doorways leading out to the ship. It took a second to adjust to the dim light and the noise with people talking loud, and distorted announcements coming from horn speakers. There was at least one floor above me. I could see men and women going up and down a double staircase and elevators. People were milling around as they do when they're in a place where most of them don't know where they're supposed to go and the ones who work there every day are trying to move them where they need to be.

I could see the black side of the ship and what I thought was the foot of a covered gangway ahead of me. I was heading toward it when I noticed the big "Information" sign above a round kiosk in the middle of the open floor. Three guys in blue uniforms were working there. The closest one said with a French accent, "May I help you, monsieur?"

"I need to meet Connie Nix. She's on the ship."

They had four clip boards with passenger lists. My guy found the right one and flipped through pages. "Yes, Mademoiselle Nix has been in Stateroom 422. She should be using disembarkation ramp three, and I believe her group should be leaving about now, but passengers do not always choose to use the proper exit or the assigned time for their deboarding group."

The guy next to him had been listening to us. He said, "*C'est une fille populaire.*"

I thought I knew what he meant and the sick feeling in my stomach got worse. "What did you say?"

"She's a popular girl. Everyone's looking for her."

"Who else? When?"

The second guy said, "Her mother. She was here a few moments ago." Oh, hell.

"Which way to this Ramp Three?"

Both of them pointed to the big signs right in front of me. I tried not to hurry too much as I pushed my way through the crowd. I'd learned when I was working for Rothstein that trying to go too fast through pedestrians on the sidewalk didn't work. Most of the people were heading toward the front of the building so I was moving against the flow. I kept exaggerating my need for the cane, so most people gave me extra room. As I got close to the ship, I saw the foot of one ramp. It was thick with people waiting to meet passengers who were getting off. That's where the gangways angled down from the deck of the ship to the pier. Lots of waving and yelling. Getting more worried, I slipped the knucks onto my right hand.

I was close to Ramp Two. Ramp Three was farther down the pier. As I went toward it, I tried to make out women's faces on the deck of the ship. Nothing. I kept moving. I can't say how long it took, going back and forth between the ramps, looking up at the faces of the people leaving and waiting to leave. I went almost to the end of the pier and had turned around heading back to Ramp Three when I heard Connie's voice. "Jimmy!"

She had to be close but I couldn't pick her out of the crowd. "Jimmy! Here!"

When I spotted her, she was about as far from the ramp as I was, and moving toward it slowly through the crowd. I yelled, "Connie," and waved my stick.

She smiled when she saw me. Then just as fast, she scowled and threw up her arms. "Goddammit, Jimmy Quinn, what the hell are you trying to do, you son of a bitch!" There was more but I couldn't understand it, only that she was really mad. People on the ship moved away from her as she hurried down the ramp.

That's when the big woman in the blue raincoat and a black hat pulled down over her ears lumbered in front of me. The moment I saw her, I remembered that afternoon on the subway platform, her blocking my way and then somebody trying to shove me in front of the train. She was moving so slow that the next part was easy. I reversed the stick, hooked the crook around her closest ankle and jerked it back. She went face down hard on the concrete. I yanked the stick loose and stepped on her back and then on the back of her head as I stomped over her.

Then Connie was right there next to me, saying, "What's the matter with you. Are you crazy? Ma'am, I'm so sorry. Let me help you up."

I shouldered in front of Connie. The big woman was just pushing herself up. I backhanded her with the stick. The black hat and a wig flew off but I didn't slow her down. Her face was dark and she wore big round dark glasses like a blind woman. She rose to her feet and caught me with a solid left that snapped my head back. There was a bad scrape on her forehead. She pulled a shiny pistol from under her raincoat, and I punched her in the face with the knucks three times as fast as I could. The pistol clattered to the concrete. People around us screamed when the blood spurted from her nose. She fell back, legs sprawled out in front of her.

"Get a doctor!" I yelled. "This woman's fainted!"

Until that moment, I'd never hit a woman. Figured it was something I wouldn't do but, hell, she had a gun.

I grabbed Connie and pushed her toward the street as people crowded around. She was looking back at the big woman and trying to ask what was going on. I said, "I'll explain later. I think there's more of them."

She held onto me and didn't argue. I tried to angle back toward Frenchy but by then people had realized something was happening. Some of them moved toward the commotion, wanting to know what it was, and some wanted to get away. At first, nobody tried to stop us. The crowd was so confused that we pushed through it slowly. There was more noise behind us. Somebody yelled "You there. Stop." We didn't.

We were close enough to see Frenchy standing on the running board of his truck when the next one tried to get me. Figure he'd been watching Frenchy, knowing that's where we were headed. Medium-sized guy, suit and hat, standing beside a support post. Couldn't see his face, but I saw him glance to his left and right, then he stepped toward us, unbuttoning his coat. There was no room or time to do anything else. I took my arm from around Connie and moved toward him fast. He tugged twice at a piece in a shoulder holster. I cocked the .38 and pointed at the center of his chest. I was maybe two paces from him. People around us backed away. He stopped when he saw the gun. Spig Dolan. He turned around and disappeared into the crowd.

Then Connie was grabbing me, throwing her arms around my neck and crying. I think she was trying to ask what was going on. I couldn't understand her but I didn't need to. We just hung onto each other until Frenchy hustled us toward the truck.

Inside the cab, she said, "What about my bags, my clothes?"

"We'll get 'em later. Something bad's going on, you just saw some of it. Get us out of here, Frenchy."

He hit the horn and cut in front of a cab, making a lane on his way out. We were going too slow. I saw Dolan slipping through the crowd, keeping up with us, moving ahead. He opened the passenger door of a big black DeSoto sedan and pointed at Frenchy's truck as we went past. The DeSoto pulled in behind us. Frenchy said, "I see him."

"Can you lose him?"

"Probably not."

Connie said, "What the hell is going on?"

Her face was flushed and her eye makeup was messed up by the tears but she looked just swell and I was so glad to see her I didn't know what to say. "Some guys are trying to kill me. I don't know why. Yet. We're working on that. They've been luring me to places where they're waiting. That's what they did today. How did they get to you?"

"Marie Therese sent a wire saying that you'd been shot and stabbed. They couldn't get you to go to a hospital. Then there was another wire saying you were in the hospital and might not make it. I needed to come back. I tried to telephone but making a Transatlantic call is impossible. The operator couldn't get it to go through and then when she did, I couldn't understand a word and the woman who answered hung up. So, I left Paris, changed my ticket and got on the first ship coming here. I've been worried sick for a week about what was happening to you. When I saw you on the dock I thought you'd made it all up to get me to come back. But you didn't and you haven't been shot."

I said, "Marie Therese didn't send you any telegrams, not like that."

"Then how did they know how to contact me?"

"I've got that figured out. We'll get to it later. Right now, we need to lose this guy behind us."

"He's still there, two cars back," Frenchy said. We were heading south. I told him to go up on the elevated highway the first chance he got. Traffic moved faster there but the DeSoto followed and it was easier for him to stay with us. Frenchy swung from lane to lane like he was drunk. It didn't do any good. I told him to take the next exit to a surface street and then head uptown. Look for somewhere with enough people around he wouldn't take a shot at us. Frenchy turned. The DeSoto stayed right with us.

On the street level, Frenchy drove under the elevated train tracks and turned north on Tenth Avenue where it was lined with small businesses and busy sidewalks. He slowed down enough that other cars were passing us for a block or so. He kept slowing, checking his mirror and cursing softly. I looked through the back window and saw that the DeSoto was still there. Dolan was in the passenger seat. A bigger guy was driving. Couldn't see his face. Frenchy slowed some more, and held up his hand out of the window, signaling a right turn. Then he goosed the truck and jumped ahead without turning. Another car pulled into the gap behind us. Frenchy kept his speed up, and slowed as we came to a yellow light. Just as it turned red, Frenchy hit the gas and scooted through the intersection.

The guy behind him stopped, trapping the DeSoto. We gained a block on them and Frenchy turned east when they got caught by another light.

"Are we going back to Jimmy's?"

"No, try to get to the Plaza Hotel, the Fifty-Eighth Street side." I had half a plan in mind.

Frenchy negotiated the traffic as well as he could, but the truck with its wooden cab didn't blend in with the other cars and taxis. The DeSoto was faster, and it figured that if the driver knew anything about following another car, he could get close enough and stay with us.

"Whatever's happening, it's worse than I thought. If they know enough to get to Connie, we've got to disappear for a while, and, it kills me to say it, but we'll have to close the place for a while."

Frenchy and Connie said, "No!" at the same time.

"Just for a day or so. They're going to be watching it. Put a 'closed for private party' sign on the door. Marie-Therese can tell Anne Green and Mrs. O'Neal she'll let them know when we reopen. I'll call you at home tonight."

Traffic got heavier as we went uptown. Frenchy said he thought he saw the DeSoto behind us on Eighth Avenue.

"What about my clothes?" Connie said. She took her ticket envelope from her purse. "I've got three bags back at Pier 57. They're new and they're expensive. I'm not going to lose them."

Frenchy said he'd take care of it.

"No," I said, "They'll be looking for you and this truck. Arch has my car. Give the tickets to him. Explain what happened in case they've got somebody watching the bags."

Connie said, "Do you really think that's possible?" She was worried.

"They know an awful lot about me. And you."

"Oh hell," she muttered, and set to work fixing her makeup.

When we got close to Columbus Circle, Frenchy turned on West Fifty-Eighth. Looking through the back window, I didn't see the DeSoto. That didn't mean anything. After we crossed Sixth, Frenchy pulled to the curb. "Call me tonight," he said. "Marie Therese will give me the business if you don't."

Connie gave him a quick kiss. "Tell her I'm fine. Paris was as wonderful as she said it would be. More."

After Frenchy pulled away, I checked the traffic. No DeSoto, but I still felt like there was a target on my back as we walked to the hotel. The reason we were there was to lose them if they were still behind us. Connie and I could go into the Plaza lobby through the doors on Fifty-Eighth Street and cross it to the main entrance on Fifty-Ninth where the cab line was. Grease the doorman, jump the line and lose them.

Connie made us stop before we got to the door. "I need a second," she said, so low that nobody but me could hear.

She stood straighter, raised her chin, pulled at her skirt and coat, adjusted her hat. Then, for the first time I noticed the dress. I'd never seen her in anything like it. Hell, I don't know that I'd ever seen any woman in something that looked so good and fit her so well. There was nothing flashy about it. It was just a simple navy-blue blouse and skirt that came just below her knee, about six inches shorter than women were wearing that year. Narrow strip of white trim at the collar. Half sleeve jacket of the same soft material. It fit perfectly because it had been made for her. I don't remember the hat, but it looked good, too.

"Damn," I whispered. She knew what I meant and tried to hide her smile.

She hooked her arm in mine. The doorman hurried to open the door for us and watched her as we walked in. "The designer altered it for me and even then, he said I wasn't right for it. He said my bosom is too big. The line's not smooth enough and I jiggle."

"He's wrong. So wrong."

All right, I'm the last person who should be saying this, but it seemed to me that all the rich folks in the lobby of that swanky joint watched us. In that dress, her stride was different, confident. Maybe all the women in Paris looked like that, but women in New York didn't, and every other woman in that lobby knew she didn't look as good as Connie. And those were women who'd paid a lot more for their clothes and had spent hours being primped and coiffed and painted. They looked at her and cursed to themselves.

The men in the lobby, they thought I was one lucky gimp. Damn right.

Out front, the doorman put us in a taxi. I told the driver to go through the park, then take a turn around it and let us out at the Pierre, which was so close we could see the top of it from where we were. And let me know if he saw a black DeSoto behind us. He probably thought I was worried about Connie's husband. As soon as he pulled away, we were all over each other. When Connie came up for air, she said, "Watch it, buster. Don't do anything to mess up this dress."

Then she kissed me some more.

• • •

It was a little after two when he let us out on Fifth Avenue at the Pierre. We'd straightened our clothes by then. Connie fixed her makeup again, wiped the lipstick off my face, and made sure my tie was straight and there was no blood on my suit. The suit, by the way, was not my best but since I was with a beautiful woman in that dress, it didn't matter. Crossing the lobby of the Pierre, I tried to saunter like a toff who carried the stick as a fashionable accessory, not a gimpy thug who needed it.

The gent behind the desk didn't look like he was buying my act. Sounding snotty, he said, "Yes sir, do you have a reservation?"

I took the registration card from him and filled it out. "The last time we were here," I said, "we were visiting our friend Miss Wray. She had a delightful suite. I believe it was on the eighth floor, four rooms on the corner overlooking the park. That would be perfect. We'll be here at least two nights, possibly more. This should take care of it. Our bags will be arriving sometime this afternoon from the *Champlain*."

I put a short stack of twenties on the card.

"Of course, sir, I believe that's available." He tapped his bell, and a bellboy appeared. He gave a key to the kid. "Take Mr. and Mrs. Patterson to the Gerry Suite."

Walking to the elevator, Connie whispered, "Who am I, Mr. Patterson?"

"Simone Patterson of Los Angeles, California."

"I don't know what's going on but I could get used to this."

We didn't say anything in the elevator. The kid opened the door of the Gerry Suite. I took the key and gave him two bucks. He said, "Thank you, sir" and meant it.

"Listen," I said. "A couple of years ago, Fay Wray, the actress, stayed here. Some funny business had to be taken care of and there was a kid, he was about your age then, worked as a bellboy. I didn't get his name but he helped out a friend of mine. I don't know that this kid's still here, but there's another dollar in it for you if you ask around, find out if anybody knows about it. Can you do that?"

"You bet."

He left smiling. I put the Do Not Disturb sign on the doorknob.

Chapter Twenty-Six

Mrs. Opperman got back to the Agency offices from Washington on Wednesday afternoon, about the same time we were checking into the Pierre. She found T.S., the Provisional Operative, waiting with a neatly typed transcript. This is the report:

Tues. July 10, Mrs. Booth left the Liberty Foundation at 6:15pm. By 6:30pm, the floor was empty. At 10:17pm, I heard the sound of a man's footsteps in the hall and then the door to the Foundation being unlocked. The man entered, and I heard newspapers rustling, liquid being poured, rude bodily noises, and other sounds that I could not identify. Soon I smelled cigar smoke through the grille. The telephone rang at 10:35pm. The man spoke.

"How the h--- are you. Yeah, that's what she said if you can believe it... Nah, me neither but what the h--- you going to do? Listen, things are starting to move... Uh huh, I got brandyboy right where I want him. I'm picking up the next installment tonight and after that, we're going to be talking about real money, believe you me... No more of this penny ante [obscenity] (long silence)

"Jerry and Doyle are finished. They don't admit it yet but they're finished. They're meeting Butler again... Yeah, the business about using the VFW and the Legion to take down Roosevelt." Laughs. "Me too but they had their Wall Street guys who said it can be done for three million and they'd pony up the cash... All of it, three million. (Listens) Right, when I see it, that's what I like about brandyboy, he says he's got the dough, he comes through... He has so far, hasn't he? ... I know a hundred and six thousand is a lot more... (long silence)

"Look, if you want to back out of this now, it's [obscenity] fine with me, I can get other guys and I'll be glad to take your share... You think I'm trying to [obscenity] you? Listen, this is what I did and it's [obscenity] brilliant if I do say so myself. I took Jerry and Doyle to meet brandyboy at his place, the one around the corner. They had the next installment of the Wall Street money—eighteen thousand in cold hard cash, the money they got for Butler, and we showed it to him. (long silence)

"I told them it was to prime the pump. Once brandyboy saw they were serious, he would come through on his side. He doesn't think they can get to Butler, even with that much money on the table. (long silence) That [obscenity] Kirk spent the first five setting this operation up... Yeah, well brandyboy really has a bug up his [obscenity] about getting his [obscenity] 'monographs' distributed. There was no talking him out of it... Cramps my style to have that [obscenity] in the other office but she's never here at night, so she's not a problem... (silence)

"What we're going to do is this, I'm going to tell brandyboy we're ready to take the next step. He wanted proof we could deliver on getting rid of the problems, we gave him proof. Lanning—his seat is empty and the way is open for her man. Shea won't be giving anybody any [obscenity] agita anymore. (Laughs) The serious money—(Listens)

"Look, that [obscenity] Quinn has just been lucky is all, and for the moment he's not [obscenity] important anyway. We've got plenty of time to fix his wagon... Don't worry about that, she'll be on the—(Listens) Even if she's not, the point is we've delivered and what has it cost these guys? Eight ten large? For them that's peanuts... (listens)

"Is the [obscenity] ready for tomorrow? I know she says she is but she's [obscenity] this up once already... Yeah, yeah, she got the other one but this is a h--- of a lot more important. The dock isn't like the subway. (listens)

"Sherman? What about him? Don't worry, Chink will show up, he always does... Look, I got things to do... Yeah, that... (listens) You want me to see if she's got a friend? Sure, but it'll cost you... Of course she's clean, you [obscenity] (Laughs) Long silence.

"Yeah, yeah, yeah, like I told you, tomorrow night, ten, here, you putz." Hangs up telephone. Sound of liquid being poured. [Obscenity]

When Mrs. Opperman finished reading, she told T.S. that she'd done good work, but she wanted to know more. "Tell me, what did he sound like? What was his tone? Was he angry when he talked about the other man trying to back out?"

T.S. said she thought he wasn't really serious then. It sounded like he was trying to needle the man on the other end of the call. The detective wrote a note in the margin of the transcript. She took another look at the part where he said 'that [obscenity] Quinn has just been lucky.' That got her attention.

T.S. said that Mrs. Booth, the Foundation secretary, had spent the afternoon cleaning Sturdivant's office. A boy had delivered something that she thought was a bucket of ice before Mrs. Booth left. T.S. asked if she and the detective were going to go back for the ten o'clock Wednesday night meeting Sturdivant mentioned.

It was two days later before I talked to the detective and saw that typed report. Even then, I didn't understand everything Sturdivant said. Some of it only made sense after the Congressional hearing they had later that year.

Chapter Twenty-Seven

I locked the door to the Gerry Suite Wednesday afternoon and felt almost safe. The guys who were after me didn't know where I was. I had a few hours to think without worrying about who might be waiting for me right outside. And Connie was there.

When I was in the Pierre before, Miss Wray's suite was filled with flowers, congratulating her on how great *King Kong* was. Every flat surface had been covered and I could remember the overpowering smell of the things. Without them, the main room seemed bigger. The views of the park were about as good as you could find on the East Side, not that there was much you wanted to look at in those days.

Connie stood with her fists on her hips. "Everything. Tell me everything that's going on and this better be good."

"Let me see about your stuff first."

I called the hotel operator and gave her the number for Jimmy's Place. Frenchy answered. Connie crowded close to the earpiece wanting to hear as much as she could. I asked Frenchy if he'd seen the DeSoto again after he left us.

"No, I was careful coming back. Nobody followed me. I know you told me to close up, but we've had a good lunch crowd. Are you sure that's what you want?"

Greed vs. caution. What're you going to do? "Wait until business slows down around three, then kick everybody out. Put the Private Party sign up. Have Marie Therese call Katherine and tell her not to come in tomorrow. And tell Vittorio we're closing for the day, but it shouldn't affect his business in the grill. What else?"

"Arch is here. He wants to talk to you."

I heard him handing the handset over. The bar sounded busy.

Arch said, "I understand Connie's back. Frenchy said there were guys waiting for you on the dock."

"It got interesting. Two of them with guns. One was the woman from the subway."

"These bastards are serious."

"I knew that but I didn't understand it. I understand it now."

"And you know what that means?"

"Yes." I didn't want to say it out loud yet, so I went back to the thing that had to be done right away. "Did Frenchy explain about the bags? Give you the claim tickets?"

"Oh, yes. I took the liberty of calling the French Line and explaining that Mlle. Nix had been called away on an emergency. They're holding her luggage."

"You're closing early today. Use my car. Pick up the bags at Pier 57 and bring them to the Pierre Hotel. Make sure nobody follows you. They've got a black DeSoto. Tell the doorman the bags belong to Mrs. Patterson in the Gerry Suite. And, for now, don't let anyone know where we are."

"Of course, and, unless you've got something else that needs my attention, I have some ideas I'd like to investigate. They concern the other matters that Mr. Kirk brought to your attention, and I imagine I'll need a small advance to pursue them."

"Sure. What the hell, I'm made of money."

Connie grabbed the telephone from my hand. "Arch, let me talk to Marie Therese."

He had something to say that made her smile. She said "O.K." a few times and "Thanks" before Marie Therese took over. Connie turned away from me and lowered her voice when she talked to her. When she'd finished, she said, "Now, tell me everything that's happened. Marie Therese says don't leave anything out."

I took off my coat. "It can wait until we've—"

"No." She crossed her arms across her chest. "You can take down the Do Not Disturb sign."

Oh, hell. I found a chair that looked comfortable. "This is going to take a while."

I hoped that telling it to her would make things clearer for me, but it didn't work that way. The more I talked, the crazier it sounded.

"It started a couple of nights after you left. I was walking back to the Chelsea after we closed up. A couple of guys were waiting for me at the corner. One had a knife, one had a gun I think. I handled them o.k. Thought they were just a couple of muggers. Then, I guess it was ten days later, I got a telephone call from a guy who said there was a problem with one of my alcohol license applications and I had to come to his office downtown to fix it."

I told her about the subway. The woman who blocked my way, the same woman she'd just seen at the dock, and somebody trying to push me in front of the train. Then the licensing bureau turned out not to be where the guy said it was. And the next day, there were the young guys who tried to shoot Arch and me, and the Soldier who killed them. She made me back up more than once to explain things that didn't make sense to her, like the Soldier just showing up there. I told her I didn't know what to make of it either but there was more to say about him and I'd get to it by and by.

About then, I realized I hadn't had lunch and called room service for sandwiches and coffee. I told her that we got our licenses and were completely legal. She said she knew that from the only telegram I sent her, and why hadn't I answered the others she sent?

"I only got one, telling me your address, and then the one to Marie-Therese today. How many did you send?"

"One a week."

"So, there were three or four more that I didn't see?"

She nodded. One more piece of the puzzle to figure out.

It was harder for me to explain how Arch found the newspaper story about an accountant who fell in front of a subway train and how that spooked me enough that I hired Theodora Opperman to look into it, and while that was going on, I got the first telephone call from a guy who claimed to work with the people who were trying to kill me, and he'd tell me about it for five hundred bucks.

When I got to the part where he came over after we'd closed, I just said that things got a little dicey and I had to relieve him of a pistol and his wallet. His name was Asa Kirk, and he had the same newspaper clipping that Arch showed me, along with another one about a New Jersey politician who died after drinking bad booze. Connie stopped me then.

"Wait a minute. Are you saying that whoever these people are, they've also killed this accountant and the politician in New Jersey, and it has something to do with you?"

"That's what it looks like and I can show you the clippings. They're in the safe, but don't worry about that now. It's going to get worse. You see, the next thing Kirk told me was that a guy named Spig Dolan was involved. Before today on the dock, the last time I saw Spig Dolan I was nine years old and he was trying to horn in on Black Sox World Series action. But I'm getting ahead of myself. That night Kirk claimed that he had more proof he could show me. I told him I'd pay for it and sent him on his way. Haven't seen him since."

"Does Mrs. Opperman know about this?" she asked.

"No, but I'll get back to her. She's still working on something else I haven't got to yet."

"That's reassuring," she said, looking like she thought I'd lost my mind.

She was even more skeptical when I tried to go through the way I located the office Kirk had rented for the National Liberty Foundation. Explaining the Foundation wasn't easy, either, since I really didn't understand what this Brandon Pelltierre III was doing with his pamphlets and mailing operation, but we were going to figure that out because I rented the office next to the Foundation, and Arch had done some unobtrusive remodeling so we could hear what they were up to. That's what the Continental detective was handling. By the time I got to Jenny Pris Kirk, it was evening and the sandwiches were gone.

"She says she's Kirk's wife and she doesn't know anything about his work except that he hated it and he told her he'd figured a way for them to get enough money to go back to Washington. And the last time she came to see me, Arch saw her talking to this Soldier, the guy I already mentioned, like they were old pals."

Her expression became softer. When I started talking, she looked like she thought I was making all this up, but the more I went on with it, she realized that I was trying to tell the truth about something I didn't understand. And that it frustrated the hell out of me. It made me mad, not screaming and busting things mad, the kind of mad that makes you stupid and careless. It was a cold anger at whoever was screwing with my life. It stayed with me for the next week, and it explains a lot of the things I did.

Connie got up and paced. "I got the phony telegrams saying you were hurt a couple of weeks ago. What day is it, anyway? When I couldn't get in touch with anyone over here, I got on the first ship I could. For the past week, I've been sending wires to you and Marie Therese from the ship, and still not getting answers. The more I thought about it, the more it seemed that something wasn't right. The telegrams just didn't sound like Marie Therese. That probably meant that you and she had cooked up something sneaky to get me to come back."

She closed the curtains on one window and did the same with the two that overlooked Fifth Avenue.

"I was on that ship for seven days. One day, I'd be angry, the next day I'd change my mind and be worried that you were dying in a hospital someplace. When we docked today and I saw you there on the Pier, at first I was relieved you were all right and then I went back to being mad at sneaky Jimmy. Until I saw you attack that woman. Then I thought you'd gone crazy."

She put the Do Not Disturb sign back on the door, opened a wardrobe, turned on a light by the bed, and carefully undressed.

I yanked off my tie and toed off my shoes. "I never hit a woman before, you know that don't you? I might not have recognized that one today if she hadn't been wearing the same raincoat and hat. I know it doesn't make any sense but I thought she was going after you. Whatever she was trying to do, I had to stop her. Hell, I don't know what I'm saying. Ever since this mess started, I've been confused. I've had to figure out what I should do from one minute to the next, and I hate not knowing whether I'm doing the right things."

Connie hung up her coat, took off her top and wriggled out of the skirt. Folded them carefully. She had new underwear but not very much. It didn't take long for her to take it off.

I forced myself to move slowly. She strolled over and unbuttoned my shirt. "I believe you and I guess I believe your whole screwy story is true but you're going to have to tell me again. I'm still mad and now I don't know who to be mad at."

"Not at me."

We finished taking our clothes off and got into the big bed.

"No, not at you," she said. She rolled over and pushed her black hair up away from her neck. "Give me a back rub. You got the last one."

I set to work with a will, starting with her neck and shoulders and upper arms, working my way down. She smelled great.

"Marie Therese told me that brown-haired girl came back. You know, I said she would. Tell me about it."

I didn't know what she was talking about, not at first, being so focused on the job at hand. It took a minute to remember the brown-haired girl. Then it came back.

"Yeah, the tall girl, that's an interesting story, and I can see why Marie Therese would think she had to bring it up. You remember the first night she came in with all those other girls? Four of them, they were celebrating her engagement. Started with champagne. She switched to a Manhattan. It was right after we remodeled the place and she was surprised at how respectable it was. Her name is Esther, Esther something. The next time she came in, she was by herself and she didn't have an engagement ring. That's right, her boyfriend jilted her. Turns out she's a buyer for Bonwit Teller, and when her boss learned what had happened, he decided to send her to Paris because something was going wrong there and she was the only person who could fix it."

I finished with Connie's back and rolled her over to work on the other side. "There was more to it, but the point of it is she was really emotional, I guess because she'd come to my place to celebrate her engagement and wanted to stop by again before she left, and the last thing she did was kiss me. Right there at the bar, in front of everybody. Then she left and I guess she's in Paris because I haven't seen her since."

"Marie Therese said you'd have a good story. If you were lying I'd know."

"When you think about it, you can hardly blame the girl. I mean, she's a buyer. She noticed that I was wearing one of my best suits." I stretched out and tried to kiss her.

She put her hands against my chest. "Which one? The Rogers Peet?"

"Yes. You know how good I look in it, and I am really tired of talking."

So was she. We shifted around so we were facing each other. She kissed me sweet and seriously and guided me home. It wasn't as great as it had been the night before she left, but nobody was trying to kill me then. And, hell, even if it wasn't great, it was wonderful enough and we were both smiling when it was over.

She stretched out on top of me and said, "What's a girl got to do to get a drink in this joint?"

• • •

Connie was in the shower when I heard the soft knock on the door. I got out of bed, pulled on my trousers, and found the little kraut automatic in my vest. Opened the door on the chain. Standing behind the room service cart was the guy who helped me with Miss Wray. He looked a lot different.

I took the door off the chain, pocketed the gun. He wheeled the cart in. Two years before, I'd guessed him to be fifteen or younger. He'd grown taller, taller than me, and he'd traded a bellboy's cap and short jacket for a black suit and tie. "Good evening, Mr. Patterson," he said. "Nice to see you again. Shall I put this by the window?"

"That's fine. Looks like you've been promoted."

"I'm assistant concierge to Mr. Phillip. If there's anything you need, call the desk and ask for Anthony."

"There is. Some luggage will be delivered this evening. There will be tags from the French Line on the bags with the name Nix. Ignore that. Bring them here."

"Of course." He took the cover off the cart. Bottle of French white in an ice bucket, Jameson, soda siphon, three dishes under metal domes. I could smell fried chicken. "Shall I open the wine?" he said.

He worked the corkscrew without making a production of it, and put out two place settings on the table.

"One more thing. I'm involved in some unusual business at the moment."

"Is it anything like Miss Wray's business?" He kept his voice level, not insinuating anything with the question.

"Could be. For now, I just want to know if anybody comes around asking about Jimmy Quinn. I don't expect them to, but if they do, let me know right away."

"Of course."

Connie came out of the bathroom, running her fingers through damp hair. She was wrapped in a towel. As she padded over on bare feet, she said, "I thought I smelled food. Wine, please."

Assistant concierge Anthony poured a glass and barely glanced at her. I guess seeing a woman wrapped in a towel and a guy without a shirt was just part of a day's work. Connie paid no attention to him and lifted the domes off our dinner. She wouldn't have come out undressed like that and knowing a stranger was in the room before she went to France. I wondered what else had changed.

"Will there be anything else, sir?"

"Yes," Connie said. "I need a robe. You'd better bring one for him, too."

Anthony said, "Of course," and backed out of the room.

I made a drink. Connie tucked into a chicken leg and talked around it.

"You wouldn't believe how good the food is over there. I'm not talking about the fancy places. I couldn't afford to go to any of those, but the neighborhood cafés and restaurants have meals you can't find anywhere here."

"Tell me what it was like." I settled back with my whiskey and enjoyed watching her eat and listening to her. And she said that all the talk was about Hitler and what was going on in Germany. That was everything you saw in the *Herald Tribune*, the only English paper she could get at the newsstand near her apartment. She'd started to learn French on the ship and was able to read headlines in the French papers but not the stories. She signed up for French classes at a language school, and that's where she spent most of her mornings. In the afternoon, she walked, drank coffee in cafés and tried to learn about French fashion. She met a French girl named Maite in the school. She was learning English, so they helped each other. Maite worked for a couturier. That was somebody who made the very best clothes, the kind Connie couldn't afford, but managed to acquire anyway.

"Was that the guy who said your bosom was too big?"

She tried to act like she was offended but she smiled and said that it was.

A half hour or so later, Assistant concierge Anthony knocked on the door and delivered two robes. He said there was no sign of her bags, but the guys out front knew what to do.

Connie unwrapped her towel and put on a robe. By then she'd had most of the bottle of wine. She poured the rest. "When you were talking to Arch, he said that these guys are serious, the guys who are after you. And then he asked if you knew what that meant. You said yes."

I nodded.

"So, what does it mean?"

I poured another drink. I still didn't want to say it out loud, but there was no trying to hide it from her. "It means I'm going to have to kill somebody to end this. Probably. If this was any kind of normal beef that I had with most of the guys I know, I might be able to talk to them, figure what was going on, work something out. I still don't have any idea why this is happening, what I've done that makes somebody want to kill me. I don't like it a damn bit, it scares me. And I can't see any way that I can go to the cops, even Detective Ellis for help. No, I've got to settle it myself."

She thought about that, thought about it hard. Then, "No. We've got to settle it."

• • •

Her bags showed up after eleven, and she spent a couple of hours taking the clothes out, showing them off, hanging them in the wardrobe and folding them carefully into the dresser. Stretched out on the bed, I drank more whiskey and enjoyed watching her. When she finally came to bed, she was asleep before I could suggest anything else.

Chapter Twenty-Eight

The cold anger kept me awake. I couldn't stop seeing everything that happened on the pier. Around three Thursday morning, I got dressed and wrote a note saying I would be back soon. At that hour, the lobby and the concierge desk were empty. Out on Fifth Avenue, the doorman whistled the first cab in the short line. I told him to take me to Sixth and Twentieth, a couple blocks from the Chelsea. It figured somebody was watching the hotel and Jimmy's Place so I walked slowly over to Eighth and then up to the alley that ran behind the joint. Once I got away from the streetlights, I stopped and let my eyes adjust. Then I stepped carefully, not scuffing my feet or using my stick. I had the .38 in my hand and tried to peer into every shadow.

I made my way to the other end of the alley without seeing anybody, then went back to the heavy gate and the loading area. The light was on over my back door. I unlocked the gate and found my Ford parked on the other side. Arch was standing at the top of the back steps. He lowered the pistol he was aiming at me and said, "Let's have a drink."

"No, let's have breakfast."

• • •

In the Cruzon kitchen I made salami and eggs. Arch made coffee and rye toast. He said Frenchy had filled him in about Pier 57, and he told me what happened after that as we ate.

"We put out the 'Closed for Private Party' sign when things slowed down in the middle of the afternoon. Frenchy and Marie Therese drove Mrs. O'Neal home. I waited to go to Pier 57 until traffic was heavier late in the evening. I didn't have any trouble at baggage claim, and it wasn't hard to spot the guy who was waiting for somebody to pick up Connie's luggage. The frog behind the counter yelled out the name 'Nix' and a feller who was leaning against a wall nearby closed his newspaper with studied nonchalance and sidled over closer to me."

"What'd he look like?"

"Forty, forty-five. Five ten maybe. Heavy on his feet. Dark suit and hat. Cold cigar. That's just an impression. I didn't want him to know I'd made him. He followed the stevedore who loaded the bags into the car. The DeSoto was right behind me when I left. I continued to play dumb as I drove. Stayed in one lane, kept the speed down which is really a shame with that lovely V-8 engine. Oh, wouldn't it be grand to take it out into the country where there are good paved roads and I could—"

"Arch."

"All right, all right, as I was saying I ambled down to the Holland Tunnel and we drove under the river to New Jersey. The DeSoto has that swept back grille in front, easy to pick out in traffic. Once we got into Newark, I slowed down until they were right behind me. I held up an envelope to the light where they couldn't help but see it, like I was trying to read directions. Looked back and forth between it and the street signs and I'd start to turn but wouldn't like I didn't know where I was going. I was so goddamned irritating that everybody who passed me was hitting the horn or giving me the single-fingered salute. Oh, I was wonderful, I must say. After a mile or so of this act, I timed it to catch them at a light and get a block ahead. Without hurrying, I turned right at the next intersection, and again at the next dark cross street. Cut the lights and the engine and waited for the DeSoto to zip past, as it did presently. Then I headed straight back to the tunnel. If that simple stratagem worked, they think that I was delivering those bags to you and Connie across the river, and they think I didn't know I was being followed."

"Possible."

"After that, as you know, I delivered Connie's new clothes, and if what Frenchy says is right about the dress she was wearing, those clothes are really something."

"That's the understatement of the evening."

"As I was driving back here, it came to me that our unidentified adversaries probably know we closed this afternoon and, if they know that, Mr. Pelltierre's thugs might attempt some mischief after hours. That's why I'm putting in overtime for which, I am sure, I shall be richly compensated."

"Does anybody but you know we're at the Pierre?"

"Not unless Connie told Marie Therese. What are we going to do now?"

"Call Frenchy and tell him we're going to open as usual. Hell, I can't afford to stay at the Pierre unless I'm making money, and it's not safe for us to go back to the Chelsea. So we're going to live like rich people for a few days while Mrs. Opperman figures out what's what with Pelltierre and his foundation. If she calls or comes here, tell her you can contact me and I'll get in touch."

"I'd been planning to look into the unfortunate assemblyman in New Jersey today but we shouldn't be shorthanded now. The assemblyman can wait."

We went downstairs to the office. I checked Wednesday's count. Not much even for a half day. I gave Arch enough cash for the register. Kept out a couple hundred to take care of things at the Pierre and locked the rest back up. As I closed the safe, I remembered that Connie's Russian egg was there. If things got tight, I could always call Bogolomov about it. But not yet.

Arch drove me to the Third Avenue El station. I caught an uptown train and got back to the Pierre as the sun was rising. I let myself into the dark room and undressed quietly. Connie hadn't moved. I got into bed beside her.

She hitched over close and draped a sleepy arm across my chest. "Where've you been," she murmured.

"I made sure things are alright at Jimmy's Place. Arch is there. It's fine." She felt great.

"I've been thinking about what happened on the pier," she said, more awake than I thought. "That woman had a gun, didn't she?"

She threw a leg over me. "So I've been lying here thinking she pretended to be Marie Therese and sent those wires to Paris that got me to come back."

"Probably."

"Then she's been working on this for almost a month and planning it longer than that."

"Maybe a lot longer."

"And that means you and Arch are right. They're serious and we're going to have to kill them."

I pulled her the rest of the way on top of me. "But not right now."

Chapter Twenty-Nine

"Your detective called. Says she has news. I told her that you were incommunicado for the moment and I would deliver whatever nuggets she had dislodged. She was obstinately uninclined to share them, even though she said it was extremely important. Apparently they are for your ears only."

Arch was behind the bar. Over the telephone, I could hear it sounded busy. It was about six in the evening, Thursday. Connie had been talking to Marie Therese for the past half hour. When she finished, I told her put Arch on the line.

"Mrs. Opperman say anything else?"

"That she's working on a preliminary report."

The business on Pier 57 still had me spooked. The fewer people who knew where we were, the better. I wanted to hear whatever the detective had to say but I didn't want Arch talking about it on the phone. Not that I had reason to think that anybody was listening in on my line, but it had happened to a lot of guys I knew and nothing good came of it.

"Do this," I said. "If she comes in, go to my office where you can be sure you're keeping it between yourselves. Tell her I'm at the Pierre under the name Patterson. Better she comes here. Anything else? How's business?"

"On the good side. For a Thursday, we're busy."

"Nobody that sets off any alarm bells?"

"Almost all regulars. The only one I'd recognize on sight is the mook from the pier last night."

"That's Spig Dolan, and there's also a big woman involved. I told you about them this morning, and maybe I'm wrong to be worried. So far, these guys are just after me. They haven't threatened the bar."

"But we can't assume that they won't. Listen, there's something else."

"What?"

I heard from a fella who's been spreading the word that we'll pay for information about Pelltierre. He says he's found somebody."

"Somebody on the household staff?"

"I don't know any of the details, and I don't know how trustworthy he really is, but there's a chance I can see this fella tonight. I told him to come here. If he can arrange a meeting with his somebody right away, should I do that or stay here overnight?"

"If you think there's a chance to learn something, take it. I'll talk to Frenchy and Marie Therese about staying."

I hung up the handset. Connie grabbed it straight away and called room service. I paid enough attention to hear that she wasn't hearing the answers she wanted. After some more talk, she got a chef on the line.

I went back to the newspapers. Nothing much in the front sections was of interest. I went to the Shipping pages at the back. The little story I wanted was between the headlines "SHIP MEN CARRY ON LIFEBOAT RACING" and "SEAMEN FLOCK HERE TO OBTAIN WORK."

It was about what I'd expected.

ALTERCATION AT NORTH RIVER DOCKS

Passengers disembarking from the SS Champlain at Pier 57 yesterday witnessed a disturbance in the French Line building. Several people reported an altercation between two men that occurred near one of the boarding ramps. At about the same time, according to Passenger Agent Martin Askins, others said that a woman was in distress. Following an extensive search of the area, no such woman could be located and Harbor Police were not notified.

I poured a short whiskey over ice and tried to figure what I should be doing. The answer was nothing until I heard from the Continental detective. So I sat back, appreciated the warm breeze blowing in from the Park and watched Connie arrange and rearrange her new French clothes. I couldn't tell you what the fabrics were or the styles. I could just see that the blouses and jackets were simple, without bows, lace and the like. The dresses and skirts were several inches shorter than most women wore. All of them looked great on Connie and she was really enjoying them.

She saw me smiling and said, "You think that this is frivolous, don't you?"

"I'm just glad you're back. Hate what you went through getting here and what you're in the middle of, but I'm glad you're here."

"Don't try to change the subject. You think that these clothes are just something that women occupy themselves with while men have more serious concerns."

What the hell had got into her? It couldn't have been the wine. She'd had two bottles of their best sent up but she'd hardly touched her glass.

Before I could say anything, she went on, "Think about all the care and time that you put into your suits. That's not frivolous, is it? How many times have I heard you say that because you're not tall or educated or rich, you've got to look your best for men to take you seriously? Don't get your back up, I'm not tall, either and I'm not going to get any taller. You think this is just some silly woman's vanity, it's not. I don't want to 'be pretty.'" She made a face like that was the worst thing a woman could do.

"I just want to look my best—like you do. Growing up it was hand-me-downs from my older sister and she was so much bigger than me that nothing fit without being cut apart and sewn back together so everything I wore looked like it had been made from a quilt, and then when I worked for Mrs. Pennyweight, she made me wear those godawful black wool sacks that nobody could even tell I was a girl when I had one on, and the stupid cap. God, I hated that cap."

She wasn't wrong about the maid's uniform. It was the ugliest thing I ever saw on a woman.

"And then I finally get a chance to go to the one place on earth where they really think seriously about women's clothes and make the best you'll ever find. I can watch what they do and learn what goes into it, and just when I'm getting started with that, you let some guys try to kill you and then you drag me back."

As she was talking, she was taking different outfits out of the wardrobe, holding them up and seeing how they looked in the mirror on the door. Putting one back, taking out another, then stripping off the clothes she was wearing to try on the one she just took out. I didn't interrupt. I enjoyed. After an hour or so, there was a light tap on the door and the room service cart was wheeled in. More wine and covered plates. Connie was in a pale yellow sleeveless number. It was my third favorite, after the navy blue outfit and the silk underwear.

She slipped the kid a buck from my wallet and told him to leave the cart. "This is a special order," she said. "It wasn't on the menu but I talked to one of the sous chefs in the kitchen. I told him about what I had at the bistro around the corner from our place on Rue Git Le Coeur and he said his mother made it every week. Chicken with garlic and wine."

She lifted the dome. I inhaled. "Oh, hell yes."

She said, "It's not the same, but it's probably as close as I'm going to get. Open another bottle of the red while I put this on the table."

We dug in, and I've got to say that it was one of those meals that I remember so well that I can see the room and remember the moment the breeze through the open window caught the gauzy curtain and blew it over my plate. Even if it didn't live up to what she had in Paris, it was the best chicken I'd ever eaten. The wine was a couple cuts above what I normally drank, too. She was happy. For a few minutes, I forgot why I was hiding out in the Pierre.

For a few minutes.

Chapter Thirty

We were still at the table when I heard another knock on the door, a harder knock than room service or Anthony the Assistant Concierge. I took the kraut automatic out of my vest pocket and looked at Connie. The way she tried to act surprised, I knew she wasn't.

I put the piece back in my vest and opened the door, not bothering with the chain. It was the Soldier and Jenny Pris Kirk. Not hard to figure how they got there. The girl came back to my place and talked to Marie Therese. Gave her a sob story and Marie Therese believed every word of it. This afternoon, Marie Therese told Connie about the girl. Connie told her where we were and said send them right over.

I said, "Good evening," like we'd been expecting them and opened the door wider. He stepped in warily. She stayed close behind him, her arms wrapped around her body like she was cold. She looked around the suite, surprised at how big it was.

Until then, I hadn't been close enough to get a really good look at the man. Make him six feet and thin. The stiff-collared uniform was loose at the neck. Figure he'd been a teenager in the war and that made him around forty but he looked older. Sharp face, short sandy-white hair, gray eyes. When he started talking later, he interrupted himself with regular coughs, not a harsh lunger's hack but you could tell the coughing bothered him. After each one, he'd pause and gather himself before he spoke again.

Connie couldn't take her eyes off him. He was paying attention to her, too. Any guy would even if she hadn't been wearing the pale yellow sleeveless number. He made an effort not to stare.

I said, "Connie, this is Jenny Pris Kirk. I told you about her. Jenny Pris, Connie Nix. I don't know this gentleman's name, but about a month ago, he shot two jackleg punks who were trying to kill me. I haven't had a chance to thank him, Mr...?"

"Renka. Caleb Renka."

Connie said, "Please, have a seat," and waved a hand toward the sofa. "What'll you have to drink?"

"I see you've got some of the good French stuff," he said. "I did develop a taste for it while I was over there."

Connie poured two glasses. Caleb Renka tasted and smiled. Jenny Pris sniffed it, took a sip and tried not to make a face before she put the glass down. She sat as close to Renka as she could.

He said, "Why are they trying to kill you, Quinn?" He stared at me like he was trying to see what my reaction was. Sounded serious.

"I'm still working on that. I think you may know as much about it as I do. Two weeks ago, her husband Asa called and said he knew who was after me. Said he'd tell me all about it for five hundred dollars. A few days later, he came to my place. We talked. He gave me some names. I asked for proof. He said his proof was close and he'd get it. He left and I haven't seen him since. The names are Herk Sturdivant and Spig Dolan. Mean anything to you?"

"Maybe. Let's say I know there's a man here who's using an assumed name. He might have more than one."

I poured whiskey for myself and more wine for him. "Do you know Asa? Know anything about what he was doing here?"

"Sure, I know Asa. From the camp in Anacostia. He was one of the volunteers who brought us food. I didn't know he was in New York until I saw Jenny Pris outside your place. She helped Asa from time to time."

Connie said, "Camp? Anacostia? I don't understand."

"It's the Bonus Army," I said. "Mr. Renka was part of it, right? Two years ago, veterans of the war went to Washington to demand the bonuses the government promised them after the Armistice. A lot of them made a camp in Anacostia, right across the river. I don't know why, but that whole business has something to do with what's happening now. Tell me about it. All I know is what I read in the papers."

I topped off Renka's glass. He coughed and started talking.

"Let me say right now, I'm not proud of anything I did that summer. I was wrong about every part of it. My wife died because of mistakes I made. I wasn't there when she needed me and I still don't know what happened or why it happened. But that was later, at the end. I'm from Masaryk, Pennsylvania.

"You've never heard of it. Just a little mountain town between Kutztown and Reading. I'm sure that clears it up for you. My story's the same as just about every other fella my age. When the Great War came along, they called me up. They really wanted young men who could shoot and read and I could do both pretty good. There's a lot of game in the woods around Masaryk. I started hunting food for my family when I was eight years old, so I knew what to do with a rifle. And I'd graduated high school. They took six of us from Masaryk. As it happened, I was the oldest of the group by a couple of years, and it naturally fell to me to be sure that the other five came back. It was 1917 when they drafted us. Put us in the 328th Infantry, 82nd Division, the All American.

"If that sounds familiar, it's probably because it was Alvin York's unit, the famous 'Sergeant York,' who won those medals and captured all those Germans. Well, the truth is I'm a better shot than Alvin. Proved it often enough on the range and in the field. But once we got into it, he took more chances than I did. Had the idea that God was protecting him. Talk your head off about God, Alvin would, if you let him. For myself, I was just trying to get me and my boys back home in one piece.

"They sent us down to Fort Gordon in Georgia to train. That was the first time I met boys from big cities. Greeks, Italians, Irish and Jews. At first, we didn't understand each other very well, but at the end of five months we did. By then, most of those boys could shoot, too, some of them pretty good. After that we went to a camp in New York and then to Boston where we shipped out to France.

"The All American saw a lot of action, and none of it is anything I want to talk about. Every minute I was in France I wanted to be back home."

"I didn't," Connie murmured under her breath so only I could hear her.

"Like I said, I was trying to get all of us back to Masaryk, and I wasn't able to do that. Frank Newton was killed by a sniper at Monsec. Sammy Bethune got blown up by a shell. We got gassed at Norroy and my lungs have never been right since. So, six of us went 'over there,' four of us came back—Bill Finn, Arvin Buchanan, Newton Thomas and me.

"Of course, when we returned the town had a parade for us and there were a lot of parties, but once those were done, it seemed like the people didn't know what to do with us. They'd got used to living their lives without us and now they had to find something for us to do. Some of 'em weren't too happy about it, either, and when I really thought about it, I couldn't blame them. They were right when they said we weren't the same boys we had been before.

"While I was gone the girl I'd been courting had married and started a family. I married, too. Miriam Bowman. She was a nurse from Reading, and she had been in France near to where I was, but we never saw each other. We didn't meet until we came home and then we got along right off the bat. I guess it was because she'd seen what we went through and knew what it was. I could talk to her in a way that I couldn't talk to any other woman. We got hitched in a month. A lot of people took pity on Miriam because she couldn't have children. That didn't bother me at all, and she'd known for a long time and she'd accepted it. Because of that and being a nurse, she sort of became the mother for the younger people in the area who needed one. We were happy with each other. Until the Crash.

"After my father retired, my younger brother and I took over his hardware store. We borrowed to improve it, and I ran the gunsmith operation. We had some good years, really good years, and we hung on after the Crash. Kept the store open. But the store could really only provide for my brother and his family. I still put meat on the table—that wasn't a problem—but we had to close down the gunsmith side of the store. That's when the Bonus Army came marching through Masaryk. Their pitch was that the government had promised to pay us bonuses based on the time we'd spent overseas, but not until 1948. It was supposed to make up for the money we would have earned if we'd stayed home and worked instead of being in the service. The man who started the march, fellow name of Waters out in Oregon, argued that the Crash changed everything and if enough of us went to Washington and stayed there until they heard us out, they'd change their mind and give us our money. Yeah, I know it sounds pretty naïve saying that now, but the men from other towns in Pennsylvania told us there were groups from Illinois and Maine and just about every state in the union, just like the All American, heading for Washington any way they could. When Bill, Arvin and Newt said they were going, and Arvin's wife Ethel was coming with them, Miriam and I decided we didn't have anything better to do, and started walking. She said I was still trying to take care of the boys, who weren't boys anymore, and I guess she was right. That's why she went, too. I never thought we would see any money from it, but I thought that by going to Washington, we might find something else, some kind of work that was worth doing. That's all any of us ever wanted, a job.

"The six of us joined the others and we walked from Masaryk to Washington. Sometimes we got rides. People in towns along the way gave us food, and some of them thought we were doing something to fight against the Depression, and they wished us well, just like the people in France did. Wherever we came across other veterans, they lent a hand. We made the last leg of the trip through Maryland in a boxcar that let us off at Union Station. The first Bonus Army camp was just a few hundred yards away. Truth is, none of us except Miriam had ever been to Washington and I expected it to be bigger. You walk out of the station and there's the Capitol dome right in front of you."

He said they got there in the first or second week of June. The camp that they saw was close to the Capitol building in a block of old abandoned Civil War buildings. One of them was an Armory. It was already full. Most of the men in charge stayed there.

"There was another smaller camp a few blocks away, the Reds' camp where the communists and Weasels were staying. A lot of the other guys didn't want to associate with them."

Connie interrupted. "Weasels?"

Renka looked at her. "What did you say?"

"Weasels? What are weasels?"

Jenny Pris said, "He can't hear very well on account of the war."

"I was too close to the mortars and the big guns for too long."

It came to me then that he was staring so hard at Connie and me because he was reading our lips when we spoke.

"Weasels. That's what we called the Workers Ex-Service League. They liked to stir things up, passing out handbills and the like. One of their men even claimed that the whole Bonus Army was his idea."

One of the flyers in Kirk's wallet was from the Ex-Service League, but it was too new to have come from the business in Washington. What did it mean?

Renka said there were several thousand people taking part in the march in the city by then. Before it was over there were more than fifteen thousand of them staying in dozens of camps around the city, one of them in a burlesque house. They were more than the city could handle and they made the cops nervous. Most of the families with kids were staying at the largest camp, a tent city they'd laid out with straight roads on the other side of the Potomac River in Anacostia—Camp Marks, named for a cop. That's where they stayed.

"It was not much more than a shantytown really. Folks made shelters out of scrap lumber, sheet metal, shingles, cardboard, anything we could find. Some had thatched roofs made with the long grass that grew in the mudflats. People tried to clean it up when the newsreels were filming us or the photographers showed up. Sometimes they made it look a lot nicer than it was. Miriam and I wound up with one of the better places. That was because of her.

"She brought her nurse's kit. Pills, a few medicines, bandages and first aid supplies, so our hut became a little clinic mostly for the women and kids. There was always somebody that needed attention. A few days after we got there the Marines set up a bigger clinic near their barracks. Miriam and I got to know them and they gave her what she needed for the kids.

"We were a ragged bunch, but we tried to enforce military order. During the day men from the Armory camp and our camp marched around the Capitol building. Some of them made speeches. When Congress was in session, they passed a bill supporting us. Everybody knew they wouldn't have done anything if we hadn't been there at the doorstep. A couple of nights later, the Senate killed it. I was outside the Capitol when we got the news. At first, everybody was mad and it looked like we might try to get inside the building but the Army band started to play 'America' and we sang along instead. Then we walked back over the bridge to our camp. It didn't seem to me like we had any hope of seeing our money. In fact, the whole enterprise was starting to feel like a Children's Crusade, and I didn't want to be there when it ended. But in the few weeks that we'd been there, so many people were depending on Miriam that she didn't want to leave. She helped anyone who asked for it, and guys were saying that as long as Congress was in session, there was a chance we could get something out of them. So, we stayed.

"They started treating us different in the press about then. At first, we were patriots who weren't asking for anything that wasn't due us. Then they said Jews and radicals were in charge and colored people were living and eating with white people. That part was true. We didn't see it in the Army. They always kept the colored troops separate and gave them the shi—... the dirty jobs. There was a colored neighborhood right beside our camp and it seemed to me we all got along together pretty good. The real problems were sanitation and food. Different organizations donated meals. Ira and Lois Kirk were with a Friends Committee. They came through with sandwiches every weekday. We saw them on weekends, too. Lois always brought a little camera and took a lot of pictures."

"Asa worked for Ira, right? Ira is his uncle," I said.

"That's right. Most days, Miriam would give me a list of things she needed from the Marines. I'd go across the river and we'd march in ranks in front of the Capitol. Later, I'd pick up what she needed and go back, unless there was a vote or something planned at night. Nothing was really very well organized. Anybody with any sense knew that the longer it went on, the less chance we had of getting anything for our trouble.

"It was in July, I think, that they first offered us 'return funds' to buy train tickets out of town. I was ready to take it but Miriam still didn't think she could leave and that's when General Smedley Butler showed up and gave a real stem-winder of a speech telling the men what great Americans we were. That got us charged up for a few days. But by the end of the month, things had gone back to the way they were. Food was still a problem, and then they brought in cranes with wrecking balls to demolish the old Armory buildings where the first group we saw was staying. The cops started moving people out and it was peaceful enough to begin with. One colored man refused to move and they carried him down from the second floor sleeping area.

"Around noon, another group of veterans showed up following a guy who was carrying an American flag. As they got close to the cops, they started throwing bricks and rocks. A cop got slugged by a lead pipe when he tried to take the flag. By afternoon, there were thousands of us around the Armory. They'd roped off an area in the middle and were trying to clear it. Three cops went up to an open area on the second floor. Men were yelling and throwing bricks at them and they almost got hit by a garbage can somebody threw from an upper floor. I heard two quick shots and two of our men went down. One dead, the other died later. That was the first real trouble since we got there. An ambulance took them away and word spread that federal troops had been brought to the White House and cavalry troops were riding across the river from the Arlington Cemetery, and the infantry was coming in trucks.

"The cops moved all of the people who'd come to watch on one side of Pennsylvania Avenue and left us on the other side."

He drained his glass. I filled it. His expression turned hard.

"They came down from the White House. First the cavalry with sabers drawn, then tanks on trucks, and then about four hundred infantrymen. They halted their march in front of us where we could see them when they fixed their bayonets and put on their gas masks. An officer moved to the front and shouted at us, 'You've got three minutes to leave the building. Three minutes,' before they threw the first gas grenades and everything went to hell."

He looked over at Connie and muttered, "Sorry."

She said, "Please go on. Tell it like you remember it."

"The first soldiers climbed the staircases and threw down more gas grenades. The wind blew the gas across the street and it got the civilians, too. Young, old, babies in carriages, black, white, it didn't matter. People were coughing and crying and trying to run in every direction. The soldiers cleared the street. As they drove us out, they set fire to the huts and billets in the building. All day I'd been with Arvin and Newton and Bill Finn, but I lost them in the confusion. I couldn't tell exactly what was going on but I knew our men were being forced out permanently. It took all afternoon and evening to empty the Armory and set it on fire.

"They shouldn't've treated us like that. Maybe we'd overstayed our welcome but they shouldn't've ordered American soldiers to attack unarmed American veterans and women and children. A lot of us, me included, refused to move. A boy in a gasmask acted like he was going to bayonet me. When I didn't move, he reversed his rifle and punched me in the gut. I doubled over. He dropped a gas grenade at my feet and he kept marching. I tried to stagger away from it but I'd inhaled so much it made me sick. Two guys helped me to my feet and got me away from the worst of it.

"When they finished, the tanks rolled off of the trucks and went south to the Weasels' camp and cleared it out. I'm making it sound more organized than it was. There on the street, I couldn't tell what was going on. By evening, the veterans were scattered. Nobody was putting up any resistance. All I wanted to do was get back to our camp but the soldiers were ahead of me on the bridge. That night, they crossed over to the Anacostia camp and drove everyone out.

By the time I got there, it was dark and somebody had brought in a searchlight. The beam of light in the sky went back and forth across the camp. It was the only light until the soldiers started the fires.

"Our hut was burning when I found it. Arvin Buchanan's wife Ethel was there looking for me. She told me that Miriam had been hurt. Ethel thought a horse had kicked her but she said it wasn't that bad, Miriam was going to be alright. The other women had taken her to the far side of the camp where we were retreating. That's where I found her and the others from Masaryk. Miriam told me she was really fine but I could tell that wasn't true. She didn't sound right and her skin was cold. I tried to ask her what had happened, but she wouldn't tell me. She just said she wasn't sure. It was confusing. She thought she'd passed out. She said I was right, that we should've left before. Now her back hurt and she just wanted to get away, to go home.

"By then, the whole camp was on fire. It lit up the sky and the heat pushed us away."

His voice was thick. He pushed tears away with the heel of his hand.

"The only thing we could do was start walking but Maryland state troopers closed the main roads. By four in the morning, it was raining and they let groups of us move if we promised to get to Pennsylvania as fast as we could. We heard that the mayor of Johnstown said veterans could stay there, and that's where Bill Finn and Newton Thomas went. Arvin, Ethel, Miriam and me hitchhiked back to Masaryk. Took us three days.

"We'd been gone almost two months. No parades, no parties this time, and we were considerably worse off than we'd been before we left. Beyond that, I was scared for Miriam. She'd never been sick, even through the Spanish flu, and seeing her so weak frightened me like nothing in the war ever did. It seemed like there was nothing anybody could do, either. There were three doctors in the area who knew her and agreed to look at her even though they knew we couldn't pay. They said she had 'renal trauma.' Her kidneys had been damaged, either by a fall or a blow. Standard treatment was 'watchful waiting.' So, we waited.

"She kept saying it wasn't really that serious, she was getting better, and I told myself I believed her. Ethel and the women in town really tried to take care of her. Not a day went by that one or more of them didn't come by our place and sit with her, and she was still able to help them and their kids, but she didn't have any energy and she tired so quickly. She died a little more than a year later."

He finished his wine.

"A week after the funeral, Ethel Buchanan came to see me. She said she knew some of what went on that last day in the camp, and before she passed, Miriam told her what happened in our hut, but she swore Ethel to secrecy."

He smiled a little. "That was a mean thing to do to Ethel because she loves to talk and gossip but if she promised Miriam, she'd keep her word. Once Miriam was gone though, Ethel just had to tell me.

"She said that on that last day, when they heard that soldiers had been mobilized, Miriam and her crossed the bridge to the city and tried to find me and Arvin. But it was so chaotic they saw right away it was better to go back to the camp. They got across the bridge ahead of the soldiers. Ethel went to their tent to wait for Arvin. He got back with Newton and Bill Finn after dark when the first soldiers started rousting people. They gathered their stuff and went to our hut where they found Miriam unconscious on floor. As they were reviving her, another soldier showed up and told them they had to leave. Arvin, Bill and Newton walked Miriam to the far side of the camp. Ethel stayed and waited for me.

"What she didn't know then and what Miriam told her later was this. When Miriam reached the hut, she found Lois Kirk, Ira Kirk's wife, a woman who brought us sandwiches, there inside the hut taking pictures. She had a camera with a flash bulb. That much, she told Ethel, she could always remember clearly, but after that, she wasn't sure. Miriam thought Lois started to explain what she was doing, but then she felt a blinding pain in her back and her head. She must have blacked out. The next thing she knew, Ethel and Arvin were waking her up, and then there was a soldier ordering them to leave while he threw wadded up newspapers into the hut and lit them with a torch."

He held out his glass. I refilled it.

"The day after Ethel told me that, I packed up and hitchhiked back to Anacostia."

Chapter Thirty-One

Before Renka said anything else, I asked Jenny Pris what she remembered of that summer. "Did you spend much time in the camp with Asa and Ira?"

She shook her head. "During the week, I babysat a group of kids at Ira and Lois's house all day. I only visited the camp three or four times on weekends. I liked it. The veterans and their families needed so much help. I was glad we could do something. Uncle Ira and Aunt Lois and Asa did much more than I did."

"What did they think of the Bonus Army? Did they talk about it much?"

"I don't know," she said and looked like she hadn't expected the question. "Uncle Ira spent more time at the camp than he did at his job that summer. He said they understood what he was doing and didn't mind the time he spent there."

"He worked for the Department of the Navy. What did he do?"

She shook her head. "I don't know. He went in early and was back by ten o'clock to help with the sandwiches. After they were finished at the camp, he went back to work and didn't get home till late almost every night."

Connie saw that the girl hadn't touched her wine. She scooped ice into a glass and filled it from the soda siphon. Jenny Pris took it in both hands and drank it straight down. Connie refilled it, and sat in a chair closer to the girl. "When you went to the camp, did you spend much time with Miriam?"

"Oh, yes. Mrs. Renka asked me to help with the kids. Even the mothers who didn't need anything came to their shelter while their men were at the Capitol building. It was the place where everyone got together in that part of the camp. Asa pitched in too. He wanted to know everything about what they were doing and what they had planned."

The first night she came to my place she said that her husband could talk to anybody. Maybe he was good at getting people to say more than they meant to. Maybe that's why his uncle recommended him to the Liberty Foundation.

Connie said, "Did you go to the camp that last night?"

Jenny Pris shook her head quickly. "Oh, no. That morning Uncle Ira said they'd put General MacArthur in charge. He was going to finish things and I should stay away from downtown Washington. It was going to be dangerous. He made Asa promise that no matter what happened, he would stay home."

"And you were with him," Connie said. "Was Aunt Lois there?"

"No, it was just the two of us."

Renka cleared his throat and said, "Jenny Pris and I talked about this last night. We talked about a lot of things. Lois Kirk wasn't at her house. Jenny Pris didn't see her until the next morning. I don't know that she was at our hut, but I think it's likely she was. I think she and Ira hurt Miriam. Whatever they did to her, that's what killed her, but I'm not certain. And I don't know why they would do anything like that."

He started to say something more but Connie interrupted him. She asked Jenny Pris when she had her last meal. The girl said she wasn't hungry. Connie turned to Renka. "How about you?"

"I could eat."

"Don't say anything more until I'm done." Connie picked up the telephone and got room service. She asked for the guy she'd talked to before and said something I couldn't hear. While she was doing that, I refilled the glasses.

Connie sat close to the girl and said to Renka, "You were going back to Anacostia."

I said, "No, before we get to that, is there anything more to say about Ira and Lois Kirk? What do they look like?"

Renka said, "Ira is big, not fat but thick around the middle. Slope-shouldered. Had a pencil mustache and never seemed to be able to keep his hair combed in Washington. About fifty years old. Served in the Navy during the war. Lois is a handsome woman, and tall, about five-nine. Both of them, and young Asa too, looked for ways to help and they tried not to make you feel like you were accepting charity from them. Always smiling. They said we'd got a raw deal and it was wrong of the government not to help in some way even if we didn't get our full bonus."

Connie said, "Anything else? Jenny Pris?"

The girl cut her eyes back and forth between Connie and me. "Well, they... No, I shouldn't say anything. It's not my place."

Connie touched her knee. "Go ahead, please. Anything might be important."

"They were about to divorce." The way she whispered it, divorce was a serious matter. She looked at Renka. "I've never seen two people fight like they did. They were friendly as could be around other people, like they were at your camp, but when they were home with just Asa and me, they didn't hold anything back. They yelled at each other. She actually hit him and dared him to hit her back. It took everything he had not to. At least, I never saw him hit her, but I saw bruises on her arms where he grabbed her. That's when she'd hit him. Asa and me made ourselves scarce when they got that way. I remember once hearing her say as soon as this was over, she was leaving so she didn't have to look at him anymore. And, sometimes she... No, I really shouldn't say that."

She bit her lip and cut her eyes back and forth, waiting for somebody to coax her. Renka looked at her like he didn't know what she was talking about. The cookie really knew how to drag it out.

Connie said, "You're embarrassed, aren't you? It's alright. Go ahead."

"Sometimes Lois wouldn't wear anything more than her underwear around the house. I guess she got used to doing that when it was only her and Uncle Ira living there but she did it around Asa. He didn't know what to do. I mean they weren't related by blood or anything, but it made him really uncomfortable. She did it when I was there, too. Uncle Ira never said anything but you could tell that it made him mad."

She stopped when she heard the soft knock at the door. The room service guy pulled out our first dinner cart and wheeled in another one loaded with hamburgers. Jenny Pris went at hers like a true trencherman. Renka ate slowly as he talked.

"I left Masaryk about a year ago. I didn't completely believe what Ethel told me but I had to talk to Lois and Ira. I hitchhiked most of the way. Hopped freight trains and walked the rest. Of course, I didn't know where they lived but I did know that the organization they worked for was called the Maryland Friends and Volunteer Society. In Anacostia, I found out that the Society's offices are in Baltimore. I went there and they told me that they didn't have any records from Anacostia, but there was a smaller office in a church there. They gave me the address on Q Street and I went back to Anacostia.

"I found the church and a nice woman who worked there said she knew about the Friends. She didn't know Ira and Lois, and they didn't keep files on all of the people who volunteered, but if I wanted to go through it, they had saved all of the paperwork from that summer. It was in a basement storeroom but nobody had the time to do anything more than put the stuff in boxes, so it wasn't in order. That storeroom also had the church's records going back to the Twenties. Most of it wasn't labelled right and none of it was in order either. She said I was welcome to go through it and the pastor let me sleep on a cot in the furnace room. Took me more than a week to find an order form from a local grocer for bread and baloney to be delivered to I. Kirk of 14 O Street SE."

I gave him more wine, and snuck a look at my watch. It was past eleven.

"The people at that address were renting the house and didn't know anything about the Kirks. I went to the realty agency. At first, they didn't want anything to do with me. But after I persuaded them that I wasn't going to go away until I got what I wanted, they looked into their files. Turned out that Ira Kirk had moved away a year ago in August, right after they broke up the Bonus Army. The forwarding address was in New York City. Five Thirty-Five East Eighty-Sixth Street."

"Yorkville," I said. "The German section." Only a few blocks from the street where the two jackleg punks tried to kill me.

"Fair number of Micks, too, I found when I got there."

"And how did you get there? Not to pry, but it doesn't look like you're rolling in dough. How have you been living?"

He laughed and that made him cough. "I left Masaryk with a small stake. Along the way I've been able to find other veterans from the All American, and men from other units and their wives that we got to know in the camp. I haven't had much trouble finding a meal or a place to sleep for a night. Seems like anybody who knew Miriam has been more than happy to help.

"It did take some time to get used to this city once I got here. There's a lot going on. At first it's confusing."

Connie said, "Ain't that the truth." Jenny Pris added an amen.

"Once I found East Eighty-Sixth, I saw that the neighborhood was nothing I hadn't seen before. It's a nice enough place where regular people live. The address was a prosperous looking apartment building. Not knowing how things are done, it took me some time to figure out that the person I needed to see was the building superintendent. He told me that there was no Ira or Lois Kirk living there, and they never had. For the moment, I was stuck but I wasn't about to give up."

Renka said that despite the Depression, the neighborhood was carrying on. Tree-lined streets, sidewalks and stoops swept clean. He didn't see as many empty storefronts as he had in some other places. He picked up odd jobs mopping floors, cleaning windows, washing dishes—anything that would bring him a few dollars and give him an excuse to stay in the area and keep an eye on the apartment house. He had to hope that Kirk was living there under an assumed name and that he'd see him coming or going. That presented another problem. The building was on a corner. It was five stories tall, twenty apartments. There were four different doors opening on two streets. People that lived there used all of them. If Kirk was one of them, chances of spotting him were not good. Renka couldn't stay in one place and watch the building for very long, either. Cops on the beat noticed things like that. He tried to get on the good side of the patrolmen he met, but they knew he was up to something. Cops are like that.

Renka stayed on sofas and cots in veterans' places, making sure he never wore out a welcome. In the evenings and at night, he went to restaurants and cafés and the big Yorkville Casino. That wasn't a place for gambling. It was more of a community center with ballrooms and motion picture theaters and restaurants. Everybody went there. Renka tried to frequent the crowded, popular places, always looking for Kirk's face. He'd strike up conversations with men he met there, eventually asking if they happened to know his old friend Ira Kirk who lived someplace in the area. Nobody did.

"I'd been at it for more than two months, and I was getting mighty discouraged. Then, just like that, one evening, I saw him. At first I didn't believe it. I mean, from the time I was back in Anacostia, I thought I saw Kirk a dozen times a week, but that had passed. I was afraid that I'd forget what he looked like, but I remembered him just fine. That evening, he was coming out of a cobbled alley a block from the apartment building with another smaller man. Both of them were carrying leather suitcases. The light was going and I couldn't get a good look at their faces but I recognized Kirk's walk. I was across the street from them. The smaller man stepped off the sidewalk and hailed a passing taxi. As they got in the back seat, I saw that moon face and pointed chin. It was Ira."

Jenny Pris nodded at the description.

When Renka knew Ira Kirk in Washington, he was always wearing old, rumpled, wrinkled clothes. Frayed collars, missing buttons, short ties, shiny pants. That meant that he fit right in with the men of the Bonus Army who wore everything from old uniforms to bib overalls to business suits. The man Renka saw getting into the cab was wearing a camelhair topcoat over an expensive suit. The mustache was gone and his hair was shiny with pomade.

"Then I knew I wasn't wasting my time. Kirk wouldn't have changed that much about where he lived and how he looked without a reason, and even that quick glimpse was enough to tell me that he'd come into money. What did he do to get it?"

Chapter Thirty-Two

Caleb Renka told us his story about the Bonus Army and his search for Ira Kirk on Thursday night. The day before, Wednesday, Theodora Opperman and Provisional Operative T.S. were in the office I'd rented. They were listening to two men in the Liberty Foundation office. This is from her final report:

Provisional Operative T.S. and I overheard Sturdivant, the subject of our surveillance, enter an office on 27th St. at approximately ten-thirty o'clock. He was accompanied by a second man, almost certainly the individual he spoke with on the telephone the night before. They had been drinking. Their voices were slurred. I heard Sturdivant open the closet doors and take out a bottle. Drinks were poured.

Sturdivant: What the [obscenity] happened on the dock?

Second man: I don't know. I stayed close to the car. She was—

Sturdivant: She [obscenity] it up, that's what happened. Twice [obscenity]. She's not going to get another chance. I've [obscenity] had it with the [obscenity]. What happened later?

Second man: Like you said, I waited around the baggage claim, and the old guy from the bar showed up with the tickets and got the bags and the trunk. Loaded them into a green Ford coupe.

Sturdivant: Did he see you?

Second man: [Obscenity] You think I'm some kind of amateur? H--- no, he didn't make me, not then and not when I followed him into New Jersey neither. He was looking for an address in Newark. Didn't know where the [obscenity] he had to turn. He got lucky at a light and I lost him.

Sturdivant: The h--- you say, he got lucky. He made you, you [obscenity] sap.

Second man (yelling): [Obscenity]! I'm telling you, they're somewhere in Newark.

Sturdivant: My [obscenity] they're in Newark.

Second man: That doesn't make any difference now anyway. I gotta go back tomorrow. Did Pelltierre come up with the cash?

Sturdivant: Some of it, not all of it.

Second man: You said he'd—

Sturdivant: I know what I said, don't worry. We've still got to be careful with him. As soon as he thinks we're trying to milk him, it's [obscenity] over. We are dedicated, patriotic Americans who are willing to make any sacrifice to stop the encroaching Red menace that threatens our shores and our very existence.

Both laugh.

Second man: Where do you come up with this [obscenity].

Sturdivant: It's like any other grift, once you get the patter down. The trick is not to go too far. With brandyboy, it's not hard. It's different with the old woman. She doesn't give a [obscenity] about this [obscenity]. She's in it for the money and she knows there's plenty to be had on her end once he's in. Not just now but for years if she plays her cards right.

Second man: She won't need brandyboy then.

Sturdivant: The dumb [obscenity] thinks he'll still be in charge, but first we've got to get her man in.

Second man: I know, I'll be in Trenton tomorrow. And Newark. Is the [obscenity] money ready?

Sturdivant: It's right here.

Sound of desk drawer opening.

Sturdivant: Here, it's a hundred each for Mace, Perkins, Magas, Perry and Moller. If you short any of them, you're [obscenity]. I'm not [obscenity] kidding. If you [obscenity] this up with some [obscenity] stupid move like that you did with the Greenpoint job, I'll—

Second man: The [obscenity] you say. I didn't short him on Greenpoint. He was drunk when he got there for the payoff, and this is different anyway. [Obscenity], Ira. I'm not that [obscenity] stupid. The big payday is so [obscenity] close I can smell it.

Sturdivant: That's your [obscenity] stinking underwear.

Both laugh.

Sturdivant: You take care of New Jersey. I'm going to flush out that [obscenity] Quinn, wherever he is.

Second man: How much did Pelltierre come up with?

Sturdivant: Two Gs.

Second man: He promised [obscenity] a hundred and six.

Sturdivant: He'll have it next week. At the meeting.

Second man: Where is the rest of the two?

Sturdivant: It's safe, what's left. I had to cover some expenses.

Second man: Yeah, well I got [obscenity] expenses, too.

Sturdivant: I took care of you last week.

Second man: Come on, give. I gotta drive to [obscenity] New Jersey again for [blasphemy] sake.

Sturdivant: Alright already, here's fifty. Don't [obscenity] spend it all in one place.

The two men left the office at eleven-thirteen o'clock.

Postscript: Mace, Perkins, and Magas are William "Big Billy" Mace, Charlie Perkins and Richard Magas. Magas and Perkins are Democratic party hacks who work with the General Assembly. Mace is the man to see in Trenton. We have not yet identified Perry and Moller. The Greenpoint job could refer to a paperhanging ring that operated in the neighborhood in the spring of 1933.

(Stenography and typescript by T.S.)

Chapter Thirty-Three

Renka said it was almost a month before he saw Kirk again, but knowing that the man was in the neighborhood, he wasn't about to change his plans. At the end of the cobbled alley where he'd seen Kirk, there were steps down to a rathskeller. It was one of those smokey, low-ceilinged places with heavy wooden furniture and booths. Renka got a job bussing tables and washing dishes. Just about everybody who worked in the place was German. That was all they spoke in the kitchen. Renka had picked up enough of it in the war to follow orders and to know what they were saying about him when they thought he couldn't understand.

"I never wore this in Yorkville," he said, meaning the doughboy's blouse. "In some quarters there, they still don't think they lost. I played dumb, pretended I didn't *sprecken*. Showed up on time for every shift. Didn't speak unless I had to."

He managed to get inside Kirk's apartment building twice by holding the front door open for people who were leaving, but he didn't learn anything. There were no names on the doors or mailboxes, and he knew the super wouldn't talk to him. During the day, he continued to walk around the neighborhood, stopping often for coffee or beer, always watching for his man. He was clearing a table at the rathskeller on a Thursday night when he heard the owner greet a customer at the door.

"Guten Abend, Herr Johnson. Wilkomen zurück."

He turned and saw the owner leading Kirk through the tables. The shorter man he'd seen before was with him. Kirk was saying "...been out of town. Can't find decent veal anyplace but..."

Kirk looked right at him as he passed, but Renka saw no sign that Kirk recognized him. "I was wearing a mustache then. Didn't have one in Washington, and I needed a haircut. I guess if Kirk had changed the way he looked because he had a lot of money, I changed the way I looked for the opposite reason."

The owner took them to a corner booth on the back wall. He snapped his fingers and the bartender brought over two Schnapps. Renka cleared the table he was working and took the dishes back to the kitchen. Kirk and the other man spent the rest of the evening over their dinner with more drinks, beer and brandy. The waiter who served them knew Kirk and moved his order to the front of the line. Cook didn't object. Renka thought that Kirk must be a good customer because Cook raised hell if somebody tried to change the way he was doing things. Later when Kirk was finishing, Cook went out to talk to him, something else Renka hadn't seen before.

As he cleared tables, he tried to move close enough to Kirk to get a better look at him and to hear what they were saying. The suit might have been top-drawer, but it was specked with food and wine. Kirk's collar was unbuttoned and his tie hung loose. He was red-faced and loud from the alcohol. As he talked, he stuck his finger in the face of the other man, digging at him, mocking him about something. The other man took it but didn't like it. Renka could see that in his face. Kirk ignored it.

They stayed until closing time and were three sheets to the wind as they staggered out. Renka cleared the table he was working, took the dishes back to the kitchen and left without saying a word to anyone. The kitchen steps led to the back door. The restaurant was two blocks from Kirk's apartment building. Renka hurried to it and got there as Kirk was going inside. The smaller man was down the street hailing a cab.

"I'd considered speaking to him in the restaurant," Renka said, "Just taking off my apron and walking up to his table to see how he'd react. But seeing that he was a lot better off then he'd been a year before, and he'd assumed the name Johnson, I knew something else was going on. The next several weeks were frustrating."

Kirk disappeared again. Renka tried to spend more time watching his apartment building but the superintendent noticed him and pointed him out to the beat cop. Renka moved on and watched the building from other angles. Still no sign of Kirk. He came back to the restaurant in April with a woman and took the same corner booth.

Renka said, "She was a big brunette who looked a lot like Lois. She and Kirk kept their voices down. The way they were smiling, they were going to make an evening of it. They left early. I didn't try to follow."

He coughed harder than before and said, "I could use some more of that wine. I'm talking too much."

I poured for him and Connie, whisky for myself. Jenny Pris still hadn't touched hers. Renka got up and paced slowly around the room. "When Ethel Buchanan told me that Lois had been in our hut that night, I didn't know that it meant anything but I did know that something wasn't right about the way Miriam died. Even considering that they burned the camp and drove us out, Miriam was hurt before the first soldiers crossed the river, Ethel was sure about that. At the beginning I just wanted to talk to Lois, find out if she'd been in the hut. But after looking for her and Ira for almost a year, I was sure there was something they wanted to hide. I wasn't going to walk away but I didn't know what to do except stay there and learn more."

The next chance he got was on Friday, June 15.

It was almost midnight and he was in the kitchen when he heard one of the waiters mutter that Mr. Johnson had just come in and wanted to order. They'd started closing down but Cook said he'd take care of it and went out to see Johnson. He came back a few minutes later and told everyone to leave except one waiter. The rest of staff didn't argue and headed for the back stairs. Renka took his tray out to clear the last tables. Kirk was in his corner booth. The shorter man was with him. Kirk was angry, the other man was worried and sweaty.

As Renka passed them on his way to the kitchen, he heard the shorter man say, "Don't worry, they'll be here."

Kirk said, "Go up to the street. Make sure they can find the place."

The shorter man hurried out. Renka took the dirty dishes and glasses into the kitchen and started washing them. Cook paid no attention to him. When he finished, he asked Cook if he should stay. Cook shook his head and told him to leave. That's when Renka had to make a decision. He'd hoped Cook would want him there. He went to the back door. Cook and the waiter were arguing about something Johnson had ordered. Renka walked quickly back through the kitchen. He was going to say he'd forgotten something if Cook and the waiter noticed him. They didn't.

Renka eased through the swinging doors into the dim dining room. The shorter man was still outside. Kirk was at the back of the booth. The partitions between booths were tall enough that Renka could crouch down and not be seen. He got as close as he could to the corner booth, dropped to the floor and crawled on his belly under a table. The partitions ended a foot from the floor. He snaked his way slow and quiet against the back wall until he was close enough to see the laces on Kirk's shoes.

If anybody bent down and looked under the table, they'd spot him and the jig would be up. If they didn't spot him, maybe he'd learn what Kirk was up to. Now, Renka didn't say as much, but I know what it's like to crawl under a table in a bar and you don't want to do it. But, hell, he'd crawled out of trenches in France.

By and by the waiter brought a plate of sausage and kraut. He tried to be friendly but Kirk cut him off and said he had business to conduct. Sometime later, Renka heard the front door open and footsteps approached the corner booth. He recognized the shorter man's voice.

"These is the guys Little Philly told us about—Ickie Eccles and Skinny Egidio."

By turning his head, Renka could make out three pairs of shoes.

One of the guys said, "Pleased to make your acquaintance. We understand you might have some work."

Kirk answered through a mouthful of sausage. "That's right. I would handle this myself but it's good to spread the wealth. Spig and Little Philly tell me that you two can be counted on to do a job and not ask questions. That true?"

One of the guys laughed. "For the right price, there's nothing we won't do."

"Good. What I need is simple. Get rid of one guy. It's got to be done tomorrow morning, understand? I know where he's going to be and he won't be expecting anything so it'll be easy if you've got the nerve."

The guy laughed again. "Ask Gando Simonetti if we've got the nerve. Course, you'll have to dig him up."

"Little Philly mentioned that when he recommended you. He also said you have guns and a car. Is that right?"

Renka heard pistols being pulled from holsters. "Yeah, I got a car."

"Put those away. The guy you're after is Jimmy Quinn. Little guy. Uses a cane. He's got a bar down on West Twenty-Second Street. Early tomorrow morning, he's going to leave there, probably in an old Chevy flatbed with a wooden body. You can't miss it. He keeps it in an alley behind his place. He'll be driving north to 442 East Ninetieth Street. Probably come up First Avenue. He's never been there so he'll be going slow, looking for the address. It's close to the intersection with First. I want you to pick him up on the way. Stay close behind him but get ahead of him right before he turns on Ninetieth. That way, after you make the turn, he'll be behind you. You stop in the middle of the street, you get out. He can't go anywhere. Boom, boom, you take care of him. Got it?"

"And we get fifty each. In cash."

"That's right. Here's twenty-five each now. The rest after the job is done and if you handle it right, I've got more work."

Kirk's feet shifted. Renka figured he was passing bills across the table. "Come back here tomorrow night for the rest."

"We really appreciate—"

Kirk said "Scram," and went back to his sausage. The two kids scrammed.

The shorter man sat in the booth. Kirk said, "A couple of punks, that's the best you and Little Philly could manage? Christ, if you and Lois hadn't fucked up on the subway this afternoon, I wouldn't be doing this."

"He's lucky is all, and I gotta tell you that Asa is getting antsy. He knows something wasn't kosher about the telephone call to Quinn. We gotta keep an eye on him, I tell you."

"So keep an eye on him, Christ, have I got to do everything here?"

The two men groused at each other until Kirk finished. He told the shorter man to leave a buck on the table. Kirk wheezed as he slid his butt across the seat to get out of the booth, then pushed heavily off the table as he stood. As soon as he and the shorter man were out the front door, the waiter came out of the kitchen. He locked the front door and collected the money on the table. Minutes later, all the lights went out and Renka heard him leave.

Renka got up from the floor and went over what he'd heard. Ira Kirk is calling himself Johnson, and he's trying to kill a guy named Quinn. His nephew Asa is working with him but he doesn't know everything that Ira is doing. More to the point, any doubts he'd had that Ira and Lois Kirk had something to do with his wife's death were gone.

• • •

I refilled his glass and touched it with my own. "And the next morning, you saved my sorry ass from those two jackleg punks."

Renka sat back down on the sofa and almost smiled. By then he'd had a lot more to drink than he was used to and the words came easier. "I was curious to see if it really was murder that Ira was planning. I went back to my room and washed up. By then I was renting a place. Didn't sleep much because it seemed like the more I learned about what Ira was really doing, the less sense it made. But, of course, there was still more to do. In the morning I cleaned the Colt and strolled up to East Ninetieth to see what I could see."

I turned to Connie. "And he saw just what Kirk said he'd see. The two punks swerved around me and stopped just like they were supposed to. But when they did that, me and Arch got caught by a red light and they had to wait."

Renka nodded. "When I heard their tires squealing around the corner, I knew what was coming, and that was the first time I saw their faces. Too young for what they were trying to do. At first they stopped in the middle of the street. Another car went through the traffic light and laid on the horn. They saw it wasn't you and moved to the curb. A few other cars passed and when the light changed, they pulled out into the middle of the street."

"I remember that part. I can close my eyes and see every detail. They charged the truck but before they got a shot off, you showed up. Both of them fired at you and missed."

"They were running. They were excited, maybe a little crazy. Not thinking."

"I've seen that before. But, tell me, why did you help? You didn't know me."

"I knew that Ira wanted you dead. You had that on your side, and it seemed likely that you'd know more about what he was up to than I did."

"I guess I do. Have you ever heard of the Liberty Foundation?"

He shook his head.

"Just to be sure I understand this next part, you heard Ira Kirk talking to Ickie and Skinny about killing me and he said I had a place down on West Twenty-Second Street. After you clipped them, you decided to look it over. I saw you that afternoon in front of the Chelsea, right?"

He nodded.

"And Tuesday night, you were there when Jenny Pris came out?"

"I thought I recognized her when she walked in, but I wasn't sure. I've been watching your place hoping that Ira would show up. I haven't seen him in Yorkville for more than a week."

"That night you and Jenny Pris talked. She told you that Ira got her husband a job in New York. Asa set up an office in a building on East Twenty-Seventh Street. He shares it with an outfit called the Liberty Foundation. It looks like the Liberty Foundation publishes pamphlets written by Brandon Pelltierre III and sends them out to libraries and colleges and such. In these pamphlets Pelltierre tells you what he thinks about all kinds of things from the Negro Problem to the Bonus Army. Did Asa ever talk about anything like that?"

Jenny Pris looked confused and surprised. "Are you sure that's where he worked? He never told me."

"Yeah, it's his office." I decided not to mention that I had his keys or how I'd come by them. "I've hired a Continental detective to keep an eye on it. This afternoon I heard that she has learned something but I don't know what it is yet. Expect I'll hear from her soon."

Renka said "*Her*?"

I ignored him. No time to explain. "Here's what you don't know. They tried to get me two other times before this. Couple of guys mugged me near my place one night when I was walking home and somebody tried to push me in front of a subway train. That's what you heard Kirk talking about. Asa made the call that lured me there. Then yesterday when Connie came back, a woman on the dock was ready to take a shot at me. I didn't get a good look at her face but I'm pretty sure it was Lois Kirk, who has been working at my place under the name Anne Green. There's also some business involving an accountant who was pushed in front of a subway train and a New Jersey assemblyman who was poisoned by bad booze last Christmas. Asa had newspaper clippings about both of them as part of his proof. He also had a handbill from the Workers Ex-Service League and one of something Hitler said. By the way, Connie was in Paris and I think Anne Green was intercepting telegrams that she sent to me."

I probably told them too much too fast. Renka didn't know what to make of me. I could tell he was trying to decide which question to ask first.

Breathing hard, Jenny Pris said, almost yelling, "How can you say all those things? Asa couldn't have been involved with anything like that, this is all a mistake, it doesn't make any sense. I can't believe it, I don't believe it."

She broke down in sobs. Connie moved next to her on the sofa and put her arm around the girl's shoulders. "Where's Asa?" she cried. "Please, why won't somebody just tell me where my husband is? He said we were leaving and now I'm stuck here. You talk and talk and talk and you make up these awful stories and everything just gets worse."

She sobbed. The emotion was raw and the naked fear in her voice made her sound even younger than she was. "Where's Asa?"

Renka and I stared at each other not knowing what to do. Connie helped her stand, kept an arm around her shoulders, and said, "I know it doesn't make any sense. They don't understand what you're going through right now. Come in here and lie down and rest for a time, go to sleep."

She led the girl into the smaller bedroom and closed the door.

A few minutes later she came out and went straight for the wine. Poured a glass, drank and glared at us. "You have no idea what it's like to be a young woman alone in a strange city like this. Abandoned. You don't understand her at all."

"What are you talking about?" I said. "He didn't even know she was here until a couple of nights ago and I've been busy with a few other things."

Connie didn't say anything for a long time, just stared at us. Then, "She's pregnant."

Renka's eyebrows went up. I said, "She told you that just now?"

"No." She gave me her cold look. "I knew it the moment she walked through the door. Actually, I suspected it when you told me how scared she was when she came into your place by herself the first time. So, Jimmy, where is her husband?"

Chapter Thirty-Four

It was about one o'clock Friday morning when Theodora Opperman came into Jimmy's Place. Marie Therese recognized her, poured a brandy and told her to wait until last call. After the customers left, Frenchy and Marie Therese joined her at the bar.

"Your boss has got himself into one hell of a mess," the detective said. They probably agreed though Frenchy didn't mention it when he told me later.

"He really needs to hear what I've got to say. Face to face."

Marie Therese blurted, "He's at the Pierre, so's Connie."

"She's back then, good, and that was him at Pier 57 yesterday. As if I didn't know."

Frenchy went to the telephone behind the bar and called the Pierre switchboard. When he reached me, he said, "Your detective is here. She says you've got yourself into a hell of a mess and she needs to talk to you."

Maybe something was working out, I thought. "Is Arch there? He could drive her."

"No, a guy came earlier, a colored guy, wanted to talk to him. Arch said you knew about it and he had to leave."

A colored guy? What did that mean? Hell, maybe something else was working out. "Tell her to take a taxi and have the cabbie watch out for a tail. Ask for Mr. Patterson in the Gerry Suite, and there's something else. Is Fat Joe still there?"

"Hell, no. You know he's the first one out the door when the lights come up."

"Figures. Since Arch is gone, can you and Marie Therese stay there tonight?"

"You think they're going to try something?"

"I don't know, but Arch stayed last night. It's better if somebody's there."

"We'll take care of it."

Frenchy, Marie Therese and Fat Joe came with the place when I bought it. Fat Joe collected his pay. Frenchy and Marie Therese thought they had more of a stake in the joint than I did. In some ways they were right.

I hung up and said to Connie, "That was Frenchy. Mrs. Opperman's got something to tell me." I turned to Renka. "She's the Continental detective I told you about. Been listening in on the Liberty Foundation. I want to hear what she has to say. So do you."

• • •

She got there about a half hour later. Connie jumped to the door at her knock. They hugged and whispered to each other before she came in.

The detective sat on the sofa where Jenny Pris had been and lit a Fatima. I poured her a whiskey. "This is Caleb Renka. It looks like he's been involved with all this longer than I have. We'll get to that by and by. What have you got?"

She opened her notebook. "All of this will be in my final report in more detail. For now, I'll give you the meat of it."

I said to Renka, "I rented the office next to the Liberty Foundation and arranged it so you can hear what goes on in there."

The detective rolled her eyes at "arranged."

"I spent a day in the office and we also have a provisional operative who takes shorthand stationed there. On Tuesday night, a man came into the Foundation office and she overheard a telephone conversation. The secretary had been told that her boss, Mr. Sturdivant, was going to be there, so we can assume it was him. We don't know the identity of the man he was talking to. Much of their conversation means nothing at the moment. It concerned men named Jerry, Doyle, and Butler who are involved with men from Wall Street who claim to be willing to pay three million dollars for something. They have already come up with eighteen thousand in 'cold hard cash.' Sturdivant said that 'Brandyboy,' presumably referring to Brandon Pelltierre, is ready to pay a hundred and six grand for something."

Renka whistled through his teeth at the amounts of money she was talking about. Figure it was no coincidence that Asa Kirk had come up a hundred and six grand in "estimated expenses."

"Sturdivant and the other man do not like someone named Asa Kirk. Sturdivant admitted to getting rid of men named Lanning and Shea. He intends to kill Quinn and he's not worried because Chink Sherman will show up eventually."

"Chink!" That was a solid punch to the gut I hadn't expected. Hearing the name surprised Connie, too, but the detective didn't notice that. She was watching for my reaction and she was pleased that I was surprised.

Mrs. Opperman explained to Renka, "Chink Sherman is a known gangster and dope peddler. Quinn knows more about him than I do."

"Only what I read in the papers. Chink and I don't get along. Never have. I hear he's laying low somewhere upstate." That was true enough. I didn't mention that the last time I saw Chink was in the Pennyweight mansion. I'd just shot his partner who was trying to queer a big dope smuggling deal that Chink and my friend Walter Spencer were engaged in. And the partner had raped Spence's wife.

"The telephone conversation was Tuesday night. On Wednesday night, there was a meeting in the office. We think it was between Sturdivant and the man he spoke to on Tuesday. They began by talking about a botched attempt to kill Mr. Quinn on Pier 57 that morning. They were unhappy with a woman who was involved. Later there was an attempt to follow the man who picked up luggage at the French Line office that evening. It sounded like they were talking about Arch Malloy, a Mick who works for Quinn. The second man lost Malloy in Newark. Sturdivant then admitted that he is playing on Mr. Pelltierre's patriotism to get money from him, Sturdivant said that Pelltierre had recently given him two thousand. Some of the two thousand was to be used by the second man to bribe Democratic politicians in New Jersey."

She looked at me. "Sturdivant said he was going to flush you out."

Connie said, "And I thought this sounded nut's when Jimmy described it."

I asked Renka if he could add anything to what the detective said.

"No, the name Sturdivant means nothing to me. Describe the man."

Mrs. Opperman said, "I can't. I've never seen him. I know he smokes cigars and drinks whiskey. He has a heavy tread and a loud voice. I suspect he is a large man."

Renka said, "I'm looking for a large man named Ira Kirk. His nephew is Asa Kirk. I knew both of them two years ago when I was part of the Bonus Army in Washington. They helped provide food.

WELCOME TO JIMMY'S PLACE • **201**

So did Ira Kirk's wife Lois. I think they were involved when my wife was injured on the night they burned our camp. She died from those injuries a year later. Right after she died, a friend of hers told me that Lois Kirk was at our hut that last night. I've been looking for her and Ira ever since. He's living in Yorkville under the name Johnson and he paid two kids to shoot Quinn."

I said, "We also know that Ira Kirk recommended his nephew to someone, probably Pelltierre, for a job in New York. Before Asa Kirk and his wife Jenny Pris moved to Brooklyn, Ira Kirk left Maryland. He told everyone he was going to the Great Lakes Naval Training Center but he probably moved to Yorkville."

"There are too many Kirks to keep up with here," the detective said. "But I think what you're getting at is that Ira Kirk, Johnson and Sturdivant may be the same man."

"They all want to kill me," I said. "And here's something else. Asa Kirk is the guy who started all this. Before I hired you, he claimed that he knew somebody was trying to kill me and for five hundred clams, he'd tell me all about it. He came to my place one night and gave me two names. Herk Sturdivant and Spig Dolan."

"Spig Dolan? That cheap con." Then Mrs. Opperman was shocked.

"I couldn't believe it either." I saw that Connie and Renka didn't know what we were talking about. "Spig's a lowball grifter who's been in business since I was working for Arnold Rothstein. He's always trying to glom his way into somebody else's action and peel off a slice of it."

Mrs. Opperman said, "The second man mentioned being part of a check kiting ring that worked out of Greenpoint last year. Sturdivant accused him of trying to cheat his partners."

"That's Spig all over. So, figure that Pelltierre hired Ira Kirk and Spig Dolan to do something that includes killing me. He also hired Asa Kirk, but Jenny Pris, that's Asa's wife," I said for Mrs. Opperman. "She says that she thought they hired Asa because he was so good at getting people to talk about themselves, and he could handle a lot of paperwork."

I turned to Renka. "Does that square with what you know?"

Renka nodded his head. "Both Asa and Ira were friendly. Like I said, they were on our side. Ira was Navy. Said if he wasn't still working for the Navy Department, he'd be there with us. The only time I ever saw him get mad was when one of the Weasels laid into him about never bringing sandwiches to their camp. Asa said the Reds had no business getting mixed up with the veterans, and he got so worked up he grabbed the man and threw him against the wall of a hut. He was a good-sized man. Knocked over the hut."

Mrs. Opperman said, "Do you think he might have been looking to infiltrate your group, to identify radicals for the government?"

She knew what she was talking about there. Continental operatives had been used often enough as strike-breakers against the Wobblies and other unions.

Renka said, "There was nothing to find, not in our camp. Sure, there were communists in some of the other camps but everybody knew who they were and we had nothing to do with them."

"Ira never asked any questions about them?"

"No. He and Lois just brought sandwiches. Lois was always asking my wife if she needed anything for the little clinic she ran out of our hut. More than once she bought things from the drug store and paid for them herself. That's why it still doesn't make sense to me that she'd hurt Miriam. They got along fine."

Mrs. Opperman looked confused. I couldn't blame her, I was having a hard time keeping all the names straight myself. In the years I'd known the detective, I'd seen her angry, determined, crafty, sympathetic, suspicious, uncertain, and disappointed. Never confused.

"You need to hear Renka's whole story to understand what he's up to, but now's not the time."

"I know," she said. "My problem is that now I have direct knowledge of the intention to commit a crime."

"It's my problem."

"And you're thinking you'll handle it by walking into that office and putting a bullet in his head."

"It has crossed my mind."

Connie said "Jimmy!" like she couldn't believe it, at the same time the detective yelled "Forget about it."

I ignored them. "I'm not going to do it because killing him doesn't tell me why. For now, keep your stenographer in place and find out everything you can about Brandon Pelltierre. Whatever's going on, looks like he's bankrolling it."

Mrs. Opperman thought about that before she spoke. "Alright. For now, I'll stay on it. My trip to Washington was not productive. There's not enough in what we've heard to take to the police, I know some men on the force who'll bend the rules to put the right people away, people like Dolan, but not with what we have. If you're still around when this is over, I want to know the whole story."

She left. Connie went into the little bedroom to check on Jenny Pris. She stayed there for several minutes. Renka and I drank. When Connie came back, she switched from wine to whiskey, and sat in the chair close to Renka. She said the girl had been asleep but she woke up and heard some of what we'd said with Mrs. Opperman.

"She's more scared now than she was before. She doesn't understand what you were saying about the Kirks. What she needs right now is for you to be in there with her. She shouldn't be alone."

Renka leaned away. "No, it's not done, her being a young woman with me in a bedroom."

"Don't worry about that. You're the only person she really trusts. She needs somebody to be close to her. You don't understand what she's going through."

Renka and I looked at each other. Connie was right, we didn't understand.

"Please," she said. "I only met you a few hours ago and I have no right to ask anything of you, but, as a favor to me, please go in there and stay with her. At least until she goes back to sleep. Believe me, I wouldn't ask you to do this if I didn't know how important it is for her."

For a long moment, Renka sat with his eyes closed. After he opened them, he nodded his head and went into the bedroom. Connie and I went into the big bedroom.

• • •

Much later, naked in bed with the covers kicked off, I asked her why she wanted Renka to stay with the girl. "You think it's that important?"

"Right now it is. She needs a friend to be close to her, somebody who doesn't scare her like you do."

"What're you talking? I don't scare anybody." I slid closer and rubbed her stomach. "He's her friend but put them together in bed and he might be something else."

"She might need that too, and you know it."

"What do you mean?"

She rolled up on one elbow and looked at me seriously. "Where is her husband? You really haven't seen him since that night he came to the place?"

"No. I've been thinking about it and I can see two possibilities. The first is that Sturdivant and Spig tumbled to what he was up to. For months, the kid has been setting up this office, making decisions, spending money—and signing checks—then he begins to understand that besides printing and sending out Pelltierre's stuff, something else is going on in the office that isn't kosher. He learns that his bosses have something to do with two accidental deaths. Then they bring him in to make the bogus telephone call to me and he knows he's in over his head. He also understands the people he's working with are dangerous. You follow?"

She nodded.

"He sees that I'm the kind of guy who might have enough cash on hand to get him and his wife out of town. He gathers this proof, cleans out his office. Or maybe he left whatever proof he had back at the office on Twenty-Seventh Street and when he went back to get it, they caught him. Or maybe they were watching my place and were waiting for him when he came out. However they did it, they got hold of him and his proof, and they killed him."

"You think they'd do that?"

"Spig's a mean son of a bitch. I wouldn't have said he had the balls for murder but the truth is I don't know him that well and until we were on the dock, I hadn't seen him in years. And if what Renka says is right, this Sturdivant or Kirk likes to have other people do his dirty work."

I rolled on my side to face her. "Until tonight, I figured that was likely the case. But now, I don't know. Suppose that while Asa's figuring out what his bosses are really up to, he learns his wife is pregnant. He thinks he's too young to be a father, he doesn't want to be tied down. Hell, he's just as scared as she is, and he does what young guys do when they're scared. He runs. Forget about her, forget about Sturdivant and Spig, forget about me, just get out of the city. Run.

"I don't know if I told you this, but he also said that what he was doing was part of some larger plan. He made it sound like something bigger than he could describe. He said Spig and Sturdivant were one team and there were other teams. Sure, he could have been blowing smoke, but he sure as hell made me believe he was frightened."

She moved closer, put her arm around my neck. "What are we going to do?"

"We're going to sit tight until we know more. There are worse places to be than this joint. Arch is trying to get to people who have worked on Pelltierre's household staff, and the fat detective's on his trail. Let's see what they come up with."

Chapter Thirty-Five

The sun woke me up around eleven Friday morning. Connie had pulled the curtains closed but they didn't do the job like the blackout curtains at the Chelsea. I got dressed and found her drinking coffee and reading The *Times*. She held a finger to her lips and whispered, "Be quiet. They're still here."

A room service breakfast tray had replaced our dinner tray. I had a bagel and lox. Renka came out of the bedroom and closed the door carefully. Connie poured him coffee. He took it to the sofa. She asked how Jenny Pris was.

Still looking uncomfortable, Renka said, "She had trouble sleeping, but I guess she's all right now." He turned to me. "Who are those men the detective mentioned, Dolan and Chink somebody."

"Chink Sherman. He sells drugs. Used to work with Waxey Gordon during Prohibition. I can't say I know him well. Don't know Spig Dolan that well, either. He's a grifter, a con man. He has a reputation as a guy who will do anything if the money's right, and he gets enough people to trust him that he stays in business. I don't think much of either one of them."

Renka said, "What's the connection to you? You say you have no idea why they're after you. You own a bar? That's it, and you're staying in a place like this? Are you sure there's nothing else about you to know?"

Connie's eyebrow arched up. "Is that it, Jimmy? You're just a simple businessman?"

"O.K., before I owned a bar I ran some booze, stole some cars, this and that. Been arrested a few times, never charged. Nothing ever came of it. Until this business started I'd never heard of Brandon Pelltierre and I hadn't laid eyes on Spig Dolan for fifteen years."

Renka said, "You were a gangster."

I was going to set him straight but we stopped talking when Jenny Pris came out of the bedroom. Connie hurried over. They whispered and Connie ushered the girl into the bathroom.

Renka said, "She needs to go back to her apartment to get some things. I should stay with her."

I found one of my cards and wrote the number of the Pierre on the back. Handed it to him. "I'm going to call the detective. I hope she'll tell me she knows about another meeting at the Foundation office. If Kirk is going to be there, I'll introduce myself and he'll answer some questions."

"It'd be good if you were that lucky but you can't count on it." Renka turned the card in his hand, fumbling for what he had to say. "I hate to ask this since you've already helped us out." He waved a hand meaning the bed and the meal the night before. "Could you loan Jenny Pris a little more money. Like I said, her rent's due on the fifteenth and her landlady's getting impatient because she's been late before. You know what it's like."

I slipped him a twenty. Why the hell not? As a man of leisure living in the Pierre, I was made of money.

After they left, I called the Continental Agency and left a message for the detective. For the rest of the afternoon, I sat around in the bathrobe. Connie gave my suit to Anthony the Assistant Concierge and told him to have it cleaned and returned pdq. She also ordered two new shirts and underwear for me from Macy's and had them delivered. I read the papers and listened to the radio.

• • •

Renka called back that evening. "He shot her. He was waiting for us in front of her building." His voice was hoarse and I could hear his cough over the telephone line.

"How bad is it?"

"I saw worse in the war but it's not good."

Connie couldn't hear what he was saying but she could tell something had gone bad and came over next to me.

"Where are you?"

"Bellevue. The ambulance brought us here from Brooklyn."

He said they'd taken a taxi from the hotel to her apartment on Lincoln Place. The cabbie double parked and Jenny Pris got out first while he paid the fare. Middle of the day, the narrow street and sidewalk were loud but

Renka still heard running footsteps. He and Jenny Pris were close to the stoop of her building. He turned toward the sound and saw a man running toward them and pulling at a pistol in a shoulder holster. Spig Dolan. Jenny Pris was between them.

Renka shoved her toward the stoop. She yelled and tried to break her fall. Without stopping, Dolan cleared his holster and fired. Renka charged, trying to put himself in front of the girl. Dolan kept running and fired again at Jenny Pris. Renka grabbed at his gun hand. He got Dolan's wrist and twisted his arm up.

The gun went off. Dolan staggered back a step.

Like the guys who came after me under the lamppost, Dolan didn't think somebody would attack him, somebody who knew what he was doing. Renka tried to knee his crotch and got his stomach. He held onto the gun arm and grabbed at Dolan's throat. Got his tie, pulled it hard. Dolan gagged and clutched at his throat. Renka swung him into the side of a parked car. The pistol went off again. The bullet hit the sidewalk at their feet and bits of concrete exploded around them. People nearby must have been yelling and running away by then. Dolan fell backward. Renka was able to keep Dolan's gun hand trapped between them. He let go of the tie and chopped Dolan's face repeatedly with the side of his fist until Dolan went still.

By then, a lot of people were milling around them, most of them crowded around Jenny Pris and Renka. The left side of her thin cotton dress was soaked with blood. A man was pressing a handkerchief to the wound. Somebody yelled to call an ambulance. The girl's face was pale. Her breath was rapid and shallow. Somebody said they thought she lived in that building. Somebody else asked Renka who he was. He said he was her friend, and he'd seen wounds like this in the war. He should stay with her. It was important that she could see him and hear his voice. He asked if anybody had another handkerchief or pocket square, and took over with the direct pressure when he got them. It seemed like an hour before the ambulance got there. He didn't know what happened to Dolan.

"On the way to the hospital," he said, "I told the medic she was pregnant and he made sure they sent her to a special emergency room. Since I'm not her husband, they won't let me stay with her."

I was holding the earpiece so Connie could hear him. She grabbed the telephone from me and said, "I'll be there as fast as I can."

She pulled a new coat from the wardrobe, put on a beret and found her handbag.

I said, "Wait 'til they bring my clothes. I don't like you going without me, and Renka's with her."

"It's broad daylight. There'll be a thousand people in the hospital. She needs me to be there and I'm going."

"You heard what he said, Dolan shot her in the middle of the street. Nothing's stopping them from trying again."

"Not in a hospital," she said and kissed me.

"Then take this." I pulled the little kraut automatic out of the pocket of the bathrobe.

She shook her head and left. I waited for my clothes.

• • •

I was still waiting and worrying when Arch knocked on the door an hour later.

"Where the hell have you been?"

"Harlem. I may have good news, but I need a drink first. Why are you wearing a robe?"

Chapter Thirty-Six

Some people said Bellevue was the biggest and busiest hospital in the world. Maybe it is. I know it was in a lot of buildings spread out over a dozen square blocks down on First Avenue near the East River. After Connie got out of the cab Friday afternoon, it took her more than twenty minutes winding through corridors to find the "special" emergency room Renka mentioned, where Jenny Pris should have been. But when Connie got to the gunshot ward, or whatever they called it where people who'd been shot were taken, the nurse in charge looked through the admission records for the day and told her that after they learned the girl was pregnant, they moved her to another ward in Obstetrics. That nurse gave Connie directions to the place but by then Connie wasn't sure she could find anything, and so she asked the woman to draw a map. She did.

Connie followed it, looking for signs as she walked, and finally found Obstetrics behind two double doors with glass panels. She was about to push them open but when she looked through the glass, she stopped and moved to one side. Spig Dolan was standing at a circular nurse's station. Even with black eyes and bandages on his face from Renka's beating, she recognized him from Pier 57.

It looked like he wanted something from the nurse who was in charge there, and the woman was having none of it. Even if Connie couldn't hear what he was saying, she could see that he was trying to persuade the woman in white, leaning close and smiling, hands held palms up. Her mouth was set in a straight line, arms were crossed over her chest, and she shook her head at everything Spig said. Finally, she uncrossed her arms and pointed to the double doors. Spig didn't stop talking until she picked up the earpiece of a telephone and dialed.

Connie backed around a corner behind the door. Spig shoved it open and stomped down the hall. She waited until he was out of sight before she went to the nurse's station.

The head nurse was still steamed. Connie said, "I think the man who was just here wanted to see my friend Jenny Pris Kirk. I'm Connie Nix. Can you tell me how she's doing?"

The nurse shook her head. "What's going on with that girl?" The way she gave Connie the once-over, Connie could tell she was still suspicious.

Connie almost told the truth. "Her husband has gotten involved with some people who promised him a lot of money. He trusted them. He shouldn't have. Nobody knows where he is now. I think those people are threatening Mrs. Kirk to get to him."

The nurse's anger cooled and, Connie told me later, she thought the woman might have felt sorry for Jenny Pris or at least been curious. She said, "Then the girl should talk to the police."

"She can't."

"What's she to you?"

"Like I said, she's my friend. I just want to be sure that she gets the best care and no one disturbs her. What can I do to make sure that happens?" Connie leaned forward and put her hands on the partition between them. The corner of a twenty peeked out beneath her fingers. It was about as much as the nurse made in a week.

As casually as Connie offered it, the woman slipped it into her apron pocket. "I'll see that doctor is aware of the specifics of her case."

"How is she doing now? How worried should I be?"

The nurse's expression was serious. "We don't know. She's sleeping. She was treated as soon as she got here. There is an exit wound so they didn't have to remove a bullet. That's probably a good sign, depending on where she was hit. I haven't seen her chart."

"The man who came in with her when she was admitted, is he still here?"

"I don't think so. The waiting area is back down that hall on your right. I tried to make it clear to him that visitors are almost never permitted on this ward, certainly not when a woman has been shot."

"And the man who was just here, what did he want?"

"He claimed to be her uncle. In a pig's eye, he's her uncle. Here." The nurse wrote a number on a slip of paper. "If you want to find out how she's doing tonight or tomorrow, give the switchboard this extension when you call. If I'm not here, tell anyone who answers that Nurse Beasley okayed it."

"Thank you. Will you be here tomorrow?"

"No, I'm here tonight and I have the weekend off. I'll be back on Monday."

Connie wrote the number of the Pierre on the back of a Jimmy's Place card. "If there's any change or anything you can tell me, please call this number. Ask for..." She paused to remember the name I'd used to register. "Mrs. Patterson."

The head nurse broke a small smile.

• • •

Connie walked more slowly and paid more attention to the people around her as she made her way out of the hospital. No sign of Dolan. As long as she was inside the building, she felt confident she hadn't been spotted. Outside, trying to hail a cab on First Avenue, where dozens of impatient men were jockeying for an empty taxi, it was different. Then she had the same stomach-clenching feeling of a target on her back that I'd been living with since the jackleg bastards shot at me on Ninetieth Street.

She jumped when someone touched her arm. It was Renka.

Chapter Thirty-Seven

Arch asked where Connie was, disappointed she wasn't there. I told him she had gone to Bellevue to see Jenny Pris Kirk. "One of the guys that have been after me, the guy who followed you to Jersey, shot her in front of her apartment this morning. She was here last night with the soldier that saved our asses. His name's Renka."

I gave him a short version of what Mrs. Opperman and her stenographer had been doing, and Renka's story about the Bonus Army, the death of his wife and his coming to New York. "The kicker is that Jenny Pris is pregnant."

"He shot a woman with child?" His soup strainer mustache bristled like it did when he got really angry. "And this Sturdivant character is actually Ira Kirk, her uncle by marriage. There's a nasty piece of work for you. How is the girl?"

I poured two whiskeys and gave him one. "That's what Connie is trying to find out. Now tell me about Harlem. What were you doing there?"

"Mr. Henderson, the gentleman who supervises the maintenance crew that cleans the Liberty Foundation office, came through for us. He's been doing the same thing among his colored associates that I have been doing among the Micks. He let it be known that he would pay for personal information about the Pelltierre family, and he had even less success than I have. For what it's worth, I did manage to locate two men who are on the Pelltierre household staff, young men. I spoke to them and made handsome offers. Neither of them accepted and both refused to explain why. I was left with the idea that it is an extremely severe place to work. Strict rules, and staff are let go regularly with or without cause. They were frightened and wouldn't do anything that would threaten their position."

"And Henderson didn't find anything because Pelltierre would never hire a colored guy to work for him. He wants to ship them all back to Africa."

"Precisely." Arch got up and started walking around the room. "Then last night Mr. Henderson came to Jimmy's Place."

Arch stopped talking when somebody knocked on the door. It was Assistant Concierge Anthony with my clean clothes. I strapped on my brace and dressed while Arch talked.

"Did Fat Joe let him in?" I could hear him saying something like 'We don't let no fucking coons in here.'

"He didn't want to but I gave Mr. Henderson one of our cards the night I met him. He showed it to Fat Joe and said it was a matter of business between him and me."

"What time did he come in? How'd everybody react?" I couldn't remember ever having a colored customer. You saw mixed crowds often enough at a few places in the Village, and I'd heard there were some like that in Harlem, but the famous joints, like the Cotton Club, were for white people. The entertainment was colored but the customers were white.

"Around eleven. Only customers who noticed him were near the door and the coat check. They probably assumed he was delivering or repairing something. Mr. Henderson was more uncomfortable than anyone."

"What did he have to say?"

"He had something I might be interested in, but it was too complicated to explain there. We needed to talk privately. Frenchy and Marie Therese and Mrs. O'Neal didn't need me at the moment, so I told Mr. Henderson to come with me to the back door, and we went up to your office."

"Where you gave him a drink."

"Of course, wouldn't have been hospitable not to, now, would it? Besides, I had a feeling we were going to be negotiating a price and a bit of lubrication never hurts."

Arch said that Henderson told everyone he worked with and trusted that he wanted to know about Brandon Pelltierre. Like Arch, he thought that if Pelltierre was serious about the back-to-Africa business, he might have had some dealings with the colored people who were trying to do the same thing. For more than a week, nothing. Then that morning, he heard from his aunt, Miss Henderson.

"She called him on the telephone and asked if it was true that he would pay for information about someone named Pelltierre. His aunt knows a young woman who lives in her building and is taking care of an old white man who lives on the next block. His name is Michael Patrick Reardon. The neighborhood's Spanish Harlem. It was Irish and Italian at one time and now you've got all colors living next door to each other and even in the same building. This old man is sick, with some kind of cancer, she thinks. The girl helps with grocery shopping, getting his clothes cleaned, and the like. He can't afford a doctor, and takes morphine for the pain. Sometimes he talks about his life and tells wild stories. She thought he was just making things up about the wickedness he'd been involved in. He claimed that for years he worked for the most evil thing in the city, a place where the richest men committed unspeakable acts. One of them was a Pelltierre. It struck her as such a funny name. That's why her mother mentioned it to Miss Henderson while they were playing Hearts. Ergo, she called her nephew."

Ergo? I'd have to look that one up.

"She said she'd take him to the girl if the price was right. By the way, Mr. Henderson says his aunt is the tightest woman with a dollar he has ever known. He said she might not be telling the whole truth but she probably wasn't lying either. He wouldn't have left work to see me if he didn't think there was something in it for both of us."

"So you went."

"We did, indeed. After a bit of haggling, we settled on ten dollars for him with ten more if it panned out, and five for the penurious auntie. He telephoned her from your office. She was in for a fiver and agreed to see us. We took your car."

Arch got another whiskey and sat on the sofa. I found my notebook and wrote *ergo* and *penurious*.

"I know what you're about to say. Did we check for a tail? Yes. I told Mr. Henderson to keep an eye out for a new DeSoto or anyone who seemed to be following us. We went up to a hundred and tenth unmolested. His aunt lives in a large parlor-floor apartment in a rowhouse, one of the nicer ones I've visited in that neighborhood, by the way. Crosses and pictures of Jesus on the walls. Well-worn bible next to her chair. She is a large woman. Wore a knitted shawl over her dress. Naturally, she was suspicious of a strange white man offering such a large sum for such an unusual item but she welcomed us into her living room. Before we sat down, she closed the curtains on the bay window, doubtless to keep anyone walking by from seeing me. Mr. Henderson knew that he was expected to sit on a long horsehair sofa that might have been made in the last century. I sat at the other end where she could watch both of us from a matching armchair that looked like a throne. He explained that the man I was inquiring about wanted to send black people back to Africa and to place those who refused to go in internment camps. He knew this because he had read the man's writings, and this man was rich enough to back up his ideas with actions.

"Then I told her that this man, Pelltierre by name, had also threatened my employer. More precisely, he tried to kill him three times. If she would arrange for me to meet with this young woman who claimed to know something, I would pay her five dollars and if this young woman had anything important to tell me, I would give Mrs. Henderson another five, and the young woman would be suitably rewarded, at least five, more if her information warranted. Mr. Henderson vouched for all I said. His aunt was silent for a moment while she considered our offer. Then she nodded her head and a girl came in from the back of the house. She crossed the room quickly to stand close to the older woman.

"The aunt introduced us, saying 'Louise, this is my nephew, Mr. Henderson. He and this gentleman would like you to tell them about Mr. Reardon.'

"The girl was twelve or thirteen, long coltish legs. Simple dark dress with a white collar. Hair pulled back, not straightened. I thought at first my being there made her uneasy but I soon learned that was wrong. When she spoke, she sounded confident and more mature than she first looked.

"She said, 'I've known Mr. Mike all my life. He's a bachelor. My mother has done his laundry for as long as I can remember, and I help with pick-ups and deliveries. He always treated me proper, even when I was little. I played with his dog and cat. When I got older, he gave me a key to his apartment and paid me to walk his dog, and to take his dirty clothes back to be cleaned. Sometimes when he was busy at work, he wouldn't be able to come home for two or three days, and I'd feed the dog and cat. He even said I could use his apartment to read and do my homework after school. He was never there and it is a lot quieter than anyplace else. Ma liked him because he always paid on delivery and never asked for anything on credit. His clothes were nicer than most of her customers', but sometimes there were bloodstains that wouldn't come out. When Ma asked what he did for a living, he said he was the manager of a men's club.'"

She said Mr. Reardon changed six months ago. When she and her mother came to pick up his clothes, they found him hung over, something they'd never seen. He told them he'd just learned that he was sick and he'd been let go from his position. He wasn't sure what he was going to do. He felt lost. Her mother said that she could cook for him, at her home, and Louise could bring meals over. He started crying then, and blessed both mother and daughter.

At first, he just stayed in his apartment and didn't go out. It wasn't long until the pain got worse. He refused to see a doctor, said it was his time, his punishment. Somebody was selling him morphine, but he wasn't a typical addict. Got it as a liquid that he drank. He wasn't using because he wanted to and so he'd let the pain go too far before he tried to ease it and that's when he'd lose touch with where he was, and begin to talk nonsense. He paid Louise to stay with him, and so she heard him talk about Cerberus, and Pelltierre, and a plot to oust President Roosevelt. She told her mother about them and her mother mentioned it to Mr. Henderson's aunt at their regular Hearts game.

Arch said, "At that point, I interrupted her and said that my employer and I would very much like to speak to Mr. Reardon and would pay if that could be arranged. I assumed both of them would jump at it, but the girl was reluctant. She stepped up from Miss Henderson's side and said, 'How do I know you won't try to hurt him?'

"I said, 'Did you hear what we told Miss Henderson while you were in the other room? This man Pelltierre is extremely wealthy. He's almost certainly a member of the men's club your friend Mr. Reardon managed. That doesn't concern me. Pelltierre has hired men to kill the man I work for. If Mr. Reardon can tell me why, we will make it worth his time. And yours.'

"She frowned and shook her head. By then it was well past midnight. I asked if Mr. Reardon might still be awake. She said he probably was. I suggested that she and Mr. Henderson walk over to his apartment, since a girl of her age should not be out on the street alone at that hour, and explain the situation. If Reardon didn't want to see me, I'd leave him alone. Of course, that was a lie. Once Henderson knew where the gent lived, we could find a way to get to him, but the girl accepted it. Half an hour later, they came back and she said he'd see you."

I finished knotting my tie. "All right, what now?"

Arch picked up the telephone earpiece and gave the hotel switchboard operator a Harlem number. "We arrange to meet Mr. Henderson."

Chapter Thirty-Eight

We drove about three miles north on Fifth Avenue across One Hundred and Tenth Street. We went from one of the swankiest hotels in the city to a loud crowded block where people were getting ready to have a good time on a warm Friday night. The colored men and women dressed with more style and flash than most of my customers, and the activity on the street reminded me of Chelsea. On a night like that I should have been behind the bar at Jimmy's Place and it made me mad that I wasn't. But, no, don't get angry, that doesn't accomplish anything. Be determined. Listen to what this man has to say and then use it against these rat bastards who are out to get you.

Arch parked in the middle of a block of rowhouses. A black man who'd been sitting on one of the stoops got up when he saw the green Ford. Mr. Henderson. About thirty, six feet or better, hair clipped short, mahogany complexion, well-tailored suit in a shade of brown lighter than his skin, bright tie, new fedora. Arch shook his hand and introduced us. He didn't move to shake mine.

"Louise is with him," he said. "I just came from there. It's this way."

We walked a block and a half in the direction we'd been driving. It must have been at least a little unusual to see two white men on that street. We got a lot of second glances, and I've got to admit that being one of the only white guys surrounded by black guys was something I hadn't experienced. I didn't have any reasons to go that far uptown for business or for fun. I wasn't used to feeling so out of place.

Henderson led us up the steps of another row house. He opened the front door with a key and we went up narrow dim stairs to a second-floor apartment. A large dog barked on the other side of the door at his knock. The girl opened the door and held the collar of a large brown terrier that pulled at her arm.

"Lass, no, stop that," she said. The dog growled until she said "no" again. It stopped growling but still didn't want us there.

Heavy curtains were closed and the place was even darker than the stairs. It smelled of the dog and a sick room. I remembered the smell from Mother Moon's last weeks, and my chest tightened at the memory. The girl said to Mr. Henderson, "I told him you were coming. He says he wants to talk, but, well, you'll see. Sometimes he's hard to understand."

A quavery voice from the bedroom yelled, "Louise, are they here?"

"Yes, Mr. Mike. Do you want me to send them in?"

"I need to see you first."

She hurried toward the back. Beaded curtains rattled as she went through a doorway. The dog sniffed at me and then went to Arch to be petted.

I said to Henderson, "Do you know this guy?"

"No, just that his family's always lived here. He was born here, in this apartment, they say."

The only light came from one small table lamp, so you couldn't tell much about the furniture or the size of the place. The girl parted the curtains and said "Mr. Mike's ready."

The bedroom was a little brighter with two bedside lamps. The man was in a comfortable chair propped up with pillows left and right, his legs covered by a lap robe. Reddish hair, thin wrists. Despite the warmth of the room and the day, he wore a sweater and sweat dotted his forehead. Books were stacked on every shelf and table and on the floor.

He turned on another lamp so he could see us better, and took a sip from a small brown bottle. It was never far from his shaky hand. "I understand you gentlemen want to know about the Cerberus Society." There was a hint of Ireland in his voice, and whatever drugs he was using gave him a half-mad look. Make that more than half.

I was tired of screwing around so I didn't go for small talk. "I don't know what that is. My name's Jimmy Quinn. I've been told you know Brandon Pelltierre. He's trying to have me killed. I want to know why. Can you help me?"

His mouth twisted up in an unhappy smile. "What's in it for me?"

"Money," I said.

"And much more. A confession and absolution," Arch said. "A soul cleansing admission of all your sins, and not to some mumbling padre who understands nothing of what you've done, but to someone who might still be able to correct a situation you helped create."

I had no idea what he was talking about, but it looked like the man in the chair understood. He said, "Forgiveness is beyond me now. This cancer is the punishment I deserve, but a confession, a full and complete testament of all that I have done in the name of the society, that is a story that should be told."

He sat up straighter, "While I still have breath to tell it."

I took a stack of books off a kitchen chair and moved it so I could see and hear him clearly. "Fire away."

"You're an impetuous young man, you don't understand. This isn't a simple 'I did this and he did that' sort of story. It began years ago." His voice dropped to a whisper, "when the baby was kidnapped."

He was staring right at me when he said those last words and I felt the hair stand up on the back of my neck.

"That was a terrible time, so terrible the very heavens opened up."

"The blizzard," I whispered. "The wind."

His expression changed. "You remember."

"How could I forget?"

"It frightened them horribly. It made them understand they were mortal. That's when the plotting started, and now they mean to bring down the president. If no one stops them, they will destroy him from within."

"Who are they?"

His voice dropped so I was the only one who could hear him. "The Governors, Brandon Pelltierre and Peter Wilcox."

If I hadn't been sitting, my knees would have buckled. Peter Wilcox had good reason to want me dead. I knew the truth about his family.

"This is going to be a long story," I said. "Let's get started."

Reardon shook his head and slumped back in his chair. "Oh, no. To tell it properly, I must prepare. I tire easily. Perhaps tomorrow."

I started to get steamed, thinking the guy was trying to pull something until Arch stepped in. "I can see how that would be difficult for you. Perhaps there is another way." he said. "Could young Miss Louise join us?"

The girl must have been on the other side of the beaded curtain. She came in, followed by the big terrier and a plump brindle cat. She went straight to Reardon's chair and adjusted his pillows. "I knew you'd tire him out, it doesn't take much" she muttered.

Arch said, "Mr. Reardon was just telling us that he feels a need to make what will be, I think, be a fairly lengthy confession. Perhaps he could put it in writing—"

"Yes," the sick man said, sitting up again, "it must be written for the world or at least for someone to know the truth. A testament."

The brindle cat jumped to the arm of the chair and then to the top where it stared at me. I'd seen a cat like that before. Like he was suddenly exhausted, Reardon sank back in his cushions. His eyes shut and the bottle he'd been drinking from almost fell from his hand. The girl caught it and said, "He needs to sleep now." She pushed us back through the beaded curtain to the front room, and then eased the bedroom door partly shut.

Trying to stay calm and sound reasonable, I said to the girl and Mr. Henderson, "I really need to know what he has to say. Tonight."

She shook her head and looked to Henderson for support.

He gave me a hard stare. "If Louise says no, that's it."

I squared up on him but before I could say anything, Arch butted in. "I think we already have a solution."

Chapter Thirty-Nine

The note I'd left for Connie read:

6:00. Arch found a guy
who may know Pelltierre.
We're going to Harlem.
—JQ

She showed it to Renka when they got back to the Pierre Friday night and said, "Those two in Harlem? What next?"

She picked up the telephone earpiece, asked for Room Service and then for the sous chef who made the chicken with garlic. When he got on the line, she asked if he could whip up a simple steak au poivre and pommes frites. Four orders and send up more of the red wine right away.

"I hope you're hungry," she said. "Would you care for a drink?"

Renka said, "I think I'll wait for the wine."

Connie took off her beret and sat on the sofa. When she told me about it later, she said she could tell Renka was uncomfortable being alone with her. She said, "Tell me more about what happened this morning."

He went through the attack again and said that after he talked to us from the hospital, he took the El back to his apartment to get his pistol. "Guess I shouldn't have been surprised, not after the way those gunsels went after Quinn, but I never thought they had a reason to want Jenny Pris dead. None of this makes sense."

"Ain't that the truth."

"And excuse me if somebody explained it to me last night, but what is your part in all this? You're Quinn's girlfriend, I think, and you just got back from France?" He gestured toward her suitcases.

223

"It is hard to explain. Yes, I'm Jimmy's girlfriend. I also work for him. I'm a waitress and the bookkeeper and I keep track of orders and payments and I redecorated the place while Jimmy was getting his licenses. His place was a speak, a speakeasy during Prohibition and he had to work like a Turk to keep from being shut down after Repeal."

She stopped to think. "What else? Yes, France. Not too long ago I came into some money. That part is really hard to explain, but I always wanted to go to Paris and I promised myself that as soon as I could afford it, I wasn't going to let anything stop me. Jimmy wasn't crazy about the idea because he couldn't leave, not while so much was going on with Repeal. I sailed on June second and had a wonderful month before I got the first telegram that said Jimmy had been shot and stabbed.

"It was signed by Marie Therese, a woman who works with us, but it wasn't from her. It was from the guys who are after Jimmy. Then there was a second telegram. I tried to call him, couldn't get through and so I got on the next boat to New York. They were waiting for Jimmy at Pier 57 on Wednesday."

Renka scratched his chin. "They really want to kill that little guy."

"That's why we're here at one of the nicest hotels in the city because it's Jimmy's idea of a swell place to hide out, not that I'm complaining."

• • •

It was around eight when Arch stopped behind the Pierre and let me out. He said he was going back to work. "Frenchy and Marie Therese will be needing me. It'll be busy, and I'll stay the night again. Don't worry, I'm keeping a careful count of my expenses and overtime hours. We'll settle up after we've fixed these bastards."

"Keep a piece close at hand. They shot the girl on a busy sidewalk in Brooklyn. I doubt they'll do anything at the bar if I'm not there, but what do I know? And remember, there's a woman involved, the woman who slowed me down in the subway and tried to shoot me on Pier 57. I think it's Anne Green and she's really Lois Kirk, but that isn't important. Just keep an eye out for her. If anything happens tonight, call me."

He drove back to the bar. I waited for a minute, watching for the DeSoto or Spig Dolan, before I walked down Sixty-First Street to the side door of the hotel lobby and the elevators.

Connie was opening a bottle of wine as I opened the door. I poured a short whiskey over ice and started to tell her and Renka about Harlem when room service knocked. Connie had the waiter set the table for three. When he lifted the first dome and I got my first whiff of steak au poivre and the sauce I forgot what I was going to say. The chicken the night before had been damned impressive. By the smell of it, this was even better. As they say, I wouldn't want to try to make a living on the difference. We weighed into it with a will, and the three of us had no trouble taking care of four orders.

Renka pushed back from the table and said, "I know it's not polite to eat and run but I want to get back to the hospital to check on her."

Connie said, "I'm sure visiting hours are over."

"Let me worry about that. There are ways to do these things."

"If she's still there, the woman in charge is Nurse Beasley. I asked her to see that they take special care of Jenny Pris. If she's not there, use her name."

I said, "Before you go, one thing. Have you ever heard of something called the Cerberus Society?"

"No, what is it?"

"I think it's a club that Pelltierre and some other rich guys belong to. A guy who used to work there is going to tell me all about it. For now, it's just something I didn't know this morning. May turn out to be nothing."

He left and I started to tell Connie about Harlem. She shook her head. "No, call Mrs. Opperman first. She needs to know about it."

I had the hotel switchboard call the Continental agency, expecting to leave a message so late on a Friday evening, but the detective was there. She spoke quickly.

"Are you still at the hotel?"

"Yes."

"Stay there. Don't go anywhere. I'm on my way."

• • •

The detective got to our room around ten o'clock. She had a manila folder under her arm. Connie hugged her and asked what she was drinking. Since we didn't have any good brandy, she took whiskey.

She gave me a bleak stare and said, "I don't know that I've ever been involved with a case that's as cockeyed as this one."

Connie said, "It's not getting any easier. Last night we talked about Jenny Pris Kirk, the girl who's married to Asa Kirk."

"I was confused about that part. Too many people named Kirk. I'm still confused."

"She's married to the young guy who said he was going to tell me who's trying to kill me. Nobody's seen him for more than a week. He's the nephew of the character who's calling himself Sturdivant."

Connie nodded. "Jenny Pris was asleep in the other bedroom while you were here. Stayed the night. When she went home to her apartment in Brooklyn this morning, Spig Dolan shot her. She's in Bellevue."

"What do the police say?"

"We don't know," I said. "Even though it happened on a sidewalk, looks like Dolan got away clean. Renka, the soldier you met last night, he was there. Laid into Spig pretty good. Renka left with the ambulance before the cops got there."

"The doctors aren't letting anyone see her."

The detective shook her head, and lit a Fatima. "That explains part of this," she tapped the folder, "but before we get to it, let me fill you in on the other parts of the investigation. On Tuesday, I took the night train to Washington and met with Ferdinand Pecora Wednesday morning."

Connie frowned. "Who's that?"

"He ran the Senate investigation that uncovered the double dealing that the big bankers had been up to before the Crash," I said. "Mitchell Shea, the accountant that got pushed in front of a subway train, used to work for him. Asa Kirk had a newspaper clipping about it in his wallet, and on Tuesday night in his office, Sturdivant copped to killing Shea."

"I wanted to talk to Pecora to find out if there was anything else in Shea's background that made him a target. The only thing I learned didn't seem to have anything to do with this. Before Shea worked for the investigation, he was fired from a job with a bank after his bosses pressured him to buy the bank's stock at an inflated price. His case was never part of the public hearings. It wasn't illegal either and it was over more than a year ago, so I thought that angle was a dead end. Until I read this."

She tapped the folder again. "Last night, I told you a provisional operative has been stationed in the office Quinn rented. That young woman has been listening and copying down what she hears in shorthand and then coming back to the Agency office and typing her reports. That's what she was doing this evening. Earlier this afternoon she overheard a conversation between Sturdivant or Kirk, if that's his name, and Dolan.

I didn't understand the first part until you told me about the girl being attacked. Sturdivant talks about it. He also talks about his attempts to kill you and..., well, I'll let you read it for yourself and you'll see that you're in over your head."

She stopped, trying to decide what to say next. "Last night I told you I'm troubled by the crimes that are being planned and admitted to. What the Agency is doing—listening and recording what we hear—that's not illegal, but it's not anything we can take to the police. I'm not sure about continuing, particularly with this young provisional operative. You'll see that she's not comfortable with her part in this either. She's willing to stick with it, and she's careful to put down what she hears and nothing more. But now that Sturdivant has attempted to murder a woman, on a sidewalk in broad daylight I can't let this girl go back there."

"Of course not," Connie said.

"I wouldn't ask her to sign on to that," I said. "What about doing something else, her and you?"

"Depends on what it is."

"Earlier tonight I met a man up in Harlem who says that he knows Brandon Pelltierre from the years when he worked for something called the Cerberus Society. Ever hear of it?"

The detective lit another cigarette. "There's been rumors of a hellfire club with a name like that for years, but nothing more than rumors."

"What's a hellfire club?" Connie said.

"A place where rich guys do things they're not supposed to do, and that may be what this is, I don't know. Anyway, this guy I met, Michael Patrick Reardon, he worked for the Cerberus Society till they fired him because he's old and sick. Now he's taking morphine for the pain. He drinks it, no needles. He nods off and his hands are so shaky he can't write. But he wants to confess. He says they're 'plotting' at this Cerberus Society, Brandon Pelltierre and someone else. Another rich guy, a banker."

I turned to the detective. "I will bet you a dollar it is the same banker Mitchell Shea ratted out to Ferdinand Pecora. Peter Wilcox."

Connie sucked in her breath at the name. She knew who I was talking about.

"What the hell's going on, Quinn?"

"I still don't know, but this man Reardon has another piece of the puzzle."

"How did you find him?"

I ignored that. "I want you and your provisional operative to go to his apartment and write down whatever he says. It's up in Spanish Harlem. He's ready to talk. A colored girl takes care of him. It may take more than one visit. Sounds like he's got a lot to say and he can't stay awake very long. You and your girl won't have anything to do with Sturdivant anymore. This is part of the same investigation so we won't need another contract. What do you say?"

"How will we arrange it?"

"Here." I found the number for Henderson that Arch had given me. "Call this number and talk to a colored guy named Henderson. He can work out the best time for you to go to Reardon's apartment."

She drew heavily on her cigarette and squinted at me through the smoke. "I don't have any trouble working with spades. Brought in several of them myself over the years, but I will not put this young girl in any more danger. First thing tomorrow, I'll talk to this Henderson and pay a visit to this apartment. If I think it's safe, we'll proceed."

Chapter Forty

It was almost one o'clock Saturday morning when the detective finished. After she left, I opened the folder. It was a carbon copy of five typed pages. I read it once quickly, then again more slowly. Connie was impatient and wanted to know what it said. I made her wait until I finished the second round. I handed it to her and poured two short grease cutters. Her eyes went wide at the same places that surprised me. When she finished, I gave her the drink. She sipped it as she read a second time slowly. This is what it said:

Stenography and transcription by Provisional Operative T.S., Friday, July 13, 1934, 5:50pm.

At 2:48pm I was in the office on 27th Street. I heard heavy footsteps in the hallway, followed by the opening of the door to the office under surveillance. Mrs. Booth, the secretary, said, "Mr. Sturdivant. I didn't know you were coming in today." His reply was loud, unintelligible and angry. Mrs. Booth gathered her belongings and left quickly. Mr. Sturdivant entered his office. He was breathing loudly. After the sounds of some activity, I heard liquid being poured and the smell of alcohol came through the grille.

Mr. Sturdivant dialed his telephone and was silent until he cursed and hung up the earpiece. He repeated those actions several times until 3:11pm when the door of the office opened a second time and another man came in.

Sturdivant: Where the [obscenity] have you been? [Obscenity], you look like [obscenity].

Second man: [Obscenity] you. I had to dodge the [obscenity] cops. Then I had to clean up the blood and get bandaged. Then I had to go back and get the [obscenity] car.

Sturdivant: What happened?

Second man: She came in a cab. There was an old guy with her. Never saw him before. I hit her once before that [obscenity] came after me. He [obscenity] near killed me, feel like I went ten rounds with Max Baer.

Sturdivant: What's he look like?

Second man: White hair, skinny. What's going on here anyway? First, you say the girl wasn't a problem, then you say I got to get rid of her. I don't like this.

Sturdivant: You think I [obscenity] like it? It's just another problem and not a big one. If she's out of commission now, that's good enough. The payoff hasn't changed. Remember that. Oh, h---, sit down. Have a drink.

More liquor was poured.

Sturdivant: Look, none of this changes anything. I talked to Brandyboy this morning and I'm meeting him tonight at his club. I told him what we need, and I'm going to show him the first part of the plan I worked out. That [obscenity] Kirk was supposed to handle the paperwork. Now it's up to me and this is where we've got to be careful. The money's almost in our hands.

Second man: Yeah?

Sturdivant: After I explained it, he said that he could have $106,000 ready by next Wednesday, and [obscenity] you wouldn't have believed how calm he was when he said it. The money really doesn't mean anything to him. With all he's got, that much is nothing. It's just a matter of choosing which accounts to withdraw it from, he said.

Second man: [Obscenity].

Sturdivant: This is it. Payday. When I got started with Brandyboy and Wilcox, I worked for nothing, h--- less than nothing. I was keeping an eye on the Bonus Army and I spent more on bread and baloney than they paid me.

Second man: What do you mean, bread and baloney?

Sturdivant: I made up dozens of sandwiches every day and spread them around in the camps where the most seditious activity was going on. I gathered my evidence carefully—and not just small talk and the usual Red [obscenity]. I got names; I got carbons of Bureau reports; I got pictures. H---, I even got my hands on a surplus trench mortar, and when I described it all to Brandyboy and Wilcox, I turned those poor starving saps into a force so threatening that now they're willing to shell out 106,000 bucks to get rid of Roosevelt.

Second man: [Obscenity.]

Sturdivant: I couldn't have done it if that [obscenity] hadn't got elected. They really hate his [obscenity] and they're willing to do anything and spend anything to put him out of commission.

Second man: It's set for Wednesday? At their place?

Sturdivant: Right. You and me and Brandyboy and Wilcox.

Second man: And 106,000 big ones. [Obscenity.]

Silence.

Sturdivant: But I've still got work to do. As a mark, Brandyboy's a [obscenity] dream, but I can't just tell him I need that much dough, I got to show him what I'm going to do with it. He wants the details of the European trips, cost of tickets and hotels, and he's got to see everything about the guys who're being bribed, how much they need to be paid, dates, and what they can do for it, and how we've got to stick with the three-year plan to put the men in the house. The little [obscenity] was supposed to handle it, but he took most of the documents about the districts we're going to recruit and maps when he [obscenity] cleared out. I'd give anything to get my hands on the little [obscenity].

Second man: Can you do the paperwork?

Sturdivant: It's almost finished.

Silence.

Second man: What now? You want me to go back, keep an eye on Quinn's place?

Sturdivant: I don't know. He's got to come back there sometime. The sooner I can tell Brandyboy he's dead, the better. Then the way's clear for her to put her man in and we seal the deal. The trick is to flush him out.

Second man: I told you, he's in New Jersey.

Sturdivant: I don't think so. I think that Mick [obscenity] made you when he picked up her bags. They went uptown after you and Lois [obscenity] it up on the pier. Quinn's a city boy. Why would he go someplace he don't know to hide out? And what about Asa's little wife? You said every time she went to see Quinn, she took the subway. She didn't take the subway this morning. She was in a taxi.

Silence, then fingers snapped.

Sturdivant: That's it. She found Quinn. Her and this old guy, they know where he is.

Second man: So?

Sturdivant: They probably took her to Bellevue. Go there and find out how she's doing. Call me or meet me later at the rathskeller. I got to think this through. And I've got to take care of her. The [obscenity].

The second man left at four o'clock. Mr. Sturdivant left ten minutes later.

• • •

After she finished her second reading, Connie said, "They were having this conversation about the same time Caleb called us."

"Right."

"I didn't have a chance to tell you I saw Dolan at the hospital. He was trying to pressure a nurse into telling him about Jenny Pris. And don't bother to ask, no, he didn't see me."

She drained her grease cutter and turned off the lamp closest to her. She opened the curtains, turned off another lamp and started to unbutton her dress. "I don't understand everything they were saying but I understand enough. We've got to let Jenny Pris know her husband's alive."

I turned off the last lamp, loosened my tie, toed off my shoes. There was enough light coming up from the street to watch her as she carefully put the dress on a hanger and hung it in the wardrobe. She crossed the room and pulled me out of my chair by my tie. Took it off, unbuttoned my shirt.

I said, "Next thing, we need to find out where this meeting is going to be."

She said umm-hmm and unbuckled my belt. Then she turned away and strolled to the bed, while she unfastened her brassiere. She put it and her underwear in the bureau before she threw the covers back and slipped into bed. There was just enough light for me to make out her smile. I stripped off the rest of my clothes and joined her. When I put my arms around her, she snugged in close.

"This changes everything," I whispered into her hair.

"It sure does," she said. "A hundred and six thousand dollars." She slid her thigh up over my hip, pulled me tighter.

Chapter Forty-One

The telephone in the room rang around noon on Saturday. It was Arch. He had a lot to say.

"Mr. Henderson called this morning. He said your detective had been in touch with him and he wanted to be sure it was the same arrangement we discussed last night. Check her bona fides, so to speak. We agreed on amounts for the girl Louise, his aunt and him, with a minimum of fifty dollars for Mr. Reardon. More if he has useful information."

"How much more?"

"Don't worry about it," he said.

"Did Henderson say anything about when they'd start?"

"This afternoon."

"Good."

"And I think I spotted your old acquaintance Spig Dolan hanging around outside early this morning. I took out trash after we closed and checked both ends of the alley. Close to Eighth Avenue, I saw the glow of a lit cigar in that shadow by the place with the garden in back, you know what I mean."

"Yeah."

"I made a show of chambering the Colt. A man spat out the cigar and ran out of the shadow down Eighth. I only caught a glimpse of him but it was Dolan, no question. I stayed the night. Slept on your divan."

I told him about reading a transcript of the conversation between Sturdivant and Dolan. "That was early yesterday afternoon. They admitted to trying to kill Jenny Pris and they said that it's important for them to tell Pelltierre that I'm dead. Now here's the part I really don't understand—they want to kill me so they can get rid of Roosevelt."

"The president?"

234 • MICHAEL MAYO

"Teddy's dead and it's not Eleanor."

"Did they say anything to explain why killing you has anything to do with the president?"

"No, but I hope to ask them before I shoot them, and there's something else. They mentioned money. One hundred and six thousand dollars. Pelltierre is going to give to Sturdivant on Wednesday night. I don't have an address yet."

"Now, **that** is interesting."

"It gets even stranger. The detective learned that the accountant, Shea, was working for Pecora because of some shady stuff at a bank that fired him. And you couldn't hear him yesterday, but Reardon said that Pelltierre has a partner in this Cerberus business. They're the same guy—Peter Wilcox."

"The dirty moving picture man!" Arch was with me on the night more than a year before when we saw a two-reel silent version of *King Kong* with a black guy in a gorilla suit screwing a girl who looked nothing like Fay Wray. Peter Wilcox paid for it to be made. He was also involved in some nasty business between his wife and his father, Learned Wilcox. Nasty business that I thought I was done with.

"One and the same."

"Wouldn't it be grand to take that swine down a notch or two."

Connie punched my arm. "Give it to me, I need to talk to him."

I handed her the telephone and the earpiece.

"Arch, as soon as you can, go to Bellevue. I'd go but Jimmy says we can't risk being seen there. Jenny Pris is in a special maternity ward. It's hard to find but you'll manage. Yesterday, they weren't letting her have any visitors. They probably won't let you in, but she needs to know that her husband Asa is alive. It was in the conversation Jimmy was telling you about. They said they wanted to kill him because he ran off with some things they needed."

Arch said something I couldn't hear, then Connie said, "They don't know where he is and neither do we, but Jenny Pris has to be told that he isn't dead. Listen, yesterday I talked to the head nurse, a woman named Beasley. I'm pretty sure she runs the place. I let her know that we want to be sure Jenny Pris has the best care possible. She won't be in until tomorrow but I think if you mention her name at the nurses' station, it'll carry some weight. If they won't let you see her, have the nurse tell Jenny Pris that her friend Connie wants her to know her husband's alive."

He said something else. Connie said, "Then write it down. Oh, and keep an eye out for Dolan. I saw him at the hospital yesterday, and on the transcript of the conversation, Sturdivant said you made him when he followed you to New Jersey."

Whatever Arch said after that made her smile.

• • •

Renka knocked on the door of the suite in the middle of the afternoon. He said he was on the way to Bellevue and wanted to know if anything had changed.

Connie said, "Sit down, Caleb, you need to read this."

I handed him the transcript, and explained what it was and how I got it. He read it the same way Connie and I had, once quick, once slow. His expression didn't change but I saw the way his hands gripped the pages and the way his shoulders tightened and the flush that came to his face and the hard set of his pale gray eyes. He put the pages down and said, "That son of a bitch. While he was smiling and dealing out dry sandwiches and telling us what a great thing we were doing, he was trying to frame Miriam and me as a couple of Reds. And Meriam said that the last thing she remembered was seeing Lois taking pictures in our hut that night."

"Part of the frame," I said. "Cops don't have evidence, they plant it, and Kirk and his wife weren't even cops. They were just trying to cook up a story that would get Pelltierre and Wilcox to shell out more dough. Figure that night at your hut, your wife saw Lois planting evidence. Kirk was close by. He came up behind her and hit her in the back so hard it tore a kidney and knocked her unconscious. Didn't matter to them whether she was alive or dead in all the confusion. They take their pictures and scram. Have I got any of that wrong?"

Renka considered what I said and shook his head.

I said, "And now they think it's about to pay off when they collect a hundred and six thousand dollars."

I stopped to make sure he was paying attention.

"I'm going to steal it."

"How?"

"I don't know yet. Will you help?"

"If you'll promise me that I will get to face both of them and make them admit what they did."

"I can't promise that, but I will do everything I can to keep them from getting away and I'll try not to kill 'em before you talk to them. Is that fair?"

Renka said it was fair, but things didn't work out that way.

Chapter Forty-Two

When Marie Therese called that night, I could hear the sounds of a loud Saturday crowd at Jimmy's Place. She kept her voice low, almost whispering. "Detective Ellis is here. He wants to know where you are. What should I tell him?"

"Put him on the line."

He grabbed the earpiece from her. "Where are you, Quinn? I need to see you. Now."

"About what?"

"Don't ask questions. Where are you?"

"None of your business. I'm laying low for a few days. What do you want?"

"Screw that. Where are you?"

"What's going on?"

"I told you no questions. Now, spill. I'll close this place down right now and get a warrant if I have to."

"All right, keep your shirt on. I'm at the Pierre. And don't let anybody follow you. Watch out for a new DeSoto."

"Be in front in twenty minutes."

He hung up the telephone.

Connie knew something was wrong. I explained who it was and what he said.

"It's got to be something serious for him to be sounding like such a hardass."

She said she was coming with me and got dressed. I strapped on the brace, considered carrying a pistol and thought better of it. Downstairs, we stayed close to the building, out of sight of most foot traffic on the wide sidewalk until an unmarked four-door sped down Fifth Avenue. With squealing tires and a short blast of the roof siren, it braked to a stop. Ellis got out on the passenger side blocking another lane of traffic. The driver behind him laid on the horn. Ellis slapped the guy's fender and bellowed, "Police business!"

Connie and I crossed the sidewalk and climbed into the back seat. A uniformed cop was behind the wheel. He hit the siren again and swerved out into the southbound traffic. Ellis twisted around, his arm on the seatback, and noticed Connie.

"You're back already."

She shrugged. "Things happened."

"You shouldn't be here. But it's good that you are. I've got questions for you, too."

Neither of us knew what that meant. The driver ignored stoplights and used the siren when it suited him. We danced through traffic down to Greenwich Village. When we got into the narrow little streets, he turned right. We wound up on Christopher Street. He stopped in front of a new-looking three-story apartment building tucked between two taller buildings. Another cop car was parked in front of it, and there was a uniformed cop in the small lobby. He handed Ellis a large manila envelope with a string fastener.

"They left these for you, sir."

Ellis didn't answer and went up the stairs off the rear of the lobby. No elevator. I lagged behind with my stick. The smell of strong soap that stung my nose started on the second floor and got worse as we climbed. It was a small building with two apartments on each floor, stairs in the middle. No cooking smells and no sound except our footsteps. Another uniformed cop was waiting on the third-floor landing. One large apartment took up the whole floor. The cop stepped away from the door and we went into a living room that had been wrecked. An armchair and a splintered console radio were on their sides. Looked like the radio had been thrown against a wall where the wallpaper was torn. Another chair was upside down in the little kitchen that opened off the living room. The soap smell made Connie sneeze.

Ellis was breathing hard from the stairs. His tie was pulled loose and he'd sweated through his hat band. He lit a cigarette with a gold lighter that matched his cufflinks and his flashy gold watch. "Is this place familiar, Quinn?"

"No, what're you talking about?"

"One of your employees lives here. Lived here"

"It's not Frenchy or Marie Therese or Arch or Fat Joe, I know where they live. That leaves Anne Green and Katherine O'Neal." I turned to Connie. "Your replacements."

Ellis said, "It's Anne Green. If that's her name. When was the last time you saw her?"

"She was scheduled to work last Tuesday, but I don't remember if she did. She and Mrs. O'Neal swapped nights whenever they wanted. She was scheduled for Wednesday but I had to leave early. Haven't been back since. What do you mean 'if that's her name'?"

"I'll ask the questions," Ellis said.

Connie broke in. "What happened to her?"

"I said I'll…" and he stopped talking when he got his first real look at her. She was back in the short blue skirt and top. She'd put on heels and had a small blue and silver hat pinned to her hair. He didn't know what to say and stalled by clearing his throat. He'd never seen her looking like that or acting like that, standing straight, shoulders squared, looking him in the eye. She wasn't the waitress he thought he knew.

"Somebody killed her. There's no sign of forced entry so she might have let him in. The Medical Examiner says it happened," He unwound the string on the envelope and read from a typed form, "between eleven o'clock Friday night and one o'clock this morning. They fought in this room and the bedroom. He killed her in the bathroom."

"Who called it in?" I asked.

He read through the report. "At first we thought the cause of death was multiple gunshots but the Examiner says those are post-mortem. Whoever killed her bashed her head against the back of the tub, but some of her facial injuries occurred earlier, more than two days. Here." He handed me six big black-and-white photographs.

They were as bad as I've ever seen. The body was in a bathtub with pieces of a shattered mirror. Blood was smeared and splattered on the white tile. Her mouth gaping open. Skull flattened against the porcelain. Bullet holes and powder burns on a white blouse I recognized. When I think about those pictures, my stomach still churns.

Connie said, "Let me see them."

"You don't want to."

She took them. Her face went white at the first one, and she handed them back without looking at the rest.

Ellis said, "What do you know about her?"

"Not much. I didn't even know she lived in a place this nice. It's got to go for seventy, eighty a month. I don't know how she could afford it on what I paid her. Her tips were good but not that good. Said she was a war widow from Chicago. Had a boyfriend who's a musician. Customers liked her, but you know that. You flirted with her often enough."

"Yeah, well."

"Neighbors must have heard something."

He shook his head. "Second floor is vacant. Landlord on the first floor says he thought he heard something Friday night but he was listening to the radio."

"Who called it in?"

"Friday and Saturday mail was still in her box."

"O.K.," I said. "Why am I here? You know I didn't have anything to do with this."

"Why did you hire her?"

"Marie Therese said she needed a job."

"That's what Marie Therese told me tonight. She said the woman came in early one day, as soon as you opened, and told her that she'd heard you were looking for a waitress. Is that right, did you buy an ad in the paper, put a sign on the door?"

"No, I was going to but as soon as Connie talked about her trip, Marie Therese said that her friend Katherine O'Neal had experience and was looking for work. I figured the same went for Anne Green."

Ellis shook his head. "She says you hired her the same day she came in."

"Marie Therese is a soft touch."

"So are you," Connie said.

"From what Marie Therese said, I thought Katherine O'Neal wanted a full-time job, but when I talked to her, she said she didn't. Anne Green was there and said she was happy to get anything. Hell, I needed somebody."

Ellis frowned. "Yeah, that's what Marie Therese said. Come here." He went into the bedroom. It was torn up like the living room. Clothes were thrown around and the dresser drawers were open. Sheets half ripped off the bed. Vanity overturned. Cosmetics scattered on the floor. I could see the bathroom through an open door. They'd taken the body away but they hadn't cleaned all the blood. Connie glanced at it and looked away.

"What do you know about Joyce Robinson? Phillipa Purcell? Amelia Harris? Mary Reagan?" Ellis said.

I shook my head. "Nothing. They're just women's names."

"They're names on drivers licenses. I found them at the back of the bottom dresser drawer. Joyce Robinson has a New York license. Phillipa Purcell is from New Jersey. Amelia Harris has one from Maryland. Mary Reagan's was issued by California. The physical information on each one for height, weight, age, eye color and hair color matches Anne Green's, and each of them is in a cheap leatherette coin purse with fifty dollars in ones and fives."

"Are they good fakes?"

"About average."

"Look," I said and wandered over to the closet. "She told me she had a musician boyfriend and she said she'd worked at speaks in Chicago, so I figured she'd been around the track, but she didn't do anything that made me think I needed to worry about her."

The closet door was cracked open. I use the tip of the stick to push it wider so I could see inside.

"Get away from there," Ellis barked.

I'd seen what I wanted. "Looks to me like she was ready to scram out of here pdq."

"And she had reason to," Connie said.

"What else do you have?" I asked.

"This," Ellis said. "It's the reason I'm talking to you. Found it in a waste can."

He handed me a creased slip of flimsy buff-colored paper that had been crumpled and straightened out. It was a French Line telegram from Connie dated July tenth, Tuesday, and addressed to Marie Therese at my place. It read: WHICH HOSPITAL? ARRIVE TWO DAYS. CONNIE

I gave it to Connie. A big piece of the puzzle.

Ellis said, "What does it mean? What was she doing with a wire from Connie to Marie Therese?"

Connie said, "I don't know what she was doing with it but I can tell you what it means. Jimmy didn't want me to go to Paris in the first place and so he and Marie Therese came up with this little scheme. She sent me a telegram saying he'd been hurt and might die at any time. I had to come back as soon as I could. I tried to make a Transatlantic telephone call and got through to Jimmy's Place but nobody on this end could understand me. I sent more telegrams but they didn't answer, so I cut the trip short and came home."

Ellis glared at me. "Is that right?"

"I got lonely. What do you expect? I knew she'd be pretty steamed when she learned the truth and that's why I booked us a suite at the Pierre."

"He was hoping it would be kind of a honeymoon without a wedding."

Put that way, Ellis bought it. "Did anybody threaten her at work? Any guys hanging around waiting for her to get off?"

"No."

"She ever mention anything else about her private life?"

"No, and you said the landlord didn't hear anything, right?"

He nodded.

"So who called it in?"

He stared at me hard before he answered. "Nobody. I found her."

I didn't ask if he had a key.

Chapter Forty-Three

Ellis stayed in the apartment. His driver took us back to the Pierre. Connie and I didn't say anything on the way uptown. We had too much to think about. I wanted to tell her what I'd seen in the closet, but the cop behind the wheel would report anything I said to Ellis. It figured I'd be talking to him again soon enough and I'd have to tell him something, but not yet, not until I knew more. It was around eleven Saturday night when we got to the hotel. Upstairs, the door to the suite was cracked open. I pushed it the rest of the way with the tip of my stick and slipped on the knucks.

Theodora Opperman had let herself in and poured a whiskey. "Don't worry about anybody else bothering you here," she said. "I know the house dick. He let me in and he's keeping an eye out for you. He also said you left in an unmarked department car."

"That's right." I went to the sideboard with the booze and picked up a bottle of wine for Connie. She asked for whiskey. Ice, no soda. I made two and said to the detective, "What brings you here?"

She looked from Connie to me, waiting for one of us to explain the unmarked. To me it was the same with her as it was with Ellis. Things were about to reach a point where I was going to have to break some laws to stay alive, and they were going to do what they had to do as law enforcement. No need for them to know too much about my plans. When we didn't answer, Mrs. Opperman said, "All right. Here's what Mr. Reardon had to say. He can only go an hour or so before the dope knocks him out. If the old guy really does have anything important to tell you, it's going to take another day, at least, maybe more to get it out of him."

She handed me a white business envelope with the Continental Detective Agency eye-in-the-upside-down-triangle logotype.

"But it's clear he's thought this out, and he's still sharp. He may forget to button his fly but he remembers what he did while he was working. Take a look at this and then tell me if you want the Agency to continue. We talked to him this morning and again in the afternoon."

I opened the envelope and took out six pages of carbons of an Agency report. It began, "The Cerberus Society was founded in 1895. It is housed in an unassuming five story building at 249 East 35th St. From the street it appears to be a single private address, but the Society also occupies the buildings on either side. Facilities for the removal of incriminating evidence are located in the basement."

Sound familiar? Yeah, you've already read this. I put Reardon's pieces where they are hoping this story will make more sense to you than it did to me while it was happening.

I gave the pages to Connie after I finished reading and asked Mrs. Opperman what she thought.

She shrugged and lit a cigarette. "He's telling the truth. Like I said, I've heard enough rumors about such a group that there has to be some truth behind them. I want to know what else he has to say."

"So do I, as soon as you can."

"The Negro girl is expecting us in the afternoon. She has church in the morning. I'll be in touch."

• • •

As soon as the detective was gone, I took off my coat and loosened my tie. Connie went to the telephone and had the hotel operator call Jimmy's Place.

"Marie Therese, this is Connie. Did Ellis tell you why he wanted to see Jimmy?... No? Listen, one of the women Jimmy hired to replace me has been killed... That's right, Anne Green. She had an expensive apartment down in the Village. Somebody beat her terribly and shot her there."

She listened to Marie Therese for a time, then said, "Don't waste too much sympathy on her. The bitch was intercepting my telegrams to you and Jimmy. Yeah, we saw one there. That's why Ellis wanted to talk to Jimmy... I don't know, we haven't talked about it yet, but it looks like she's been helping the people who're after him. And she and Ellis were screwing... Right, anything you can think of that was out of the ordinary, anything. Call me, or if you and Frenchy aren't too tired, come by here after you close. We'll be up, Jimmy hasn't had anything to eat for a few hours… O.K. but if you change your mind, the invitation stands. Good night."

She hung up the earpiece.

"There's something else you need to know," I said. "When I looked in 'Anne Green's' closet, I saw an oversized blue raincoat on a hanger and a black hat and curly wig on the shelf. She was the woman on Pier 57."

"You didn't recognize her?"

"No, she must've had on some kind of make-up that made her face dark and she was wearing those big black glasses that blind people use. The first time, in the subway, I didn't see her face at all."

"Based on what Caleb and Jenny Pris said, she was Lois Kirk."

"Of course, along with those other aliases she had ready to use."

"And her husband killed her. Had to be him," Connie said.

"He admitted it. Where's the transcript Mrs. Opperman gave us last night, of the conversation between Sturdivant and Dolan?"

"It's in the drawer of the bedside table."

I found it and read through quickly. There it was. "Look at the last thing Sturdivant said. 'I got to think this through. And I've got to take care of her. The [obscenity].' He wasn't talking about Jenny Pris, he was talking about his wife, and he was still angry that she hadn't killed me."

Connie hugged me tight from the back. "We still don't know that, do we, and it's the most important part—why they're trying to kill you."

"We will, but you know it's odd. Jenny Pris and Lois Kirk were almost family back in Washington and, what was the name of that other place, Anacostia? If Lois had been working any of those nights that Jenny Pris came in asking about her husband, everything would've been different."

"Or if she'd seen Caleb before that night he saw Jenny Pris."

She hugged me harder and my stomach growled. "You said something about food when you were talking to Marie Therese."

• • •

Connie told her sous chef to whip something up but I don't remember it. We'd seen too much and learned too much. We reread the transcripts from the detective. The conversation Friday between Sturdivant and Dolan a few hours after they'd tried to murder Jenny Pris. That's when he said the sooner he could tell Pelltierre that I was dead, the better. Parts of it still didn't mean anything. What was their "three-year plan to put the men in the house"? Kirk said "the way's clear for her to put her man in." Who was "her"? So much of it made no sense, but there was no use spending more time on it. I went back to Reardon's testament and his tales about doping girls and getting rid of the bodies of "common street mongrels." At first they were just words on a page but the more I thought about them, the more real they became. And I knew nobody would ever answer for that.

Connie took that part harder than I did. There were tears on her cheek after the third or fourth time she went through it. She shook her head and whispered, "Those poor poor girls."

I said, "Those murdering bastards."

It got worse with the next parts of Reardon's testament.

Chapter Forty-Four

On Sunday afternoon, Connie called Bellevue to check on Jenny Pris. The way she frowned, I could tell she wasn't happy with what she heard.

"You can't tell me anything else?" she said. "Will the doctor be in today? Fine, I'll talk to him."

She was still frowning when she hung up the earpiece. "I couldn't tell what that nurse was trying to say except that Jenny Pris still has a fever and they're not sure about her baby. I wish Nurse Beasley was there."

She put on another of her Paris outfits, a pale green suit that looked not as terrific as the blue number. I slipped fifty bucks and the kraut automatic into her bag. She gave me a look.

"Dolan could still be hanging around and maybe the people at the hospital are worrying about getting paid for taking care of her."

She gave me a serious kiss and whispered, "You really know how to sweettalk a girl."

• • •

Connie was still at Bellevue when Mrs. Opperman came back late that afternoon. She had the next two pieces of Reardon's testament, where he told about getting canned and how the Lindbergh kidnapping scared the bastards who ran the Society so much that they decided they'd have to do something to save the country. That's what led them to hire Ira Kirk, alias Herk Sturdivant, to infiltrate the Bonus Army, and then to his telling them how he accomplished it.

The detective drank some of the good whiskey and smoked a cigarette while I read the pages. She saw how confused I was when I finished.

"What the hell have you gotten yourself into, Quinn?"

Again, I thought about how much I should tell her. "I think I understand more of what he's saying than you do, but not enough more. How's the old guy doing?"

"His attention wanders, and he nods off every so often, but he only uses the dope when the pain really gets to him."

"How much more does he have to say?"

"I think we'll wrap it up tomorrow. He wanted to finish today but the colored girl said he was too tired. Sounds like he's coming to the end unless he thinks of something else."

"Good."

"You know, he thinks you're going to do something to make up for what the Governors did to him. If what he says is even partly true, that wouldn't be easy. It'd be dangerous, maybe even fatal."

I couldn't disagree with her so I didn't say anything.

"Are you going to ask me to help you?"

"I'll plead the fifth on that."

She stubbed out her cigarette. "It figures. You don't know what you're going to do."

She was wrong.

• • •

It was just after dark when Connie and Renka came in. She wanted whiskey. He asked for red wine. Looked like he needed it.

"I told him about Lois Kirk," Connie said.

He shook his head. "Hell of a thing."

"Remember that Jenny Pris said Ira and Lois argued and talked about divorce that summer of the Bonus Army. I think I know what happened after that. Pelltierre and a banker named Wilcox offered Kirk some kind of well-paying job. Kirk needed help with the job. Maybe he and Lois were separated by then, I don't know and it doesn't matter. They left Anacostia at the same time but lived separately when they got here. She moved into a nice apartment down in the Village and he went uptown to Yorkville. He also convinced Asa and Jenny Pris to move to Brooklyn. All neighborhoods where they wouldn't be running into each other. He told Asa that his new boss was Herk Sturdivant. The first night she came to my place, Jenny Pris said part of the reason Asa hated his job was that he never met Sturdivant. He got his orders from messages that came through the office secretary, Dolan, or by wire. And sometime while Ira Kirk was setting up shop, he ran across Spig Dolan, a fellow grifter. He'll do anything for a price and with Spig the price usually isn't that high. He's also been in the business so long that he knows guys. Probably didn't have much trouble worming his way into Sturdivant's con."

"That's one screwy story."

"And here's how it got started." I gave Renka the first pieces of Reardon's Testament. I handed Connie the sections the detective had just given me.

"These came while you were gone."

As they read, I poured a drink. When they finished, they traded and after they finished those, they traded again. When he finished the first two parts for the second time, Renka said, "Is this real?"

"Sure it is. I think you don't understand how rich Pelltierre and Wilcox are. They've got I don't know how many millions between them."

Connie said, "They can spend as much as they want to get anything they want, and it sounds like they believe they can take over the government or at least change it to suit them."

"And they think they've got to kill me to do it. That part, I still don't understand."

I waited for one of them to explain it. They were no help. "Mrs. Opperman thinks she's going to get another part of Reardon's Testament, the last part, tomorrow. Maybe that'll help, but I'm working on some ideas anyway. There's no sense talking about them now. Anybody else hungry? Connie, call your sous chef. And we need more wine."

Chapter Forty-Five

Connie was on the telephone to the hospital early Monday morning. I stayed in bed and tried not to wake up. Didn't work. She and Renka hadn't got anywhere with the nurses and doctors they talked to on Sunday. Nobody could tell them anything about how Jenny Pris was doing and they wouldn't let them see her. Nurse Beasley's shift started at eight o'clock. Connie talked to her for a few minutes before she started getting dressed.

"You learn anything?"

"Nurse Beasley says she doesn't seem to be any worse, but she just got in. She thinks she'll be able to convince the doctor to let me see her."

"Take some more money from my wallet. Show them you're serious. I don't need to tell you to watch out for Spig but I'm telling you to watch out for Spig."

"Caleb's going to meet me there."

Room service knocked on the door and wheeled in a breakfast tray. I tipped the guy and told him to bring all the morning papers. Connie had coffee and left. I drank coffee and listened to the radio until the guy came back with the newspapers. I went through the back pages quickly looking for anything about Anne Green. There was nothing. Ellis must've put a tight lid on it.

I spent the rest of the morning going back over the typed pages from the detective. I made notes as I read. I remembered what Arch said back when this got started and listed what I knew, what might be true and what I didn't know. It didn't make complete sense but it made some sense, and I worked on the few ideas that had come to me.

• • •

Mrs. Opperman knocked on the door as I was finishing my lunch. She took another Agency envelope out of her handbag. She didn't hand it to me.

Instead, she sat back on the sofa and said, "I don't suppose you know anything about a Jane Doe who was killed Saturday night on Christopher Street."

How close to the vest should I play this? "I knew her as Anne Green. I hired her and another woman to replace Connie. I've been told that her real name might be Lois Kirk, from Anacostia, Maryland. Ellis has the case."

"I know that."

"He found the body."

Her eyes got wide. She didn't know that. She tried to cover it up by fishing a smoke out of her bag and lighting it. She slid the envelope across the coffee table. "We finished with Mr. Reardon this morning."

I opened the envelope and found three pages of carbon copies. As I read, I tried not to let any reaction show on my face.

Continuation of statement by Michael Patrick Reardon; Monday, July 16, 1934; 9:20am.

(Personnel same as Sunday, July 15 sessions.)

Stenography and typescript: T.S.

After Mr. Sturdivant had brought out the Stokes mortar, the Governors examined it and the other photographic evidence he'd brought. They were extremely impressed with his work. Sturdivant answered all of their questions.

"Before I go any farther, I have to tell you that Sturdivant is not my real name. It's my current nomme de guerre. I've been doing clandestine work for the government so long that I've forgotten the name I was born with. When I infiltrated the groups that invaded the Capital, I was known as Ira Kirk. I tell you this now to keep everything above board between us from now on."

Curiously, I thought, the Governors seemed to be impressed by this admission of a lie and they accepted everything else he said enthusiastically.

"It was my observation that many of those who were not already subversives were ready to be persuaded. That is the key point of my report. The Bonus Army represented a powerful and as yet unfocused force that continues to grow. It is a demand for change that was born within the ranks of the unemployed after the Crash. As you have noted, Mr. Pelltierre, the American economic system has failed them. As their numbers grow, so does their political power.

"You believe that despite Mr. Roosevelt's many obvious weaknesses, he is popular with the people and he will almost certainly win the election. To openly oppose him is futile. You have told me that to effect change, you will recruit attractive young men to run for state and federal offices. On the hustings, they will claim that they support the new President but will actually vote as you tell them to. Once you have a man in office and he is behaving as you wish, you will be able to persuade other wealthy men with the resources and the nerve to follow your lead. They will find young men they can ease into office. With a dozen counterfeit Roosevelt Democrats in the House of Representatives, they could be in a position to limit his more destructive ideas. One of them might even manage to replace Roosevelt when the time comes.

"I think this is a wise plan. It does not promise immediate unrealistic results. You are playing a long game. Your first step is to locate a suitable candidate, and you say you have done that. The next step is for me to clear the path for him. I can do that easily."

That very afternoon, with only the three of them—and me—in the library, he said it was best if they did not tell him what to do or ask him questions later. "We all know what we want to accomplish. If you provide the means, I will reach the desired end. Are we agreed?"

They said yes. He was not finished. "Understand, gentlemen, once we set out on this path, we have to be committed. It is not for the sunshine patriot. We will do difficult things. We will break laws. But I believe with every fiber of my being that you and I must do this to save America."

That was the last time I saw Mr. Sturdivant in the Cerberus Society building, but not the last time I heard his name.

Last year, one night after Christmas, Governor Pelltierre ordered me to bring a bottle of the 1858 Croizet Cognac, one of our finest, from the cellar. He and Governor Wilcox were alone in the library. I opened the bottle and poured two snifters. Smiling broadly, they toasted.

"Sturdivant's success!"

"The first of many..."

After they left and I was cleaning up, I found a copy of the Newark Evening News with their empty glasses. It was folded open to an article about the poisoning death of an Essex Fells assemblyman who would soon need to be replaced.

• • •

The detective lit another cigarette. "I took the liberty of checking that last part. Do you want the Agency to look into the death of Assemblyman Lanning?"

"How is Reardon doing? He's had a lot to say over the past few days. Is he dipping into the morphine more than he should?"

She shook her head. She was pissed that I didn't answer her question.

"So he's thinking straight and talking straight?"

"Yes, and that means that two of the richest men in New York are still trying to kill you. A smart man would clear out right now. You are blued, screwed and tattooed."

I couldn't disagree. "Complete your report and send me a bill."

She stabbed her smoke in the ashtray. "You can be damned sure I will and you'd better pay it quick. The Agency will have a hell of a time collecting from your estate."

She grabbed her bag and slammed the door on the way out. I found the number that Arch had given me for Mr. Henderson and gave it to the hotel switchboard. Got no answer, so I had them call my place. Arch answered.

"I need to get in touch with Henderson. I called your number and got nothing. Reardon answered a lot of questions with his 'testament' but I need to talk to him face to face. The girl won't let me into the apartment without Henderson."

"Hold on. I've got another number... Yes. I'll call you right back."

Fifteen minutes later, he did. "Mr. Henderson will meet you at Reardon's building at four o'clock. He wants more money. Says this wasn't part of the agreement."

"O.K."

"What's going on?"

"I'll know more after I talk to Reardon. Don't want to jinx anything now."

I went over all the carbon copies one more time and made a few more notes about what I needed. Names, addresses, schedules, exits. When it was time, I strapped on the brace and went downstairs for a cab. I left a note for Connie with the last section of Reardon's testament. It said "Read this. I'm going to see Reardon. Probably back late."

Chapter Forty-Six

Henderson was waiting on the sidewalk in front of Reardon's building when I got out of the cab, Monday afternoon. He said, "My aunt tells me the women you sent up here have visited the old guy every day, more than once sometimes. Have you been keeping your side of our agreement?"

"Five dollars for each visit, right? Mrs. Opperman's been taking care of it. So am I."

I held a folded fiver between my fingers. He glanced at it and said, "Inside."

Upstairs, the dog started barking before we got to the door. The girl opened it and held the big terrier's collar. The place still smelled of the dog but some of the curtains had been opened and more lights were on. Made the room bigger. Reardon's sleepy voice came from the back, "Who is it, Louise? Did they come back? I told them what they wanted."

"It's Mr. Henderson and the gangster. Do you want to talk to them?"

He didn't answer.

I wasn't sure how to say what I wanted. "I know this whole business has been unusual, but it's important to me. Maybe you didn't believe me when I told you that this Pelltierre character is trying to kill me, but he is. It's too complicated to explain now but what Mr. Reardon has been saying to the detective has helped me understand what Pelltierre and some other guys are up to, and now maybe I can do something about it. I need to talk to him alone."

I gave Henderson the fiver and the girl a ten. She said, "All right, but he's getting tired."

• • •

Reardon sat up with a start when I came into his room. I sat in the kitchen chair facing him. By then he was awake. The brindle cat was on his lap. The bottle of morphine was on the table beside him. More than half full. Good. Out of habit, his hand moved close to it.

"I read your testament, all of it. Read it several times and I don't doubt a word. I know Peter Wilcox. I knew his father, too, Learned Wilcox."

The old man's eyes opened wider. So did the cat's.

I took out my notebook and pen. "Now, I need a few more details about the Society."

"Why?"

"We'll get to that by and by. First, the kid who replaced you," I looked at my notes. "Henry Brevet, tell me more about him."

I asked questions for almost an hour and then told Reardon why I needed those answers. It took another hour. After that, he was exhausted, excited about what we'd been talking about but exhausted. He had enough energy left to dictate the note I needed. When we'd finished, he said, "Indeed, you are an impetuous young man. Good luck, you'll need it."

• • •

The taxi let me out at the corner of Lexington and East Thirty-Fifth Street, a couple of blocks from the Cerberus Society. According to Reardon, members almost never took meals at the Society on Monday and Sunday. The place would probably be empty but there was a chance that Sturdivant or Dolan might be there so I approached it carefully. It was a typical cross street in a prosperous business and residential neighborhood. Narrow sidewalk and traffic lanes. Apartment buildings, closed lunch counters, storefronts, and garage doors. Streetlights had just come on. Nothing identified the Society by name. Wide steps went up to wooden double doors with a mail slot, brass address plate and knocker. I walked past it on the far side of the street and crossed Second Avenue before I turned around and passed it a second time. Nobody else on the sidewalk. I went down to an unmarked door to the left of the double doors, three steps below street level. Pushed a button and heard a faint buzz inside. Waited. Buzzed again. Waited. Waited some more. The little spy door slid open.

"Henry Brevet?"

"Yes?" The voice was wary.

"Mr. Reardon sent me. I have a note from him. He said I should tell you Cecilia needs flowers." I had no idea what that meant. Reardon said when Brevet heard it, he would know I was on the up and up. It worked.

The spy door slid shut and I heard locks being disengaged. He opened the door and motioned for me to come in quick. We were in a large room, part kitchen, part storage. Brevet was a young guy about my age. Tall, short hair maybe red, narrow worried face. He wore a stained white steward's jacket with a stiff collar. "What's going on? How is Mr. Reardon?" Keeping his voice down.

"Not well." I gave him Reardon's note. His lips moved as he read.

> Henry,
>
> This man is Jimmy Quinn. I have told him what has gone on at the Society. For reasons concerning the political activities that you and I have witnessed, the governors are attempting to kill him.
>
> With our help, he means to prevent them from carrying out their plans. I urge you as strongly as I can to give him your full cooperation.
>
> As we have discussed, there is no future for you with the Society. You have seen the ledgers. You know that the older members are no longer active. The members who were once the young Turks are middle-aged and indifferent. Whatever happens now, you know it is unlikely that the Society will still be in existence a year from now. This is your best opportunity to leave before you are ordered to commit more acts that will damn your immortal soul and could result in your imprisonment.
>
> With Mr. Quinn, it is possible that you will be able to leave the city with enough money to build a future for yourself.
>
> Please believe all that I have written here. I have only your best interests at heart.
>
> Your friend, MPR

When he'd finished, Brevet said, "What does he mean about the money?"

That's what I wanted to hear. "We'll get to that, and it's more than you think. First, Reardon said you know everything he does about Sturdivant, the guy that Wilcox and Pelltierre have hired to do their dirty work. Is that right?"

He nodded.

"Have they said anything to you about a meeting on Wednesday?"

"Only that the building is to be closed. I'm to have a cold dinner ready for the Governors. I've been telling the members."

"Closed how long?"

"All day."

"I just need to take a look around to—"

"No." He lowered his voice. "We can't talk. There are members in the library. Wait here. They'll probably leave soon."

He hurried up a narrow set of servants' stairs on the far side of the room. Reardon said the library was on the Mezzanine level above the lobby. I made myself familiar with the basement. The kitchen setup was bare bones with a work table in the middle. Even though this joint was bigger than Jimmy's Place, their cooking facilities weren't up to Vittorio's at the Cruzon Grill. Must have used caterers. The ice machine and walk-in refrigerator were huge. Easy enough to store a body there for a weekend. There were lockers and clean uniforms in a small staff room. The Major Domo's office had a big rolltop desk and a wooden filing cabinet both locked, a cot, and bath with a shower. Two steps led down to an unlocked subbasement wine cellar. I was impressed by their stock. Reardon said they had the best and he was right.

Young Brevet came back almost an hour later looking even more worried and scared than he had when he let me in. "They're leaving now," he almost whispered. "Don't say anything until I know they're gone."

He went up a second set of servants' stairs on the right. About ten minutes later, I heard him say "All clear." The stairs he'd taken opened onto a wide lobby on the first floor. It was two stories high with a marble floor, paneled walls, and a huge glittering crystal chandelier. A curving marble staircase on the right led up to the Mezzanine. A coat room with Dutch doors was tucked beneath the staircase. I went up the stairs, gawking at the tall ceiling and the chandelier. Brevet finished locking the front doors and scurried behind me, saying something about what to do if anyone came in.

On the Mezzanine, the paneled library was as clubby as Reardon had described. It smelled of the fireplace and cigar smoke. Dusty books nobody had touched on tall shelves. Wingback chairs, expensive hooch and smokes on the sideboard, the biggest Oriental carpet I ever saw on the floor. Sliding wooden doors opened onto the dining room. Four-tops and six-tops with seating for thirty. A good-sized butler's pantry with a dumbwaiter served both rooms. The first set of servants' steps came up next to the dumbwaiter. The pantry had wide countertops and open cabinets. No wasted space. There was a telephone mounted on the wall.

Brevet said it was connected to the kitchen. I asked him if the dumbwaiter went to the upper floors. He said it did. I tried the doors. They wouldn't open, so I pushed the call button.

Brevet, sounding almost panicked, said, "What're you doing?"

"Finding out how loud it is. Nice and quiet. That's good. You can feel a little vibration in the floor but nobody in the library or dining room would notice it, right?"

He looked at me and gulped, and I realized how frightened of me he was. He looked just like Asa Kirk had when I strung him up in my basement. That kind of fear did me no good. I tried to sound reassuring.

"Look, don't worry. You said it's not likely that any of them are going to come knocking at the door, and if they do, I'll stay out of sight in this pantry. I know I'm springing all this on you, but I'm going to make it worth your while."

If he bought it, it didn't show on his face.

"Show me the upstairs."

Two sets of stairs went from the library and dining room to the upper floors. The billiard room and card room took up the third floor. On the fourth were two bedrooms and a well-appointed opium den with low beds and tables. They had a collection of dusty pipes and lamps, and another cabinet with the works for shooting heroin. The fifth floor was two larger bedrooms, one with a velvet swing suspended from the ceiling, and the other with shackles, whips, and chains.

I asked if there was anything else up there, maybe an attic? He said no and we went back to the library.

I found the Croizet Cognac that Pelltierre and Wilcox had used to toast Sturdivant's first success on the sideboard. I poured two snifters and tried to give one to Brevet. He stepped back, horrified.

"What are you doing?" he whispered even though we were the only people in the building.

"None for you? All right, I'll drink both of them." I breathed in and got that smooth soft nose tickle you find with the best brandy. It tasted even better. I raised the glass. "This is for Horace Lanning, a state assemblyman in New Jersey who died after he drank bad booze. I don't know how he poisoned it, but Sturdivant was responsible. It's only right that somebody remember the poor son of a bitch they murdered."

I finished that one and started on the second. "I want a better look at the butler's pantry." Harrison picked up my used snifter and followed me.

"You use this to prepare food for the dining room and drinks in the library, right? And both doors can be locked. Of course." That could be useful.

"What is all this about? I don't understand." Sweat beaded on Brevet's forehead and upper lip. My being upstairs was driving him nuts. I didn't want that so we took the stairs back down to the basement where he was more comfortable and sat at the work table.

"Does this place have another exit?"

"Through there." He pointed to a door in the side wall. "It goes to a gated alcove. We keep the trash cans there."

"Do you know what's going to happen next Wednesday?"

He shook his head. That's what I'd expected. "O.K., this is where the money comes in…"

Chapter Forty-Seven

It was after midnight when Brevet and I finished talking. By then he'd thrown in with what I was proposing. He was reluctant at first. Anybody would've been. It wasn't really a plan that accounted for everything that could happen. It was more a possible plan, and if it played out as I described it, then we wound up with a lot of money. It was the money that convinced him. I also told him that if we saw that this possible plan wasn't going to pan out, then we'd come up with something else. If we saw there were no possible plans, we'd back off with no one the wiser. That was a lie but he bought it. The money was more than he could say no to.

The pages of my notebook were crammed with the details of the Society that Reardon and Brevet had given me, and I needed to work through those before I did anything else. Brevet let me out through the alcove they used for trash. Less chance of anyone seeing me near the front door that way, and besides, I wanted to know where it was. Turned out to be a stub of an alley with a tall locked gate, the kind that's meant to keep people out, not to look good. Then I spent a good half hour walking back to the Pierre. Figure there wasn't much chance Sturdivant or Dolan was lurking about to spot me, and I think better when I walk. First thing, I had to make a list of the things we'd need.

• • •

Connie and Renka were waiting for me, and Connie was steamed. "Where the hell have you been?"

"Where I said I'd be, talking to Reardon. After I heard what he had to say, I needed to see the Cerberus Society building, so I did that. Cased the place pretty good. Talked to the young fellow who replaced Reardon. Name's Brevet. He had a lot to say, too, and I'll tell you all about it but not until I've had something to eat. Can't remember my last meal. Call your sous chef. See if he can whip up something. Now, let me sit down. I've got to write this list of what we're going to need before I forget something."

Connie shook her head, thinking I'd gone nuts, probably. I couldn't tell what Renka was thinking. I scrawled down my list. She picked up the telephone.

"Get coffee," I said. "A lot of coffee, and then call Arch. Tell him to come here, he needs to hear this. So do both of you." I went back to my list. Crossed things off, added others.

Connie finished her calls, picked up the whiskey and asked me if I wanted a drink. I said no, I still had too much to do. Then she understood I was serious. She poured wine for herself and Renka. I had seltzer.

"How's Jenny Pris doing?"

"Maybe better or at least not any worse," Renka said. "They're still worried about the baby."

"You saw her."

Connie said, "Yes, we had them move her to a private room in that same obstetrics ward. Nurse Beasley says that's the best we can do for the moment."

"I trust her," Renka said. "A lot more than any of the damn doctors."

"They let me sit with her for a time. I had to tell her about Anne Green, or Lois Kirk as she knows her. I thought she'd be upset, but so much has happened that it didn't seem to bother her at all. Really, she's relieved that her husband is still alive. She thinks that Jimmy did something to scare him off and once he's had time to think about it, he'll come back for her."

The first part of that was right, but it wasn't the time to tell them how I strung him up, so I didn't say anything.

The food arrived. Some kind of French ham and cheese sandwiches that Connie ordered special. I was so hungry by then that I was ready to bolt it all down, but I made myself slow up and appreciate each bite, every sip of the strong black coffee. After all, I thought, if we go through with what I'm thinking about, there's at least an even chance that this is the last good meal I'll ever eat.

Arch Malloy arrived as we were finishing. He went straight to the bar. "Marie Therese filled us all in on 'Anne Green.' At first, it was hard to believe, but as I think on it, the needle never really pointed to true north with that one. Can't say I begrudge Detective Ellis having a tumble with her. Still, if she was looking for information about you, I was a much better source and I'm sure I would have enjoyed her trying to worm it out of me. Well, more's the pity."

"Here." I handed him the five chapters of Reardon's testament and the transcripts of the conversations between Sturdivant and Dolan in the office. "Read these. There's no point in my saying anything until you do."

"Caleb and I went through all of it this evening," Connie said. "It's just about the screwiest story I ever heard."

"No one could argue with that," I said. Renka added an amen.

When Arch finished reading about twenty minutes and another drink later, he said, "Screwy doesn't begin to describe this. Wilcox and Pelltierre think they're going to buy enough seats in Congress to stop Franklin Roosevelt?"

"Kirk has promised them he can do it for a hundred and six thousand dollars. They're going to bring the cash to the Cerberus Society building on Wednesday."

I let that sink in. "We're going to steal it. Pelltierre and Wilcox have told the members the joint will be closed that day. I learned tonight that they've ordered the cooks to prepare a cold dinner for the two of them. They want it to be laid out by eight o'clock. Sometime after that, I think, Kirk and Dolan are going to make their pitch, showing them how Kirk is going to put a dozen phony Democrats in Congress. I don't know that it's a dozen, I'm just saying that. I do know he told them it's going to set them back the hundred and six thousand. Pelltierre says that raising that much money isn't a problem."

Nobody said anything. We just looked at each other for a time. Then the three of them looked at me. "I have figured two or three ways that it might play out, so I can't say exactly what will happen. And there are some other important things I haven't mentioned yet. I'll get to them, but I think there's a chance the four of us, with a little help from Frenchy and Marie Therese, can steal that money. Are you game?"

Renka said, "I'm not really interested in money. I want to face Kirk."

"Sure you do. I understand that. Kirk and Dolan aren't going to let the money go without some kind of fight. And even if Pelltierre says that a hundred and six thousand dollars isn't a big deal, he and Wilcox aren't going to roll over, either. It's not going to be easy, and there's something else. If we're able to pull it off, we can get out of there with some—what should I call it?—'insurance' that they'll never bother us again, but I'm not going to worry about it now. Renka wants to face Kirk. I want to face Pelltierre and Wilcox and tell them that I know they've been trying to kill me. When I do that, I'm going to have a gun. They won't."

I stopped talking and waited for somebody else to say something. Nobody did. "O.K., are you game?"

"Of course," Arch said. "Why wouldn't I be?"

Renka said, "If it gets me to Kirk, I'm in."

Connie didn't say anything. Then, "They'll kill Jimmy if we don't stop them."

"Good." I found my list. "For what I'm thinking, here's what we need."

Handcuffs—6 sets
Bolt cutters
Shotguns—2
Ammunition
Wide adhesive tape—6 rolls
Bandanas—4
Straight razors or sharp knives—2
Liquor or wine crates—12 or more
Commercial laundry bags—6 or more

I said, "This plan of mine depends on them not bringing too many guards with the money. They have a dozen heavily armed guys, we're sunk, but I don't think they will. Figure Wilcox and Pelltierre have been picking up smaller amounts of cash for the last month. They want to keep it on the quietus so it won't be a big deal when they bring it to the Cerberus Society. Once they've got it in that building, they'll think it's safe. And we've got one other thing working for us. Surprise. They don't know we've been listening to them. It's gonna work like this…"

We talked until sunrise Tuesday.

Chapter Forty-Eight

At quarter past three Wednesday afternoon, a long brown Packard and an Ashton-Wilcox Bank armored car stopped in front of the Cerberus Society. That time of day, it wasn't busy. I was watching from the third-floor card room. A heavyset guy in a black suit got out of the front passenger seat of the Packard. The chauffeur hurried out and opened the rear door for Peter Wilcox. Wilcox crossed the sidewalk quickly and rapped on the front door. Brevet opened it. I found I was holding my breath because this was the first time that things could go completely wrong. If Brevet let on that anything wasn't on the level, the jig was up. Wilcox gestured toward the armored car. A uniformed driver got out and hauled open the back door. He drew a big revolver from a holster and held it pointed at the ground. Two guards got out, each carrying two locked canvas bags. Another guard followed them with a short-barreled shotgun. They must have dropped the bags in the lobby because they came right out and went back to the armored car. They moved twenty-seven bags into the lobby. The chauffeur stayed with the Packard, the rest of them inside. Two guards, the armored car driver, the heavyset guy in the black suit and Wilcox. Shit.

I made my way down the stairs being quiet with the stick, and stopped when I got close to the Mezzanine. From there I could hear guys climbing wide stairs from the lobby. Wilcox was ordering them around but I couldn't make out what he was saying. I went back to the third floor and then down the servants' stairs to the basement. Connie, Arch and Renka were waiting for me to give them a number. I held up four fingers and a thumb in a white glove. Arch and Renka mouthed "shit" silently. So did Connie.

• • •

We'd been there since four in the morning, half an hour before sunrise. Brevet let us in then. He'd slept in the place the night before and was expecting us.

Tuesdays, he'd told me, were moderately busy. It wasn't unusual for the Major Domo to stay overnight, particularly if a special gathering or event was coming up. The cooks had prepared a cold dinner for the Governors to have on Wednesday. They left as soon as they'd put it in the refrigerator, happy to get a day off midweek. Since Brevet had been promoted to Major Domo, there was only one Steward. Brevet told him and the Sergeant at Arms they could take the day, too. That was his first lie. The Governors had declared the building closed to members. They didn't say anything about the rest of the staff. That meant Brevet had the place to himself for the rest of Tuesday night and all of Wednesday.

He looked about as nervous as I expected when we walked into the kitchen early that morning. First thing, we put on the white gloves Brevet had for us. I'd told him there would be four of us. Didn't say anything about Connie. He was surprised when he realized there was a woman with us and she was a knockout. To beat that, she was wearing trousers, something else you'd didn't see every day. But Connie said the black coat and pants were her favorite French outfit. To me, they didn't measure up to that first blue skirt and jacket but I didn't say that to her. Besides, the clothes fit with the plan.

I started to introduce them when I heard a light knock on the basement door. Brevet opened it to Frenchy and Marie Therese. They were wearing gray coveralls. Brevet gave them gloves. Without saying anything, Frenchy, Arch, Renka and I went outside to Frenchy's truck and unstrapped the stuff he'd brought. We offloaded and carried it in without wasting any time. Then Brevet brought out the boxes he'd packed during the night. There were a lot of them and they were heavier than Frenchy's stuff. Books are like that. Marie Therese and Connie paid no attention to us as we did the heavy lifting and lugging. They talked. From the little I heard, the subject was Jenny Pris. Since they didn't sound or look worried, I guessed the girl wasn't any worse.

Marie Therese and Frenchy were driving back to Jimmy's Place before the sun came up. Brevet drew coffee from an urn, and we opened Frenchy's crates.

• • •

Before I left Brevet Monday night, I told him he wouldn't hear from me until I showed up with my associates on Wednesday morning. The cops could check telephone records and I didn't want there to be anything that connected the Society to the Pierre Hotel. We spent Tuesday in the suite making arrangements to get the things we needed and talking through the various problems we might run into. Everything was based on the assumption that Kirk was right when he said that Pelltierre and Wilcox would bring a hundred and six thousand dollars in cash to the meeting Wednesday night. Arch tried to figure how much space that much money would take up and how much it would weigh, but since we didn't know the denominations of the bills, he couldn't come up with a number. If they brought it in big bills—hundreds, five hundreds, and thousands—it would be worthless to us. And it would be worthless to Kirk. He needed cash he could spend. So, figure it would be small bills and figure it would be damn difficult to deal with. The real question was how many men would they have guarding it.

If they brought a dozen armed men, we were sunk. If it was three or four and they were the same kind of low-rent gunsels Kirk liked to hire, we might be able to handle them, but Wilcox would use professionals. Figure if things broke right, we could deal with two guys, but if it was any more than that, I had to come up with another plan.

Then there was the timing. Reardon's testament said that Kirk's big presentation about the Bonus Army, complete with used trench mortar, had been done in the late afternoon. The other times Kirk visited were later, around nine or ten at night, and he always arrived after Pelltierre and Wilcox. Figure they'd tell him when to be there and he wouldn't be early. Brevet was supposed to have the cold dinner ready by eight o'clock, set up on the sideboard in the library. The spread was for two. Of course, the cooks had prepared enough for six, but it sounded like Kirk wasn't invited. Figure Governors Pelltierre and Wilcox arriving between seven and eight and Kirk around nine or later.

When would the money get there? Arch and Renka thought they'd wait until evening to move it out of the bank, or wherever they had it.

Connie said no. "Think about it. We don't know how they got the cash together, but it must have involved moving money around from different accounts. Even if you own the bank, you can't just take more than a hundred thousand dollars without somebody asking questions. And Pelltierre said it would take him some time to make the arrangements. It would be less conspicuous to move that much cash during the day, when the bank is open. That means, we've got to get there early, really early."

Thus, we knocked on the door at four. Half an hour later we were opening the crates Frenchy left. Actually, most of the crates he'd brought were empty and they were stacked along the wall. Three were filled. One had the rolls of thick adhesive tape, handcuffs, ammunition, bandanas, tack hammer, brads, and white cotton gloves. As it turned out, we didn't really need the gloves. Brevet had dozens of pairs. The Governors demanded that staff members wear the gloves at all times. Another box had seven big commercial-sized canvas laundry bags. The long crate had the bolt cutters, padlocks, two Remington riot guns wrapped in a towel, the cleaning kit Renka had asked for, and more ammunition. Shells for the shotguns, bullets for the handguns. Arch had also thrown in the kraut dagger that Asa Kirk had strapped to his leg.

We didn't know how much time we had, so Renka spread out the towel and cleaning kit, and set to work on his first job, taking apart the shotguns. Fat Joe had one that he kept in the back of the coat room. As far as I knew, he never used it. Arch told him we needed another one. He said he got it from a cop friend and he told Arch it was going to cost twice as much as you'd pay for it in any store. I didn't trust Fat Joe or his cop friend and so I asked Renka to go over the guns. The man knew what he was doing. Using a few tools, he broke the pieces down, cleaned them, oiled them, checked the action and loaded them. He did the same with our pistols, then set to work on the dagger with a whetstone.

When Brevet saw the weapons spread out on the table that morning, a sick look came over him. Until then, he'd been able to think about the money I promised, not what we were going to do to get it. Now it was real.

I distracted him by mentioning his part in the proceedings. "What have you got for us to eat?"

It worked. He quit staring at the guns and got a big tray of sandwiches out of the refrigerator. We were going to be there all day, and we needed to have everything ready. Brevet had told me the Governors never came down to the basement. As long as we were there and stayed quiet, it was unlikely anybody would know we in the building. But eventually we were going to be seen, so each of us put on a steward's white jacket with a stiff collar, and the white gloves. Then Brevet took Renka, Arch and Connie upstairs, one at a time, to learn the layout of the building. I'd drawn diagrams and told them about it, but they needed to see the place to understand what we were going to do.

After that we waited. Brevet stayed in the lobby area. The rest of us kept to the basement or took one-hour shifts in the upper rooms where we could watch the street. I had the three o'clock shift when the money arrived.

• • •

When I got down the servants' stairs to the basement, I could hear men moving things above me. It sounded like they were rearranging the tables and chairs in the dining room. Brevet was still with them. I found a scrap of paper and wrote, "3 armed guards, 1 bodyguard, Wilcox" Arch, Connie and Renka looked grim.

We waited for almost half an hour before we heard footsteps going down the steps from the Mezzanine, several guys moving slowly. The heavy front door opening, closing moments later and locking. Then more footsteps, one man.

Brevet wiped sweat from his forehead with a pocket square as he came down the servants' stairs from the Butler's Pantry.

We stared at him. "How many stayed?" I asked.

"Just one. Governor Wilcox's bodyguard. I know him. He's been here before." He was almost whispering.

"Where is he?"

"They've moved the money into the dining room."

"Is it still in the locked bags?"

"Yes, they're stacked on the tables. I can't believe how much it is. Governor Wilcox opened one."

"The sliding doors between the dining room and the library, open or closed?"

"Closed."

"Where's the guard?"

"Sitting at a table. He's reading a newspaper. Asked for coffee."

That was a break. "All right. Let's go."

Brevet laid a white linen napkin on a silver tray. He drew coffee from the urn into a silver pot and put it on the tray with a cup and saucer, cream pitcher, sugar cubes, spoon and a small rose in a bud vase. Arch and Renka made masks out of bandanas and tied them around their faces. They got the shotguns and crept up the other servants' stairs to the lobby and then up the curving stairs to the Mezzanine. They crossed it and waited by the closed dining room doors.

Connie grabbed me and kissed me as hard as she ever had. She hissed in my ear, "Don't get killed, goddammit."

Anything I said would've been wrong, so I tied my bandana on and checked the jacket pockets. Handcuffs in the right, knucks and tape in the left. Brevet put the coffee service in the dumbwaiter. He sent it up and climbed the narrow stairs to the Butler's Pantry. I followed without my stick. I'd need both hands. The coffee reached the Mezzanine before we did. Brevet got it out of the dumbwaiter, and backed through the door to the dining room.

"Here you are, sir," he said, loud enough for Renka and Arch to hear. I stayed behind him in the doorway of the Pantry.

They'd moved the tables to the far side of the room. The canvas bags were stacked on several of them. The heavyset guy in the black suit was at a two-top with a *Daily Mirror* open in front of him. He sat where he could see the door to the butler's pantry and the sliding doors. Brevet had taken two steps into the room when Renka and Arch yanked the sliding doors open. Brevet dropped the tray and dove under a table. Arch went to the right, Renka left. Both of them had the shotguns locked against their shoulders, leveled at the sitting man. They were close enough that they couldn't miss, far enough apart he had no chance to shoot at both of them. He still started to reach for a pistol on his hip.

Renka yelled, "Don't do it, asshole!" Loud, a sergeant yelling at a private.

His voice level and reasonable, Arch said, "Don't be a hero. You can walk away from this."

It seemed like time stopped then. I couldn't see the guy's right hand but I could tell his arm in the tight sleeve was moving slightly. I stepped in behind him and said, loud and commanding, "Don't touch it. Stand up. Hands behind your back."

His thick neck twisted and he gave me a dead-eyed glare. I took out the handcuffs. He glanced at them, then at Arch and Renka, then back to me. He nodded, stood slowly, and turned so his back was toward me, fists behind him. As I moved closer, Arch yelled, "No!" and jumped forward.

I can't say exactly what happened after that. The guy spun so fast I didn't really see him. They told me later that he snapped around and hit me on the ear with his elbow. Then Arch and Renka were on him, both hammering his head with the butts of the guns. I wound up on the floor. Didn't lose consciousness but I went deaf, my vision was blurred and I had trouble standing up for a few seconds.

Brevet was smart enough to stay under the table while Arch and Renka worked the big guy over. By the time I was thinking straight, Connie had run upstairs. We rolled the guy over on his stomach. I grabbed one thick wrist and twisted it palm out before I ratcheted the cuff on. Did the same with the other. Arch held the guy's head off the ground so I could wind several turns of adhesive tape around his eyes. I did the same around his mouth, and relieved him of his keys, wallet, and a .38 in a holster clipped to his belt.

The dumbwaiter was barely big enough to accommodate him, so we crammed him in and sent him down to the basement. He came to after we unfolded him and herded him into the walk-in refrigerator. Being the big-hearted guy that I am, I turned over a wooden milk crate and sat him on it while I taped his ankles together.

The tape around his eyes also covered his ears. I said, "Nod your head if you can hear me."

He hesitated, trying to decide if he should fake it. Then he nodded.

"I've got no beef with you. You were only doing your job. Don't give us any more trouble, we'll let you live. You can't identify us. All we want is the money," I lied. "If you want to sacrifice your life for it, that's your business. If you don't, just stay here and be quiet. Somebody will let you out tomorrow. Got it?"

He didn't do anything.

I said, "Don't screw around. I don't have time to waste."

Then he nodded. We'd have to check on the big bastard. One more thing to keep in mind.

I left him in the refrigerator and found they had started moving the money bags down on the dumbwaiter. Arch and Renka were working upstairs. Connie and Brevet were taking the bags out and moving them to the work table. The bags were made of thick canvas with flat leather bottoms and leather tops that folded and locked with a strap and padlock. I found the right tiny key on the bodyguard's ring. We wouldn't need the bolt cutters. Unsnapped the first lock, pulled the strap loose and dumped the contents. There it was.

The money was a mix of new bills and the old gold certificates that were still in circulation. Most of them were in paper wrappers, some held together by rubber bands. Most of the bills in that bag were fives. I opened another bag. It was ones and twos. Large amounts of cash had come into my possession before, but both times I had no real claim to it and no opportunity to take it for myself. This was different, but there was no time to appreciate it.

We'd talked about how we were going to do this and set to work without saying anything. We dumped the bills into the big laundry bags. As we emptied the bank bags, Brevet stuffed them with linen napkins, towels, stewards' jackets, newspapers—anything that made them look full and relocked them. Arch and Renka came down after the last dumbwaiter load. We'd emptied a dozen bags when somebody pounded on the front doors.

Brevet looked at me, not knowing what to do.

"See who it is. If it's not Wilcox or Pelltierre, don't let him in. I'll go with you." I put the Detective Special in my jacket pocket, found my stick, and followed him upstairs. The pounding resumed.

I found Brevet looking through a brass peephole in the front door. "I don't know who he is."

Brevet moved away. I raised up on tiptoes and was able to see Spig Dolan's ugly mug trying to look through the wrong end of the fisheye lens. He backed away from the door, glanced to his left and right, and fumbled at his coat pocket. I couldn't see what he had but I knew what he was up to. A few seconds later, I heard the scratch of a pick and tensioner.

I whispered, "It's Spig Dolan. He's with Sturdivant. Actually right now, he's trying to break in here and steal the money from Sturdivant. Think he can get in?"

Brevet shook his head and pointed to a deadbolt between the doors. There were floor bolts and ceiling bolts in both doors, all of them engaged. I looked through the peephole again. I could see the top of Spig's head as he plied the tools. Even through the fisheye lens, I could tell that people on the sidewalk were noticing what Spig was up to. I can't pick a lock myself but I've watched guys who make a living at it. Spig wasn't one of them. I whispered to Brevet and took out the pistol.

Brevet put his eye to the peephole and spoke loudly, "You there. State your business."

Spig turned and ran. It might have been better to let him in, cuff him and put him in the refrigerator, but when he didn't show up before the presentation, Kirk would know something was wrong. Besides, I knew that wasn't the end of it for Spig. He meant to grab as much of the cash as he could carry, likely that night if he thought he could get away with it. Figure Kirk didn't trust his partner, either. He wasn't stupid.

• • •

When the laundry bags were full, we had five bank bags unopened and still locked. We left them with the laundry bags and sent the restuffed bags back upstairs.

Wilcox had supervised moving the money. He knew they'd brought in twenty-seven bags. Eventually he'd notice some were missing. By then it wouldn't matter. At least, that was one possibility. We didn't know exactly how the night would go. It depended on when the various parties showed up and what they did. So we waited for the rest of the afternoon. That was the hardest part of the day for me. It didn't bother Renka. He went to sleep on Brevet's cot. Arch went up to the library and found a book. He moved one of the leather chairs so he could read and watch the front door.

Brevet had two small suitcases packed and ready to go, and ten thousand dollars, the cut I'd promised him. As soon as his part was over, he was heading for Pennsylvania Station and the first train west.

Connie and I helped him prepare the Governors' cold dinner. Vichyssoise, shrimp, oysters on ice, pheasant, pâté, pickled vegetables (Governor Pelltierre's favorite), two white wines, mineral water. We sent it up on the dumbwaiter. Brevet took serving pieces and china from the Butler's Pantry and set it all out on the library sideboard as he'd done dozens of times before and covered the dishes with glass domes. Then we waited.

By seven o'clock we were stretched pretty tight. Renka was up, having more coffee. He got rid of the steward's jacket and put on his doughboy's blouse. Arch put his book away. As I'd thought about the different ways the evening could develop, one possibility, and the best thing for us, was Kirk and Dolan showing up early with their presentation materials, before Pelltierre and Wilcox. Brevet lets them in. We greet them with riot guns and handcuffs, and put them on ice. We do the same for the Governors when they show up and then work out our differences. But, no.

Connie and I sat with Brevet and went over what he would say when his bosses arrived. In the normal course of things, he told us, Pelltierre would arrive first. As a Governor, he liked to be sure the proper preparations had been carried out for any function at the Society. With Wilcox, it was different. No matter what was going on, if he was supposed to be there at eight, expect him at eight thirty. It would be unusual for both men to arrive at the same time. That had never happened.

As it got dark outside, Brevet turned on the lights in the big chandelier and all of us went to the lobby. As soon as the first Governor showed up, we'd move to the places we'd worked out. Renka and Arch with riot guns in the Butler's Pantry. Connie in the basement with the money, ready to come upstairs if she heard trouble. Brevet at the door. Me hidden in the coat closet where I could cover Brevet who was keeping an eye on the street from a narrow window by the doors.

"Governor Pelltierre is here," he said, and unlocked the deadbolts.

Arch and Renka trotted up the wide staircase. I kissed Connie and said, "Don't get killed."

"I don't have time," she said and dashed for the servants' stairs. I opened the bottom half of the Dutch doors to the coat closet between the staircases and slipped inside. I left the top half open wide enough to see what went on. Brevet opened the front door before Pelltierre could knock and went straight into his spiel. Then, maybe it was because of the adrenaline pumping through my body or something else, the world snapped into sharper focus. Colors were brighter, sounds crisper and louder. Whatever happens, I told myself, don't hurry, don't hesitate.

"Governor, thank God, you're here, sir," Brevet said, his voice rising. "I was just about to call."

"What is it?"

Brandon Pelltierre the Third, also known as Brandyboy, was a tall thin gent. His dark hair was slicked straight back, giving him an exaggerated widow's peak. He wore a black suit and a tightly knotted tie. The stiff collar of his old-fashioned shirt came right up under his chin.

"The guard who accompanied Governor Wilcox and stayed here this afternoon, he complained of not feeling well. He had to, uh, use the facilities several times. It was clear to me that he was in distress but he declined any help. Finally, he rushed to the bathroom where he was violently ill. I heard him fall but I was able to revive him. Given the circumstances, I thought it best to call the special number we always use for Doctor's Hospital when there's a medical situation. The doctor I spoke with advised that I put him in a taxicab to the hospital right away, and that's what I did."

"Has the money been disturbed?"

"Of course not, sir. I did take the precaution of locking the dining room—"

"What's going on here?"

Pelltierre turned to look at a second man coming through the doorway. "Good, for once you're not late."

The last time I'd seen Peter Wilcox was a little more than two years before. He still had the mustache and little glasses that reminded you of Teddy Roosevelt, but the mustache and hair were streaked with white, and his suit hung loose around the shoulders.

Pelltierre said, "Major Domo says your man was taken sick. Off to Doctor's Hospital."

Wilcox headed straight up the stairs. "Is the money all right?"

Brevet locked the front door and went after him "Of course, Governor, the dining room's locked."

Pelltierre started after them but stopped when he heard the brass knocker banging on the front doors. Brevet paused, too, halfway up the stairs, and before he could do anything, Pelltierre opened the door. I could make out the silhouette of a large man, larger than Pelltierre. He pushed the door the rest of the way and stepped in. I smelled aftershave.

Pelltierre said, "Good evening, Mr. Sturdivant."

Wilcox, on the stairs, said, "You're early."

"I know, sir." Kirk or Sturdivant was well over six feet tall. I put him at close to two hundred and fifty pounds. Clean shaven, pink cheeks, pointy chin, some kind of pattern to the navy suit, hat in hand.

Wilcox looked at his wristwatch. "We're not ready for you."

"If there's a problem, I can—"

"Come back at nine, as you were told. We will discuss nothing until then."

Both men stared at each other, Wilcox on the stairs, Kirk at the door. I knew he was thinking that it might be time to quit playing his game with the rich men. But he couldn't be sure the money was there.

"Very well, sir, I'll see you at nine, and, by the way, there is news and it's better than expected."

Wilcox continued up the stairs without answering. Kirk hesitated before he left. Pelltierre locked the door and followed Wilcox and Brevet up to the dining room. When they were gone, I took the servants stairs to the basement, moving as slow and quiet as I could.

Connie grabbed me and hissed, "What's going on up there?"

I kept my voice low. "Pelltierre and Wilcox got here at the same time. Kirk may have been following one of them, because he showed up right after. They told him to cool his heels and went to check on the cash. Are Arch and Renka up there?"

She nodded. I asked her if she'd checked on the guy in the cooler. She said no, but she hadn't heard anything. I opened the door to the cooler and found him standing right in front of me. He flinched and shuffled backward on taped ankles until his legs hit the milk crate and he sat clumsily. I closed the door without saying anything.

Chapter Forty-Nine

"At times, the man's confidence borders on impertinence." Wilcox said. "I've never been completely certain we were right to have engaged him."

"It's late for doubts, Peter."

That was Wilcox and Pelltierre in the dining room. Arch heard them from the butler's pantry where he and Renka were waiting. He knew that Kirk had been there, too, and so he wasn't sure how to proceed. We'd agreed that if we had the chance to take either Wilcox or Pelltierre alone, we'd show ourselves, cuff and gag them, then wait for the rest. If we had them together and there were three of us, we'd do the same. Renka put it this way, 'We act when we have surprise and numbers on our side, not before.' But at that moment, with me in the coat closet, they waited. If they'd been sure Kirk was out of the picture, they'd have taken the Governors. Or if they'd gotten a sign from Brevet, but he wasn't sure what to do either.

Pelltierre noticed the stain on the floor where the coffee set had been spilled and said, "Is that where Governor Wilcox's man was sick?"

"Yes, sir," Brevet said, "I haven't had a chance to clean it yet."

"See to it."

Wilcox approached the bags of money and looked them over. "Is dinner ready? I'm famished," he said, and went to the library, apparently satisfied with what he saw. Pelltierre followed.

"Shall I lock the dining room?" Brevet asked.

"Indeed," Wilcox said as he loaded a plate. "Wouldn't put it past that man to try something, even at this late date."

Brevet locked the doors. "Will there be anything else now, Governor?"

Neither of them answered. He went into the butler's pantry and saw that Arch and Renka had already gone to the basement. He followed.

• • •

In the basement, my four fellow thieves looked at me, waiting to hear what we were going to do next.

"This is working out well enough," I said, not believing a word of it. "We stick with the plan. Now that we've got Pelltierre and Wilcox alone, we take care of them. Then we wait for Kirk. Arch, Renka and I will go into the library through the butler's pantry. Less chance of being heard that way. Connie stays with the money for now."

She gave me a look. "Somebody's got to," I said.

Brevet said, "What about me? I thought all I had to do was let the Governors in."

"Right. You've done your part."

Without saying another word, he yanked off his steward's jacket, found his coat, hat and suitcases, and headed for the exit to the trash alcove.

"Wait a minute," I said. "Give me your keys."

I made sure the door was locked behind him.

"Gentlemen, let's ruin their evening."

Renka said, "Masks?"

"If you want. They know who I am."

I led them upstairs. I waited until we were all crowded in the butler's pantry before I opened the door to the library.

Peter Wilcox sat in one of the big wingback chairs, an untouched plate of food on the table beside him and a glass of mineral water in his mitt. Pelltierre was getting a second helping of the pickled vegetables at the sideboard. At first, he just saw three guys, two in steward's jackets. Then he noticed the riot guns. Arch and Renka came around me on both sides and stopped about four feet away from their targets. If you've ever had the business end of shotgun stuck in your face, you know it's as big as the world. You don't see or think about anything else.

I yelled at Wilcox and Pelltierre, "Hands out, both of you. Now!"

Neither of them moved. I yelled again, louder, "Now, goddammit!"

Arch gestured with the muzzle of his gun for Wilcox to stand. He did, slowly. I stepped in front of Pelltierre and knocked the plate out of his hand with my stick. He stared at me, blinking rapidly. I cracked his elbow hard with the stick, got in his face. "Hands out!"

I ratcheted the cuffs on his wrists and pushed him toward a chair.

"This… this is a kidnapping, isn't it?"

I shoved him into the chair and moved to Wilcox

"You," he said, "You're Quinn."

"Give the man a Kewpie doll." I got the cuffs on him. He collapsed into a chair.

Pelltierre and Wilcox looked at each other, then at me. "That's right, I'm Jimmy Quinn and you're screwed."

Nobody said anything for what seemed like a long time. Wilcox stared at me like I was a ghost. Pelltierre was quicker to try to weasel his way out.

"I'm sure there has been some kind of misunderstanding. This is a private club and you have no right—"

"Can it. I know all about the Cerberus Society and I know you two common cocksuckers have been trying to kill me. Now you're going to tell me why."

"Kirk betrayed us," Wilcox said, his voice sounding strangled. "He sent you to kill us."

"Maybe I'll kill you, maybe I won't." Let them believe what they wanted. "Kirk had nothing to do with it."

The two men were in wingbacks facing away from the fireplace. I stayed in front of them, about seven feet back. Renka was on my left where he could cover both of them. Arch was on my right, close to the stairs leading to the lobby. He could see down to the front doors from there.

Pelltierre tried to take control of things. "This is really about the money, isn't it? I'm sure it seems a lot to you, but I can deliver twice that amount in a few hours if I can simply contact my office."

"Don't worry about the money. We're taking care of it. Right now, you just have to answer one simple question. That's it. Understand?"

They looked at each other and at me, then at each other again. Finally, Pelltierre said, "What are you talking about?"

I spoke slowly. "Why are you trying to kill me?"

They didn't say anything while they tried to come up with a story I'd buy.

"Look, I know most of what you've been up to. It doesn't matter how I know it for now. You started cooking it up right here in this room after the Lindbergh kid was snatched, and you hired Kirk to infiltrate the Bonus Army, and now you've got him working to help you put somebody else in office and somehow—I really don't understand this part—that's going to lead to getting rid of Franklin Roosevelt. To accomplish that he killed a

New Jersey assemblyman out in Essex Fells. Kirk also killed an accountant named Shea by pushing him in front of a subway. Shea embarrassed you," I said to Wilcox, "in front of the Pecora commission by getting you to admit how you fleeced your employees."

Pelltierre glared so hard at Wilcox I knew I'd hit a raw nerve. "And you've come after me three times. What the hell's going on?"

Pelltierre said, "I don't know where you are getting this incredible information."

I lunged forward and cracked my stick down hard across his forehead. I drew blood. A lot of it. I meant to. "Don't lie to me! Next one of you dickwads lies gets a bullet."

Pelltierre screamed and sobbed. I had the same sick feeling I had when I strung up defenseless Asa Kirk with the white tablecloths. It went away when I thought about what they'd done to me and what they wanted to do.

Pelltierre raged at Wilcox, "I told you it was too risky to go after Shea, but no, you had to be sure Sturdivant really had the balls to do what he claimed."

"Shut up, you idiot. Don't say anything if you want to get out of here alive."

Pelltierre started saying it was Wilcox's fault but he stopped when Wilcox began to pant and his heels drummed against the floor. He seemed to go rigid for a moment before he collapsed back into the chair and stared at the ceiling.

"He's faking it," I said.

"No. Here," Renka handed me his shotgun and loosened Wilcox's tie. "It's shock."

"Is it going to kill him?"

"Maybe, but probably not."

"O.K., leave him there." I gave the shotgun back and turned to Pelltierre. "Why are you trying to kill me?"

He glared at me through smudged glasses and shook his head once.

"Fine." I looked at my watch. "We'll wait for Kirk. He's been doing your dirty work."

We didn't wait long.

• • •

The brass knocker on the front doors clacked right at nine o'clock. Renka stayed in the library. Figuring I'd need both hands, I left the stick in the library when I went to the lobby. Arch came halfway down the stairs and trained his gun on the front doors. I cocked the Detective Special, opened the door and stepped back quickly, out of Arch's line of fire. The short-barreled riot gun threw a wide pattern of shot. The door swung open. There was a large shape on the other side of the threshold, bigger than one man. I could make out two faces, nothing else.

Kirk said, "Quinn. Don't shoot. Here's your partner." He lifted a man high off his feet and threw him inside. It was Brevet. He didn't raise his hands to break his fall, just landed on his face and slid across the marble floor leaving a bloody streak. He'd been beaten bad. Face and hair bloodier than Pelltierre. After a moment, he tried to rise to his knees. Kirk stepped in behind him and closed the door. He glanced at Arch and at me, trying like hell to look unconcerned about the weapons trained on him.

"I'm expected." He started up the stairs.

I said, "Stop" and moved farther out of Arch's range. My pistol was aimed at the center of Kirk's chest. "Open your coat. Turn out your pockets. Pull up your pantlegs."

He unbuttoned his jacket and revealed an automatic in a holster clipped to his belt.

"Take it off. Carefully."

He tried to put it on the newel post.

"No. On the floor. Empty your pockets too. Raise your pantlegs." He put down the pistol. Took out wallet, keys, pocket square, comb, coins. When he pulled up his pantlegs, he revealed hairy white calves and socks held up by garters.

Arch moved backward up the stairs and kept the gun leveled on Kirk. I knelt by Brevet. "What happened?"

"They promised they'd…" Pain forced him to stop and he clutched his stomach. "They hurt me bad. Something's not right inside, I can feel it." He gasped and curled into a ball. So the son of a bitch ratted us out.

I set all the locks on the front doors, collected Kirk's belongings, and followed him and Arch. Kirk climbed the curving stairs with that odd grace that some fat men have, like he was aware that people were watching him and he wanted to put on a good show.

As he stepped through the door to the library he said, "My God, Caleb, what are you doing here? Good to see you." He sounded so genuinely delighted that I might've bought it if I hadn't known his game. He raised his arms like he was going to embrace Renka. He stopped when the shotgun didn't move.

"Put your hands behind your back, Ira. We're going to cuff you."

Kirk looked at his two bosses like he hadn't noticed them before, and knelt beside Wilcox's chair. "What's going on here! This man needs medical assistance."

I said, "Can it. Stand up, hands behind your back."

Kirk paid no attention. He said, "I don't understand what's going on, Caleb. Why are you here? Where's Miriam?"

"What the hell are you talking about, you know about Miriam. You killed her, you and Lois."

Kirk's mouth dropped open like that was the most dumbfounding thing he'd ever heard, and when he spoke, he sounded absolutely sincere. "That's impossible. Miriam helped us. When she learned what we were doing, she asked if she could join us. She must've told you about it. That last night, she brought us a mortar that the Reds had. We got separated when the first of MacArthur's troops showed up."

Renka moved toward him, getting too close, and I saw the first flash of anger on his face. "You goddamn liar."

Kirk stood and said, "Wait, I can prove it, Caleb. Here, look," as he raised a hand.

Renka glanced at that way and gave Kirk the split second he needed to grab the muzzle of the shotgun and twist it out of his grasp. As Kirk tried to get to the trigger, Renka bulled into him, driving his shoulder into the fat stomach. That carried both of them into Wilcox's chair. It went over backward. For the next few seconds, I couldn't tell what was going on. I could see arms and legs flailing but I didn't know where the shotgun landed. Pelltierre scrambled out of his chair and crawled toward the sideboard. Arch stepped over him and edged to his left to get closer to Renka and Kirk. I went to the other side, around an empty chair, and found them wrestling on top of Wilcox. Then, faintly, over their grunts and thuds, I heard two quick shots, and then a third shot, much louder. All from the basement.

I can't say how long the two men went at it—thirty seconds, five minutes—neither able to get an advantage. They tumbled away from

Wilcox, still on the floor. Renka was on top but the larger man had him in a headlock. As they rolled over, Renka was able to gouge at one of Kirk's eyes. Kirk bellowed and twisted around behind Renka. They wound up with Renka sitting on the carpet, legs straight in front of him, Kirk crouching behind him, one meaty arm around Renka's neck in a chokehold. Kirk saw that I was trying to angle for a shot at him, so he kept his head behind Renka's as much as he could. Both men were gasping for breath.

"Don't do anything, Quinn," Kirk said. "You heard the shots. That was Dolan taking care of your girlfriend. You leave us alone, let us take what we've earned and we're square. Otherwise, he kills her and I kill Caleb."

His head moved away from Renka as he spoke. I almost had a clear shot. Kirk shifted and strongarmed Renka back in front of him. Then a cheap little four-barrel pocket pistol appeared in his fat hand. He pressed the muzzle against Renka's temple.

Kirk yelled, "Dolan, bring her up here." He wrenched around again, moving farther from me. That presented his back to Arch, but Arch couldn't use the shotgun without hitting Renka. Kirk knew that too so we stayed that way.

Renka croaked to me, "If you get the shot, take it."

Kirk shoved the pistol harder into his temple. "Shut up." Then louder, "Goddamn it, Spig, get her up here now!"

There were footsteps on the servants' stairs. I glanced at the door to the Butler's Pantry, then back at Kirk and I saw that he was smiling. The bastard was enjoying this. Just like he'd enjoyed killing his wife down on Christopher Street. My finger slipped inside the trigger guard. I let the front sight rest between his eyes and tried not to think about Connie. Not now. Later, but not now. Arch slid a quiet step closer to Kirk's back.

The door to the butler's pantry moved. Spig Dolan pushed it open. Arch didn't look at him. His eyes didn't move from Kirk's back. Dolan had an unopened bank bag in one hand and a big revolver in the other. He looked behind him down the stairs and took two steps into the library before he dropped the bag. At the sound of it hitting the carpet, Kirk turned away from Renka, and Arch took a long step forward. He held the shotgun's muzzle six inches from Kirk's shoe and pulled the trigger. The foot burst into a cloud of red smoke.

The blast and Kirk's scream filled the room. As Renka jerked away from him, the cheap pistol went off and blood smeared the side of his scorched head. Then Renka twisted toward Kirk and I saw the dagger in his hand.

I shifted my aim to Spig Dolan. His legs were giving way and his dark slacks were shiny with blood. Still holding the pistol, he sank to his knees on the carpet and stared at nothing. I turned back to Kirk and Renka. The fat man was still on the floor, looking at the bloody ruin of a foot and the dagger buried in his thigh. Caleb leaned against one of the wingbacks. There was a wide smear of blood stippled with black dots around his bleeding left ear which was missing a chunk, and an oozing red groove above it.

I grabbed a napkin from the sideboard and gave it to him. He pressed it to his head and winced.

"How bad?" I asked.

"Not very," He shrugged. "I think." He drenched another napkin in mineral water and tried to wash it.

I couldn't see the little pistol Kirk had pulled on Renka or the other shotgun. I wanted to find out how Connie was, but I had to account for those guns before we did anything else. I kept my pistol aimed at Kirk.

"Arch, where are the guns? Check Dolan."

I stepped closer to Kirk, trying to see if the pistol was behind him.

Kirk grunted, "Get me a torniquet."

"Screw off. Where's the little piece?"

"For the love of God, man—"

I hammered the pistol butt down on the top of his head as hard as I could. "Shut up. Where's the gun?"

"I don't know," he whined. "I need a torniquet."

I didn't make the son of a bitch turn out his pockets in the lobby, that was my mistake. Arch found Renka's shotgun under the overturned chair. To hell with the cheap pistol for now. I gimped over to the butler's pantry and down the stairs as fast as I could. I met Connie on the landing as she was coming up. We grabbed each other and said at the same time, "Are you alright?"

I said yes. She said, "I think so." She was still trembling and angry—so was I—but she was able to tell me what happened.

• • •

After we went to the library, Connie heard the commotion that went on up there, yelling, plates hitting the floor, cursing. What she'd been expecting to hear. Then right before Kirk knocked on the front door, she thought she heard something outside. First, she checked the door to the alcove, the one Brevet had left by. Heard nothing, saw nothing. She went to the door to Thirty-Fifth Street and put her ear to it. Nothing. Then she heard a really loud noise directly above her. Kirk throwing Brevet onto the lobby floor. She was distracted by that when Spig Dolan opened the alcove door. She pulled out the kraut automatic before she saw him.

Figure that when Brevet left, he opened the alcove gate for Kirk and Dolan. They pumped him for anything he could tell them about what we were doing. Then instead of cutting him in on their action as they'd promised, they laid a serious beating on him. Kirk dragged him out front while Dolan picked the lock on the alcove door. Or, more likely, used a spare key Brevet gave him.

Connie said, "I knew I should have pulled the trigger right then, as soon as I saw him, like you and Caleb said, but I couldn't. He looked like he was unarmed and I just… I couldn't do it."

Connie backed away from him, putting herself between Dolan and the laundry bags of money. Even if she couldn't make herself shoot him, she knew how to handle the pistol. She raised it with a two-handed grip, pointed at his chest.

"Then the strangest thing happened. He raised his hands and said, 'Wait a minute, mister, you've got me wrong' and I realized that he didn't know I was a woman because I was wearing trousers and a steward's jacket and my hair was pulled back. I could tell by the look on his face exactly when he realized it, and this is the strange part. He frowned and said softly, like he was talking to himself, 'Christ, it's her.'

"Then he started with the smooth-talking, 'Why don't you give me the gun, little lady. Nobody needs to get hurt. We just want the money.' And he walked toward me with his hand out and smiling like he really expected me to give him my gun. God, that pissed me off! That's when I shot him the first time. I hit his hand."

It surprised both of them so much that Dolan stopped and looked at the hole in his hand before he lunged for her, grabbing at her right arm. She got off a second shot and backed away. He was able to grab her and twist around behind her with his arms wrapped around her, trapping her gun hand. She felt his breath on her neck. Dolan was about a head taller and a lot heavier so he pushed her forward into the laundry bags. They toppled over the money and wound up on the floor. Connie was able to free her gun hand and got off another wild shot.

Dolan cursed and held onto her as he tried to stand. She kicked and twisted so he couldn't get to his feet. He could stand or he could let her go but he couldn't do both. He shoved her to the floor and stood over her. She rolled onto her back and brought the pistol to bear. While Dolan was trying to pull a gun out of a shoulder holster, she put two shots into his stomach.

Spig's pistol caught on something. He tugged harder. It went off, and he staggered back a step as a voice came from above, "Dolan, bring her up here."

He looked at Connie, then at one of the bank bags on the floor in front of him. His eyes weren't really focused. He bent slowly to the bank bag. Connie said it seemed to take all of the concentration he had to wrap his fingers around the handle and pick it up.

"Goddammit, Spig, get her up here now."

He staggered up the stairs, still trying to pull the pistol out. She saw he'd blown a hole in the back of his coat.

• • •

Connie and I went back up to the library. It stank of blood and gunpowder. If Spig Dolan hadn't died by then, he was close to it. He'd fallen to his side, half on top of the bloody bank bag, the pistol still in his loose fingers. Somebody had coaxed Pelltierre out from under the sideboard and put him in a wingback. Wilcox was sitting up. His breathing was still shallow and he kept his head down. Maybe he thought if he didn't look at us, we weren't real. As long as he was cuffed, I didn't care. Arch stood where he could cover Dolan. But there was something else, something that bothered me, but I couldn't remember what it was.

Kirk was still on his back. Renka yanked the dagger out of his thigh and wiped it clean on his pantleg. Judging by the look on Kirk's face, he was still in so much pain that he wasn't a threat. Renka moved around behind the big man, grabbed him under his arms and lifted him into a wingback like he weighed nothing. Kirk howled when his wounded foot dragged across the carpet, leaving a dark stain.

Renka stood where he could face him. "Cut the shit about Miriam helping you and Lois. I know the truth, most of it anyway, and now I'm going to hear it from you."

Kirk grimaced and grabbed at his thigh. He was panting like he'd run a hundred yards. "It is the truth, Caleb. The second week we were there, her and Lois talked. She agreed with what we were doing. She knew that the Reds were up to no good. We gave her extra medical supplies and money. I assumed you knew."

"That's a bunch of baloney."

Connie walked over to them. "And you tried to kill Jenny Pris."

I think that was the first time Kirk noticed her. His laugh was ugly and short, and he cursed. "You, Christ. Finally." His hand moved to reach inside his coat. Arch raised the riot gun to his shoulder and I drew my pistol.

"I'm getting a smoke," he said, his voice fading. "You wouldn't deny the condemned man a last cigarette, would you?" He brought out a pack of Chesterfields and a box of matches, and I remembered what I'd forgot.

"Where's that cheap little gun he had, the one he shot Caleb with." I moved to the other side of the room, looking under furniture. Connie did the same. Arch kept his gun on Kirk. Kirk smoked.

Renka didn't move. "We know everything you've been doing," he said. "At that office down on Twenty-Seventh, the things you said to this man Dolan, and the things you did here."

Wilcox's head snapped up at that.

Kirk tried to look unconcerned. "Anything the old Major Domo told you is a lie. He's a sick, senile old man. Means nothing."

Renka might have smiled. "And I was there when you hired the two young punks to kill Quinn. The game's over, Ira. You're not getting any money."

"If you've got any chance of walking out of here alive," I lied, "you better start telling the truth right now."

Kirk hesitated, looking at Renka and then at me, trying to figure his best play.

"You know what I did. These two," he waved his cigarette at Wilcox and Pelltierre, "think they can buy anything and I showed them what they wanted to see. A way to stop all the terrible things they read about in the papers. I started with the truth, all things I could back up with Bureau reports, and I made them seem bigger than they were. When they bought those, I invented more. They followed me with every step. It was easy."

"You liar!" Pelltierre came out of his chair waving the cheap little four-barrel pistol in his cuffed hands, not aiming at anyone until he turned toward Connie. I shot him in the chest. So did she. He pitched forward and fell on his face. The little pistol flew out of his hands.

Kirk snapped his cigarette at Renka and dove for the gun. He twisted out of the chair fast as a cat and had his hand on the piece when Renka stomped on his fingers. Kirk screamed again, and when Wilcox heard the scream, that set him off. He threw back his head like a dog baying at the moon and let out a shriek I've never heard from a human being. It was long, loud and full of pain. He didn't stop until Arch gave him a sharp slap across the mouth. His face had turned bright pink and the veins in his temples looked like fat worms under his skin.

Wilcox jumped up from the chair and began to babble, sputtering nonsense, "Call the Sergeant at Arms, this must cease immediately, such behavior will not be tolerated, someone must help the governor, he's been overtaken by strong drink. Fetch Reardon, he'll set everything aright."

Arch pushed him back into the wingback, but he bounced right up, his face an even deeper shade of pink, forehead veins swollen. His eyes rolled wildly, and I could see that a blood vessel in one eye had burst, turning the white to red around the wide black pupil. Arch shoved him down again, and that time he stayed there. He froze and his mouth sagged open.

Kirk was still screaming, his voice rising high and hysterical. That's when the stink of the blood and the dead and the dying and the madness became more than Connie could take. She dropped the .22, and ran to the butler's pantry to throw up in the sink.

Kirk's screams finally stopped. They trailed off like he'd simply run out of energy. He had. After he went quiet, I looked down and realized that colors in the deep pile of the Oriental carpet had turned to black as Kirk bled out.

Connie came out of the pantry and none of us said anything. I'm sure Renka had seen worse in the Great War and maybe Arch had, too. The last night Connie and I spent at the Pennyweight mansion, a lot of people got killed. But she didn't see most of it, and this… this was more personal. I didn't have any regrets or second thoughts about what we'd done and I still don't. The three dead men in that room had been trying to kill me. Brevet, on the marble floor of the lobby had sold us out.

But, I thought, the why of it still isn't answered, not all of it, and I've got to know that. First, though, there was more to be done.

Connie, Arch and Renka went back to the basement with the money. I went to the lobby to check on Brevet. He hadn't moved and when I felt his neck for a pulse, the skin was cool. I wondered when he'd sold us out. Maybe he and Kirk already knew each other from when Kirk made his pitches to the governors. More likely, Kirk came to Brevet on Tuesday. Brevet told him what I had planned. Then Kirk decided to let us take the risks dealing with the guards. I tried to think it through but I was stalling. Got a good grip on my stick and went up to the library.

Damn, it smelled awful and I knew it would get worse. The carpet under Kirk was soaked through with blood. The dagger I took from his nephew had sliced through that big artery in his thigh. Trying to keep my feet out of the blood, I put my .38 in his right hand, closed his fingers around it, and let it drop to the soaked carpet. My hands clumsy in the thick white gloves, I pulled open his coat. As I'd guessed, the thick stack of bills I'd given Brevet was in his breast pocket. Let the cops puzzle over that. I picked up the kraut .22 Connie had dropped.

Wilcox was still unconscious or pretending to be. He opened his eyes and glared at me as I took the cuffs off. The eye with the burst blood vessels had turned red and black. He opened his mouth like he was going to say something but when he moved his lips, no words came out. I wanted to do what I had to do and get out, but I couldn't. Not right away. I pulled up a wingback and sat almost knee to knee with him.

"Do you understand me?"

He nodded.

"Can you speak?"

He tried again. Then he shook his head. He looked even less like the man I dealt with two years before. This guy was smaller, angrier.

"All right, like I was trying to tell you, I know about this business with Kirk, getting rid of Roosevelt, etcetera etcetera, and I've also learned a lot about this place, what you guys have done here at your little society. I talked to your old Major Domo, and I've been able to check out his stories, some of them anyway. And what he said about the way the members liked to bring their women here and juice them up to make them more cooperative, that sounded kind of familiar. Your chauffeur—what was his name, Hobart, yeah, Hobart—he said that your father raped your wife, Mary Ashton Wilcox in June, 1917. He thought it was done in the library of your mansion, but he could have been wrong about that, because on the night of Friday, June 20, he was here, and he was accompanied by a young female guest. Don't ask me how I know that. I do."

He shook his head, spit flying from his open mouth.

"You denied it before with Hobart but you know it's true. You know it."

"No, no, you've got it wrong, all of you. Hobart filled you with lies. My father was a fine man. If he did anything like that, it was because the wanton little whore threw herself at him."

That cut it. I grabbed his right wrist, stuck the .22 in his hand backward and wrapped his thumb around the trigger. There was no strength in his arm.

"What is…" he was trying to say when I jammed the muzzle into his mouth and pressed hard on his thumb.

After that, I gimped into the butler's pantry and threw up in the sink. Then I went back to the basement with my fellow thieves to finish.

While the others got to it, I put on a bandana mask, and opened the door to the cooler. The bodyguard who'd been with the money had managed to get his hands in front of him. I'd heard some guys could do that and even though he was a big guy, I figured he might manage it. He'd torn off the adhesive tape blindfold and gag, too. Thus, my mask. I didn't point the pistol at him, just motioned for him to sit on the milk box. He didn't look angry, just fully alert with his eyes open wide trying to notice and memorize every detail about me.

"You heard that a lot has gone on upstairs," I said.

He nodded.

"We're taking the money, but you should know, if you don't already, this whole business is not on the up and up. Your boss may have been smart enough not to break any laws collecting that much cash, but he didn't want anybody to know what he was doing. Understand?"

He nodded again. I still couldn't read what he was thinking.

"I'm telling you this so you can decide what to tell the cops when they show up. I was you, I'd stick to the truth, as little of it as possible. Wilcox ordered you to guard the money and left you here. Three masked guys got the drop on you and locked you in the cooler. Tell them who your boss was, and if you think they don't know what they're doing, make sure their captain knows. End of story."

He nodded a third time.

"You want me to put another blindfold and gag on?"

He waited a long moment before he spoke. "Yeah, a blindfold but no gag, and take that other tape with you."

Sure, I was taking a chance by talking to him, but I didn't have the stomach for any more killing, and the man had just been doing his job.

Arch ditched the steward's jacket, found his coat and hat, and left. As we'd planned, he walked a couple of blocks west and caught a cab to Jimmy's Place. We'd been closed all day on account of a plumbing problem in the bathroom. Frenchy had jimmied the toilet in the men's room that morning and gone to a hardware store in the afternoon to buy parts to replace the ones he'd broken. I wanted a legitimate excuse in case anybody questioned us about not being open. Nobody did.

Frenchy's truck and my Ford were parked in back. The three of them drove the car and the truck back to East Thirty-Fifth Street and stopped in front of the Cerberus Society. Frenchy and Marie Therese were back in their coveralls. By then, it was after midnight Thursday morning, and all of us were stretched thin, but this was the payoff. Frenchy had put up the wooden siderails so the truck would hold more. We began with the money. Seven big laundry bags and four bank bags full of cash went quickly from the basement to the truck bed. We left the bloody bank bag Dolan had carried in the library. Let the cops worry over it and the bank bags in the dining room that we'd stuffed with filler.

Once the money had been stowed, we started on the booze. That afternoon, Arch had identified the best and rarest parts of the Society's inventory, a lot of it still in the original crates. That made it easy. The rest we repacked into our cases and anything else we could find. Later, we counted two hundred and eleven boxes of their best brandy, liquor, and wine. It was a shame we didn't have room for more, but with the material we'd removed that morning, it was enough. Took almost two hours to load the truck. When we'd finished, Frenchy, Marie Therese and Renka left for Jimmy's Place. Arch waited in the Ford. Connie and I went back to the basement to make sure we hadn't forgot anything.

I checked the guy in the cooler again. Nothing had changed. Then I went upstairs for one last look. Connie didn't volunteer to join me and I didn't ask. After that, we didn't hang around. Connie and I made sure both basement doors were locked and joined Arch in the Ford. Damn, it felt good to pull off those blood-stained white gloves. With three of us on the bench seat, we were crowded so close I could feel how Connie was still trembling. I was, too. We rolled down both windows and let the sweet city air wash over us. Arch drove carefully downtown. He stopped on Seventh Avenue at a row of telephone booths. I fed my nickel into one of them, without closing the door. I didn't want the light to come on. I dialed the number I'd memorized.

A guy who sounded like a bored sergeant answered, "Seventeen Precinct."

"I just heard gunshots coming from 295 East Thirty-Fifth Street. That's 295 East Thirty-Fifth."

I hung up before he could ask any questions.

Frenchy had parked in the loading area behind Jimmy's Place and left the gate open for us. Arch pulled in beside the truck and I locked the gate. The laundry bags and crates were too heavy for Marie Therese and Connie, so they went up to the Cruzon kitchen to make breakfast and coffee while we pulled everything off the truck and moved it into the cellar. We left the booze with our legal stock for the moment, knowing that it would go into the hidden storage area as soon as we noted down what we had. The money we stashed in the storage area. The material we'd taken from the society that morning was up in my office. Once we had all our contraband secured, we climbed the stairs to the kitchen. Even though I thought I was completely out of steam by then, the wonderful smells of toast, coffee and eggs revived me. It had the same effect on Frenchy, Renka, and Arch. Connie and Marie Therese were setting out plates and silverware and coffee cups. The familiar sounds made me smile a little.

I found six brandy snifters and uncorked a fresh bottle of Croizet Cognac. I poured generously. We all raised our glasses.

"I should have something important to say, but I don't. I'm drained. Maybe I didn't really believe we'd be able to pull this off, and now that we have, I still don't believe it. So, here's to us. For tonight, at least, we are the best goddamn thieves in New York."

We dug in and enjoyed every bite. It was near sunrise when we finished. Over the last of the coffee, I said, "We agreed on the split, but I guess we've got to count it first. Here's a hundred for each of you in case you're short." I passed out the bills I'd taken from one of the bags, and tucked the rest in my pocket.

Arch said, "Time enough for the count later, but I'm thinking we don't want to leave this bounty unguarded. I'll stay one more night here and commune with my ghosts."

Renka said, "I'll join you, and I understand your ghosts."

"As soon as I'm able to do anything tomorrow," Connie said, "I'm going to the hospital to check on Jenny Pris."

Frenchy and Marie Therese just wanted to go home.

Before Connie and I left, I went back to my office and picked out four of the books we'd taken. Connie asked what they were. I told her I'd explain after I read them. We got into the Ford and drove back to the Pierre. It felt good to be behind the wheel that early in the cool morning. Arch was right, it was a really nice car and I should drive it more than I did.

Connie stared out the window, brooding. I knew what she was thinking. When she said it, the words came out slow, almost one at a time. "I killed a man tonight."

"When a guy points a gun at you, you shoot him."

"It wasn't pointed at me yet."

"Better still."

"You don't understand!"

"Yes I do, you feel rotten. There'd be something wrong with you if you didn't."

I didn't say anything while she mulled over that. Then, "And there's something else."

"Yeah?"

"Yeah. I think Spig and Kirk were after you, too."

Chapter Fifty

Sometime in the middle of the morning Thursday, I woke up and heard Connie in the shower. The day before came to me in pieces and much as I wanted to go back to sleep, there were still things to do, things to learn. When she came out of the bathroom I asked her if there was anything on the radio.

She dropped her towel and said, "I haven't turned it on."

I hit the switch and we waited for it to warm up. "Did you order breakfast?"

She shook her head. "Don't get anything for me. I'm going to Bellevue."

Still not awake, I stumbled toward the telephone. She stopped me. "What you were saying last night about them being after me, I still don't understand."

We'd been exhausted when we got back to the hotel. As we undressed I tried to explain what I thought I knew, but I couldn't make sense of it to her. We agreed to sleep on it, but a few restless hours hadn't changed anything. "Let me shower and eat something," I said. "Order breakfast."

I turned the dial to WJZ where news would be coming up soon, and got under the shower. I stayed there for a long time and was beginning to think clearly when I turned the water off. Connie had dressed by the time I came out. She was wearing a rose-colored outfit, not as nice as the blue number but not like you'd see on any other woman in the city. She was looking through one of the books we brought back.

"What is this?"

"It's one volume of the Archives of the Cerberus Society, or it may be a ledger of a year's expenses and purchases. It could also be a part of the Major Domo's Journal. They've all got the same binding and the covers aren't labelled that I can see. They're not in order, either. All of them were in that big bookcase in the Major Domo's office, sixty-seven books. Reardon says they make up a complete record of everything that was done there."

She leafed through the pages and frowned. "You're kidding. If I was running a boy's club where guys were doing things they had to keep secret, I wouldn't want anybody writing down who did what."

"They didn't know about it. The Governors trusted the Major Domo to run the show and didn't ask questions. Reardon said the Governors never even came down to the basement. The members did what the Governors told them. I thought these four books were the first journals, but they're not. Once I've got them sorted out, we'll see what they say."

I was putting on my clothes when the breakfast cart arrived. Once she got a whiff of it, Connie changed her mind and poured two coffees. More eggs and flaky rolls. When the news came on WJZ, we both quit chewing so we could hear better. There was no mention of dead multimillionaires. As expected. Figure if word had got out, they'd interrupt their regular shows.

Connie said, "Did you expect to hear anything?"

"No, I called it into the Seventeenth Precinct for a reason. For years, I've delivered payoffs to the guy who's the captain now. He knows what's what and he'll clamp things down until the brass above him are clued in. I'm also counting on somebody in the department knowing about the Cerberus Society, and knowing that there are several influential men out there who do not want to see anything about it in the papers."

"That could help."

"There's nothing in that building that connects us to it or them. We didn't leave any prints in the place. The weapons are there. There's one bank bag of cash that Dolan carried upstairs, and the money that we gave Brevet is in Kirk's pocket. If anything ever comes out, somebody will call it a 'falling out among thieves,' and I think the bosses at the Ashton-Wilcox Bank and Pelltierre Weapons and Matériel will see to it their names aren't mentioned."

"What about the money," Connie said. "A hundred and six thousand dollars?"

"I don't know how the hell things work at that level. Let's say Wilcox sold some stock or tapped into his savings account—fat chance!—or pulled the cash out of somebody else's account he could get into. As soon as the top guys at the bank tumble to it, they're going to keep it quiet. We're going to do the same. We do nothing. We don't buy new cars, we don't buy fancy clothes, or more fancy clothes. We keep our heads down. If anybody asks, you and I have had our little 'honeymoon,' and we're heading back to work."

"After I go to the hospital," she said.

"If you get a chance to talk to Jenny Pris, tell her that we're going to take care of her, but don't say anything else."

She gave me a look that said I didn't need to tell her that. Then she kissed me and left. I called Assistant Concierge Anthony, and told him we were checking out later. I asked him to tote up our bill and bring it personally. He did. The envelope he handed me felt thick.

We'd run up twelve pages of impressive room service charges.

Anthony said, "Sous chef Phillipe asked me to tell you how much he enjoyed cooking for Mrs. Patterson and how much he appreciated her kind comments. His boss, chef Marcel, wasn't too happy about it, but nothing pleases him. If you and Mrs. Patterson ever visit again, please let him know. And me."

The total was about what I'd expected. I counted out hundreds and fifties to cover it, and added a good tip. He counted the bills without appearing to and nodded his thanks when I gave them to him.

"One other thing," he said. "You wanted to hear about it if anyone asked about a Jimmy Quinn. No one did. Should I expect anything more?"

"Not likely, but you never know." I gave him a Jimmy's Place card. "Next time you're downtown, stop by for a drink."

• • •

"A hundred and six thousand dollars, my bleeding ass. The cheap bastards short changed us by more than ten grand, taking into account the ten you gave the unfortunate and traitorous Mr. Brevet." Arch threw down his pencil in disgust.

It was midafternoon. We were in the cellar and he'd just finished his count—eighty-five thousand, five hundred and sixty-seven dollars. Stacks of ones, twos, fives, tens, and twenties filled the table. Arch and Renka had started counting that morning. As soon as I got there, Renka left for the hospital.

Arch and I divided the cash by denominations, put it back in wine and liquor boxes, and stowed them in the hidden storage area. The bank money bags, bloody steward's jackets and gloves had gone into one of the big laundry bags. Arch knew an incinerator where he could get rid of it. The Cerberus Society's books were more important. Once we started looking at them, we found that there were three different kinds with slightly different bindings and sizes. The largest, the ledgers, were about sixteen inches tall. There was one for each year beginning in 1896, detailing expenses and inventory, all hand written in ink some of it faded to light brown, with receipts and notes tucked and paperclipped between pages. The Archive books were the same size. Members were listed by name with notes of meal charges, liquor tabs, dues paid and owed, and special fees. At a glance, it was hard to tell what most of them were.

The seven Major Domo's Journals were no easier to understand. When I talked to Reardon on Monday afternoon, he told me they were the key. That's where he and the first Major Domo kept their own record of the members' activities. He'd told me which of those books to check for the entry on Learned Wilcox, his daughter-in-law, and the other Governors.

As soon as Arch and I had the money counted and the books separated, we stashed everything away and got ready to open. I called Frenchy and told him they could come in whenever they were ready. He asked if I wanted Mrs. O'Neal to work since Connie was back. I said yes and caught a taxi to the Pierre. The Ford was back in the garage where I kept it parked.

I found Connie packing her suitcases. She said they were going to release Jenny Pris the next day.

"Caleb and I decided that it would be best if I got rooms for them at the Chelsea. She doesn't want to go back to the apartment in Brooklyn, and I don't blame her."

"Some guy shoots you on your doorstep, you might want to find a better neighborhood."

"Caleb is clearing out his place in Yorkville. He'll move in today. I just called the hotel and arranged everything. Anthony is ordering a car for you and me in an hour. It's also going to meet me tomorrow morning at Bellevue to move Jenny Pris to the Chelsea. And there's something I'm forgetting, what is it? Oh, yes, I'm going to need a bigger room, and tonight..."

She saw the way I was looking at her. "What?"

"A month in Paris changed you a lot."

"A month in Paris, a week at the Pierre, getting shot at, shooting a guy, becoming a thief. It all adds up."

I had to smile. "This is going to take some getting used to."

"You better believe it, buster."

• • •

Jimmy's Place reopened that evening. The first regulars who came in saw that Connie was there and word spread through the neighborhood. Before long the joint was packed and everybody wanted to talk to her—'How did you like Paris?' 'I thought you were going to stay all summer.' Her story was the same one she told Ellis when he questioned us after Anne Green's murder. Marie Therese and I had cooked up a story to get her to come back and since she'd been conned out of her trip, she'd demanded a week at the Pierre. Hell, that was more believable than what really happened.

I'd planned to get started on the Major Domos' Journals but we were so busy that I stayed behind the bar with Frenchy until midnight. We closed at two. After the last customer left, we cleaned up and I put Mrs. O'Neal in a cab. I locked the door and the five of us sat down to talk. Arch explained how much money we'd taken, and said he'd spend his nights there until we figured exactly how we were going to divide it and got it out of the cellar. I said I'd relieve him in the morning.

We'd agreed at the beginning that since we didn't know exactly how much we'd wind up with, if anything, I'd guarantee at least ten thousand dollars each, more if we had it. I hadn't told Frenchy and Marie Therese much about Michael Patrick Reardon and how sick he was. Everybody understood that he'd been the key to the whole business and nobody complained when I said that I was going to make sure that he got the best care for however long he had left. Maybe it meant getting real nurses to stay with him, or a private hospital room. There was also going to be something extra for Miss Louise, the colored girl who'd been looking after him. The same went for Jenny Pris.

Connie said, "I'll talk to her and Caleb tomorrow after they've moved in. She doesn't want to stay in the city and there's nothing for her to go back to in Anacostia, but I've been thinking about it. Let me take care of it."

• • •

When Connie and I walked into the lobby of the Chelsea, it was the first time I'd been in the building in more than a week. She'd been there that afternoon to unpack. I'd gone straight to Jimmy's Place. The first thing I noticed in the lobby was that it smelled right, a combination of old upholstery, the Spanish restaurant next door and other things I couldn't identify. Home. We went to my rooms. Her bags were in the middle of the floor. Before we turned in, I opened the lockbox in the back of the closet and got the spare pistol I kept there. I was almost sure that nobody else out there was threatening us, almost.

For the second night in a row, I slept poorly. I could still smell the Cerberus Society library and see Wilcox's angry red eye. I wanted to believe that he'd set Kirk on me because I knew about his family, just like he set Kirk on Shea because the accountant embarrassed him in front of Pecora, and he wanted to be sure that Kirk had the spine to do what he said. I wanted to believe that but I didn't. Something was still missing.

• • •

I got up and dressed around six Friday morning without waking Connie. I stopped at a newsstand on the way to my place and bought three morning papers. Arch heard me when I let myself in through the alley gate. He opened the back door.

"Nothing to report. A blessedly quiet night."

"Go home. Get some sleep. Come in whenever you're ready."

"I've been going through the Ledgers. If I understand it at all, the amount of money they spent is monumental. Fascinating material."

He left. I made coffee and toast in the Cruzon kitchen, and read the papers. There was nothing in the *Times*, *Daily News* or *Gotham Comet*. Only the *New York American* thought the story was worth covering, and they added a "recreated" picture of a guy lying on his back. His eyes and mouth were open and he looked scared or dead.

**THREE SLAIN
IN EASTSIDE
MASSACRE**

Police are baffled by what appears
to have been a robbery that proved
deadly for the three men involved.
After receiving a report in the early

hours of Friday morning that a
torrent of gunfire had been heard at
294 East 35th Street, officers attempted
to gain entry to the building but the
front door was locked and securely
bolted. When they forced the door
open, they discovered the body of
David Brevet, 25, of 50 Lincoln Rd.
Brooklyn. The cause of Brevet's death
has not yet been determined but
officers on the scene said he had been
severely beaten.
Upstairs, two more bodies were found.
One was Raymond "Spig" Dolan, a convicted
felon who served two years at Sing Sing
for extortion in 1927.
A third victim is yet to be identified.
Both men had been shot and stabbed
repeatedly. Several weapons and an
undisclosed amount of money were found
at the scene. Nothing else had been
disturbed in the building. Detectives believe
the three men slayed each other.
Neighbors said they thought the
Establishment was a social club because
gentlemen were often seen entering at night.
No mention of the address could be found in
records at the 17th Precinct.

I don't know how they managed to remove Wilcox and Pelltierre, but three days later on Monday, Pelltierre Weapons and Matériel announced that Brandon Pelltierre III had suffered a stroke and died peacefully in his sleep. A week after that, Peter Wilcox, who had not made any public appearances since he attended Franklin Roosevelt's inauguration, died at his home after a long illness. But that didn't concern me on Friday morning as I read the papers. I still didn't know why.

• • •

Mrs. Opperman came in when we opened at one o'clock. She brought the bill and said we needed to talk. I told Frenchy to call the kitchen and have them send an order of tea to my office.

The preliminary report and the original typed pages of the surveillance conversations and Reardon's confession added up to more than twenty pages. The final bill would have dismayed me before I was so well heeled. That first report listed the dates of our meetings, the actions I requested, and what she did. Nothing else. She sat on the divan, smoked a cigarette and drank her tea as I read.

When I finished, I said, "Do you want me to take care of this now, or wait for your final report?"

"Do you want a final report?"

"Sure, I paid for it."

"You saw what happened to Spig Dolan and where it happened."

"I read about it in the papers. Didn't know he was out."

"Like hell you didn't."

I took my wallet out of my breast pocket and counted out bills. "I'll need a receipt."

• • •

I spent the rest of Friday afternoon in my office going through the Major Domos' Journals, looking for something that would tell me why. I started with the most recent years and worked backward. Came up with nothing. It was interesting reading just the same. Reardon had written out how much they had to pay Doctor's Hospital on the dates that members had overindulged, along with the names of the members and how much they were charged. None of the girls and boys who were injured or killed were named. They were noted as "the young man with member H.T." or "Governor W's companion."

I had to go all the way back to the first volume to find it, and even then, I didn't see it right away. The binding was coming apart, and the dry pages crumbled at the corners as I handled them. No surprise, the book was almost 40 years old. The hand written entries began with "completion of building interior expected January 4, 1895" and went on to list the activities that were planned for the month. Most of it was abbreviations I didn't understand. I opened each page carefully and tried to find something I recognized. Nothing. As I was closing the book, the spine cracked and I noticed the endpaper at the front. The two marbled pages seemed to be stuck together. I worked a fingernail between them to pry them apart.

Another piece of paper had been glued to the inside of the front cover and folded over lengthwise. The book was sixteen inches tall. The paper was thirty-two inches long. It was the membership roll, beginning with the three original founding Governors, Learned Wilcox, Brandon Pelltierre, and Ethan Pennyweight.

What the hell? I thought about that for several minutes before I found the Major Domo's Journal for 1928-1929, and there it was.

Chapter Fifty-One

Connie spent most of Friday helping Jenny Pris check out of Bellevue. Renka had moved into a room at the Chelsea. Connie thought the easiest thing was for her to take everything she needed out of her room on the fifth floor, and put Jenny Pris in there. The girl didn't want to deal with the landlady in Brooklyn, so Connie said she'd handle everything. I wish I'd been there to see it.

Jenny Pris had been scared of the woman. Hell, she was scared of Catholics, Jews and everything else in Brooklyn. When Connie got to her building, she saw that the landlady, a Mrs. Klopernick, really was an old dragon. She'd padlocked the door and said she wouldn't let Connie in until she'd been paid every penny that Jenny Pris owed her. Connie asked how much that was. The old gal took a look at how well-dressed Connie was and she noticed the Cadillac limousine that the Pierre had sent, and she came up with a ridiculous number.

Connie got right back in her face and said she knew exactly how much the rent was and she knew Jenny Pris's husband had taken care of the last month when he signed the lease and if Mrs. Klopernick didn't open that goddamn lock right now, she'd be back with a court order and she'd make sure that everybody on the block knew that Mrs. Klopernick had thrown a girl who was expecting a child out onto the street. By then a crowd was gathering on the stoop, so the old woman decided to cut her losses and unlocked the door.

"You wouldn't believe how shabby it was," Connie said when she came into the office that evening. "No wonder Jenny Pris hated it the way she did. Her clothes and toiletries were the only things worth packing up. We really need to get her some new things."

"Is she in your room now? How's she doing?"

302

"Still unsteady on her feet. Nurse Beasley thinks she really shouldn't travel until after the baby is born."

"What does she know about everything else?"

"I'm not sure. Caleb said he was going to talk to her about it."

"About her husband? Does she understand he's not coming back?"

Connie shook her head. "You don't know that."

I agreed that I didn't. I didn't mention how scared he'd been the night he left.

"What did you do today?" She asked.

"Mrs. Opperman came in with the bill. Took care of that. Arch and Frenchy and I moved the rest of our new stock into the storage area. And I figured out why they were trying to kill you and me."

"Oh?"

"Ethan Pennyweight was one of the founding Governors of the Cerberus Society."

"What does that mean?"

"He died a year or so before you went to work there. I never met the man but Spence and him hit it off the minute they met. You know the story, I've told you this. It was, when? The summer of 1928, Spence and I drove a load of liquor to the Pennyweight mansion for a party. While Mrs. Pennyweight haggled with me over the price, Spence wandered up to the house and met her husband. Maybe it was because they were both veterans, I don't know, but that afternoon they got blind drunk together. I couldn't roust Spence so I left him there. Never been so damn mad in my life. That's when he met Flora, and you know the rest.

"Once I knew that the entries in the Journal that referred to 'Gov. E.P.' meant Ethan Pennyweight, I went back to 1928 and found what I was looking for."

I turned the book around and held it open to the important page. "Read the line that begins Dec. 24."

She moved her finger to the words. "Gov. E.P. introduces son-in-law to Govs. B.P. and L.W. Possible member/gov."

She opened her mouth to ask a question, then shut it and thought for a time. "I'll be damned."

"If Renka doesn't come in tonight, call him. Jenny Pris, too, she's got a right to know. We'll explain this to everybody after we close."

• • •

We didn't lock the doors until two thirty. It was one of the best Friday nights we'd had since we were legal. After we kicked out the last customers, Frenchy and Arch pushed two four-tops together. Marie Therese moved chairs. Renka was there, not Jenny Pris. She was too tired to go out.

I said, "If you've seen the papers, you know that somebody managed to get Wilcox and Pelltierre's bodies out of that building without the papers finding out. Like I said before, I think the people at the bank and Pelltierre Weapons aren't going to be interested in chasing down ninety-five Gs. They want to say nothing to nobody never about this business. Maybe they know their bosses were trying to overthrow the government, maybe not, but if that got out, it would be bad for business so they don't talk about it."

"I doubt it's going to be that easy," Connie said, "but until this afternoon, we didn't know what Jimmy had to do with any of this. What could killing him have to do with getting rid of Franklin Roosevelt?"

She looked around the table, waiting for an answer. Nobody said anything.

I explained. "Funny thing, it goes back to the Lindbergh kidnapping, again. You see, back when Prohibition began, I did this and that, mostly driving booze and stealing cars. My partner was an older guy, Walter Spencer. What you need to know about Spence is that he's a really good-looking guy—Gary Cooper good-looking—and since he was my partner, I taught him how to dress. Conservative suits, nothing flashy that would embarrass the swells who were buying the product. The long and the short of it is that one afternoon we delivered a truckload of quality booze to a party in New Jersey where Spence met Flora Pennyweight. Yeah, Pennyweight Petroleum. They got hitched and had a kid.

"As it happened, at the same time the Lindbergh baby was snatched, Spence had to go out of town. He asked me to come out to his place in New Jersey, Valley Green, and look after his wife and new baby. You see it's not that far from Hopewell and Flora was sure that they were next on the kidnappers' list. She didn't want Spence to leave but he had to. He said that he was going to take the company Tri-Motor down to Louisiana to look after some exploratory wells."

The two men looked at each other like they didn't understand what I was saying.

Connie chimed in. "I was working for the Pennyweight family as a maid at the time. Things had been tight for months. Salaries frozen, bills not paid. Don't worry, they said, it was all going to be fine when Mr. Spencer brought in those new wells."

"But there weren't any new wells, "I said. "Instead, Spence flew to Mexico where he picked up six crates of one hundred percent pure, pharmaceutical quality drugs from Germany, still in the factory boxes. It was a deal him, his mother-in-law Catherine Pennyweight, and a neighbor who's a kraut doctor cooked up. Chink Sherman, one of the biggest dope peddlers in the city, was in on it with them, but Catherine was the brains of the outfit."

Arch said, "Kirk mentioned the name to Dolan one of those nights in their office."

"I can't tell you how their deal finally worked out. Connie and I left the day after they brought the stuff in, and we haven't been back, but Spence said he was going to move their profits straight into Pennyweight Petroleum, and the company seems to be a going concern again."

Renka said, "What does that have to do with Wilcox and Pelltierre and Kirk?"

"Flora Pennyweight's father was Ethan Pennyweight. He and Learned Wilcox and the first Brandon Pelltierre were the founding Governors of the Cerberus Society. When their sons or grandsons, I guess, started looking for somebody to run for office, they settled on Spence and they brought Catherine Pennyweight in on the deal. Remember, Kirk said something about getting 'her' man into the house. The first step was to find an open seat in the New Jersey State Assembly."

Arch said, "Remove the local assemblyman by slipping him some bad booze, then drop a few hundred dollars in the right pockets of the Democratic machine, and install their man so he'll be in position to run for Congress in the next election."

Arch paused while he figured the rest. "But before his silent sponsors stand Mr. Spencer for election, they have to make sure that everyone who knows about his drug dealing past stays quiet. Permanently. That means getting rid of Chink Sherman and Jimmy and you," he said to Connie.

She smiled. "That's right. Tomorrow Jimmy and I are going to have a talk with Mrs. Pennyweight and settle some hash."

• • •

Now, if you are saying to yourself that is the dumbest idea for a conspiracy you've ever heard, I won't blame you. But I'll go you one better.

Four months later, on November 20, 1934, General Smedley Butler, the same Smedley Butler who told the Bonus Army what a terrific thing it was doing, that Smedley Butler testified before the McCormack-Dickstein Congressional Committee. He told them he was offered $17,000 in cash to take over the American Legion and use it to force Franklin Roosevelt out of office. That part was easy to understand. The Legion thought that labor unions, Jews and black people would take over the country unless they were stopped, and Roosevelt was helping them. The money was going to come from a couple of rich New York guys. Gen. Butler dealt with the middlemen, Gerry McGuire, a fat man with a silver plate in his head, and Bill Doyle who was with the Massachusetts American Legion.

Their idea was to get friendly newspaper editors and radio stations to run pieces saying that Roosevelt's health was failing and he wasn't able to lead the country. Butler would then bring a group of American Legion members to Washington, and because he was such a trusted public figure, everybody would go along with him becoming the "Secretary of General Affairs" who'd run things instead of the president.

The Committee called McGuire to testify and he denied everything. General Butler named the guys who were ready to supply the money, but the Committee thought it wouldn't be right to make such esteemed gentlemen appear before them. When it was all made public and the final report came out, they said that Butler told the truth. But even if it was the truth, everybody treated it as a joke. Such a wild scheme never had a chance of succeeding. Yes, these millionaires meant to overthrow the government, but in the end, they were conned by a couple of grifters who knew an easy mark when they saw one.

Just like Wilcox and Pelltierre. Happens every day.

Chapter Fifty-Two

We left around eleven o'clock Saturday morning in the Ford. Connie was wearing another skirt, blouse and coat combination cut like the navy number, but this one was a different shade of blue, almost gray. I had on my lightest tropical weight, a tan two-piece. The paper said it was getting into the nineties in the city. Once we were through the tunnel and past Newark, it felt fine in the car with the windows down. I'd forgot how green everything was out there in the summer. Didn't care for it. All that fresh air didn't smell right, either. As we got closer to the Pennyweight house in Valley Green, the road was lined with white rail fences, low stone walls, pastures, and tall trees. Connie and I talked about how we were going to play it, but we knew it was hard to predict how Mrs. Pennyweight would react.

Connie had the book on her lap. She fretted. "We should have called. What if she's not here?"

"We'll leave a message."

"You don't know what that woman's like."

"Yes, I do. Don't worry. We hold good cards. Remember, you're younger and better looking than her. You're better dressed and you're smarter."

"Maybe not smarter."

I could feel Connie tensing as I turned at the stone gate and we drove down the long gravel drive that led to the Tudor mansion. I was wound up myself. It had been two years since we'd last seen the place. Looked like it had been painted. I parked at the front doors under the overhang. There was no sign that anyone was there, but the garage was around back where you couldn't see it. As we walked to the door, Connie said under her breath, "Give me your knucks."

O.K., she was taking this seriously. I gave them to her and rapped on the door with my stick. We waited. I rapped again and waited some more before I tried the knob. It was unlocked. I pushed the door open and ignored whatever Connie was hissing at me. It took a second for our eyes to adjust to the gloomy interior. I heard shuffling footsteps and saw an old gent with a walrus mustache making his way from the servant's stairs across the long room. Up close, I could tell that he thought he recognized me but couldn't remember who I was.

"Mr. Mears, it's Jimmy Quinn, and this is Connie, you remember her."

"Hello, Mears. It's me, Nix."

I'm pretty sure he smiled behind that lush mustache when she hugged him.

"Tell the lady of the house she has visitors. We'll see her in the library," I said and walked away as he sputtered something to my back.

"What the hell are you doing?" Connie was still hissing as she followed.

"Taking the offensive. Keep her off balance."

The library hadn't changed. The one at the Cerberus Society might have been copied from it. Dark paneling, Oriental carpet, cold fireplace, books nobody read. I sat in the swivel chair behind the desk so I could act like I was in charge. The book we'd brought was in front of me. We waited for Catherine Pennyweight to come down from her rooms upstairs.

We heard her quick footsteps on the stairs, then she swept into the room, her eyes angry and worried at the same time. She wore a long, light summer outfit. Her hair had turned more gray than brown in two years, and she still had a way of tilting her head back so she seemed to look down at you. "What is the meaning of this!" she thundered.

"Hello, Catherine," I said. "How's tricks?"

She got even angrier, but then Connie stepped next to me and Mrs. Pennyweight's expression turned thoughtful.

"Nix? Is that you?"

Connie stood a little taller. "Yes, it's me… Pennyweight."

The older woman flinched at the lack of 'Mrs.' and tugged at her flowered blouse to compose herself. "I see you've made yourself at home."

"I knew this was the best place for us to talk politics. You see, a little bird told me that Spence is about to run for office."

She sat in a chair facing the desk and leaned back to look down her nose as she forced a laugh. "Nonsense. Where did you hear such a thing?"

"Where I heard it doesn't matter. You need to know there's been a change in plan."

"What on earth are you talking about? If you'd like to talk to Walter, he and Flora are in Newark today." I thought she'd play dumb but I thought she'd do it better.

"Figures, but we don't need to talk to Spence. We know who really runs the show and we know that some parties have been easing the way for you, in Newark and in the city. That's over. You're on your own now."

"Really, Mr. Quinn, I have no idea what you're talking about."

"In a pig's ass you don't, but nobody cares about that, not any more. Like I said, things have changed. You'll hear about it soon enough, but this is the important part. We drove all the way out here to tell you in person so you'll understand how serious we are."

"This is nonsense, I'm afraid you'll have to—"

Connie stepped around the desk to face her. "Stop pretending you don't know what we're talking about. They tried to kill us. You paid them to do it because we know what you and Mr. Spencer did."

"Insanity! This is—"

Connie gave the old girl a light tap with the knucks on the point of her chin, hard enough to click her teeth and cross her eyes but not serious enough to hurt.

"She's not going to admit anything, but so what? This is the important thing." I paused and stared straight at her. "Are you listening?"

For once she shut up and nodded her head.

"We know about the Cerberus Society and what your husband and his friends did there. We have these." I held up the book.

"What is that?" She looked worried. Sounded worried.

"It's the first part of the Society's records from the founding in 1895. The members' names, when they joined, what they did for fun, their expenses, all of the details in 67 handwritten volumes. You can see, here's your husband's name." I closed the book and put it down.

"Don't worry about how we happened to come by them. They are stored in a safe place where nobody will look at them. For now. If anything happens to Connie or to me, they will be sent to men who know what to do with them. Might be Walter Winchell who could read parts on the radio or publish them in one of his columns. The District Attorney might be interested. The thing for you to remember is, as long as we're alive, they stay private."

"My late husband belonged to several clubs. I'm sure some of them went beyond the pale, but it hardly makes any difference. It has nothing to do with Walter, should he decide to accept the offer that's been made. Whatever it is that you think you're talking about will make no difference."

I stood so I could look down at her for once. "You think I'm a common gun thug and maybe I am, but pretty soon you'll learn that your sponsors in the city aren't there to help you any more. So, do not screw with me."

Connie gave her another tap with the knucks. "Or me."

"Just leave us alone. That's all you have to do. Stay out of our business. Are we agreed?"

Connie and I stood and stared long enough to make her nervous. "Honestly, Mr. Quinn, I really have no idea what you're talking about but of course I will stay out of your business."

Connie put away the knucks and smiled sweetly. "Then we've got nothing more to say."

As we drove back out to the road, I felt the tightness easing in my shoulders, the tightness that had been there since the first night the goons tried to kill me. Then I realized how much more there was to do. It wouldn't be right not to make sure Michael Patrick Reardon's last days weren't as comfortable as possible. And there was Jenny Pris Kirk and her baby. And Renka. And, it finally hit me, the money!

Without thinking I blurted out, "What the hell are we going to do with all that cash?"

Connie smiled even more sweetly. "I've got some ideas."

Thanks and Acknowledgements

Sarah Gay and Florent Crayssac at the French Line Archives provided information, photographs, and film of the company's glamorous liners.

Dr. Martha Mayo-Magnuson helped with information on the treatment of kidney injuries in the 1930s.

Fearless beta-readers Rachel Ratliff Warren, Robert Kintz, Jan Harrison and Tom Bergin provided much needed criticism and suggestions. They made this a better book.

Like the other Jimmy Quinn novels, this one is based on fact. Details of weather and current events are accurate. The newspaper articles are based on similar contemporaneous stories.

General Smedley Butler and Ferdinand Pecora are genuine American heroes who should be much more famous than they are. The plot that Gen. Butler refused to be a part of was one of several that meant to stop or reverse the Roosevelt administration's early efforts to lift this country out of the Depression.

I continue to thank Rian James who wrote with the lightest of touches about the city in the early 1930s and Reginald Marsh, John Sloan, and Berenice Abbott whose paintings and photographs capture everyday life so vividly.

About the Author

Michael Mayo has reviewed films for numerous publications, including The Washington Post. He has worked extensively in radio and was co-host of the nationally syndicated Movie Show on Radio and Max and Mike On the Movies. Among his books are *American Murder, Videohound's Horror Show, War Movies,* and the *Jimmy Quinn* suspense novels.